... British writer of novels, essays, literary journalism and a memoir. Her most recent novel, *The Mermaid of Black Conch*, won the Costa Book of the Year Award, 2020, and was nominated for eight major awards. Her other Caribbean novels, *The White Woman on the Green Bicycle* and *House of Ashes* have also been nominated for major awards. *Archipelago* won the OCM Bocas Award for Caribbean Literature in 2013. Her work has been translated into many languages. She is a co-founder of Writers Rebel inside Extinction Rebellion and she is a Senior Lecturer in Creative Writing at Manchester Metropolitan University.

Read more at moniqueroffey.com

PRAISE FOR *THE WHITE WOMAN ON THE GREEN BICYCLE*:

'This is a powerful, juicy novel about the tragedy of Trinidad, one of the most beautiful places on earth. Personal, political, physical – you feel you've been there' Carole Angier, author of *Jean Rhys: Life and Work*

'From its opening pages, I was entranced by the world of this novel. Monique Roffey's Trinidad is full of strife and languor, violence and also hushed moments of peace, so beautifully and lushly evoked ... What a vibrant, provocative, satisfying novel – I can't stop thinking about it' Suzanne Berne, winner of the Orange Prize for Fiction

'Vibrant and vivid; passionate and true. This is a powerful tropical mix; a compassionate book that needed to be written' Amanda Smyth, author of *Black Rock*

'Extraordinarily vivid ... beautifully observed' *The Times*

'Rich and highly engaging' *Guardian*

'Brilliant, brutal' *Independent*

'Packed with meaty themes, from racism and corruption to passion and loyalty' *Sunday Telegraph*

'Superb ... shatters Caribbean clichés by depicting the explosive tensions of post-colonial Trinidad with fierce affection ... intoxicating and gritty' *Metro*

'Monique Roffey's understanding of the human character is boundless. Gentle and sensual, stinging and frustrating in equal measures. Roffey weaves a story of human love and determination, and the emotion and impact of an evolving society – both of whic[...] nd they're set in. A beautiful, m[...]

'Searing ... [...] rith West Indian heat'

'Sharply observed and engrossing' *Waterstone's Books Quarterly*

'Days after reading it, I can still smell Trinidad' *Sunday Telegraph*, Australia

'An epic and strikingly original love story' *Australian Women's Weekly*

'Roffey draws an intriguing portrait of a marriage that resonates long after the last page is turned' *Sunday Times*, Australia

'This unforgettable love story will enchant the reader' *Daily Liberal*, Australia

'Roffey creates a terrific sense of place: heat and languor, politics and passion, tropical smells and the heady music of the local patois, all combine to make the novel memorable' *The Age*, Australia

'Fascinating, provocative, funny, beautiful . . . does what few novels successfully pull off: capturing, like a newsreel, the state of a society' *Caribbean Review of Books*

'Move[s] literary awareness and focus of this conflicted Creole space firmly into its bewildering contemporary state of fear, loathing, and dark beauty . . . The Age of Innocence in West Indian fiction is over' *Trinidad Guardian*

'Dares to speak about an unravelling as it happens' *Trinidad Express*

'Roffey undertakes an examination of the Trinidad & Tobago Independence Movement and, a generation later, its bitter fruit . . . A millennial portrait of a new republic' Lisa Allen Agostini, co-editor, *Trinidad Noir*

'Eloquent, sometimes poetic, always passionate . . . paints an intriguing, sometimes disturbing picture of Trinidad in the turbulent post-colonial era . . . Riveting, fearless' *Caribbean Beat* magazine

'Compelling and original. A bruised, sensuous love-letter to Trinidad which grippingly unfolds the violent aftermath of colonial rule and also speaks fearlessly of love and hatred across the lines of 'race' and class' Maggie Gee

'There might be an implicit nod to the Caribbean classic *Wide Sargasso Sea*, but Monique Roffey's story of contemporary Trinidad seen through European eyes breaks entirely new ground. It is a major contribution to the new wave of Caribbean writing: energetic, uncompromising, bold . . . and a great read. Roffey is a magical storyteller . . . *The White Woman on the Green Bicycle* is boundless in its understanding of the human spirit. It will resonate with readers everywhere' Olive Senior, winner of the Commonwealth Writer's Prize

For my mother, Yvette Roffey

Also by Monique Roffey:

Fiction
Sun Dog
Archipelago
House of Ashes
The Tryst
The Mermaid of Black Conch

Non-fiction
With the Kisses of His Mouth

First published in Great Britain by Simon & Schuster UK Ltd, 2009
This edition published by Scribner, 2022

SCRIBNER and design are registered trademarks of The Gale Group, Inc.,
used under licence by Simon & Schuster Inc.

1 3 5 7 9 10 8 6 4 2

Simon & Schuster UK Ltd
1st Floor
222 Gray's Inn Road
London WC1X 8HB

Simon & Schuster Australia, Sydney
Simon & Schuster India, New Delhi

www.simonandschuster.co.uk
www.simonandschuster.com.au
www.simonandschuster.co.in

A CIP catalogue record for this book
is available from the British Library

PB ISBN: 978-1-3985-1409-6
EBOOK ISBN: 978-1-84737-802-6

Typeset in Palatino by M Rules
Printed and bound in Great Britain by CPI Group (UK) Ltd, Croydon CR0 4YY

MONIQUE ROFFEY

The
White Woman
on the
Green Bicycle

SCRIBNER

LONDON NEW YORK SYDNEY TORONTO NEW DELHI

Love for an island is the sternest passion . . .

– Phyllis Shand Allfrey

HURRICANE

They took him to the top of Paramin Hill. Right to the top, where there was no one around, where no one could hear him call for help. Four of them. Four to carry out such a job. They wanted to teach him a lesson. He'd no business complaining. *So what* if the police had stolen his mobile phone, they can damn well take what they like. And poor Talbot – well – yes. Mixed up with the local thugs, the badjohns up on this hill, the ones causing all the problems. The police already knew Talbot. And now they wanted to teach him not to go making more trouble.

Talbot was in the back of the police vehicle, squeezed up between two of them, handcuffed. They'd already hit him about when they picked him up – slapped his face, told him to shut up or they'd return for his sexy younger sister, Chantal. They told him to shut his *damn blasted mout*.

'Leave mih sister *outa* dis,' Talbot shouted. But they hit his face hard. Then Talbot shut up. They parked and left the headlights on full. It was dusk, darkness about to settle. The biggest of them, a man called Johnny, was laughing like he knew what to do. Last week he gave the same treatment to another man, some poor-fuck up in Debe.

'De damn blasted people need to show some respek, man,' he'd said then and meant it. They pulled Talbot out shaking and blabbering and begging, saying he was sorry, sorry he told his girlfriend about the mobile phone, sorry he made a fuss. He didn't need it, he didn't want it. They took off the cuffs and Talbot rubbed his wrists.

Badap. The first blow sang out. Then Johnny went at him with another big punch, *whaddap*. This time he hit Talbot in the belly. Talbot doubled over. He spewed something out onto the grass. Talbot staggered, holding his sides. He looked up.

'Show some damn fockin' respek, man.' Johnny smiled; his eyes were wild and dark. It was he who stole Talbot's phone at the fête the week before. Later, Johnny got a ticking-off from the Superintendent – nothing big, but Johnny'd had a lot of pressure recently. Too many complaints.

'Hol' him, nuh,' Johnny said. Two of the men held Talbot back by his arms, across the broadside of the police vehicle. The head-lights sprayed light across the hillside bamboos.

Badap. Another punch. Johnny had some boxing experience. He took off his uniform shirt and his muscles glowed in the heat. He flexed and shadow-danced a little. He laughed as the other men held Talbot down. Talbot said nothing. His eyes were open wide. Johnny and his friend Marco, a policeman on another force, took turns with Talbot. *Bam, badap*. Each punch brought Talbot's eyes out of his head. Blood sprayed out. Sweat flew from his chest. *Bam, baff*. Talbot took the punches, but he cried like a little boy. Each one made him jump off the ground and made him weak, so weak they had to hold him upright. Then Talbot went limp. They straightened him up and pinned him across the door of the car. He was crying, crying for them to stop.

And then Johnny got really mean. He set in. His eyes gleamed like he was enjoying himself and then he lashed out like a kung fu expert, executing all manner of kicks. He round-kicked at Talbot with his big police boots and he swung around, kicking him again and again, in his stomach, in his mouth. *Crunch*, a sound like something had split in Talbot's chest. *Crack*. Bones were breaking. Talbot groaned, blood trickled from his mouth.

Then they both started kicking him: flying kicks and blows, karate chops. Talbot couldn't stand up. His face was mashed up, his chest bleeding; he was black and blue and sweating. The man poured with sweat and blood. They continued punching and kicking him. When they stopped, because they had tired themselves out, they drank rum from a bottle of Vat 19. Johnny and Marco were sweating, too, from all their kicks. They spat out some rum on the ground.

'He go dead,' one said, looking at Talbot.

'Nah, man,' Johnny replied. He hadn't finished yet.

Again Johnny went at poor damn Talbot, this time with his fists, and he worked him over, *smack, crunch*. A rain of blows to Talbot's face. Blood spurted out. Blood on Johnny's hands that he wiped on his uniform trousers. Johnny smashed up the man's nose so it folded across his face. Talbot was unconscious.

'Enough,' one of the policemen told Johnny.

But Johnny hit him again.

Then Johnny and Marco took turns. They hit Talbot one and two and three while Talbot's head bounced back and forth.

When they stopped, Johnny went up close to Talbot. His face was all swollen and his eyes were sealed shut. Johnny whispered to Talbot, close into his ear. He told Talbot he deserved the beating. He said, 'You part of what wrong wid de country. It your fault you get licks. We watchin' you. De licks, dis a warnin', yes, an' if you ever complain again about anytin' to do wid de police force, we go *come back*.'

They let him go.

Talbot sank to the ground.

They left him like that. It was dark. No one else was around. They thought no one saw what happened.

TRINIDAD, 2006

CHAPTER ONE

THE BLIMP

Every afternoon, around four, the iguana fell out of the coconut tree. *Bdup!* While sunbathing, it had fallen asleep, relaxing its grip, dropping from a considerable height. It always landed like a cat, on all fours, ready to fight. The dogs always went berserk, gnashing and chasing after the creature as it fled, scuttling across the grass, a streak of lime green disappearing off into the undergrowth.

'It never remembers the day before,' Sabine remarked. 'Never remembers its dreams, either, I suppose. Brain like a *peanut*.'

The lizard's daily plummet acted like an alarm clock, prompting Sabine to make their afternoon pot of tea. She went to put the kettle on.

'Jennifer, tell your son Talbot to come and kill that damn lizard.'

But Jennifer only rolled her eyes. She'd dominated the kitchen all day, baking gooey cakes and sweet-breads, stewing chicken with brown sugar. She'd been making pellau for the weekend. On the kitchen table, two halves of Madeira sponge were just out of the oven, cooling on racks.

'Why?'

'It upsets the dogs.'

'So?'

'It's driving me crazy.'

'Let de dog go bite it, nuh, den dey go see somptin!'

'I don't want it to bite the dogs.'

'Dem dogs chupid.'

'Not my little one, *ma petite*.'

'She de *woss*.'

'Oh Jennifer, how can you say that?'

'If dat lizard go fall on she, she go dead.'

'Don't say that.'

Jennifer chuckled, enjoying the thought of the lizard falling on Katinka's glossy Pomeranian head.

'I want Talbot to kill it.'

'He won't kill it.'

'Why not?'

'Talbot 'fraid dat lizard too bad.'

'Don't be ridiculous. He can cook it, or do whatever he wants with it.'

'Put it in a pot,' Jennifer teased her.

'Uggghhh.'

'Stew it up.'

Sabine flinched, making a wincing-chewing face.

'It taste *nice*, boy.' Jennifer stifled a laugh.

'No, thank you.'

'You never taste it?'

'Of course not, eh, eh,' Sabine steupsed, sucking her teeth.

Jennifer laughed and Sabine poked out her tongue in response.

Jennifer was mostly African, mixed up with some Spanish blood, or so she claimed. Her arms were heavy and her hips had spread, but she was proud of her heart-shaped face, her round polished cheekbones. She waxed her kinky hair and pinned it up. Jennifer smelled rich, coconut oil and Paramin mountain herbs, fresh rosemary, wild thyme, scents she knew well. And yes, these days Jennifer was much too fresh by half, never did what she was asked any more; did what she liked and when she liked, in her own time. Jennifer hoovered when she wanted to, polished the silver and cleaned the crystal only when she felt like it. Jennifer ran things now: good for her.

'Oh Gyaaaad,' Sabine complained loudly. 'The heat! Jennifer, I cyan take it.' She lifted up her voluminous house dress and fanned it up to her face, exposing her pink cotton knickers.

'*Phhhhhut!*' She made a loud hissing sound, fanning herself. '*C'est un fourneau.*'

Jennifer shook her head. 'Take cyare Mr Harwood ent come in and ketch a fright.'

'Ha ha,' Sabine cut back. As if George looked at her any more; as if he cared to look.

'You can talk. You're almost as fat as me.'

Jennifer gasped. 'I not *fat*.'

'You were skinny once, like a piece of spaghetti when you first came to us. Now look at you.'

Jennifer pursed her lips. 'I does look *healthy*.'

'You'll get fatter if you're not careful. Your daughter Chantal is already getting fat.'

Jennifer stopped her mixing at the stove; she turned and fixed her hands on her wide hips. 'Oh gorshhh, nuh. I don't want to see your panties.'

Sabine kept fanning herself. 'Oh, don't be so prudish. Who cares?'

'I does care.'

'Oh! It's too hot to wear clothes.'

Jennifer stared as if Sabine was crazy.

Sabine smiled and slowly fanned her dress downwards. She made the tea and carried the tray out to George, who was reading out on the porch, researching his next article for the *Trinidad Guardian*. Reading, reading, reading, he was always reading, sometimes not speaking for hours. But at four, he'd put down his book. They would discuss their plans for tomorrow. It was about all they had, these days, this teatime catch-up. But at least her husband wasn't boring. Or short. Sabine detested little men and boring people. George was still brilliant, somehow, despite it all, maybe even more so. He turned heads, George did, with his skin turned red as rum and his hawk-like nose. In his later years, he'd come to resemble a totem pole. And his eyes shone brighter, his blue eyes were turquoise now, like a wild liqueur. No, despite it all, she'd never stopped wanting to talk to George.

'Jennifer is baking cakes in the kitchen,' she told him.

'Oh, good. What kind?'

'Banana.'

'The best.'

'I know you like to eat banana cake when it's still warm. She'll bring it out.'

'Thank you. Give an Englishman cake, tea and cake every day of his life.' George rubbed his hands with impending pleasure, trying to catch her eye, his gaze shy of hers.

Tea. At 4 p.m. every day on the porch out back. Tea and cake and the keskidees swooping to drink from the swimming pool. Earl Grey. White sugar in lumps. No one else around drank tea like this, no one on the island cared for tea, not like them. 'Allyuh white people crayzee wid all dis tea.' That's what Jennifer always said.

'So. Who's next to be interviewed?' Sabine pressed; George often didn't say.

'The coach.' His voice was hesitant.

'Beenhakker?'

'Yes. Why not?'

Sabine grimaced.

'I'm going to ask Ray later.'

'They've spent a fortune on this man.'

'Indeed.'

'Football, they spend millions. Hospitals, *zero*.'

George stared at his tea.

Sabine stirred hers. The Soca Warriors, Trinidad and Tobago's national team. A ragbag collection of players, some just out of high school. Only two professionals, both almost forty. She made a sarcastic smile.

'It's an important event.'

'Of course, darling.'

'Trinidadians are good at football.'

Sabine nodded. 'I know. Talented bunch. Good all-rounders.'

'Try to see it as a good thing. Try, darling.'

Sabine squinted. 'Ugh. Football, football. The world loves football. Men kicking a ball around, so proud of their countries, most run by imbeciles.'

'Oh, Sabine!'

'Eric Williams loved football, didn't he?'

'So? Where did *that* come from?'

'Never mind,' Sabine brooded, surprised at herself.

'Pass the cake, please.'

But she didn't want to pass the cake. She watched the keskidees swoop at the pool. The air was like glue. Her face glistened. George reached forward and speared banana cake onto his plate, his long hair undone. A strand hung over his face. His eyes were a little vacant. She'd made him angry again.

'Sorry, darling. I'm so hot. *Phutt!*' She fanned herself. The brown-yellow birds shouted *Qu'est-ce qu'il dit* – What's he saying? He wasn't saying anything; he was just trying to understand her, as usual.

*

After tea, George escaped Sabine and her holier-than-thou ideas. Pain in the neck with her righteous questions: as if he didn't know or care either. Well, mosst times he didn't: caring never helped things along. He drove away from the house towards the chaos of Port of Spain. It was March. Dry season. George melted in the pickup truck. The liver spots on the backs of his hands seemed to double before his eyes, the windscreen acting like a magnifying glass.

How he loved this city. Port of Spain. Poor old blind-deaf city. It spanned back, in a grid, from a busy port and dock; worn out now, ruined and ruinous and suffering, always suffering. It had survived military invasions, great fires, meek hurricanes, riots, mutinies, half a century of jouvay mornings, carnival Mondays and Tuesdays. No wonder it looked fatigued. Port of Spain: assaulted again and again and risen again and again, each time leaving the remnants of what had once been. Parts of the city still renewed themselves, rising up against the odds. These days it was garish and glittering office blocks, government housing projects, Honda showrooms. But in other parts, the ornate balconies and balustrades, the twee romantic town houses and gingerbread cottages of Great Britannia, of French Creoliana, were visibly tumbling into the dust.

George peered upwards and cursed. There it was. Staring, just like the sky stared, another pair of eyes. Something very new had risen in recent months. Not up through the streets, no. It hovered high above, farcical, spectral.

The blimp. Or, more commonly, *de blimp*, for great fun was made of it.

'Where was de blimp, nuh?' people joked every time another murder was reported.

Every day, the blimp now circled over Port of Spain. Sabine hated it, of course. It had cost 40 million dollars. This was the second blimp, in fact, the first having had problems staying up. Its mission, officially, was surveillance. The PNM had informed the country that the blimp was part of their crime-busting initiative, stationed up there to spy on the slums of Laventille and Belmont and other trouble spots, where the gangs roamed.

The blimp hovered high above the coughing city. A stout blue mini-zeppelin, it puttered around, resembling a huge udder escaped from a pantomime cow. George often fantasised about shooting it down. But it wasn't just the blimp. Sometimes the air above Port of Spain hammered with the drone of metal wasps. Attack helicopters. These, according to reports, were supposed to strike the slums from the sky, snatch and scare bandits, run them down. So far they hadn't been lucky either.

*

The *Trinidad Guardian* offices stood on St Vincent Street, a stone's throw from the Red House, in the west of the city, close to some of the colonial buildings which still survived. An air of academia faintly existed, what with the infamous Woodford Square and the National Library. Two black women, bulging in their security uniforms, ate warm nuts at reception. They both had large dolorous eyes and wore their hair coiled in ringlets; they rang up for him without so much as meeting his eye. He studiously overlooked their manner.

The newspaper offices spread across the first floor, air-conditioned and open-plan, existing in a moody, far-too-quiet smoked glass environment.

Ray looked relaxed, recovered from a busy afternoon, eating Kentucky Fried Chicken from a box, feet up on his desk.

'George, how yuh goin.' Half-Chinese, Ray was young and good-looking. Most of the *Guardian's* staff had quit a few years back, following a conglomerate takeover, leaving George with a steady stream of work, increasing his profile. The new owner was an economic superpower on the island. People thought him in favour with Patrick Manning, the supreme leader.

'De Tineke interview a big hit. She sexy, eh?'

'Yes, a nice girl. Clever, too.'

'Who you wanna do nex?'

George's heart surged. Ray was in a good mood.

'The coach. Beenhakker.'

'Ahhh.' Ray laughed in appreciation, sucking up a French fry. 'Somptin tell meh you go aks dat. De Warriors comin' soon, yes. We already try him. He not givin' one-on-one interviews yet or even at all as far as we know. An' if he do, de editor go give him to de boys in de newsroom. Dey already fightin' over it. It go be a big ting, George.'

'I see. Of course.' George tried to hide his disappointment. Trinidad and Tobago had qualified for the 2006 World Cup. Thanks to their expensive Dutch coach, the Soca Warriors were going to Germany. A huge story. He was OK with his status at the paper. Crazy-ass ol' white man; good writer, though. Besides, he'd invented himself; the personal interview was his forte. George Harwood – Soft News Man. He covered features, fluffy stuff. He interviewed women, children, elderly people, award-winners, priests, nuns, monks, comedians, calypsonians, businessmen, birdwatchers, dog lovers, forest-dwellers, potters, painters, Rastamen, Baptist shouters, and, occasionally, members of the government. He'd interviewed almost everyone on the island and wrote his interviews with love and care. He did all the *up*beat stories, the good-news stories the younger men on the paper refused to touch.

'I'd like you to do Boogsie for me.'

'Again?'

'Dey name a trophy after him.'

'A Boogsie Sharp trophy?'

'Yeah.' Ray laughed. 'At de music festival. Just do us somptin small. For next Sunday.'

'Anything else?'

'I hear Lara coming back after New Zealand.'

'Brian Lara?'

Ray nodded. 'Have you met him?'

'Actually, I haven't.'

'If he come, ah go ring yuh. I know you hot on cricket.'

'Thanks.'

George left Ray's office whistling. Lara, he was happy with that. Brian Lara was a great man.

The newsroom boys were back from an editorial meeting, a young bunch, all in ties and Clarks' desert boots, hair slicked back.

'What are the stories for tomorrow, boys?' George asked.

'Cop on murder charge,' Joel read from his screen.

'Cop on drugs charge,' Ramesh read from his.

'Policeman chopped chasing drug traffickers,' chipped in Corey.

'Family claim police brutality charges,' said Joel.

'Surely there must be one baby rescued from a burning building?'

'Yeah, *right*.' The boys smirked at him pityingly.

'You wanna interview my mother?' Joel laughed. Joel was the chief reporter, serious about his work, but also the office joker.

'Is she as ugly as you?'

'Uglier. But she like your interviews. She aks meh if yousa single man. Ah could fix you up.'

George walked past them, shaking his head.

'Goodbye, boys.'

'Bye George,' they chorused.

'Ay, how de lips dese days,' Joel called after him.

George turned round, blushing and smiling with shame. 'Get lost,' he mouthed.

The boys fell about laughing.

At the last Christmas staff party George got rat-arsed, taking a shine to a pretty, skinny Indian girl in the subs department. He stayed on far too late, fancying his chances, that she had liked him back, for he hadn't *completely* vanished, damn it. The girl was at least ten years younger than his daughter; tiny tits, round and

hard as apples, tiny backside, tiny T-shirt, tight jeans. Finding himself alone in the lift with her on the way down, he became
confused, missing the curves of his wife, the luscious wife of his
youth. Knowing he'd always been lucky with women. He lunged.
The girl dodged. He'd ended up kissing the wall.

*

Sabine smoked in their air-conditioned bedroom, curtains drawn,
the covers pulled up over her knees. She liked to smoke in the
cool and the dim light. At least she no longer took pills, no longer
slept for days at a time. Lucy, many years she worked for them,
years ago now; her tonics had brought her some relief, pleasant
fragrant drinks made of hibiscus petals. The *Cavina*, the banana
boat which had delivered them to the island decades ago, she saw
it drifting towards the dock. Those black birds in the sky, corbeaux.
She still saw them, too, circling overhead. Saw them every day,
picking at her carrion flesh, the dead meat she was. Now she
couldn't remember how to leave the island. And to where? Her
skin was black now, just like them. Being like this was a soft experience, as though she were nearing death. Of course she was
near death. But at last she was from here now, like it or not. She
was part of things. She no longer lived in the past, or dreamt of the
future, no one could accuse her of that. She lived day to day, thinking for the moment. She avoided the newspapers, of course, never
even read George's articles any more. Life was simple, like a
hermit's. She ate very little. She drank a lot, though. Never mind
about that. She smoked her cigarette to the nub and crushed it
out, then rolled over and curled herself up into a ball under the

covers. Eric Williams – the football. She remembered taking him in her arms. Those bleak days, Port of Spain in flames. She shut them out but they returned again and again. The letters she wrote. Hundreds. The air-conditioner hummed. It lulled her into a vague, comforting doze and once again she forgot.

*

On his way home, George slowed his truck to let cars pass at the bottom of Morne Cocoa Road, at the T-junction joining Saddle Road, next to the gas station, opposite the route-taxi pickup spot. La Pompey stood in the gas-station forecourt in ragged shorts and a bright white pair of trainers, his mahogany chest aglow in the evening's dim heat, his girlish pointy nipples erect. He counted through a roll of red dollar notes, the money he had earned from washing cars.

'Yess, Mr Harwood.' La Pompey grinned across at him.

La Pompey wasn't mad. Maybe a bit simple. But no madman.

'Good evening, sir.' George waved from the cab of the truck.

'Man, yuh truck a *state*. Looking like it been tru de pitch lake.'

'Yes. Sorry about that.'

'How yuh could drive dat ting so wid no shame?'

George shrugged. The rust was so bad it resembled a spray of machine-gun bullet holes, but he was very attached to it.

'It need a wash, man. Ah comin' to fix it up.'

'Yes, sir. Come round any time.'

'How's Mrs Harwood?'

'Very well.'

'You is keepin' her well den. You know what dey say.'

'What's that?'

'A kiss a day keep de doctor away.'

George made an amused half-sour face. 'You should write greet-ings cards, sir.'

'Yes, man. Kiss your woman every day and keep her sweet and she will always be a treat.'

'You're a poet, too, Mr La Pompey.'

'Just La Pompey, *La* Pompey,' he corrected. 'Yes, man, ah does write a little verse from time to time.'

'And your favourite poet, do tell.'

'William Shakespeare.'

'Shakespeare?'

'Yes, man. Learn him well in school and ting.'

'And what poems did you learn?'

La Pompey smiled, only three teeth showing before his face went calm and serious. He studied George with careful attention, his eyes a little wet. 'Shall I compare de to a summer's day?'

George stared.

La Pompey mock-wooed George through the car window. 'Dou art more lovely, man, yes, man – an' more tem-per-ate!'

George wanted to kiss him.

La Pompey slow-winked. 'Nice, eh?'

'Yes.'

'Poetry say everytin.'

'Maybe.'

'Summer, man.' La Pompey grinned. 'Summer all de time in Trinidad. Heat in de place. Heat an' sunshine.' He glowed, his face like a big sun.

'I like that poem.'

'You *know* it?'

'Of course.'

'You does speak poems for Mrs Harwood?'

'Not these days.'

'I'm sorry to hear dat. You should speak more poems fer she.'

'She wouldn't like it if I did.'

'Really? You never know.'

'Yes, I know.'

'You mus speak of de love inside you, man. Or else where it go? It go rot, form a lump inside you. Rot and swell and make you sick.'

'How did you know . . . that's how it feels?'

'I's a sweet-man.' He winked again. 'Can't you see? Ah does love plenty women. Keep me healthy.'

'Good for you, La Pompey.'

'Yes, man. Take care Mrs Harwood. Treat she sweet. Mrs Harwood a plenty good woman an' yousa lucky man. Summer every day, man, in Trinidad.'

A car behind beeped George and he turned left, driving on through the village.

Winderflet village spread itself beneath the green hills of Paramin. The valley, rich in soil, once boasted nine flourishing estates, several mills and four rum distilleries. A brown river, Winderflet River, sometimes slim, sometimes fat, according to the season, slithered through the valley and the village embraced its shallow curves. Our Lady of Lourdes dominated the settlement, a grand square church peering down from an excavated mound; French, Catholic, it was carnivalesque with its gaudy red and vanilla exterior. The church cast a long shadow from up there on the mound, a shadow which fell directly onto Winderflet Police Station, much to the disdain of Superintendent Bobby 'Big Balls' Comacho. Between the church and the police station, they had things all sewn up. A quiet place, Winderflet. The church boasted a robust choir, tenors, a soprano, the whole range of gospel voices. Sometimes, when driving through the village during choir practice, George listened to the hymns sailing out, songs to God, songs floating upwards, lifting his heart. One voice was always very particular, more celestial than the others, mournful: the boy's voice.

It was dark by the time he arrived home. The house he had built nestled at the foot of the same imposing green hills. Sabine had always seen a woman in the hills, a colossus, asleep on her side, half-exposing her loins. The house was a Spanish finca in design, arches and courtyards and wide porches all around. Sliding glass windows opened so the hummingbirds could flit through, siphoning nectar from the cut ginger lilies. A pool out back in which George paddled like a duck. He stopped at the wrought-iron gates which stood seven foot tall and peered through the bars.

The sticky Julie mango tree nodded at him.

Don't look at me like that.

Like what?

Like you know how.

No, I don't.

One day she lit up, one day *I* lit her up; the next, nothing. When did it happen? I don't recall the day.

It's not your fault.

Sabine was right about this country. She punishes me.

It's not your fault. Anyway, you're sure it all happened in one day? Think.

What? Think?

Eric Williams, remember him?

Yes.

It's all *his* fault. More than you care to know.

George snorted. You going to quote Shakespeare to me, too?

I am going to let down my bucket where I am, right here with you, in the British West Indies.

Who said that?

Eric Williams.

When?

A long time ago.

Yes. Poor bastard. Whatever became of him in the end?

Ask your wife.

What's that supposed to mean?

You know.

No, I don't.

You do, you just don't want to remember.

I miss her.

Yes.

We survive off our past glory.

It's not your fault.

No.

Her eyes are evasive, that's the worst part. I should let her go.

Maybe you should.

But I would miss her so.

*

22

George clicked the buzzer. The gate slid backwards and he drove through. The big sandy ridgeback dogs woofed and jumped up at the doors to greet him; they wagged their whole bodies with delight, trailing the truck.

'Good evening, boys,' he greeted them, taking each by the muzzle and rubbing it down, rubbing each dog, especially his favourite, Henry, into a shambling stooping ecstasy. 'Good, good dogs, that's right.' They crowded him as he entered the courtyard out front.

The television was on too loud, as usual, blaring American cable TV. Sabine lounged on a sofa, the back of her head to him. Her hair had recently been clipped to an inch of her skull, because of the heat, she said.

'Hello, dear,' he called.

Sabine turned, dabbing her face with a tissue.

When, when did this Sabine materialise? Her face so clammy, her skin diseased. Chocolate-brown flecks, eruptions of melanin, splattered her forehead, her cheeks, her shoulders, too. Large brown spots on sun-ravaged skin. Bumps had clustered on her once enticing cleavage. Her face and chest were scourged, mapped with crevasses.

'You're late,' she said, turning back to watch the television. She smoked, nursing a rum and soda. Katinka flopped next to her, head buried in Sabine's lap, eyes rolled upwards as a form of greeting.

'I've seen Ray,' he said, tucking the tag of her dress back in. 'I'm going to interview Brian Lara.'

'This is incredible, what's going on!'

'What is?'

'*Who Wants to Be a Millionaire*?'

'Oh.'

'This man is two questions away from winning a million dollars.'

'Good.' He checked his watch, 7 p.m. Time for the local news. 'Can we turn over?'

She shrugged.

'Please.'

Sabine flicked channels reluctantly, stroking her lapdog. The animal lifted its tiny glossy head and yawned.

CNC came on. George sat down in his armchair. The newscaster, Carla Foderington, spoke in posh creole tones. She was a starchy-looking, well-dressed black woman whom he rather fancied.

Sabine rose and disappeared into the kitchen. The little dog jumped off the sofa and trotted after her, also bored by what was happening in Trinidad.

George pressed his fingers along the line of his brow. *Hello, my love*, she used to say. *Hello, my love, my loving love-cup, my darling-heart. How was your day?* Once, she'd glowed when she saw him. She would throw her arms around him, reach up to kiss his cheek. Sometimes she would pull him into the bedroom.

Sabine returned with a two-foot canister of Flit, blasting a thick mist of insecticide ahead of her, crop-dusting the once expensive Spanish rugs. If the sun was her primary enemy, mosquitoes were a close second. George tried to watch the news but she stood in the way, spraying. Mist everywhere. A newly lit cigarette was clamped in her other hand.

'Darling, one day there'll be an explosion.'

'What?'

'I can't see.' He waved the mist away, coughing. 'Could you move over a bit?'

But she was now engrossed in the local news, too, watching with an air of impatience.

'Oouf. Another murder,' she snapped. Even her tone of voice had changed. It made him ashamed of himself. Sometimes, when she spoke to Jennifer, it was in Jennifer's way. She steupsed just like Jennifer, and *eh, eh, ohoed*. Her third language, after French and English. Sabine was an excellent mimic. Her French was Parisian, her English like the Queen's, her Trinidadian dialect, whenever it emerged, was bold and rhythmic.

The news stories of the day:

Basdeo Panday, the leader of the opposition, in court on charges of corruption.

The murder toll had reached a hundred in a hundred days.

Thirty-nine police officers were flying to the island from Scotland Yard to help with the kidnapping epidemic.

A shoot-out in Laventille, the infamous slum of Port of Spain. Images of a man lying dead in a gutter, thick black blood pooling from his stomach. Laventillians standing around watching.

The Soca Warriors in training.

Sabine disappeared in disgust, still Flit-ing, mounting the stairs, bent on poisoning the entire house.

Later, she brought out two trays with plates of microwaved left-over goat curry. They ate on their laps, watching the weather report. Then Sabine flicked over to watch ice-dancing, dabbing her sweat-damp face and feeding titbits to Katinka. After game shows, Sabine mostly glued herself to foreign events, watching hours of figure-skating and tennis; always a tournament on, always something big somewhere else.

George heard a familiar whistling from the opposite sofa.

'Darling?'

Sabine sat in a half-fallen position, the ballast of her swollen stomach keeping her from toppling completely. Her lips billowed, reverberating, the sound like a small puffing engine. He rose quietly and went over to her, kneeling next to the sofa. He liked to look at her while she slept, so unguarded. His eyes wandered over her, picking over the bulges and sloping lines of her form. He'd caught sight of this body, here and there, in mirrors, in the bathroom. Under her house dress, her stomach looked like an uneven pile of red clay. Her breasts had grown slack, pendulous, running to her waist. Her arms were thicker, the tender white underskin yellowed and doughy. Her legs were pudgy now, marbled with blue-purple veins. Her toenails were dry and papery. No trace of her former beauty; the sun had taken it.

Sabine stirred. Her eyes flickered sleepily, then flew open. 'Oh.' She jumped awake.

'What's wrong?' she asked accusingly, as though he were an intruder.

'Nothing, my love.'

'What are you doing?'

'Looking at you.'

'You frightened me.'

'I'm sorry.'

'I was dreaming of the *Cavina*.'

'Were you?'

'The day we arrived. Laventille Hill, remember that? I thought we'd live *there*.'

George nodded. 'You were nervous, weren't you?'

'I was . . . sick with nerves.'

George gazed at her. How he still liked to look at her, puzzle at her face, how it once was, how it was now. He smiled, daring to put out his hand, look into her eyes. She watched his hand as he placed it on her belly. These days it was like trying to touch a wounded bear, which made caressing his wife somehow more thrilling. Sabine's eyes were suddenly full, expectant.

'What are you thinking?' he asked.

'My green bicycle. Remember it?'

'Yes, of course.'

'Arriving from the hold. People laughed when they saw it.'

'Yes.'

'I travelled everywhere on that bike – at first. Didn't I?'

'I remember it well.'

Often, Sabine would arrive at the dock to meet him after work. Her shorts revealed long, slim, honey-coloured legs. A halter-neck top, Dior sunglasses. Blonde curls. Every man behind her stopped dead in their tracks to watch her pass.

'Riding round the savannah, I liked that.'

'Holding up traffic with those legs.'

'I saw Trinidad on that bike. You know . . . saw the sights.'

'And you were seen, my love.' George smiled. 'Don't we still have that old thing, somewhere?'

She nodded carefully.

'Where?'

'I don't know. Somewhere.'

CHAPTER TWO

FLY AWAY

In the morning, Jennifer was sobbing in the kitchen. She was hot-faced, salt tears flowing down her cheeks. She gushed out pieces of a story, something about her son Talbot, about a mobile phone, the police beating him up.

'Sit down, sit down,' Sabine soothed. 'I'll make you some tea.'

Jennifer nodded, blinded by tears.

George asked her to start again, to try and get it all out in order.

'Las week,' Jennifer began through her sobs, 'Talbot go to a fête. Der was a roadblock on de way. He get search by de police. One o' dem fine his mobile phone and tek it from him, fer himself.'

'Bastards,' Sabine spat.

'Then what happened?' George pressed.

'Talbot have a girlfrien who in de police force. He tell her what happen and she say she know de policeman who took de phone. A real badjohn name Johnny. De girl den went to dis policeman, tell him to give Talbot back he phone.'

'And?'

Jennifer began to cry again. 'Dis Johnny police fella come fer Talbot two night ago. He bring tree odder policemen wid him. Dey take him up de hill, up Paramin Hill, Mr Harwood.'

'Right up there?'

Jennifer started to cry again. 'Yes. Dey give Talbot licks. Dey mash up his face, break his nose. Brek his *ribs*. De policeman who took de phone vexed wid him exposin' what he did. He treaten Talbot. Tell him if he ever see Talbot again and Talbot alone, he go make him dead.'

'Where's Talbot now?' George asked, thinking fast.

'He by me, he at home.'

'Has he seen a doctor?'

'No. I come here first. I cyan drive. Chantal cyan drive. Route taxi doh come up by us.'

'He's been lying two nights with a broken nose?' Sabine gasped.

'Yes.'

'Oh, Jennifer! Why?'

'Furs night he stay up on de hill. He cyan come down, he too weak. Nex mornin somebody fine him, all mash up. Dey bring him dong by me. I ent fine him till ah reach home after comin' from here.'

'He needs to go to casualty, Jennifer.' George squeezed her hand. 'Immediately. We need to take him there now, before his bones start to set. Come on, we'll go now. I'll take him.'

'I'll come, too,' Sabine decided.

George didn't fancy his chances crossing her. 'OK. Let's bring the camera.'

*

29

Music boomed from the house across the road from Jennifer's home, domineering reggae of the most pastoral and sober kind, *conscious* music they called it. Jennifer's teenage nephews played it night and day, peace piped over the poorest of neighbourhoods. Jennifer hated it. Restless buggers, they limed out on the street ambling around in circles, trousers hanging from their arses. They shot George and Sabine looks, bad looks from their bleary black eyes.

'What wrong wid you,' Jennifer scolded them. They steupsed and walked away, but not far enough.

Jennifer's home stood amongst tall grasses. A miracle. Her Aunt Venus had lived there, too – their whole family, in fact. Seven generations. An ancient slave chattel house, it was rust brown all over and had a much-patched galvanized roof; even so, it still bore a faint trace of grandeur with its gingerbread design. It stood of its own free will, walls leaning against each other like praying hands, the nails having dropped out long ago. Holes dotted the wood and, where one or two nails remained, they were orange and withered. The shack loomed there up on the hill, to the left of a treacherous bend in the road, surrounded by a wire fence. It stood on columns of rubble and furniture and pillars of flat river-stones. It always looked down on George, or so he felt.

'Can we go in?' he asked, tentatively.

Jennifer nodded, still scowling at her nephews across the road.

Inside, it was darker and it took a few moments for his sight to adjust. George was always awkward coming here, which wasn't often. He tried not to glance around, not to notice the familiar objects in the house, their cast-off armchairs, their listing sideboard, the kitchen appliances. Sabine had fallen morbidly silent. They followed Jennifer straight to the room at the back of the house.

Talbot lay on an iron-framed bed, the thin mattress covered in bald winceyette, his face to the wall. The room was airless, the walls patterned with brown shadows. Stained pyjama-striped sheets hung for curtains; their worn sheets. Talbot groaned, turning his head.

'Dear God,' George muttered.

Sabine gasped.

Jennifer began to cry again.

The bruises were so bad it looked as though a butterfly had settled on Talbot's face, a curious blue-green, purple-yellow butterfly. His eyes had exploded, so damaged they were gooey, leaking a clear glistening fluid. One of them was bloated, lopsided and sealed closed. His nose was smashed and swollen and the jagged break loomed through the skin. Talbot's bottom lip was still encrusted with gems of congealed blood.

'Jennifer, I'm so sorry!' Sabine whispered under her breath. 'Talbot, *who did this*?'

Talbot made no attempt to reply. His eyes were vacant; he was past caring. George felt his bile rise, a flush of pure hatred spread outwards from his gut. Talbot lay bare-chested, his ribs grazed; his torso appeared as if it were smudged, bruises over bruises on his young pearl-brown skin. The breaks were plainly apparent, where the lines of the bones underneath didn't meet. George worried that Talbot's lungs might puncture if they moved him hastily.

Sabine put an arm around Jennifer. 'It's OK now, it's OK. We'll get help. Shhhhh.'

Jennifer sobbed. 'Dey *beat* him, dey beat my son. Dey beat him like a dog. Dey beat him up on de hill. Where it so peaceful. Two men held him and two others beat him.'

Sabine held her tight, shooshing, her lips close to Jennifer's bowed head.

George thought fast: Talbot needed immediate medical attention, so they wouldn't drive him to the General Hospital in Port of Spain, where stray dogs roamed the wards. No, no, no. Talbot would go to the A & E at the private medical centre in St Clair. To get there, they would need to lay him flat on the back seat of the car and drive with great care to save those lungs. Then he would pay a visit the *Guardian*, take the camera straight to Joel on the news desk.

'Talbot, would you mind if we took some pictures?'

Talbot's eyes flashed open, he looked alarmed. 'Uhhh?'

'Don't worry. It won't make things worse. I promise. These men need to be punished, taken off the force.'

'Mr Harwood, dey make sure der were no witnesses. Dey take me up to de hill.'

'Yes. I know.'

Talbot's face twisted.

'Talbot, this is *evidence*,' Sabine cut in. 'These bruises tell a story. This is GBH. You've suffered a serious assault. And your girlfriend on the force will back up your story. We will back you up, too.'

'Oh gorsh,' Talbot whispered through his swollen lips. 'I doh know, Mrs Harwood. No one see what happen. I doh know. I doh want more trouble.'

George cleared a space on the bed, sitting down carefully. 'Talbot, one of these men threatened you with your life. Do you think he was joking?'

Tears appeared in Talbot's gummed eyes.

'Don't you *see*?'

'I doh know.'

'I think you *do* know. They did this because they can, because they assume you won't dare speak out. Will you let us help you?'

Jennifer sobbed harder.

'Oh gorsh.'

'Let us help.'

Talbot nodded.

Sabine left Jennifer's side, snapping some close-ups of Talbot's battered face, his ribs, his chest. Flies landed on the forming scabs and she shooed them away. Gingerly, with Jennifer's help, they lifted Talbot from the bed, helping him into the car, all the while Talbot moaning in pain and Jennifer moaning with grief.

At the medical centre the A & E nurse studied Talbot with sombre eyes. They escorted him to a small room with three beds, leaving him there with Jennifer. There would be X-rays, tests.

'Jennifer, we'll be back soon,' Sabine reassured her. 'You stay with your son. We're taking these pictures to the *Guardian*. Mr Harwood knows someone who can write about what happened.'

Jennifer nodded. She looked taken upon by a different person-ality, aged, melancholy, another woman.

In the car, George glanced at his wife: Sabine's mood had turned lethal. For a few moments they drove along in silence.

'I'm going to beat that man myself,' Sabine declared.

'Who?'

'That idiot should be *shot*.'

'Who?'

'That Bobby "Big Balls" Comacho. I'll do him in myself.'

'Darling, Bobby's no man to get on the wrong side of.'

'Bobby is a thug. He should be locked up. The men on his force are a disgrace. I'm going to make a complaint.'

'Please don't.'

'I'm going to go into that police station and kick up a huge damn fuss.'

'Please don't, Sabine. What good will that do?'

'I don't care.'

'The *Guardian* may well run with the story about Talbot. The pictures are very strong. That's enough.'

'I don't think that fat idiot ever reads the newspapers. I don't think he can read *at all* in fact. Illiterate pig.'

'Sabine, please—'

'Don't Sabine me. I'm going to give him a piece of my mind – if you won't.'

'What's that supposed to mean?'

Sabine stared upwards, out the window. 'There it is.'

George looked up. The blimp was following them, puttering high overhead. '*Please* don't distract me, Sabine. I'm driving.'

'I'll shoot it down one day.'

'Good. Go out and buy a gun.'

'Maybe I will. I'll shoot Mr Manning, too, whilst I'm at it.'

'Darling, please.'

'Talbot's face. If that was *our* son. If the police had beaten Sebastian like that, then there'd be trouble. God. Then there'd be a fight. But the police don't beat up white people. They beat up each other.'

'Do you want me to go and beat up Bobby Comacho, Superintendent of the District?'

'Yes.'

'I'm seventy-five.'

'Good. Old men are dangerous. Can't knock an old man down.'

'You want me to put on my boxing gloves?'

'If you won't, I will.'

'You're seventy-five, too.'

'That bloody thing is following us.'

'Don't be crazy.'

'Eric Williams.'

'What?'

'It's all *his* fault.'

George went silent, not wanting this conversation again. Sabine, he could see, was brooding up a storm.

'Things could have been so different,' she said in a sullen tone.

*

Sabine followed George through the maze of desks. The newsroom was air-conditioned and quiet and yet suitably ramshackle, half library, half common room; people with their heads down, on the phone, laughter and ol' talk, a mostly young staff. She'd always been curious. George had been allowed into this world late in life, when Ray had first asked him to cover the golf tournaments in Tobago. He had retired from his working life long ago – and Ray had given him these odd assignments. Turned out George could write. He was funny, too, fluent and erudite with it – and soon he had a following. More assignments followed. In those days, she typed his articles out from his longhand; she was part of things then, this second career, before he bought a computer and learnt to type.

'Darling, this is Joel.' They were at the news desk. Six desks facing each other at the far end of the room. A poster of Malcolm X on the wall behind Joel's head. Next to it, Fidel Castro biting a cigar.

'Joel, this is my wife, Sabine.'

The young man stood up and shook her hand. The other reporters all looked up with open interest.

'Oh, dis a surprise, de ol' man talk about you a lot.' Joel winked at George but Sabine could tell he was intrigued, sizing her up. Sabine let him stare into her ravaged face.

'Likewise,' she smiled sweetly. Joel was handsome, a dougla, afro hair and Indian features. His eyes were inky black and his skin the colour of cocoa dust.

'What brings you in today?' Joel eyed the camera Sabine held like a grenade.

'Spot of trouble,' George explained.

Joel grinned at this Englishman's understatement. He rubbed his chin.

'Fucking bastards beat up our maid's son,' Sabine blurted.

Joel raised his eyebrows. 'Mrs Harwood, who beat up *who*?'

'Bloody police. Three of them, beat him half to death. Left him up there to die. Top of Paramin Hill, left him for hours. Days even. You know it gets cold up there. Cold. Damn cowards. *Cochons*. He's in the medical centre in St Clair.'

Joel whistled. The other reporters were now plainly aware of this white woman with a foul mouth.

Sabine smiled, apologetic. 'Pardon my French, boys. Wait till you see the pictures.'

'You have pictures?'

'Not of the event. Of his injuries.'

'Will he speak?'

'I doubt it,' George cut in. Sabine could tell he'd hoped to handle this.

'Witnesses?' Joel pressed.

'None,' said George.

'Just those hills,' Sabine added. 'The hills witnessed the attack.'

George coughed, trying to cut her off.

'Those weaklings threatened to kill him,' Sabine continued. 'For a mobile phone.'

'Policemen bad dese days, Mrs Harwood. We run a story like dis every day.'

'I stopped reading the newspapers, I'm afraid. Some time ago.' She shot George a dark collusive stare.

'We go take a look at de pictures,' Joel said. 'We go run de story, nuh. We always do. Our own little campaign.'

'Good for you.' Sabine handed over the camera.

'Thanks, Joel,' George said.

'We'll need to speak to dis fella, aks him questions.'

'I'll give you directions.' George came forward and the pair began to make notes.

On the wall behind, Malcolm X stared right at Sabine. The young men at the news desk looked up under him, their faces young and bright and scrubbed, proud of themselves. They all stared, as if she were a hologram.

'What about *him*?' Sabine pointed to the poster.

Joel turned round to see what she was looking at. He raised his fist. His face, like the others', was open, boyish. 'Black Power, man.'

'Really? I'm surprised you say that.'

George sighed. 'Here she goes.'

Joel's face was amused, trying to please.

'What kind of *power* does Talbot have?'

His face fell.

George looked awkward.

'Yes, Mrs Harwood. The Chief of Police in de pocket of Mr Manning. Everyone know dat.'

'But you can't *write* anything about that. Can you?'

Joel shook his head. 'Mrs Harwood, maybe we should hire you, too. We could give you a news column. Mr Harwood, eh, watcha say?'

George looked appalled.

Sabine fluttered her eyelashes. 'I'd like that.'

Joel went serious; his voice dropped so he was speaking in confidence. 'We criticise, we do. We try to. The news speak for itself. Manning cyan law enforce dis country – enforce all he friens at top level? But de PNM cyan argue wid fact. Fact is fact, man. No one can stop me from writing down fact.'

'Good.'

Sabine felt a dull glow of pleasure. 'Will that loathsome fuckwit Patrick Manning get in next year?'

Joel erupted with laughter. The boys behind him hooted. 'Of *course*. Wid all de votes he buy.'

'Black Power,' Sabine said. 'That's what it's been since the PNM took over. Black Power for one man only, or for the few.'

'Sabine—' George made as if to go.

Joel looked genuinely surprised by her words. He winked at George.

'See?' George half smiled. 'See how I live?'

Sabine made a grim face, unperturbed. Let them think what they liked.

'Lady, it real nice to meet you at las.' Joel shook her hand.

'Nice to meet you, too.'

'I jus write de news.'

'I'm glad you do. Thank you, and thank you for helping us.'

At the medical centre in St Clair, Talbot was dozing. He'd been expertly patched up. Four broken ribs, a broken nose; two mangled fingers were splinted. No internal bleeding, though. His ribs were bandaged, his head wrapped so heavily his face was nearly hidden behind all the padding. He'd been bathed and his unbruised skin glowed. He smelled clean, medical and citrusy from Limacol. Jennifer had her son back again, in almost one piece. If that had been Sebastian – dear God, what hell then. What would Granny Seraphina make of this, eh? She would turn in her cardboard-box grave.

Talbot lay on clean white sheets, probably the cleanest and whitest sheets he'd ever had. Jennifer sat next to him on one of two metal chairs. Sabine sat down next to her and reached for her hand. Jennifer, usually so verbal, so quick to tease and retaliate, to picong and ol' talk and giggle and make noise and fun for her and George, was speechless. She looked aged, but somehow dignified, like Granny. Some of that old woman's resolve set in her face, her shoulders. Some of that slave silence.

'I told Mr Harwood I'm going to give Bobby Comacho hell.'

Jennifer didn't stir.

'Shoot him in the balls.'

Jennifer's shoulders shook.

'I mean it.'

'Yeah, man. Watch out, den dey trow you in a cell.'

'*What* – then they'd have trouble on their hands.'

'Jesus Lord.' Jennifer pressed her palms to her forehead. She steupsed in a long miserable way. 'I wish I could . . . fly away, yes. You know? To another place.'

Sabine put her arm around Jennifer. Tears spilled from Jennifer's eyes. 'Dis not fair. It not right. Dey leave him up der, Mrs Harwood. He try to crawl dong on his hands and knees, den a man fine him and bring him down by us. And when I see him in mih house, oh gorsh. I ent recognise mih own son.'

Sabine squeezed her shoulders. 'He's better now. He'll be OK.'

'I wish I could fly far away.'

'I know.'

'Far away, man. To another place.'

'Yes. I know.'

Jennifer raised her head and looked at her, harshly. 'You *shoulda* lef, man. I cyan understand why you never leave.'

Sabine exhaled. 'I almost did, once.'

'Das what Mr Harwood say. Das what Venus say before she lef.'

'I can't even remember those days, Jennifer. I was another woman then. Young. Naive.'

'You wanted to go?'

'Yes. I missed my son. And there was trouble here in 1970. Mr Harwood's business was burnt down. They poisoned our dogs. Oh, and worse . . .'

'You still vexed? Venus say she miss livin' wid you and de chilren.'

'Yes. Me, too. We were great friends.'

'Aunt Venus say you used to ride a green bicycle all over Port of Spain. You was famus ridin' on dat bike.' She chuckled.

'Yes, I think I was.'

'De same bike all rusted in de garage?'

'Do we still have it?'

'Must be.'

'I thought we gave it away. Didn't we? So much I can't remember.'

Jennifer steupsed. Jennifer never liked it when Sabine talked around things, what she called *English-talk*. Even though she knew the Harwoods well, she disapproved of any vagueness; she saw it as cowardice, somehow even as lying. Trinidadians had the tendency to be explicitly honest about everything.

'I mean it,' Sabine repeated. 'I've forgotten myself.'

'Forgotten Eric Williams, too?'

Sabine winced. 'Eh, eh. Why do you ask?'

'Aunt Venus say you used to write to him, always. Letters. She say you like to put dem in a box. Put Dr Williams in a box.'

'Oh. *Venus* told you that?'

'Long time ago.'

Sabine felt blank about it all. She felt none of her long-ago feelings, nothing of those early days. 'Venus was right.'

'So, you forget about him?'

Sabine had never spoken to anyone about him at all, only Venus. Careful, she looked at Jennifer, trusting her. 'No.' Her eyes welled. 'No. In fact, you know what? I *dream* of Eric Williams. From time to time.'

'Wow.'

'Funny, isn't it?'

'Yeah, man.'

Sabine laughed at herself. 'Don't tell Mr Harwood.'

'He would be vexed?'

'I don't know. I don't care, either. But sometimes I dream of Eric Williams, you know. In Woodford Square. He was impressive then. A sight to see.'

'You *saw* him then?'

'Yes.'

'Wow. Legend time, man. A famous man.'

'Yes.'

Jennifer looked at her, as if she had lit upon a sudden idea. 'You stay here in Trinidad because you love Mr Harwood?'

Sabine stared away from her, out through the jalousie shutters at the car park. Love Mr Harwood? What a question. Did she? What had happened between them? She could no longer be sure of things any more. She knew she loved him once, long ago, loved him fierce as a hurricane, fiercer. But now? Hard to tell, hard to know anything.

'The truth?'

'Yes.'

'I can't remember, Jennifer.'

CHAPTER THREE

THE AFFAIR

Midnight. A clamorous hour in the house beneath the hip of the green woman. The temperature had dropped causing the cicadas to make a sound like constantly shaking maracas. Tiny tree frogs croaked, brassy. Crickets shouted, trying to compete. The house groaned, shifting with the coolness of the night's shade. Sabine snored in their bed down the hall. The dogs whimpered in their dreams, chasing the iguana round and round.

'Now *where* is that file on Brian Lara?' George muttered. Sabine used the office in the mornings for letter writing; he used it in the afternoons. It worked well enough, except for her tidy-ups.

'Bugger,' he cursed, finding a torch in the desk drawer. He climbed up onto the office chair, sliding back the hatch to the storage space above. Everything ended up stashed there but he'd never dared search the space, left it to Sabine; it was her hidey-hole.

'Jesus,' he gasped, as the beam swept across the cavern.

Boxes, mostly, stuffed with letters, postcards, papers, cards.

Years-out-of-date bills. Piles of magazines: *TIME*, *Newsweek*, *Vogue*. Sabine's rusted Remington typewriter.

Then, in a corner, an uneven stack, covered with what looked like an old tablecloth. He shone the beam across it. The cloth was filthy, lacy with cobwebs and mould; the stack appeared hunched over, like a tramp crouching in the dust. He pushed himself up so half his body was in the darkened space and tugged at the cloth. It slipped off easily, revealing a dust-caked pile of small boxes, shoeboxes, twenty or so, each with the same two words written across the side: *Eric Williams*.

'Dear God.' He reached forward and pulled one of the boxes towards him. There was a date on the lid: *1958*. Years ago. Decades.

'Oh, no . . .' he whispered, dragging more shoeboxes towards him. Each bore a different date.

George dragged more and more across, throwing them down onto the desk below, silky grey dust cascading, powdering the office floor. Quickly, he pulled down every single box in the stack, until the desk below was a shipwreck of hidden loot, piled high and precarious. Dust everywhere. His hands were blackened, his hair caught up with cobwebs. He got down and roughly lined the boxes along the floor, running in order of year. Each box bulged, heavily stuffed with papers. Each was precisely marked up. Eric Williams. Twenty-six years, twenty-six boxes. Williams had ruled for twenty-six years. Each box was precisely dated. *Sabine, Sabine, what on earth had she been doing?*

1956. The year the boxes started. They arrived in Trinidad that year. January 1956, to be precise. Eric Williams launched the People's National Movement the same month and won his first election later in the year; a famous year in the history of Trinidad.

Eighty per cent of the nation turned out to vote him in and the British out.

George snapped open *1956*.

Newspaper clippings. Yellowed and crisp. Hundreds of time-worn *Trinidad Guardian* clippings. Tidily snipped. Each dated in Sabine's hand.

He scooped the whole lot out in one. Kneeling down, he spread them across the office floor.

'Jesus Christ.' A compendium of Williams: comment, op-ed, reports, photos of him with members of his cabinet, with the Beatles, for God's sake, with the Mighty Sparrow. With Harold Macmillan, with Gerald Ford. Phrases, comments underlined in blotted blue ink. Sabine's hand. An asterisk in the margin. An exclamation mark.

George groaned long and loud, expelling a grand and pent-up disappointment, a disappointment held in for so long he'd almost forgotten it. Stupid fucker. He knew. Sabine had seen Eric Williams speak in Woodford Square, once, maybe even twice, early on when Eric Williams was in his prime; she had been over-whelmed. Sabine had so many theories about Eric Williams. But he'd blocked them out after a while. They had even *met* Williams at the Hilton once, a strange meeting. They'd fought afterwards. Then 1970, Black Power: Sabine was never the same again. Granny Seraphina – his wife had caught something from that old slave woman.

Everything was in the box. Not just his political career, but photos of Williams' daughter, Erica. His dead wife, Soy. Photos of Soy and Williams together.

George opened *1957*. More sheaves of yellowed newspaper cuttings. More Eric Williams. Quickly, he opened box after box in the row: everyone the same. Fragments of Eric Williams' life. His speeches. His essays and commentaries in the *Trinidad Guardian*. His comings and goings. Photo-portraits. Eric Williams had been a striking man, as imposing as Churchill or Chairman Mao. His glued-on hearing aid, the heavy dark glasses.

The *1962* box felt lighter. He opened it.

'Dear God.'

Letters! Tied with a red ribbon, twenty or so. A few newspaper clippings beneath them. Letters, letters. All *addressed* to Eric Williams. George scrabbled at the ribbon's knot, his fingers stiff.

Dear Mr Williams, the first letter began.

George dumped the box upside down, shaking it. Clippings tumbled out. Letters from his wife to Eric Williams, the Prime Minister of Trinidad. He stared at Sabine's delicate handwriting. So nonchalant, evoking another woman. Sabine, writing as she talked, free as a schoolgirl. Independence Day. Memories of that day. They'd watched it all on TV. The red, black and white flag hoisted up, the Union Jack fluttering down. Sabine, here in his hands – writing to congratulate Eric Williams, saying something bitchy about Princess Margaret, something very Sabine. His first wife, here in his hands. The wife he'd lost.

George opened the box for 1963.

More letters, a bigger sheaf. *Dear Mr Williams*. He couldn't read past this opening line. What had been going on? This was madness. Had the letters been *sent* to Williams? Then sent back? Opened? Unopened? Had there been a correspondence? An affair? He thought hard. Those years, long ago; difficult to know any more. Bad years between them, and then they had almost left Trinidad. And then Williams had died. Had Williams written *back*?

On his hands and knees George crawled across the office floor, opening box after box. In each, like a corpse, a sheaf of beribboned letters. Sabine! Her questions, her voice. What had happened? He knew. He'd turned a blind eye. Crisp curled pages of Sabine's writing on her favourite onion-skin paper. Sabine's hand. His wife's outpourings to the Prime Minister of Trinidad.

George read till dawn. Sitting on the office floor, his back against the wall. He read every letter, mouthing the words. Three hundred and fifty-eight letters in all. *Dear Mr Williams*. Nothing as straightforward as a love affair: passion, guilt, betrayal, all the usual to and fro. No. They were far worse. He stopped several times to ponder, lost in reveries of their life together. He only knew the half of it, only half her despair.

The letters were originals. Unsent. Communiqués to the self in some respects. He found no replies and wondered if they were in another stash, other boxes hidden elsewhere in the house. From what she had written, he began to understand.

I'm sick of George.

I'm sick from loving him.

I can't see past the bars on the gates of this wretched house. There seem to be thousands of them.

Some of the letters were eloquent tirades. Others were pleas: tender, touching, moving, letters only a woman could write to a politician. She had been worried about Williams at times, early on, genuinely concerned. Many, though, were lacerating critiques.

Some were inane ramblings, losing themselves like a drunk mid-speech. There were conversations, too, diary entries. Every letter was personal. They brought on an ache of loss, of grief. When, when had he lost his wife?

George has gone mad. He sleeps with other women, flaunts his charms. All this has gone to his head. He owns land, he's head of the company now. People here laugh at George behind his back. A grand blanc – like those in Haiti once who went power-crazy with their little kingdoms. Yes, he's like them. He wasn't like this when we came. He's changed, become less than he was, he's deranged. Too much rum. Too many beautiful women on this goddamn island.

George was still sitting there when Sabine woke. He looked up and she was standing in the office doorway, her short hair in grizzled tufts, her blue cotton nightie clinging to her bulging form.

She quailed visibly, bowing her head, holding it with one hand. She was too ashamed to look at him. The office floor, the desk was coated with soft grey dust.

'I was looking for my file on Lara,' he explained, his voice tender. 'You cleared up.'

'Those boxes are private! None of your business.'

'They are indeed.' Letters were scattered around him.

Sabine covered her face with her fingers, peering through them. 'Leave them alone. They're my affairs.'

Bombs, they were letter bombs. He stared up at his wife, in awe. 'All these letters, Sabine?'

'I stopped writing them long ago, when . . . he died.'

'Sabine, *why*?'

'I started one day, and then I just carried on. They helped.'

'Helped?'

'To understand this stupid country.'

George gazed at her, at the wife he no longer touched, made love to.

'Sabine, all those other women I've . . . been with. They have meant nothing to me.'

Sabine's face twisted.

'Do you want to leave me?'

Tears fell from her eyes.

'You can go now, if you wish. We could sell the house, I'd give you half of everything. You can go back to England, live near Sebastian, wherever you like.'

'It's too late.'

'I'm sorry.'

'You're too late with that, too.'

'What about all *these*?' He held up a fistful of the letters.

'I cared.'

'Cared?'

'Yes. I cared about him once.'

'About someone you didn't know, only met once, at the Hilton?'

'I knew him.'

'What?'

'We met again.'

'*What*?'

'Once or twice. We . . . talked.'

'Talked?'

'Yes.'

'You met to *talk* with the Prime Minister of Trinidad, for God's sake?'

'Yes.'

George stared. 'When?'

'It doesn't matter . . . I can't remember any of it any more.'

'Was it . . .'

'No. Nothing like that.'

'What, then?'

'I don't want to explain it. What does it matter now? It's history.'

'But all these letters, you never sent them?'

'No.'

'Not even one?'

'Yes. I sent one.'

'It's . . . absurd.'

Sabine glared at him then, her eyes bloodshot. 'To you. You've never cared about anything here. You fell in love, lost your senses.'

George escaped in his rusted pickup truck, driving around for hours, ending up in Paramin, at the top of the hill. Clouds hung in the air, tiny explosions gone still. The air was spiced with chadon beni and wild thyme, his favourite perfume. But he was tired again, always tired. Another headache moving in, a storm at the back of his skull. It was quiet up here. Quiet and still. He came up here again and again. This spot. To admire the shapely mountains, marvel at their sloping flanks. The spine of the northern range loomed across a valley so curved and deep it was like peering into the mouth of a gigantic clam. This spot – where Talbot was beaten.

'Shit,' he said aloud.

The world had mattered once. Years ago, before he'd drunk the amount of rum he had, enough to kill a bull elephant. Women. They could do that to a man. Take everything away in a moment. Too damn serious, too damn earnest. All he wanted was to swim in his pool. Read books. Think about the Soca Warriors.

'Bloody Eric Williams,' he shouted at the mountains.

He got out of the truck and slammed the door.

Out in the Gulf of Paria, a cruise ship was under sail, exiting the harbour, a huge white swan paddling off. He cringed. Truth was, he preferred Trinidad – always had. He preferred these wild emerald hills, the brash forests, the riotous and unpredictable landscape of Trinidad to the prim hazy pastures of his own country, England. He wanted this bold land. Not the mute grey-drizzle of Harrow on the Hill. He liked the extrovert people, not the prudish and obedient couples his parents had mixed with. He felt alive here; unlike Sabine. But now he should say something, do something, finally. Please his wife, for once. Go and see Bobby Comacho on his way home, take him on. Show Bobby the photos of Talbot's face; let him know the story would appear in the morning's papers. He should go and give the bastard a fright.

I'm sick of you.

George spun round.

What?

You selfish man.

He stared into the hills.

Sick of you. Sick from love.

What did you say?

You heard.

George stared. The hills groaned. The groans of a man beaten, spreadeagled across a car door, punched in the gut. *Crack.* Ribs broken. *Crunch.* The butterfly of bruises on Talbot's young dismal face.

It's not my fault.

*

Sabine began to gather all the boxes up. She'd burn them, then they wouldn't exist. Stupid woman. Younger and foolish in those days. *Idiote!* Burn the evidence. Juvenile to have ideals. George said that once and he was right: George had a clearer sense of these things. He was more understanding of human failing. All a long time ago. Granny Seraphina, those crystal-yellow eyes. Granny had written letters, too. She'd almost forgotten about those goddamn letters. Almost. What had she written about George? She didn't know; loose mindless rants she'd written on those long evenings, suffocating in the heat. She already needed a drink, a stiff rum. Rum and milk for breakfast. First she'd make a pile, outside in the corner of the garden. Find some kerosene.

Jennifer arrived. She came to bring Sabine a cup of tea.

'How's Talbot?' Sabine asked.

'He fine fer now.' Jennifer looked at the chaos of dust all around. 'Eh, eh, w'appen here?'

'Nothing. Mr Harwood found some rubbish up in the attic.'

Jennifer didn't believe her for a moment; she noticed her red eyes. 'What you cryin' about?'

Sabine pressed at her eyelids, forcing the tears back in. Her fingers were soon wet and slippery. Jennifer had witnessed her crying many times.

'Oh gorsh.' Jennifer stood, waiting for her to get it out. The office ceiling was all opened up, like a big chimney that had belched its contents onto the office floor. Sabine's face was smudged with soot.

'You should leave dis damn place,' Jennifer said.

'And go where?'

'Back to England.'

'I can't.'

'Why not?'

'I'm too old. What would I do? Live on my own? In a little two-up two-down?'

'Live near your son.'

'He's busy. He doesn't want his mother hanging round.'

'I thought you liked England.'

'I thought I did, too. It's . . . changed.'

'How?'

'It's expensive. Dirty . . . it's . . . oh, I don't know it any more. I'm a foreigner there. Shopping trips once a year. Harrods. Harvey Nicks. A friend's flat in Chelsea. Play tourist.'

'What about French land?'

'My brothers are dead. My sister lives elsewhere. There's no one to go to now, not any more.'

'Mr Harwood tink he should send you back.'

'I know.' Sabine laughed inwardly: no secrets between the three of them.

'Don't worry, Jennifer.'

Jennifer steupsed.

'Worry about your son.'

'I worry enough about him.'

Sabine wanted to be alone but Jennifer was on to her.

'Dese de letters you write to Eric Williams?' she asked, nodding at the open boxes.

'Yes.'

Jennifer went sullen. 'We have some of Granny's at home. Some she never posted.'

'Poor woman.'

'Granny dead, man.'

'Yes.'

'Mr Harwood vexed?'

'Yes. I think so. Baffled. Men . . .'

Jennifer's mouth turned down and she shook her head as if she didn't want to know any more about men, about the crazy letters. As if she wanted to know nothing about anything.

*

George drove back down the hill, approaching the T-junction by the gas station in Winderflet village. A line of women waited for a taxi, hands out. They stared through him. This was the worst of all their looks: like he actually *was* invisible, like he was already dead and gone. He turned right, spotting the skinny black figure up ahead, on the left, in khaki short pants and white school shirt. The boy lurched along the dusty pavement, one arm longer than the other; this longer arm hung limp, twisted at the joint. This was how he got his nickname, Clock.

George slowed down. 'Where you going?'

The boy's face lit up. 'Boissiere.'

'Get in. I'll take you there.'

The boy was a local legend. Invited to sing at the Queen's Hall. George had interviewed him once. After that George often stopped to pick him up, dropping him back and forth between the village and his aunt's. The boy never wanted to waste his pocket money on a taxi fare, so he'd set off on foot. He was blessed, people said. *He Sparrow's son.* Sang like a bird. More talented than the man himself, even, his voice purer. Talk was the famous calypsonian once had a lover out here in one of the houses behind the road.

'Have you just been to choir practice?'

The boy nodded.

'Up at the church?'

'Yeah.'

'What have you sung?'

'Holy songs.'

George needed a song. For his soul. But he dared not ask. They drove along in a boy–man, black–white silence. Clock sat bolt upright, staring out the windscreen. Three miles to Boissiere village; the boy would have walked it. His legs were worse than his arms, twisted at the ankles.

'Mr Harwood. I never see you in church.'

'I don't go.'

'You don't love God?'

'I don't *believe* in God.'

'People say that. But they still cry out his name when they get vexed.'

'It slips out sometimes, yes.'

'I love God.'

'I know.'

'He give me bad arms but good lungs. Bad legs, but a good brain.'

'Your singing is magnificent.'

The boy grinned. He was ten or eleven, black as the universe; his face placid and serene from all his worshipful singing. His eyes were huge and baleful, full of knowledge. *I'll be your father* – the thought came from nowhere. George changed the subject.

'What do you think of Brian Lara?'

'Lara? He a man of God.'

'Why do you say that?'

'He gifted.'

'I may meet him soon, to write about him for the newspaper.'

The boy's eyes glistened. He nodded.

'If you could ask Lara one question what would it be?'

'Me?'

'Yes.'

The boy thought for a moment, peering up out the windscreen. 'Look!' he exclaimed.

The blimp hovered high above, tumescent. 'Funny, how sometimes you don't see it,' George said, looking up.

'How it do that?' Clock asked. 'It make you feel as if it following you.'

'*God* knows. It's a trick. There's a little man up there with binoculars. He spends his time staring down, picking us out.'

The boy smirked at his saying the holy name in vain.

'OK. I say "God" a lot.'

'You shouldn't.'

'I'm sorry. I won't in future.'

'We'll see 'bout that,' Clock laughed.

'So? What would you ask Brian Lara?'

'I would aks Mr Lara about the blimp.'

'Really?'

'Yeah, man. Lara world famous. He go away a lot. Has he noticed it following him?'

'Good question,' George hummed, a shadow of guilt crossing his back; why, he didn't know. He squirmed and kept his eyes fixed on the uneven road.

La Pompey was in the driveway when George returned, lathering Sabine's car in suds. The dogs were round the back, tied up. La Pompey was afraid of them. The big gate slid back and George drove in, wanting to ask the man in for a drink; anything rather than face Sabine. La Pompey whistled a tune. He raised his hand, smiling a cavernous, toothless grin.

George's headache hadn't melted. He rubbed the back of his head. He dearly needed a bath. Parking, he tiptoed through the garage into the house. Something was burning somewhere, some-thing burning outside. A bonfire? He stopped, gazing out into the garden. Black smoke billowed from one corner. Sabine was stand-ing over it, the dusty shoeboxes in a heap at her feet. He watched her feed sheets of paper onto the fire.

Too late. He could recall them at will, alive, fresh. Dancing in his head. The things she said about him, the things she'd never said to him. *I hate him, he stinks. Sometimes his sweat smells like acid. He does-n't bath enough. Or worse, sometimes he smells of* them, *of cheap cologne, of cheap women's pussy. An* egoiste! *A bore. I am stuck and cannot get back.* There were conversations he had never wanted to have.

Eric Williams? All along Sabine had *cared* about another man. Her own affair of sorts, maybe worse. She cared. This was a type of love. And what a poor show she had made of it; to love a man she didn't know. God, what had become of them? Yes, too late to burn the evidence. He ran a bath and when it was full he shrugged out of his dusty clothes, immersing himself completely in the clear warm water, massaging his aching scalp.

He'd seen Williams speak, too, of course. Once, in Woodford Square. Eric Williams was an orator of Athenian dimensions, an educated man who could also speak *like them*. Williams was a man of words. He preached politics to the fruit vendors down in Charlotte Street. He abbreviated world history to the single mothers of Laventille, condemned slavery with the boatmen from the docks, lambasted the evils of colonialism with anyone. He took on any opponent and always won. He spoke the way they spoke. This was his gift: Eric Williams was a teacher.

And Williams was short. A small man: was that why she hated short men? Not at all handsome. But highly erudite: Oxford, later a professor at Howard University in the States. An historian. Williams wrote books, history books of the Caribbean. Slaves. Slavery: that was his thing.

Williams liked big flashy American cars. He liked to mix the drinks.

Williams was also paranoid, suspicious, prone to listening to the gossips around him.

Everyone knew this.

Everyone knew the man.

Was he, George Harwood, *jealous*?

No, he told himself. No.

The bath water had turned lukewarm. He let some water out, then filled it back to the same level with hot. His skin had puckered but he didn't want to get out. Eric Williams had aroused his wife. Switched her on, to politics, to possibilities, damn him to hell; she had soaked it all up, asked too many questions. But then, Williams had moved everyone. He'd made love to the nation. A brilliant man. And a failure. Was this Sabine's type? George stared at his feet. He became aware of Sabine, standing at the door behind him.

'I'll cut your hair when you get out,' she said.

George's hair was long and unruly. He tried to keep it tamed in one direction but it always flew the opposite way in the wind. Most days, it looked like a hurricane had passed through the centre of his head. Deep russet once, his hair was now sun-bleached several shades lighter, to an indefinite singed tobacco-rust. It was still good hair, though, never thinned; strong curls which, when wet, hung down to his shoulders.

He dried himself off and wrapped a large towel around his waist. In the kitchen Sabine stood at the stove. He sat down wearily, behind her, in the chair against the wall. When she turned, her eyes were expressionless. Now even his wife had the look, the same look that came at him again and again. He was detested, *detested*. Outside La Pompey sang off-key, a Kitchener calypso, enjoying his work, soaping down the pickup truck parked a few feet from the kitchen.

Sabine disappeared, returning with a pair of scissors and a comb. She began to tug through his long wet hair.

'Oww,' George cried out. 'Oww, that hurts.'

His wife's voluptuous body was up close. He wanted to press his head into her stomach, say something. *Shall I compare thee to a summer's day?*

Sabine combed all his hair out straight; it fell about his face like a curtain. The scissors were cold and clean across his nose. *Snip, snip, snip.* Sharp steel flashing blades. His chin was clasped in her hands. La Pompey sang louder and more off-key.

'I'm going to ask him to clean up your green bicycle,' George said, surprising himself.

'What for?'

'So I can see it again.'

She snipped.

'Good for you.'

Snip.

'Who was that awful little man who met us that day, the man from the company who took us to the hotel? Never saw him again, did we?'

Snip.

'No, we didn't.'

George sighed. He was afraid for his ears. 'Eric Williams became a dictator,' he said.

'Yes.'

Snip.

'We're living with his mistakes.'

Snip.

'It's hard for a man to do the right thing all the time, you know.' He dared to look up. She pushed his chin down.

'He had good people round him once,' Sabine replied carefully.

Snip.

'They were all dismissed,' she continued. She picked up a handful of hair.

'Oww. That hurts. Oww. Why – oww – do we expect people in power to be different? We treat politicians like parents, it's the same relationship. We never forgive them if they fuck up.'

'He fucked up all right.'

Snip.

'He was just one man.'

Snip.

'I suppose you understand him better than I ever did,' Sabine said coldly.

'We're weak.'

Snip.

Sabine stopped cutting, snapping the blades shut. 'God, politicians, husbands, all given the job of fathering. Holy God on earth, these islands and their father figures.'

'The islands were children.'

'Bullshit.'

'Men rule the world badly. It's everywhere.'

'And you don't care.'

'I'm afraid I don't.'

'Maybe I'm stupid.'

'We've both disappointed you, then.'

Snip.

She took a step back, surveying her work, avoiding his eyes. 'There. You're done.'

George wanted to fall on his knees. He wanted her respect. He wanted to respect himself.

La Pompey appeared at the open kitchen door, his bare chest slippery with soap. 'Two new cars,' he grinned. 'Clean as newborn babies.' He cackled at George. 'Mr Harwood get a bath, too,

I see. Lookin' baby fresh. Yousa lucky man, to have such a good woman to take care of you so nice.'

'I am lucky, yes,' George agreed.

But Sabine had disappeared.

The whore sat on the pavement with her legs open. Drunk or on drugs, her eyes glazed. George slowed the truck and she shot him an unfocused look of insolence. The backstreets of St James, the small hours of the morning. He was drunk, drunk on white rum since early evening. Had drunk himself stupid and then sober again. He left the house in the end when Sabine went to bed. Quite plainly this whore had had enough, could no longer be bothered to stand up. Her belly hung over her miniskirt and the straps of her silky black camisole flopped from her shoulders. Her hair was all this way and that, standing around her head in a star.

George stopped but kept the engine running. She half swayed upright and then climbed in, slamming the door shut. She gazed forward. George nodded, looking at her fallen straps.

'What's your name?'

'Luna,' she whispered in a hiccup, rum on her breath.

'Like the moon.'

'Das right.'

'Very beautiful.'

She ignored this comment.

Luna's skin lacked lustre. Matt black, black as tar, pimpled, her shoulders scarred with vaccination marks. She slouched back against the seat, mumbling, her legs open, twisting at her panties, itching or restless down there. From the back pocket of her miniskirt she brought out a tiny bottle of perfume, spraying at her pudenda.

'Please don't do that,' George winced. 'I like you as you are.'

She sniffed loudly and looked out the window. 'Where yuh wanta park?'

'At the docks.'

George drove on through the night. The city lay quiet, sleeping off the day. They bumped along the broken-up paved streets, gazing out opposite windows. He was nervous. Nervous, every time. What was he *thinking*? What did he think every time? That he liked sex, still needed it, no matter how, no matter what. Luna was light. Moonlight on his parched soul.

He drove towards the spot of the *Cavina's* arrival. A strange wheezing rattled from Luna's side of the bench-seat. Had she fallen asleep? He glanced across. No. Only breathing heavily, chest heaving. She coughed up phlegm, hawking it out the window. She wiped her lips, sniffed up snot and coughed that, too, spitting it out. She opened her legs wider, reaching across, placing his left hand on her thigh.

'Dis what yuh buyin'.' She guided his fingers inside her.

Oh Jesus, Lord. Hot there and dry as fuck, dry and fuckless. What had he done? He was ashamed. Ashamed to fuck a woman with no glow in her. Feeling made women glow and wet and he knew the difference between dry and wet when it came to women. What the fuck was he doing? He didn't care. Could he love Luna? Make her come? He wanted to. Wanted to fuck her and make her come, release himself from the death he'd caused in his wife. He wanted to fuck a woman into life.

The dock was close. Ships were moored up, containers on the wharf. He knew a place. He accelerated. Luna rubbed herself and her legs were now open wide, one foot up on the dashboard.

He crash-parked in an empty lot. There was no one about, the night watchman asleep in his hut. Stars up in the sky, the moon like a lamp. The salt sea breeze was fluttering in from the Gulf of Paria into the cab and Luna was rubbing herself, her heavy breasts spilling from her black camisole, and he could smell her now, sharp and saltier than the sea. Luna rubbing her dry cunt, a cold meaningless expression in her eyes. She was drunk, so drunk she was either going to fall asleep or become violent.

Hands shaking, he unbuckled his belt and unzipped his flies. He was soft. His elderly cock lay flaccid against his thighs, a dribble of its former self. Luna lay back, her head propped up against the door, legs splayed, panties pulled to one side. He could see into her, a place he could fit his hand, like a purse, or a secret crevice in a wall. *George is a drunk, a second-rate specimen.* There, he could store his misery. Store his sins right there: inside Luna.

Luna's eyes were vacant as Sabine's.

He threw himself onto her, thrusting and thrusting until he became lost and out of breath. But he was soft, had nothing in him, nothing for anyone. He sweated, thrusted and thrusted, sweating and furious. He thrusted until he thought he'd give himself a heart attack, sweat trickling from his temples, from his hair. He stopped, his heart pounding, his chest heaving.

'I'm too old,' he said, by way of an excuse. 'Too old for you.' And he was too old. He'd die soon, he knew.

'You're very beautiful,' he muttered.

Luna steupsed, throwing him a look that said she'd seen and heard it all before. She glared at him. 'Dis still a hundred dollars, eh?'

CHAPTER FOUR

NICE TRY

Early evening, the sky was pink as pomegranate seeds. The keskidees squabbled over the pool in their eternal family argument. A horn beeped outside the front gate.

'Let me in, let me in, *Daddyyy*,' Pascale called, her headlights spraying a lemony wash all over the driveway. The dogs rushed out, barking and jumping up, wagging their tails. George sped out with the buzzer to let her in. Sabine stood in the kitchen, holding her breath, counting: one, two, three. She took a clean plate from the rack and began washing it again slowly, listening.

'Daddy, eh, eh.' The car door slammed. Pascale's loud boisterous kissing of her father on both cheeks.

'How yuh goin'? Nuttin in de paper dis week? W'appen? Eh, eh, dese damn blasted dogs. Down. Down. Henry, *down*, man. Jesus, dogs. Dey diggin' up de damn blasted roads again. Just like you said. Dey fix dem, den dey go damn well dig dem up again. Write somptin about dis, Daddy. Der's a huge blasted hole in de middle of de road, just outside Linda's. I almost drove straight in. Eh, eh. Down, you chupid dogs. Jesus Christ. Where's Mummy?'

Tears pooled in Sabine's eyes. Her beautiful daughter. Her daughter's rich sing-song voice, part of the island now. Those letters George found, all those years she thought they were about to leave. Another three years, another three, and then, and then. Now her daughter spoke like them.

'Mum's inside. This is an unexpected pleasure. What a surprise. Lovely to see you. And the kids.' Joy in George's voice. A ring in it.

'I'm here,' Sabine called, from her pretend washing-up. She stayed still; best let them enjoy each other first.

They'd moved into the living room, Sabine could tell; George, she knew, was already mixing drinks, three-fingered measures. Pascale could drink, like her father. Sabine wiped her hands on a tea towel, patted her forehead dry. *Dear Mr Williams*; what had she been doing? She blushed with the shame of being so naive. She went to join them.

'How are you, my love,' she said.

Pascale invaded the living room. Tall, blonde, her curly hair straightened and cut like a boy; she was always in heels, always made-up. Always talking and joking. Pascale stood with the glass of rum in her hand, breathing a jet of cigarette smoke up to the ceiling.

'Eh eh, Mummyuh, howyuh goin'?' She smiled in a half-frozen way.

'You look well,' Sabine managed.

The women air-kissed.

'Hello, Zack, Tabitha,' Sabine greeted her grandchildren, who swarmed to their mother's long legs. They stared up at Sabine, unspeaking.

'Come, come, here,' Pascale chided them. They clung, climbing all over Pascale as she sat down. Both had milk-chocolate skin. Both snuggled into Pascale's lap as she talked, a continuous stream of news, questions and laughing at her own jokes. Pascale fingered her children's wiry curls as she laughed. George sat on one of the bar stools, Sabine on the opposite sofa. They stared at their daughter, as if they'd never seen her before.

'Hey, Daddy, who you interviewin' nex?'

'Brian Lara.'

'Wow! Can I come, too? Hold de tape recorder for you?'

'He's coming back from New Zealand soon. It's not yet confirmed.'

'I wonder when he'll retire.'

'Oh, sometime in the near future. Perhaps after the World Cup in 2007.'

'It won't be the same when he goes. I'll miss him.'

'Maybe he'll never go. He may be indispensable.'

'He cyan disappear.'

'The ladies like Lara, eh?'

'And he likes *dem*.'

'Children like Lara, too,' George grinned.

'An ol' people.'

'The man's a national hero.'

'Of *course*.'

'That'll make him hard to interview.'

Look at them. Glowing in each other's presence. Glowing and laughing like old friends. Just like him, her father's daughter.

Something about the way they sat, stood, held themselves: so similar, both so confident. Pascale drank a lot and smoked and limed and fêted till dawn when she could.

'Your brother's coming out in a few days,' Sabine intervened.

'Oh, dat go be *fun*.' She winked.

'He'll be here for two weeks.' Sabine ignored her sarcasm. 'You know, I told you months ago. He's coming for Easter.'

'He bringin' any of his snobby friends?'

'They're not snobs.'

Pascale exhaled a long jet of smoke. 'Mum, anyone who hates calypso is a snob.'

'I hate calypso.'

Pascale laughed.

'I'm not a snob.'

George snorted. Sabine shot him a look.

'I don't know why he comes. He doh really enjoy himself.'

'Yes, he *does*.'

'Oh God, Mummyuh, you blind when it come to *him*.'

'No, I'm not.'

'He damn well tink everyone here chupid.'

'Well, most people here *are* stupid.'

Pascal bunched her jaw, pushing her lips out.

'My son is a very educated man.'

'So? Sebastian shy and English when he come home. Trinidad too bold fer him. He look down on everyone. He not clever *enough* is my opinion.'

'He cares about you very much.'

'I care for *him*. He just too damn stiff.'

'Gracious, some call it.'

'Bite up, I call it.'

George got up and went to mix himself a fresh drink.

'Dad, I'll have another one, too.' Pascale studied her father's movements as he crossed the room.

Sabine appraised her grandchildren's black skin. They were black, truly black. Not suntanned, not olive-skinned. Her grandchildren had Negro blood. African. They stared in the same mistrustful way the Africans did.

'Anyway,' Sabine continued, 'he's coming out for Easter. Alone.'

Pascale nodded. Sabine knew Pascale liked her brother despite their differences. Sebastian wasn't stiff at all; he won over his sister like he won over everyone with his charming manner, his civilised ideas. Sebastian with his handsome open face; she had made beautiful children; no one could take that away from her. Tabitha had fallen asleep on the sofa. Zack picked his nose, still staring, like he always did. Sabine poked out her tongue and Zack half-smiled back, unsure.

Pascale leant over and stroked one of the dogs behind the ears. Her eyes drifted. 'Daddy, you OK?'

'Yes. Why?'

'You lookin' a bit . . . peaky.'

'I've got a headache.'

'Want an aspirin?'

'No. I've already taken one.'

Sabine wanted to talk more, but Pascale wasn't interested. No one wanted to talk about the things she did.

'So. Brian Lara, eh? I want a signed photograph. And his phone number.'

'He's already taken.'

'So?'

If only Pascale had got away, too, escaped to the London College of Fashion, like she'd once planned. If only she hadn't married that weak-chinned, jumped-up French Creole midget. As a child, Pascale covered the walls of the house in murals and graffiti, tiny flowers, bumble bees, all three feet from the ground; they scrubbed the walls of her room every other month. Now Pascale was getting fat, she mothered the children full-time, with the help of maids. Her children's dark skin had been a surprise to them all. They'd come out much darker than their father, who wouldn't admit he had *any* African in him at all.

Pascale left still gushing, tipsy, disappearing like a comet, leaving a trail of conversation-dust in her wake. George staggered to bed, sloshed. Sabine drifted out onto the grass, staring up at the hill above the house, the hip of the green woman, a woman lying on her side, never any doubt about that. A woman trapped in the mud, half sculpted from the sticky oil-clogged bedrock, half made. She was also stuck. Half out, half in. Hip, breast, a long travelling arm. Half her face, half her bushy tangled hair. Usually, she slept heavily and the earth hummed with the timbre of her snores. It could be chilly in the evenings. Cool fresh air, the mountain woman's breath. Moments of peace, sometimes, out here.

You, Sabine addressed the hill. All you do is watch. That's all you've ever done. Sit back and observe the disaster going on.

It's my privilege.

They can't even fix the *roads*. Lay them down and then dig them up again. In all this time, no proper hurricane. They all veer away.

I don't bring the winds.

George found my letters to Eric Williams.

Oh.

I'm glad.

Really?

Yes. After all these years. I'm glad. It even feels good. So, there it is. He can think what he likes. Think me mad. Maybe I was. All I know is *you*, you haven't changed.

No, I don't change.

I've changed. I hardly recognise my face in the mirror. Another version of myself, of that woman who rode around so carefree on her bicycle. I thought loving George would be enough. But he loves you.

They all love me.

Yes. But you show no concern.

You're free to go. *Go.*

You know I won't, so long as he's here.

Your son is coming soon.

Yes. Sebastian. He'll make it all better for a short time.

Late morning, George strolled with the big dogs along his strip of Trinidad. A Carib in his hand, his hair blowing over to one side. La Blanchisseuse – the washerwoman – the name of this part of Trinidad's northern coast. The women of the village once washed their clothes in the river near by and this coastline was named after them. Early morning and the sea ebbed and flowed in tame, measured swells; the white sand under the waves illuminated the water to a brilliant duck-egg blue. Tiny iridescent fish marauded through it, chased by larger silver fish, careet. November to March the sea was rough, heavy rollers breaking onto the shore. Today it was a lido out there between the shore and the black rock poking its snout from the water. In the rock a pool had formed, full of grunts and boxfish and feathery algae. A crowd of hoary pelicans sat about on the flat part and, when they took flight, in threes and fours, gliding with aerodynamic grace inches from the sea's surface, the dogs leapt into the waves, paddling after them, woofing.

The beach, his beach, constituted a narrow strip of the coast. He owned, from the high-water mark-up, one acre of land between the beach and the road. Up here, past the busy tourist beach of Maracas, the road narrowed and the hills of the densely forested northern range gathered, protecting the coast. The remote village had emerged after the 1783 Cedula, higgledy-piggledy, by the sea, when the Spanish were settling new French Creole immigrants. Some of the colourful wooden creole homes still existed, perched precariously on the black rugged cliffs, above the waves, the spume floating up into their kitchens. Gulls hovered at the windows. The gardens were studded with conch shells. A thin beaten-up road ran past, no shops, no fresh water most of the time. In recent years the coast had turned into prime real estate with gargantuan Miami-style condos and homes blocking the view of the sea. A cluster of canary-yellow apartments were now selling for a million dollars each.

George had never built a beach house. He visited his plot once or twice a month to gaze out to sea, to walk the dogs, skinny-dip when the sea was calm, paddle about. A narrow sand-spit stretched from one end of the beach out to a craggy rock sprouting with cactus and sea-almond and manchineel trees. Harwood's

Spit, he called it. At low tide he could walk to the island along the strip of sand, observe the frigate birds diving and swooping, stealing what the smaller birds had caught, or watch the terns swinging on air-thermals. The spit's water was transparent, it was like standing in a pool of gin. Translucent crabs skittered about on the sandy floor. Tiny fish pecked his toes.

Those letters – was he upset? Hell, yes. At first it had been a shock, a dull weird fact unearthed. But now he was furious and an impotent seventy-five years old. *George isn't here tonight, God knows where he is. I wonder about you all the time, your little girl. I know how you feel now that you've lost your wife. I know what that's like. I wonder if we'll meet again. Goodnight.*

If only he'd known *then*. Eric Williams – of all people! Jesus Christ. Williams had died a broken man. He had fucked up. George was like her, though, he could admit that; the same as Sabine, a cheat. He had cheated on Sabine all along, from that very first day, the day they arrived, stepping off the *Cavina*. It had been immediate, a strong physical attraction. He had fallen, and that was that. Head over heels, with the sounds and smells, with the smiles and shapes, with all the bewitching qualities of another woman called Trinidad.

George drove his truck into the forecourt of Winderflet Police Station. Everyone knew his crud-heap truck, the state of it. Can't hide in a small place, can't sin in a village, can't fart without anyone hearing it and knowing what you had for lunch. Superintendent Bobby Comacho visited Winderflet once a month and George happened to know Bobby came, primarily, to visit his mistress. Bobby dropped round to see the boys at the station after sex, after lunch. He liked to have coffee at the station around four. George walked in to find him right there, sitting at the front desk, relaxed and happy, chatting to the officer in charge.

'Hey, Bobby.' George grinned.

Bobby turned. He recognised George instantly and stared with malice. Bobby was a fat man, eyes like a goldfish, sweat patches under his armpits. On his feet he wore caramel-coloured plasticated slide-on shoes, at least size fifteen. He had the balls of a moose, George had heard.

Bobby looked George up and down. 'What you doin' here?' he growled.

'Been reading the papers recently?'

'Dat why you following me arong?'

'Yes.'

'Go home nuh, Mr Harwood. Go home to your fat ugly lady wife.' Bobby laughed loudly. 'When de last time you screw she, eh? You done brushin' every odder ting rong here. And you comin' in aksin' if ah read de goddamn newspaper?'

George stood his ground. *Dear Mr Williams* danced inside his skull.

'A friend of mine was badly beaten recently.'

'Oh yeah?' Bobby's eyes were blank, his manner icy.

'Yes. He says four policemen took him to the top of Paramin Hill. Only last week. Beat the crap out of him.'

Bobby raised his eyebrows. 'Dat a very serious allegation.'

'Yes.'

'Which policemen?'

'My friend could identify them. Says they came from Winderflet.'

'Oho . . . an' *who*, apart from your friend, see dis happen? Eh?'

'No one.'

'No one see dis serious ting happen apart from dat lying lazy good-for-nuttin Talbot up der on de hill?'

'I didn't say it was Talbot.' George smiled with relish. 'But now you mention it, yes, I mean Talbot. Four broken ribs. A broken nose. He was in the St Clair medical centre for days.'

'Dat son of an ass have plenty enemies.'

'Don't be ridiculous!' George snapped. 'Talbot isn't a *criminal*. He's a young man, a poor illiterate young man; he's too stupid to have enemies. He stuck his neck out and complained. One of your thugs took his mobile phone. He wanted it back. And he got it back all right.'

Bobby rose from the chair, standing to his full height of six foot four, peering down at George. 'And you run straight to de goddamn newspapers, widout checkin' your facts, print one setta nonsense?'

'I didn't write the story. I'm sure the news boys tried to check the story out, talk to someone here. No one is ever here, though.'

Bobby's face hardened. That look came at him, from out of the centuries, blatant, powerful. Bobby, a giant black man glaring like he could kill, just with his eyes.

'Talbot not so innocent,' he breathed. 'He a damn *fockin'* tief. Bad as de resta dem. He mixin' with some of de badjohns up der on de hill. We catch him in all kinda business. He runnin' errands, he drivin' car for dem ruffians. We watchin' him all now and you come here tellin' me how to do my job, *eh*? You wid your hoity-toity English accent, expekin' me to jump to your attention, eh? Catch me off guard?' Bobby steupsed long and loud, looking about.

The officer in charge nodded in passive agreement. The room pulsated with a garlicky odour: Bobby's breath, Bobby's lunch.

'You some chupid ignorant white man. Dat Talbot had it *comin'* to him. He dare complain? He up der laughin' at us all now. He have you runnin' circles. You asshole. How long you live in Trinidad?'

'Long enough,' George spat. 'I've lived here long enough. Seen enough. You're a disgrace. Your badge is a child's toy. Your hat is a clown's hat. You're ridiculous. Justice? Serve and protect? Serve yourself. That's your game, just like Mr Manning. You're pathetic. Tiny-minded. So what if Talbot is in with the wrong sort. Your men have no right to *bludgeon* him. No right. You and those thugs. Your police force. He could've died up there on the hill. Those men should be had up in *court*.'

Bobby glared, incensed. He squared up to George and peered down into his face. He held his large hands high, as if proving to George that he had hands, letting George have a good look. He spread his long strong fingers into a fan in front of George's nose, smiling, before slipping them under George's armpits, squeezing his ribcage tight. He grabbed George hard, lifting him up against the wall, his toes barely touching the ground. 'Why ent you *fock off*, eh?'

George felt the blood rush to his head. No words could come out.

Bobby looked like he was vividly alive, glowing with bloodlust. George fought the urge to urinate, copiously.

'Eh? Mr Harwood. SIR. Why ent you leave long time? Wid de rest of dem? Eh? Leave we to run tings. Eh?'

George stared. He heard a dangerous interior sound, the porous creak of his ribs. His breath was short inside his lungs; he could hardly breathe. The garlic odour swam up into his nostrils. Bobby's eyes were dilated, his lips swollen and parted.

'You tink allyuh white man done any *better*? Eh? When allyuh run tings, you ent beat de black man? Eh? Allyuh superior? Better? Whiter? I sick an' tired hearing all dis about black cops. You can kiss my black ass. Kiss my friggin' black balls, too, kiss de friggin' grong I walk on.'

He stared hard into George's eyes, like any moment he might kiss him savagely or rip out his vocal cords. George tried to struggle, but it was no use. He was decrepit, old and frail, and his body had gone slack.

'Go fuck yourself,' George gasped. A hot dampness spread from the tip of his prick, a sharp ammonia stench spread with it, lacerating the air.

Bobby peered downwards and laughed and his eyes glistened.

'Poor man,' he said, releasing his grip. George slid down the wall.

For a moment they stood inches apart. Bobby's face was serene and his heavy goldfish eyelids flickered, as if at something inconsequential.

'Get outta here,' he whispered. 'Before I have you arrested for botherin' me.'

Outside, in the forecourt, George pulled a strip of aspirin from the top pocket of his shirt, bit two pills from the blisters and swallowed hard. A headache like a hurricane in his head. A ball of pain in the back of his skull. The sun beat down and the church, Our Lady of Lourdes up there on the mound, gazed down. *Repent*, it said. *Nice try*.

CHAPTER FIVE

SEBASTIAN

Piarco Airport, late afternoon. The Tobago terminal was far too quiet. Grim, Communist-style canvas portraits of Trinidad's five prime ministers dominated the forecourt: Eric Williams, A.N.R. Robinson, Chambers, Panday, Patrick Manning. Above the exit an ageing Sparrow, Calypso Rose in full flow, her kaftan waving in slow motion with her full-bosomed frame. A frieze of stuffed carnival costumes from the previous year crowded a centre dais.

It was all a bit much considering only a handful of tourists on the big jets to Tobago flew on to Trinidad these days. George liked it so, that this island was uncompromising and hard for tourists to negotiate. Not all welcome smiles and black men in Hawaiian shirts, playing pan by the poolside. No flat crystal beaches, no boutique hotels. Trinidad was oil-rich, didn't need tourism. Trinidadians openly sniggered at the sunburnt American women who wandered down the pavement in shorts and bikini top. Trinidad was itself; take it or leave it.

George hid in the café, absorbed in *Newsweek*. Sabine was

overdoing it, as usual, sunglasses like coasters clamped to her face, hovering near the baggage-hall exit, chain-smoking, pressing a tissue to her damp chin.

George buried his head in the magazine. He wouldn't be drawn into rows with his son. Not this time. His only son had shunned Trinidad for the metropolis, for brighter lights; fair enough. But Pascale was right, he could be an unbearable know-it-all. George vowed on the letters he'd found to be good. A better man. A better father to his son. Not envious or antagonistic. This visit would be different; this time he'd be thoughtful, careful. He'd watch how much he drank.

'There he is!' Sabine gasped.

George got up slowly, folding the magazine.

Sabine rushed forward as the smoked-glass doors slid back-wards, revealing a tall man, craggily unshaven, fortysomething, but still youthful. Clear green eyes, honey-olive skin. Dark curls, hair like a girl and still not at all grey. An etching of the younger Sabine, Sabine's straight nose, her strong arched eyebrows, her open and direct way of looking. All this was underpinned by a cool reserve George knew and understood; this came from his English way of living.

'Hello, Mum.' Sebastian enveloped his mother in his arms, hugging her tightly. Sabine melted, her face glistening. George stood back and watched.

'Dad.' Sebastian reached forward and the men clashed in an awkward half handshake, half hug, slapping each other on the back.

'I'll go and get the car,' George replied stiffly. He left Sabine to fawn and fuss and headed out towards the car park, apprehension breaking in waves through him. No use fucking pretending. His son brought on a reaction and it was all Sabine's fault: she made it so difficult, with her wet eyes and her tension. She made *him* tense.

George drove the car to the drop-off point, helping his son with his suitcase. Sabine climbed into the back seat.

'Sebastian, you sit in the front with your father,' Sabine urged.

'No, Mum, *you* sit in front. I'm happy in the back.'

'*No, no, no,*' she insisted. 'You men can catch up.'

'Mum, are you sure?'

George tried to hide his embarrassment and got in. Sebastian slid into the front seat.

Words fled from him, his stomach churned. But he'd try, for once. He tried to think of something to say. 'Got tickets for the football, yet?'

'Yes, actually.' Sebastian smiled, effortless with his charm.

'Which match?'

'The Trinidad–England game, of course.'

'Oh.'

'And you?'

'The team are coming for a friendly match against Peru soon. I'll go and see that.'

'That'll be fun.'

'Big story here.'

'I bet. And will you interview the Dutch coach, what's-his-name, Beenhakker?'

'Of course,' George lied.

'How was the food on the flight?' Sabine interrupted.

'Fine, Mum.'

'And what about Tony Blair?'

'What about him?'

'How much longer will he last?'

'Not too much longer, Mum.'

'And what about that George Brown?'

'*Gordon* Brown.'

'Yes, him. What's he like?'

'I've never met him!'

'I know, my son.' Sabine laughed at herself and pulled his hair, pinching his cheek.

'Oww.'

'Did you sleep?'

'No.'

'And what's the weather like in London?'

'Raining.'

'We could do with some rain here, the heat! *Phhuut!* The hottest dry season in years. Hot like hell.'

'It's always the same here, Mum.'

'No, it's not. It gets hotter every year.'

'Global warming, I guess.'

'Yes. Anyway. Jennifer made you your favourite meal. Callaloo, crab-backs.'

'How is she?'

George squeezed the steering wheel, not wanting to go there quite yet.

'Awful. Her son was beaten by the police. Almost killed.'

'Who? Talbot?'

'Yes.'

'That's terrible. Is he OK?'

'No. He was beaten black and blue. Like a dog, up the top of Paramin Hill. For a mobile phone. Some argument.'

'We took it to the papers,' George added.

'Is Talbot stealing phones?'

'Oh God. Who knows? We don't know exactly what happened. But the bloody police beat up whoever they want these days.'

George stared out towards the blackness of night sky. Great. Not even out of the car park yet. They drove along in silence for a few moments.

'*Pardonnes-moi*,' Sabine said, from the back seat.

'That's OK, Mum.'

'Jennifer made you your favourite meal.'

'Yes, you said. That's kind of her.'

'Welcome home, *mon fils*,' Sabine said, her voice sarcastic. 'Welcome to Paradise.'

At home, George badly needed a drink. *Dear Mr Williams* thrummed against the walls of his skull. His hands shook as he forced himself to pour half his usual measure of rum. The big dogs were unsure of Sebastian, sniffing and circling him. Katinka, the little one, ran away.

'George, put the outside lights on,' Sabine instructed. With his half-rum, George disappeared to switch on the lights which showed off the pool and back-lit the garden. *Put the lights on. Lord Muck has come.*

He returned, dutifully, hovering on the edge of the living room.

'My son, would you like a drinkie?' Sabine asked, her face gleaming. 'A beer, a rum, a glass of wine?'

'A Carib would be great.'

A David Rudder CD was playing, too loud. Sabine poured herself a glass of wine, a steady stream of chatter slipping from her. It was embarrassing. George bit his tongue, pretending he'd forgotten something, reversing, walking round the back garden into the kitchen, where he perched on the table, contemplating Jennifer's pot of callaloo. Lights, music. He peered into his glass. It was miserably half empty. The dogs appeared, wanting to talk to him, wet-nosed, wagging their tails. They didn't cheer him up.

Dear God. Sebastian, the two of them. Their son with his impeccable manners, his impeccable morals; their son who was kind and patient with Sabine. *George has become selfish, greedy, buying all this land, naming it all after himself, Harwood's this and that.* He'd bought land in Trinidad for next to nothing, years ago, so what? Then there was the oil boom in Trinidad – was that his fault? Land prices went through the roof. He was a rich man and hadn't worked hard for it. So what? Was that what this letter-writing business was all about? Her grand sulk: letters to the Prime Minister. *My husband is just like all the others, greedy. A lush. He drinks and lords it up.* That was her line, that was what she said in at least one letter. *George is mad.* His glass was empty.

A car honked at the gate.

'Thank Christ.' He went outside to see who it was, recognising the car. 'You're a saviour!' he shouted, clapping his hands.

'Is this a bad time?' Irit called out, driving through. 'I'm just stopping to drop something off for your wife.'

'Not at all.' George bent into the window to kiss her cheek. Irit. His favourite person.

'Come and have a drink. Your godson has just arrived.'

Irit accepted a rum, was bamboozled into dinner. Dear, lovely, glorious Irit. Irit wrapped in the scent of sandalwood, her knuckles decorated with moonstone, topaz, and tourmaline rings. Irit, one of their first friends in Trinidad. She'd kept herself radiant all these years, had stayed out of the sun's death-gaze. Her Hungarian accent hadn't softened, her love of Trinidad had never waned.

George relaxed. He poured himself another rum. He felt himself again. Dinner was noisy, cheerful, full of gossip, thanks to Irit. They sat out on the back porch, eating callaloo and stuffed crab-backs, fried plantain, a crème brûlée, coconut ice cream, a box of Bendicks mint chocolates that Sebastian brought from England. George was overwhelmed with a sulky-resentful feeling: Sebastian, damn it, still had those sceptical eyes, watching everything. Judging them all. Who did he think he was? James Fucking Bond?

'Sebastian, my handsome man, have you any news of Venus?' Irit asked.

'No, I haven't seen her for a few years.'

'You never visit her?'

'No, not really.'

'She lives in London, no?'

'Peckham.' Sebastian nodded.

'She's an old woman now, you know,' Sabine explained. 'Like me. A grandmother. Why would he go to visit her?'

'To *visit* her!' Irit laughed.

Sebastian shifted in his seat.

'You don't see her sons?'

'In London? No.'

'Really? I remember you three, like little badjohns. Your best friends. Always climbing trees, jumping off walls. Gave your mother and Venus such trouble.' She laughed.

Sebastian nodded, remembering. 'I know.'

'They were clever little boys. What do they do now in London?'

'Bernard has a job with London Underground,' Sabine chipped in. 'That was the last I heard. The other one, Clive, got into trouble with the police.'

'That's a pity.'

'Sebastian is hardly going to mix with them *now*.'

'Why not?'

'Oh come on, Irit, they're worlds apart. They were my *maid's sons*. Yes, they grew up together, but they have nothing in common now. I mean, what would he say to them?'

'Hello. How are you?' Irit joked.

'We lost touch,' Sebastian cut in. 'I've lost touch with many of my childhood friends.'

Irit raised her eyebrows and set her chin.

'Irit, don't look like that,' Sabine reprimanded.

'Besides,' Sebastian added, 'they probably wouldn't be seen dead with a posh white man like me. I did meet up with Clive once. We met for a drink, years ago, in Brixton. He's become very . . . English.'

'So have you,' said Sabine.

'We're English in different ways. Clive looks like one of those rap stars – all gold chains and expensive trainers. He looked down on me.'

'Clive looked down on *you*?' Sabine gasped.

'Yes. Why shouldn't he? I work regular hours, for someone else. He's his own boss. Running scams, this and that. I have a girlfriend, on and off. He has a harem of beauties. Drinks champagne every night. I'm sure he thinks I'm boring.'

George laughed.

'You're not *boring*. How dare he?'

'I imagine my London life is tame compared to Clive's, Mum.'

'A great pity,' drawled Irit. 'You three were thick as thieves.'

'He shtill is a thief, by the sound of things,' George slurred, chuckling. He'd had too much to drink. It felt good. Look at his son, all adored, all loved and marvelled over. Another wave of irritation rose.

'So. How's the love life, these days, eh? Who's the latest unhappy woman?'

'George!' Sabine snapped.

'Only joking.' He smiled, pleased with himself. His son was a big hit with women – all blondes, all at least ten years younger, none his intellectual equal.

'Your dolly-birds, who's the latest? You haven't brought one out for a while.'

Sebastian half stared, half smiled. 'No,' he said, frostily. 'Not since the last one you pawed and spilled your drink over.'

'That's enough,' Sabine commanded.

'Oh, let them fight.' Irit didn't care at all; she was family. 'It's good for them.'

'She pawed me first.' George smiled. No one smiled back.

'George!'

'That's unlikely, Dad.'

'Oh for fuck's sake, don't look like that . . . what was her name, anyway?'

'Rosie.'

'I beg your pardon, then. For whatever I said or did, again.'

'You said, *Nice arse.*'

'Did I?' George smiled, proud. 'Yes, she did have a lovely arse.'

'Dad, go to bed.'

Sabine glared. Irit smiled.

George let out a long exasperated breath. Fuck the lot of them. Fuck those prudes. He couldn't remember any Rosie at all. No face came to him, no smells or words. They were looking at him as if he was past it all.

*

The next morning Sabine and Sebastian drove towards the savannah.

'Mum, this is very odd.'

'What?'

Children, hundreds of children, were causing a jam; young children, primary-school age, in bunches and ribboned pigtails. Holding hands, holding up banners, placards; teachers with them, walking in well-ordered lines, shouting, chanting slogans. Sabine leant forward to read their placards.

STOP CRIME NOW
HEAR US PRIME MINISTER
STOP CRIME
TIME FOR ACTION
JUSTICE FOR SEAN LUKE

'Who's Sean Luke?'

'Oh. There's been a horrid murder recently,' Sabine explained.

'A six-year-old Indian boy. Disappeared one evening, his mother went to the police but they ignored her. His body was found two days later in a sugar cane field, a cane pole rammed straight up his anus and out through his mouth.'

'How awful.'

'Yes. All his intestines mangled.'

'Dear God.'

'They arrested three older children for the crime. The newspapers and news channels were full of it a few weeks back.'

'Like the Bulger case.'

'What's that?'

'Kids killing kids, something similar.'

'Yes, awful. Look, everyone has their headlights on.'

'What for?'

'To protest about *de crime*.'

'*De crime*?'

'Yes.'

'I come back each year. Always think it's the same place. But it's not anymore, is it? I sometimes even read about Trinidad in the *Guardian* in England.'

'A murder a day.'

'Isn't Dad *ever* scared or worried?'

'Your father? Nah. No one's going to hurt him. He's become a celebrity here, you know.'

Sebastian let out a rueful snort. 'So I hear.'

'People love him. The paper likes him. He writes well. He sees nothing wrong. He gives everyone the good news. He's a Force of Good.'

'Dad? My old fucker of a father?'

'Don't be rude.'

'Mum, he is an old fucker. Rosie. I made that name up. It was Lucy, actually. He doesn't even remember which of my girlfriends he's ogled or made a pass at. Don't you care?'

'No.'

'Haven't you had affairs?'

'No.'

'Not even one? Not even with Uncle Frank?'

Sabine laughed. 'Actually, Frank did like me . . . he did make a pass at me once. And there was Jules. Remember him? He loved me. What a great friend. And, of course, Sebastian Baker was very dashing.'

'My namesake. He's still rather dashing. You were beautiful.'

'Just like my son and daughter.'

'I remember you, Mum. On that green bicycle. Remember?'

Sabine exhaled and looked across the road, at the children.

'Yes.'

'Bet you were quite a sight. Causing cars to crash.'

Sabine smiled. The children waved their placards and chanted. Babies, babies out there in the hot sun.

'Eric Williams saw me once, on that bike.'

'No!'

'Yes.'

'Really? Ha ha. Just his type, I bet he fancied you. Did he wind down the window, pinch you on the bum?'

'Don't be ridiculous!'

'What, then?'

'Nothing.'

'Did you ever meet him?'

'Yes.'

'And?'

'And . . . he was very short.'

'And?'

'Chippy. Chip on his shoulder. You know. Drop of white blood.'

They drove round the savannah to the bank at Ellerslie Plaza, circling the car park several times before finding a space. Thousands more cars on the road now, mostly Japanese nearly-new imports; thousands of cars and the roads still one lane each way. Traffic was always bad and parking was almost impossible anywhere. Sebastian browsed the bookshop while Sabine went to the bank. Inside, twelve people stood in the queue, mostly white or light-skinned. One young female member of staff was helping them. Three half-attended customers sat in a row on some chairs near by. The counter-woman was attractive, chalky red-black skin, her long hair straightened. She spoke in barely audible tones.

Twenty minutes passed. Sabine waited in the queue. But it didn't move. The young woman disappeared. Other bank staff were deep in conversation behind the partition, not the least bit concerned.

Sabine began to stew. She wanted to scream, run bellowing at the counter. But she waited in line, like all the others. White people standing in a row, waiting patiently in the Republic Bank of Trinidad, for what they could get. White people not daring to complain or protest. One man was served. The line inched forward. Twenty more minutes passed. Sebastian would come in if he got bored. Come in and join the queue. Sabine worked it out: it would take, at twenty minutes per person, four hours to be served. Four hours, once a month, for a lifetime, to pay. Pay for what? For her sins, for the sins of all the white people who ever lived in the Caribbean.

*

George woke up much later than usual to find a message from Ray on the answer-phone. He called the *Guardian* straight away.

'George.' Ray sounded flustered. 'Somptin come up. I need someone to do somptin tomorrow.'

'Oh, good. I'm free.'

'Tomorrow afternoon. One of mih staff off sick. She cyan make it. It a big ting. I ent know when we go run it. Ders no peg. But we get de chance to interview de man. He flyin' to New York tomorrow. I was gonna send someone from de office.'

'Who is it?'

'Sparrow.'

'You're kidding.'

'Ever met him?'

'No.'

'Well, he not here often. He come and go a lot. He expekin' a reporter to go to his house in Diego Martin.'

'What time?'

'Arong four.'

'I'll do it.'

He put down the phone. The big dogs came wagging their tails. He patted them. 'Good dogs.' The Mighty Sparrow: the father of the little boy from the village? If so, the boy did have a more refined voice. Sparrow was a Father of the Nation, Godfather of

Calypso, PNM supporter turned critic. George made a mental note to ask Sparrow what he thought of the blimp.

La Pompey was in the garden when Sabine and Sebastian returned home, riding around the driveway on Sabine's green Raleigh bicycle.

'God . . . look, Mum. Isn't that your old—'

'Bicycle. Yes. What has your father done now?'

La Pompey was laughing, playing the fool. The sight of the bicycle made Sabine dizzy. She groaned in an exaggerated manner. Jennifer and George stood watching La Pompey, laughing, too. The bike shone like new. Even the bell was fixed. La Pompey rang it, amused at the tinny tinkling. Katinka, Sabine's little fluff-pot, sat atop a knoll in the garden, glaring with disapproval.

'Eh, eh, she *back*.' Jennifer's face filled with glee.

Sabine got out of the car and advanced cautiously, scooping up the little dog. '*Good* girl,' she whispered in the dog's ear.

'Mrs Harwood, come an' try it, nuh. Ah fix it up real nice,' La Pompey invited, whizzing past.

George gave her his *Sorry* face.

'George, what have you *done*?'

'Jennifer found it. Under some junk in the garage. We polished it up.'

'You expect *me* to ride that thing again?'

'I thought you'd be pleased to see it.' George looked delighted. La Pompey laughed. 'Yeah, man. Try it, nuh.'

Jennifer cackled, blushing through her black skin. 'Mrs Harwood, give it a try, nuh. I cyan believe you ride it once.'

Everyone turned to look at Sabine.

Sabine backed away, holding onto her dog. 'Are you *crazy*? Jennifer, give it to Chantal.'

'How she go ride it up dat hill?' Jennifer retorted.

Sabine stared at George: he was blushing, heat in his face. Was he *hurt*?

'Well, give it away to your friend who runs the charity shop at the church. Take it away. I can't believe we still have it lying around. Give it away, for God's sake.'

Sabine looked at their expectant faces, all of a sudden crowded-in. Memories flooded up. Eric Williams in his flashy American car, sailing past. The look he gave her, through the window, questions in his eyes. She felt faint, woozy, the wind in her hair.

La Pompey stopped his clowning, perplexed.

'She doh want it?'

Sebastian frowned. 'No.'

'She'll ride it,' Jennifer assured. 'She just take a turn.'

'Maybe she'll try it tomorrow,' La Pompey reasoned. 'When nobody arong. She mus feel shy to ride it now. Mr Harwood, you mus encourage her. Why you look so sad?'

Sabine wasn't particularly looking forward to dinner; she wore black to match the mood which had descended since the bike had been cleaned. Pascale and her husband arrived early, Pascale looking like she was dressed for a carnival fête, as usual, in an Indian-style shirt dress, slit to the thighs, high-heeled mules, a candy-pink gloss on her lips, her eyelashes luxurious, like hummingbird's wings.

'Ayyy, brudder, howyuh goin',' Pascale gushed, loosening up her accent so she spoke like she was from the bush. She kissed Sebastian noisily on the cheek, her eyes aflame.

'I'm very chipper. You look *awfully* lovely.'

Pascale laughed.

Her husband Jacques, like a twit, hovered behind her, waving a curt hello. He stood at least a foot shorter than Pascale. Why had her daughter married a short man? And Pascale so tall, legs like a show-girl. Jacques was almost blind, his pale eyes peering through tinted round spectacles. He looked sick, like he lived off bird seed. The bald patch on the back of his head was exactly the same size as the goatee on his chin. The man barely spoke; he had nothing to say. He was the runt of his large rich French Creole family. Sabine had once overheard other French Creoles gossiping, referring to him as *Bobo*.

'Drink?' Sebastian suggested.

'Of course.' Pascale pulled out a bar stool and perched on it, wrapping one long leg over the other. Jacques hovered behind her. Pascale bit her cigarette and examined her handsome brother.

'*So*, how long yuh here?'

'Just a couple of weeks.'

'One o' your flyin' visits?'

'Two weeks is all I can get off work.'

'An' how many times yuh had yuh "favourite meal"?' She winked.

'Just once.'

'*Only?*'

Sabine kept her cool. 'Pascale, don't be mean, come and say hello.' The women brushed cheeks. Sabine barely glanced at Jacques.

'Where's your father?' Sabine asked.

'Daddyyy!' Pascale called.

'He's outside tendin' de barbeque.'

'*Daddyyyy!*' Pascale yelled again, from her bar stool.

George staggered in, his hands blackened with charcoal, his hair a shock of crisp wild curls. His glass was empty.

'Oh, there you are!' He went to kiss Pascale.

'Not with dose hands!' Pascale squirmed.

'George, go and do something to your hair, your clothes.' Sabine tutted.

Jacques stood like a short stone pillar, unhearing, unmoving.

'Jacques, how are you,' Sabine asked, enunciating her words.

'Ohh gorsh, nuh, doh frighten de man,' Pascale said.

'I'm just saying hello,' Sabine retorted.

Jacques smiled.

'He's *fine*.'

'Well, he doesn't look it. He looks like he's been stuffed.'

Sebastian burst out laughing.

'Mummyuh!' Pascale bellowed.

'Well, he does.'

Jacques didn't react.

'Good gracious, woman!' Pascale raged. 'How can you say that?'

'Because I felt like it.'

'Are you *drunk*?' Pascale shot at her.

George turned round and went straight back out to his barbeque. Sabine made a sarcastic smile: no, she wasn't drunk. Yet.

'How would you like *me* to say what I damn blasted well feel?' Pascale stared her mother down.

'Please, Pascale, don't. Mum's tired,' Sebastian intervened. 'Come on now. Make friends. Mum doesn't mean to be rude. Do you, Mum?'

'Oh, what do *you* know about Mum? You're never here. All she do is mope an' wait for your emails. And den we all have to hear about them. Mum, *you're* stuffed. You look dead. Sometimes, man, only your eyes move.'

'Pascale, how did you get so coarse?'

'Me?'

'Yes. You were such an intelligent child.'

'When de las time you look at yourself in de mirror?'

'I'm seventy-five.'

'And I cyan remember you happy. I only know you to be sorry for yerself and above everytin. How dare you take your unhappiness out on Jacques. You apologise.'

'I will not.'

Jacques shrugged. He looked like he was trying to vanish.

'Right, we're going!' Pascale snapped. 'Sebastian, call me if you'd like to go to the beach or down the islands. It would be nice to catch up. Tanks for de drink, eh?' She winked at Sebastian but her eyes were glossed.

'Oh Pascale, you're making a fuss. Please don't go. I'm sorry. I'm sorry, Jacques.'

'No, ol' woman. You behave like odder people ent have feelins. We gone. Tell Daddy we couldn't stay for dinner. Goodbye.' Pascale was quivering, pushing Jacques in front of her across the rug.

Sabine winced.

'Oh, Mum,' Sebastian said, shaking his head.

'What?'

The sound of their car starting up, headlights flashing, sweeping the drive, the dogs barking them out.

'What have I said wrong? Why should I apologise? I hate that midget.'

Sabine escaped to the front lawn, to smoke, to stare up at the hills.

'Mum?'

She turned. Her son stood there.

'Talking to the hill again?'

'Yes.'

'Do you know there's a word for talking to hills?'

'No,' she chuckled.

'Starts with talking to plants. Then trees. Then, you know, hills, mountains . . .'

'Then what?'

'The hill starts talking back. Then you're in trouble.'

'Oh, she talks back. Not always, but sometimes.'

'She?'

'The woman, up there. All around. Can't you see her?'

Sebastian looked up.

'Yes, now you mention it.'

'I'm glad.'

'You OK, Mum?'

'Yes, of course. Was I very horrible to Jacques?'

'Yes.'

'I'm not sorry.'

'I know.'

'Pascale will become an alcoholic like the rest of us if she's not careful.'

'She loves him. She told me she does.'

'No, she's made an economic decision. She likes money, my

daughter. She loved a man before; he broke her heart. She married Jacques for his bank balance.'

'Maybe he has a big cock.'

Sabine laughed out loud. 'Maybe. I hope so.'

'Maybe he *does* talk, maybe he just doesn't like us.'

'Maybe he's a good man. I know. In fact, I'm sure he is. Just dull.'

'Is that a crime?'

'No.'

'It is, isn't it?'

'Oh God, I just hoped . . . for more for her.'

'Mum, Pascale *is* happy. She's married, she has two great kids. They're rich. She's doing a lot better than me. I'm unmarried, I live off a salary. I love what I do but that's it.'

'You're different.'

'No, I'm not.'

'You work for a publishing house in a big city. Your life is full of books, interesting people.'

'Many of these people can be pretentious and spoilt.'

'At least they read.'

'Trinidad boasts several fine authors. Masses of fine poetry and prose comes from this region. Caribbean people are richly artistic and literate.'

'Oh, look, don't argue. You live in the *real* world.'

'And where do you live?'

'In a screw-up of a country the world has forgotten. Who cares about this dot on the map?'

'Mum, please. Will you come in? I'll make you some tea.'

'In a moment, yes.'

'Sure?'

'I'll just stand a while.'

'See you inside, crazy lady.'

Sabine turned quickly. 'Don't tell your father.'

'About what?'

'About me talking to the hill.'

CHAPTER SIX

THE MIGHTY SPARROW'S ADVICE

In the morning, George woke and turned over in bed to gaze at the hills of his sleeping wife. Asleep, she looked at peace. Asleep, all the lines fell from her face and he could see who she once was. Sometimes he gazed for a long while and it was only then, in this early-morning time, before she was awake, that he could reclaim the memories which had amassed between them. He could gaze on her sleeping face with the same open love he'd felt from the moment he saw her. He still experienced a faint swell of well-being when he looked at her; she still affected him in a way he'd never understood. He stretched his hand out so that it hovered an inch from her, caressing the air above her shoulder, her stomach, her hip. He leant forward and pressed his lips lightly to the inside of the joint, the tender part he'd kissed a thousand times, his favourite spot on earth, this curved loin, this soft hidden place, his place in the world. 'Eric Williams never loved you,' he whispered into her flesh.

*

He rose and left the house at dawn and while Sabine and his son slept he drove up the Morne to Jennifer's. It was just past dawn; the air was chilly, the hillside neighbourhood was tranquil. No other cars were on the road, which was hairpin bends all the way up. The grass on the verges was wetted down with dew. Jennifer was standing on the top step of the antiquated shack, holding Chantal's baby girl; she looked surprised to see his truck. He parked and let himself into the yard.

'How is he?'

'Better, but he still get pain in he chest.'

'Can I come up?'

She nodded, balancing the toddler on her hip, turning to lead the way.

This time George allowed himself to look around. Everything was neat – shabby and gloomy, but well ordered. The inside of the house looked like the outside, everything so exhausted it appeared soft, as if made of silk. Objects stood in state, resting. There were more of their cast-offs than he first realised: the sagging double bed he and Sabine had thrown out years ago; a broken-down chest of drawers, now even more broken-down. Pillows, cushions, their pump-by-hand orange squeezer.

In the back room Talbot nursed a cup of black coffee. His face looked clearer, the swelling had reduced. His chest was still bandaged and he could sit up a little. George sat down on a stool next to him.

'Talbot, how are you?'

'Ah feelin' much better except mih rib.'

'I'm glad. I want you to stay indoors. I want you to keep your head down.'

Talbot steupsed. 'Ah already do dat.'

'These . . . police men won't return. We've exposed them now.'

'Mr Harwood, dem fellas bad.'

'I know.' George looked him straight in the eye. 'Talbot, if there's anything I don't know about, you'll tell me, won't you?'

Talbot looked away.

'Won't you?'

'Ah know what yer sayin'. Mr Harwood, it hard not to get mix up wid summa dem fellas up here.'

'Some of them live across the road, your cousins?'

'Nah, dey not bad.'

'Then who?'

'Nuttin and nobody. I done wid alluh dat. I get mix up, some time pass. But I stop, long time. I done nuttin wrong, Mr Harwood. Nuttin.'

'Good. Because I want to pay for a lawyer to represent you in court.'

Talbot's eyes flew wide open, the whites shining.

Jennifer clicked her throat. 'What?'

'Yes. It will mean you'll have to be strong. You'll have to give evidence, you'll have to identify these men. Not now. Eventually. You may even have to move away for a short time. But I think it's time we took this to the court of law and sought justice. This is a serious crime. These men should be taken off the force. They only do this kind of thing to poor people. They would never dare beat up my son because I have money. I can pay for your defence, Talbot. Will you let me help you?'

Jennifer hovered, still holding Chantal's little girl. She kissed her on the forehead, nervous.

Talbot's eyes flitted back and forth, trying to understand.

Jennifer hummed.

'My friends at the newspaper will support us,' George urged. 'Report the story. Fact by fact. You will have the press and the law on your side. There is still legal redress in this country, for the rich. And you will have my support, too. No one will hurt you, Talbot. I give you my solemn promise about that.'

Tears fell down Jennifer's face.

George felt ashamed. Ashamed of what? He didn't quite know. Ashamed of himself, perhaps.

Talbot nodded slowly. He inhaled deeply and George could see that even this breath hurt him. Talbot had planned to fade away. That was the best tactic. Take the beating, say nothing. Bobby's garlicky breath came to him. His own ribs creaking.

'Talbot, I won't let you get hurt again.'

Talbot's eyes filmed.

'I give you my word.'

The young man squirmed. His injuries seemed to crawl across his face.

'If it comes to it, I'll pay for a private bodyguard.'

'I doh need that.'

'I'll keep you safe. Trust me.'

'OK,' he said but his eyes held no trust in them. 'For Mummy, yes. For Mummy ah go do whatever it take.'

'Good boy. I'm glad. I know just the man to call in. Just the man. I'll make some calls now, today. And Jennifer—'

'What?'

'Please don't mention any of this to Mrs Harwood. That's my

only condition. I don't want her to know about this . . . not yet. I'll explain it all in my own time.'

'Yes, Mr Harwood.'

George left the shack in Paramin just as the sun was rising, blessing the hill. On his way to the car an emaciated bitch covered in sores slinked out from under Jennifer's neighbour's house to stretch and yawn. Four emaciated puppies clung to her ragged teats. They sucked and sucked.

'Dat dog bad.' Jennifer scowled at it, still nursing the infant.

'Why?'

'She had many more puppies.'

'Oh?'

'But she eat dem all.'

'What?'

'She eat dem when dey born.' Jennifer made a chomping gesture with her mouth. 'She eat dem.'

'Good Lord.'

'Mash!' Jennifer shouted and clapped at the bitch, scaring her off into the dust, back under the house.

George drove to the famous calypsonian's home with a churning knot in his stomach. The Mighty Sparrow. Slinger Francisco. Calypso King of the World. Chief of the Yorubas. Holder of numerous honorary university doctorates and awards from foreign governments. Winner of eleven Calypso Monarch competitions. Over seventy albums produced. In New York, 18 March was the Mighty Sparrow Day. In Trinidad, Sparrow was a god every day.

George remembered the young hustler of the 1950s: even then

he was a hurricane, blowing other singers off the stage. The resounding baritone, his charismatic persona. Sparrow could do it all: extemporise, satirise, sing with the grandeur of opera, with the sleaze of vaudeville. His calypsos were often political, all were original. They swung votes. Early on, the PNM courted Sparrow and he became their number one vote-getter, the only other black man on the island who could pull a crowd like Eric Williams. Sparrow penned many calypsos supporting the PNM, until even he turned against them. 'Get to Hell Outta Here' was the song which nailed Williams.

A headache chewed at the back of George's skull. They came every other day now, in hot, acid waves. He arrived early and sat for several moments in the close cabin of the truck, massaging the back of his head, the pain dulling as he rubbed. He stared into the rear-view mirror. His eyes were bloodshot. He looked like shit. Like he was dead. His skin was liverish. Damp. He patted his cheeks dry. Was he ill? Finally?

He got out of the truck and rang the doorbell. A young coffee-skinned woman of around twenty-five appeared gazelle-like at the gate.

'I'm from the *Trinidad Guardian*. I've come to interview Mr Francisco.'

She raised her eyebrows, openly surprised. 'Come this way. Daddyy . . .' she called out.

Sparrow's house, Sparrow's Hideaway, was famous, too. Gigantic, gaudy, it was a sprawling arrangement of buildings, more a mansion turned memorial park than a home. The house was Trinidad's Graceland. Sparrow's daughter led George to a garden out back, to a round wrought-iron table and chairs.

'Would you like a drink?' she asked.

'A cup of tea would hit the spot.'

She made a face, disappearing.

George found he wasn't just nervous. Waiting for Sparrow was like waiting for a panther to pounce on him.

'Eh, eh!'

The voice. God, the voice was enough to kill him off.

'Is *you* dey sendin'?'

George was upright without consciously moving, his hand crushed in Sparrow's steel grip. Sparrow laughed long and loud and sonorous. Baseball cap, wraparound sunglasses, shorts, an American-style checked shirt, Nike flip-flops. Like Elvis Presley crossed with Idi Amin.

'Where de young chick? Dey tell me dey sendin' a nice young woman to interview me today.'

'She has a cold.'

'I know you.'

'Really?'

'Yes, man. Yous famous. George Harwood, man. Dey send me de crack shot. De ace reporter.'

'Flattery will get you everywhere.'

'Good.'

Sparrow's daughter brought out a mug of tea, a glass of orange juice and a bottle of pills on a tray.

'Ahhh yes.' Sparrow groaned as he sat down, taking the weight off his legs and rubbing one knee. He had recently turned seventy. He was an old man now.

'Excuse me while I take some of these little beauties for mih bones.'

George smiled. 'Actually, I think I'll join you.' He fumbled in his top pocket for a strip of aspirin.

'Cheers, man.' Sparrow held up his orange juice, throwing the pills down his throat.

'Cheers.' George toasted him with tea and aspirin.

Sparrow licked his lips and shook his head so his cheeks wobbled like a big cat's. His black skin was hairless, polished. The man was huge, lean in the arms and legs. Even his paunch looked lean. George found himself staring and realised that Sparrow was letting him, getting it out the way. The face was familiar in more ways than one. The young boy, Clock; could he see a resemblance?

'You're a father,' George began.

'Yes.'

'Your daughter is charming. How many, if you don't mind me asking.'

'Two daughters.'

'Have you been a good father?' It slipped out.

Sparrow looked taken aback. 'Jesus, you get stuck in der quick, man.' He inhaled sharply. George squirmed. 'I'm a famous man. What do you think?'

'Famous people are famously bad parents,' George dared.

'Hmmph. I doh know about *dat*. You go aks mih daughters.'

'Your children must be very proud of you.'

'Dey *better* be.'

'You have thousands of children.'

'Howyuh mean?'

'You're one of the Fathers of the Nation.'

Sparrow laughed. 'Das bullshit. I's an entertainer.'

'The clown is a serious figure. Always the straight man in disguise.'

'Calypso give de poor man a voice. De poor man usually have nuttin to laugh about.'

'But you're rich.'

'I born poor.'

'I have a friend who sings like a bird. Sings in the choir at his local church.'

'I was a choirboy, too.'

'Really?'

'Yeah, man. Latin and ting. I was head choirboy at St Patrick's Church in New Town.'

'My friend is a boy, about eleven or so. He leads the choir, too. At the church in Winderflet.'

Sparrow froze momentarily, staring hard at George. George was sure he'd be thrown out. Ejected over the wall.

Then, wearily: 'I know de boy you mean. Dat little cripple boy from de village down der in Winderflet? Look. Man, you is stickin it to me. De one dey say is my son?'

'That's the local tittle tattle.'

Sparrow leant forward. 'Do you know how many women claim dey have a chile from me?'

George shook his head.

'Plenty.'

'One in every village?'

'At least.'

'See, you're a Father of the Nation. You and Eric Williams.'

Sparrow steupsed. 'Ohhh, gorsh. Pressure, man. I cyan believe dey send me you. I want de girl. De nice young ting.'

'Why did you go to the PNM celebration in January, the one in Woodford Square to mark their fiftieth anniversary?'

Sparrow paused, looking at George with dawning caution. 'I is part of their history. PNM history. I was invited, nuh.'

'But you turned on them.'

'We all did.'

'Didn't you love Eric Williams once?'

'Yes, man. Everyone loved Eric at first. We were all in awe of him. All excited by what he might do. Of course. He was a great man.'

'And then he failed.'

'Yes.'

'I met him once. With my wife.'

'Eric was popular wid de ladies. She liked him?'

'Yes and no.'

'Howyuh mean?'

'My wife . . . *wrote* to Eric Williams.'

'What?'

'For years. Hundreds of letters, actually. I found them recently. I think she developed . . . *feelings* for Eric Williams.'

'Feelins?' Sparrow's eyebrows danced.

'Like you. She saw him speak once, maybe twice. In Woodford Square. She was taken in. I think she . . . *respected* him.'

'Your wife loved Eric Williams, too?'

'She had feelings.'

'What kinda feelins?'

George exhaled loudly. 'Compassion.'

Sparrow whistled. 'Crazy. Eric didn't like white people.'

'I know.'

'Massa day done, eh?' Sparrow chuckled.

'Yes. Quite.' George felt his throat tighten. So far he'd toughed it out. But since finding the letters he'd thought of little else. What she had said, what had been going on behind his back. She'd *cared*. Just like Sparrow, like everyone else. There had been a love affair going on for a short time, when Williams was alive: Williams and the whole damn island.

A look of regret came into Sparrow's eyes. 'Eric hurt everyone who loved him.'

'Why?'

'He was very . . . up and down.'

'Tell me more.'

'Eric was a moody man. Light and dark. Happy, joking and then vexed. He trusted no one.'

'You hurt him back.'

Sparrow's eyes went dark. 'Yes.'

George nodded.

'You never ketch your wife writin' dose letters?'

'No.'

'Never suspect somptin goin' on?'

'No.'

'I tink I can understand why she write to Williams. Eric was brilliant, man.'

'My wife was very naive when she first came to Trinidad.'

'You jealous?'

'No,' George lied.

Sparrow noticed his discomfort. He smiled. 'Yous an old man, Mr Harwood. You telling me your wife had a ting for Eric long time past and you not jealous? You still man and wife?'

'Just.'

Sparrow laughed.

'You ever worry about losing your wife, Mr Francisco?'

Sparrow laughed so hard the hairs on George's arms stood up. '*What*! If I ketch my wife writing letters to Eric Williams, boy . . . dat would be a story, too. Of course, I is a jealous man. Write to Eric? Man, dat woulda been trouble fer she.'

'What would you do if you found your wife's love letters to another man?'

'I'd sing fer her, man. Win her back.'

'What if you couldn't sing?'

'Nah man, I'd win her.'

'But I can't sing.'

'What about dance?'

'I can dance.'

'Den we go launch an attack. I go sing fer she, under your window, and den you take her in your arms, dance wid her. She'd love it.'

'Like Cyrano de Bergerac. That's ridiculous.'

'Das romance.'

'I was romantic once.'

'You still are. You write like a man who have a romantic heart. I does read you.'

'Really?'

'Yes, man. Write poems fer she. Like William Shakespeare and ting. You know . . . '

'Yes, I know. Poetry isn't my thing.'

'Women like poetry. Red roses.' Sparrow's eyes shone. He was a performer through and through, a persuader with devastating charm, a man of love.

'Take my advice. You say she write letters to Eric. Write letters for *she*. Write back to her.'

'Maybe I can try. In my own way.'

'Yes, man. Write to she.'

Sparrow cackled.

'When are you going to write a calypso about the blimp?' George asked.

Sparrow laughed again, long and loud. 'Dat blasted ting. Oh gorsh. I write one already. I recordin' it all now.'

'Can you sing it for me?' George took his tape recorder from his briefcase and placed it on the table.

'You want de exclusive?'

'Of course.'

George switched the tape recorder on and Sparrow began to sing the catchy tune, closing his eyes. The rich baritone brought on a rash of goosebumps, a spreading feeling of guilt. George's eyes filled. The great man crooned his caustic words, eyes sober and bright as stars. The voice, of course, was related directly: father of the child's higher, purer voice. He, George Harwood, was somehow related, too. Sparrow sang. George could hear the little boy singing along. Sabine once wrote letters, crazy, mad, desperate, honest, even loving letters to Eric Williams; she wrote with thoughts and intimacies she'd never shared with *him*. She was young, beautiful and she ran into Eric Williams one hot afternoon, when he was in full flow, launching a political party, an angry black man in his prime, at a time in history when black men around the world were standing up and saying the same thing. *Massa day done.* Eric Williams. Just one of a generation of black leaders who wanted to wake up the world. He thumped his fists on the lectern, bellowed for change. Sabine had encountered a scholar, a player, a man poised to mean something and be someone. She'd witnessed that powerful potential and she was still mourning its failure.

*

Sabine woke with a groggy head. She'd overslept, something more common these days. A cup of tea gone cold stood on the side table. George had brought her a cup of tea before he left; he'd brought her a cup of tea every morning of their life together. She put the cup to her lips and grimaced at the tea, sipping it first and then knocking it back with a few stiff gulps. She inspected her body under her nightie, its runaway curves and generous swells; she poked at her breasts and hips, sinking a finger into the flesh. 'Mon Dieu,' she gasped, and felt a spasm of self-disgust, and loneliness for her youth, for the loss of her husband's attentions. She tried to spring out of bed. The muscles in her back groaned, her knees cracked. She tried again, this time lifting off from the bed in a more optimistic manner, hoisting herself upright. Her eyes were wet from her dreams. What had she dreamt about? She couldn't remember, only that she'd woken with that lost, thick-headed feeling. She put her feet into slippers and threw open the curtains. The garden quivered with a pure white light. Two dragonflies, battimamzelles, their slender bodies locked in sexual battle, skimmed the surface of the pool. The keskidees bickered. Vermilion, saffron, ochre, scarlet – her eyes smarted at the garden's lewd and rapacious blooms, ginger lilies, chaconia, heliconia, anthuriums, moussianda. The stout-bellied iguana was already inching its way up the bough of the coconut tree. Every morning Sabine recognised her competition. This island flexed its charms, laughed in her face as she withered.

A skittering sound echoed over the terrazzo. Dog nails on a hard slick surface; one of the big dogs trotting over?

Click, click, click.

Then – Sabine rejected what she saw. Henry, one of the big ridgeback dogs, George's dog, was on the run, an entire deck of sponge cake between his jaws. The cake had been swiped from the kitchen table again; it was a perfect fit, a coin in a slot. Jennifer must have already started making cakes for the weekend.

'*Henryy*, damn dog!' her voice bellowed from the kitchen.

'Henry, drop that cake!' Sabine commanded. But the dog paid no heed. Henry was trotting straight towards her. More skittering, the dog's claws flailing, unable to grip the glassy surface. 'Henry!' Sabine tried to corner him, arms outstretched. Henry dodged easily. Then he was off, tail low, cake clamped.

'You stupid animal!' Sabine shouted, and charged after it, her nightie billowing.

The dog galloped round the side of the house. Sabine followed. 'I'm going to *kill* you this time. Jesus Christ! This goddamn dog and those stupid cakes. Give it back!' Under a mango tree she spotted pieces of the abandoned sponge, a trail of crumbs scattered on the ground.

She followed the crumbs across the front garden and back into the house.

'That stupid dog!' In the living room she stopped, panting for breath. Her bones creaked, all of them at once.

Jennifer appeared. 'Oh gorsh, nuh man, leave de damn dog alone.'

'I'm going to kill him this time.'

Up the stairs – cake crumbs on the stairs. The dog's giant paws jutted from under the hem of the office curtains.

Jennifer laughed. 'Henry hidin' from you.'

'The rotten coward,' Sabine cursed. The dog pressed its muzzle flat to the wall and the curtain bulged over its body.

Sabine removed one of her bedroom slippers.

'Oh *gorsh*, leave de poor dog,' Jennifer complained.

Sweat dripped from Sabine's face like rain. 'I'm going to *kill* you this time,' she vowed, mounting the stairs on tiptoe. She entered the office. The dog shuddered, pressing itself against the wall.

Sabine towered over him. 'You stupid animal.'

The dog whimpered.

Jennifer came up behind her.

Sabine snatched the curtain back. Henry's eyes were pressed closed, long eyelashes like spider's legs, jittering. Those eyelashes, like a beautiful girl's, reminding her of dancing, of those days when Dr Baker pressed himself to her. Sabine hesitated, arm raised.

'You stupid animal,' she whispered, bringing the slipper down on the dog's slim head. *Whack.*

The dog cowed its head, sinking to the floor.

'Oh gorsh, leave de dog,' Jennifer begged. 'Doh beat de poor damn animal.'

'The dog's always stealing from the kitchen table. How many times does he have to be told?' Sabine cried. *Whack.* The dog bowed its head, hiding its nose between its front legs.

'I'll kill you,' Sabine gargled.

Jennifer went silent and left the room.

Tears in Sabine's eyes. Her breath quickened and her lips

curled. She beat and beat the dog. She wanted to kill it dead, kill herself dead.

*

George spotted the skinny black boy, stumbling along the pavement, a tiny fragile bird, a sparrow in the dust. His movements were jerky, his one long arm swinging like the arm of a clock. His real name was Joshua Pierre. His mother was Lavinia Pierre, a deep-black, good-looking woman who lived in an unpainted concrete house the other side of Winderflet River, near the bend by the fruit stall. The little boy stumbled with his head up, eyes looking straight ahead, a small knapsack on his back. George slowed down, pulling in alongside.

'Hop in,' he called through the window, opening the door of the truck.

The boy smiled, as if he'd been expecting to see George. On the seat he wriggled from his knapsack, pulling it onto his lap, loosening the tie.

'What have you got there?' George asked.

'I bring you something.'

'Oh, that's good of you.'

'It a present.'

'But it's not my birthday.'

'It not that kind of present.'

'What kind is it then?'

'It something to help when you call out the name of our Father in Heaven.'

'Oh? What?'

From the knapsack the boy pulled out a small figurine, made of plaster. Mary, Mother of Jesus.

George blushed, dumbstruck.

'She have a little sticker underneath,' the boy explained, peeling it off from the bottom and leaning forward. 'So you can see she.' He stuck the statue of the Virgin to the dashboard of the truck.

'See? Now she there all de time. A good woman. You can speak to her. Talk to she when you get vexed.'

Mary's hands were outstretched, palms open; horribly, ridiculously holy. It made George uncomfortable just to look at her, so saintly on his truck. His truck – in which he'd fucked a dozen women along the bench-seat, at least one of them a virgin.

The boy beamed.

Who is your father? George wanted to ask the little boy. The Mighty Sparrow? Patrick Manning? Eric Williams? All had failed him. No wonder the boy loved God, the great Papa in the Sky.

George kept driving. Clock began to sing, quietly at first, to himself. George glanced across at his birdcage chest to make sure he was seeing right, that the sound was really emanating from such a small space. *Glory to God on high, Peace to those on earth.* The boy's voice grew as he sang, as they drove on up Saddle Road, past the Country Club. Clock's voice doubled, then trebled, sounding like brass, hot and fluid. The cab of the truck filled with the sound of holiness and the hairs on the back of George's neck stood erect. Joshua, son of Sparrow – or maybe not. Son of Patrick Manning? The little boy threw back his head, a beatific smile on his face, a halo of light around him; yes, the boy glowed like a frigging divine apparition. He sang a chorus of *Hosannas*, eyes closed, in a swoon. George swooned. A hundred memories fluttered from his head, women like birds, all his infidelities, flew out and up and away from him, on a bold band of song, away and up and into the sky above the road up to Winderflet village.

When he got home, George immediately set to writing the Sparrow interview up. Henry came to the office door looking sorry for himself. 'What's the matter, eh?' He stroked the dog's slim head. 'What's up?' The dog slid to the floor and folded his nose into his shins. Had Sabine scolded him, had he stolen a cake again? 'We'll go to the beach soon,' George told the dog.

He didn't get a story, as such, from Sparrow. But a scoop – yes. He had the new calypso on tape. He listened to it again on his portable tape recorder. It was vintage Sparrow, not his usual party stuff of late; old-school calypso, critical, political. 'Shoot Dong de Blimp'. The man was still dangerous to those in power. Maybe he'd written it secretly with Sabine – nothing could surprise George these days. His headache had come back and his skull throbbed, as though there were another person inside, banging to get out.

'Hi, Dad.' Sebastian popped his head round the door.

'I thought you were at the beach.'

'I was. Not for long, though. Almost had my wallet stolen at Maracas. Little bugger, about ten years old, chased him across the car park.'

'Did you report it? There's a station on the hill just behind the beach.'

'Of course not.'

'Don't tell your mother.'

'Why not?'

'I'd just rather you didn't. You know . . . she'll get . . . like she does.'

'How does she get, Dad?'

'Tired.'

Sebastian laughed. '*That's* your word for it.'

'What's yours?'

'Depressed.'

'She's not *depressed*.'

'Her face is always damp. Clammy. It's torturous for her – just being here. Getting through each day.'

'Oh, we're *all* too hot sometimes.'

'You're not. Mum looks like she's melting.'

'She doesn't complain.'

'You don't hear her. Or choose not to.'

'This is my house. I choose what I like.'

'Exactly.'

'If you don't like it here, why do you keep coming back?'

'I was born here.'

'Yes, I was there that day.'

'Mum loves you, Dad . . . more than she hates Trinidad.'

George looked directly at him. 'You're judging *my* marriage and you've never been married at all, eh, Father Sebastian?'

Sebastian glared. 'They don't make love affairs like yours any more, Dad.'

'Oh no? That's an interesting observation. Why not?'

'Most women of my generation would have left you, years ago.'

'Oh good. All those feminists and whatnot. Good for them. Marriage is dying, I hear, isn't it?'

'Women have changed.'

'And I'm a dinosaur.'

'Actually, Dad, you have no idea at all. I've watched you and Mum for years, since I was a boy. I've always *envied* you, Dad.'

George stared. 'What have you envied?'

'You and Mum. I remember you.'

Slowly, carefully, George rubbed at the pain gathering in the back of his head.

'You were quite something. My role models. I've tried to find what you have for myself and I've failed. I still think of you as the most glamorous couple I've ever met.'

'I doubt that. Your friends all seem quite chic.'

'Few have loved like you and Mum.'

'What about you?'

'I've loved and lost as well,' Sebastian cut back. 'More than once. I wish . . .'

'Oh, save the sermon.'

'OK, Dad, *stay* ignorant.'

George wanted to spit. He stared up at his younger, more handsome self. Sebastian could go to hell. Why had he abandoned the island? His so-called glamorous London friends were far less interesting.

'I'm ignorant. And you're not. Is that your line of reasoning? I'm a fool and you aren't?'

Sabine appeared in the hall doorway, sleepy-eyed from an afternoon nap. 'You two woke me up.'

George stared. No one spoke for a moment.

'Sebastian almost had his wallet nicked,' George said coldly.

'Where?'

'Maracas.'

'I overheard what you were saying.'

George didn't try to hide his irritation. 'Oh, good.'

'I wish you wouldn't argue. You're as stupid and foolish as each other. Stop this battle. Or I'll crack your heads.'

'We. . . just see things differently. We weren't arguing.' Sebastian tried to smooth things.

'Just shut up.' Sabine eyed them both, deadly calm. 'Did I also overhear Mr Sparrow's new calypso?'

'Yes.'

'You interviewed him?'

'Yes, this afternoon.'

'He's back on form, then.'

'Seems so.'

'I've always liked Mr Sparrow. Time he started to write again.'

'Sparrow knew Eric Williams well. We talked of him.'

'Oh yes? You should invite Mr Sparrow round for tea, then.'

George smiled.

Sabine smiled back for the first time in a long time. *Win her.*

Sabine left the room. Sebastian looked at George with shrewd and rueful eyes that held the glimmer of an apology. George went back to work, thinking of the Mighty Sparrow, the man of love, thinking of his words. *Win her.* Maybe he could. Not with his songs or dancing or poems, no, bollocks to that. He would write, write. Write something which might actually matter, for once.

CHAPTER SEVEN

BRIAN LARA AND HIS STRANGE IDEAS

Easter Sunday. Long lines of cars, people on foot, families, couples, old people, young people, black people, white people, long silent strings of the newly innocent, the penitent, the hungover, the starting over, the resurrected. All wordless, climbing up the hill to the red and vanilla church in Winderflet village. Nine in the morning and the heat was still on hold.

'Let's sit near one of the side-exits,' Sabine said to Sebastian as they parked at the top. 'So we can feel the breeze.'

A life-size statue of Joseph prayed down at them from the crèche cut into the hill-rock. Joseph and Mary, cast in plaster, prayed there all year round.

'He's looking straight at me,' Sebastian joked. 'He knows something I don't.'

'Ha, him. He knows everything. I thought he was looking at *me*. To hell with all this penitence. You know, we could just go to the beach instead. Sit in the shade. Take a bottle of champagne.

It'd be empty today. The whole of Maracas to ourselves. Half the country is at church.'

'No. I *like* going to church here, Mum.'

'You do?'

'Yes. Only here, actually.'

'Why?'

'I was baptised here. So was Pascale. She was married here.'

'Pascale was born at Easter. It's her birthday soon.'

'I want to be married here one day, too. And if I never marry, I want my funeral held here.'

'What a thing to say!'

'I mean it.'

'Well, I'll be long gone. I won't be buried here.'

'No?'

'No. Send me back in a box. Bury me anywhere but here.'

'I'll try to remember that.'

'You don't go to church in London?'

'No. No one I know goes to church *ever*. I only go here.'

'Why?'

'I feel more aware here.'

'Of what?'

'Of myself. Of my sins.'

'Good God.'

'It's peaceful up on this hill, don't you think?'

'No.'

'I find praying hard, don't you?'

'Yes. Sometimes.'

'There's a knack to it, isn't there? It's an art. You're supposed to know how to do it.'

Sabine nodded. Joseph was peering down at her over his praying hands, hands like the walls of Jennifer's holy shack. Patient Joseph. Patient shack, patient Granny Seraphina. Granny who waited for so long for nothing to change, who, when time ran out, ran riot with the rest of them. Bless her.

'Whenever I try to pray my head goes blank.'

'Sometimes you pray by accident. In passing. A wish, a hope. A thought.' Sabine smiled at her son and blushed. She wanted to keep her son here with her, in Trinidad, her good handsome clever son; have him enrich her life, make things better, just like George did once.

'That Joseph is starting to get to us, Mum,' Sebastian joked.

'Yes. Let's get this over with.'

Our Lady of Lourdes was light and airy. The church had a high bowed wooden ceiling, like the innards of an upturned pirogue. The floor was a mosaic of tiles. The slim arched windows were interspersed with woodcuts of Christ's passion, iconised; the Stations of the Cross. The images were grainy, roughly cut into wood. They made Sabine sadder than usual, somehow ashamed of herself. Ashamed of what? She wasn't sure. They sat down and watched as the pews filled slowly. Little black girls filed in wearing white nylon tights and red ribbons like butterflies settled in their hair. Teenage boys with wet hair slicked back, wearing oversized jeans and oversized Caterpillar boots. Old thin black women in flouncy sherbet-coloured Easter bonnets. Old thin white people, speckled with chocolate flecks of melanin, their skin like an advancing leprosy. Everyone standing. Backs straight, eyes forward, waiting.

Facing the congregation were two pews for the choir. Six or seven black men and women stood there, peering into hymn books. A little boy stood among them, his clean white shirt tucked into ironed black trousers. He clutched a tambourine to his chest, his eyes large and bold and serious. The boy was familiar, yes. George had once picked him up in his truck; they were on their way into town. She rarely travelled with George in that rusty old thing, but her car had been in the garage; George had stopped abruptly. 'Hop in,' he'd called out to the boy. There was a familiarity between them she didn't expect, a small friendship. Sabine had felt hurt. George had never even mentioned this little boy, and yet they seemed to be friends. Maybe George had lots of friendships he never shared with her. The little boy and George had been comfortable together that day; they had chatted easily. She had felt envious.

'My guardian angel,' George had remarked, casually, when they had dropped him off.

The choir began to sing the first notes of the opening hymn, the adults taking their lead from the boy, his high pure voice holding the other voices up. The organist joined in, a man on a guitar, too. The boy shook his tambourine, crooning, his voice filling the entire cavern of the church, right up to the rafters. It seemed to fill Sabine, too, entering through her spine and filling the cavity of her chest, warming her insides. The boy's voice made her skin tingle, her scalp prickle; it made her feel self-conscious.

A flock of priests in pastoral green proceeded up the aisle, standards held aloft. Altar boys wafted smoking bombs of frankincense to the left and right.

'Hi there.' It was Frank Farfan. Uncle Frank, patriarch of a large local white family they knew well. Dear Frank.

'Can I share your pew?' Frank was six foot five and singed to a crisp, his skin papier-mâchéd to his bones. His eyes were small brown polished balls, twinkling with mischief. Sabine squeezed his hand and moved up to make room for him.

Frank stood erect, gazing at the priest, absorbing every word. This was how Trinidadians behaved in church: alert, composed, peering respectfully at the altar, awaiting a miracle. Carnival and Lent. Bacchanal and guilt. Trinidad in a nutshell. This was a nation of sin-loving people who made a point of praying for forgiveness.

'I don't like the look of *him*,' Sabine whispered to Sebastian.

A man had wandered in. He loitered by the open side door a few feet away. His body was sinewy and well-muscled, black as earth. He had short gingerish dreadlocks and his eyes were drug-bleary and red. He was glancing around, surveying the congregation.

'Eh, eh, who does he think he is?'

'A local badjohn,' Frank whispered back.

The badjohn stood his ground and the mass continued. Father Andrew proselytised about peace. Peace handed down from on high, peace and love to our neighbours. Peace for Easter. The man was goat-eyed, his dreadlocks like stubby horns. A hundred parishioners ignored him and prayed for his sins. Sabine stared him down. He stared back. What had he come for?

The man stood by the door throughout, not listening to a word, eyes scanning the pews. Minutes ticked by. Sebastian had his eyes closed, trying to pray. Then there was movement in the aisles, as the congregation prepared themselves for the collection. Old black women, bonneted, grim-faced, scattered through the church, hovering at each aisle with a collection basket on a long pole. In the central aisle, a few feet away from the badjohn, a large flat basket lay on a table, awaiting the entire cache.

Slowly, the old women emptied their collection baskets into the main basket until it contained a hill of red, blue and purple banknotes.

The badjohn glared at the hill of money.

The church glared at the badjohn.

The badjohn rubbed his chin.

The woman guarding the basket peered down her nose at him. To get to the money, he would have to knock her down. But she would howl and kick him and bite his ankles. Then he'd have to deal with hardman Frank Farfan, seventy-two and mad and wild and passionate about his God, and the black man in front of Frank, the one with the big muscles and the small baby in his arms.

The badjohn stared at the money. Sabine's stomach twisted; she was sure there was about to be an ugly fight.

Dignified and slow, the woman turned her head and cast her stern eyes in his direction. Facing him, asking him, with cold and furious intent, just what he had planned.

The badjohn didn't move.

Sabine felt faint. She saw herself that day, with the man the whole country had rejected. A man crushed, the streets in flames. A man who had come to the end of things. Eric Williams, his head hung in bitter shame. Was it wrong of her to care, to put her lips to his neck?

The woman picked up the basket.

The badjohn glared.

The woman dared him to try and steal the money. She steupsed and clicked her throat.

The rest of the church turned away.

The badjohn licked his lips, his throat dried, his soul parched.

The woman carried the money up to the altar with small measured steps.

It was time to give peace. Frank reached for Sabine's hand, holding it high like a trophy as Father Andrew commenced the blessing. The entire congregation raised up their hands in a form of salute, arms stretched across the church in a long row of Ws. Sabine looked across at the door. The badjohn stood there, clearly confused.

'Let us offer each other the sign of peace,' Father Andrew intoned.

The congregation went on the move, shaking hands, giving peace, chatting, exchanging hellos and Easter greetings. Hugs, kisses. Handshakes. Blessings. *Howyuh goin'?* Everyone was aware of this man in their midst. The man was outnumbered, outpeaced. The church shifted, moving together like a shoal of fish.

A young black woman, a baby in her arms, approached the goat-eyed man with an outstretched hand.

Sabine wanted to shout: *Get away from him.*

'Peace be with you,' she said, offering the badjohn her hand. Her baby gurgled.

The badjohn whispered something in reply. He shook her hand cautiously. The young woman moved on.

The badjohn looked around.

Uncle Frank stared him down.

Sabine stared him down.

The badjohn vanished.

Sabine sank to her knees. She crossed herself and prayed: *Marie, pleine de grâce*. She was sorry, sorry for her sins, mostly for the way she'd treated George for so long, for the way she was so distant with him, for the way she'd come to look at him like she looked at the man with the goat-eyes. When had her innocence left her? In those years when she had been writing to Eric Williams, when she was pleading and young and confused, just like the badjohn? Back then she had been hopeful. Look at the little boy up there, his big black eyes full of belief, full of love. Where had she disappeared to? She hated coming here; why had she come again? To please her son. Her son who couldn't pray. She had stopped trying to pray years ago. She wished the boy would stop looking at her so, like he knew something. Go away. At least her son was here, thank God. She would try, try to be nice again, try to find her former self – how, where? Those black birds, corbeaux, circling overhead. The day they pelted stones at her. Did she die then?

*

Not only had Ray loved the Sparrow interview, he'd gone big, running it as a spread in the main paper. He loved the exclusive on the calypso. Unexpectedly, on Easter Sunday morning, he rang George again.

'Lara just named Captain of de team again, man!' He sounded excited. 'We want another scoop! Lara arrivin' in two days, Tuesday mornin'. I want you do de interview. Get him to talk about what he'll do different, for God's sake, how he gonna turn de team back into champions. Or is it just a PR job before de cricket World Cup in 2007? Aks him tough questions, man.'

'Of course.'

'None of de usual tra la la.'

'No.'

'We need the story by Friday.'

'You'll have it.'

In the office, George saw that his file on Lara had been recently excavated from the heap of other files, left on top of the desk for him to find. Brian Lara – so famous on the island he was common, he was everyman. Lara was thirty-seven. Finally, ripe for the captaincy. At eighteen, he was way too young, but now he stood on the mountain of his career, primed for leadership. Everyone knew the stories: Bunty and Pearl Lara, his parents, had eleven children, a house in a village in Santa Cruz. His brother Rudolph had carved Brian his first cricket bat. As a child, Brian had played cricket with an orange.

On the file, George saw a note, a white envelope with his name written on the front in Sabine's hand. Years since she'd left him a note. A feeling overcame him, like he was ridiculous and out of his depth; this was the feeling he'd nursed for some time now, with his wife. She'd got the better of him, over the years. He opened the envelope and unfolded the single white page inside, hoping that it might say something of love. On it was written in Sabine's unmistakable slant: *Can you ask Mr Lara what he thinks of the blimp?*

Fifteen minutes by car from Paramin to the Hilton Hotel, which clung to Belmont Hill. The hotel overlooked the savannah and the district of Laventille. Once, a great house had existed on the same spot, occupied by the early governors of Trinidad; the governors had held court, overseeing the city, discussing the price of cocoa. The hotel was in some ways still a fort, perched up above it all. George was early. He made his way down to the pool area. Behind it ran a glass balcony with a view across the city.

George recognised Brian Lara instantly, even though Lara's back was turned to him. Lara stood on the balcony, talking into his mobile phone, peering out over Port of Spain. The clean-cut clothes, the voice. Lara was five foot nine at best. That was him all right. George felt a surge of relief: excellent, excellent, this was an amiable setting for an interview.

George coughed. Brian Lara turned.

'Hello, Mr Lara,' George said, coming forward. 'Seems like we had the same idea. I'm George Harwood from the *Guardian*.'

Lara's face relaxed. An imp, a Puck, bearing the wide, capricious smile of a boy of ten. His eyes, though, held a halting quality, flashing with a seriousness of intent, of responsibility.

George joined him at the railing, switching on the tape recorder in his pocket.

'Some view, eh?' he ventured. Port of Spain was spread out before them, right out to the Gulf of Paria. The savannah was dry, threatening fire. The sky was white. The blimp hung about in it.

'Apart from that thing.' Lara pointed.

'Yes. What do you think of it?'

'I hear it have a bar up there. That they mix great cocktails.'

George laughed.

'It have rooms and a dance floor, and a setta beautiful women, man. And the bes seats for all the matches at the oval and the stadium. Bes place to watch the Peru match when the Soca Warriors come.'

'Who's up there, then?'

'Manning. The government. That's where they spend de day.'

'Maybe you'll get invited up.'

'I already have!'

'I have a friend who'd like to go up. A little boy. Can you fix it?'

Lara's eyes twinkled. 'Yeah, man.'

George stared out at the hills surrounding the city, the green, voluptuous hills.

'My wife . . . ' He blushed. 'My wife wants me to ask you a question.'

'Oh yeah? What?'

'What do you *really* think of it?'

'Your wife aks dat?'

'Yes.'

Lara bit his lip, silenced for a moment. A shadow fell over his face and he became serious, even more glamorous, somehow. 'It not what people think.'

George nodded.

'It not watching the bandits.'

'No.'

They both gazed out across Port of Spain. The blimp hung languid, stupid.

'What then?'

'It watchin' the coast, man. It watchin' the oil installations.'

'Yes.'

'If the blimp see something it don't like. Then it go call in the helicopters.'

'The Americans are scared of Chávez, his influence,' George chipped in.

'Yeah, man. That is the point. They think he the new Castro in the Caribbean; they hate the way Chávez and Castro are friends. Imagine if Manning and Chávez paired up, too, eh? Then trouble for the US. Two oil-rich countries and a big ol' mudder-arse Communist like Fidel – that would be something to worry about.' Lara steupsed and smiled mischievously.

'You think the Americans asked – or even forced – Manning to buy it?'

Lara shrugged, but his eyes twinkled.

'It may even be American-funded,' George suggested.

'Maybe.'

'George Bush must be shitting it. A raving socialist lunatic so close to all the oil in Trinidad.'

'*Exactement*,' Lara chuckled. 'They say they get the choppers from Israel, man. Israel! They say they even have Mossad and alluh dem boys in the jungle up so.' He pointed to the hills surrounding the city. 'Waitin' to stage some kinda attack.'

'Wow. Where did you hear *that*?'

'I have my sources.' Lara grinned.

The tape recorder pulsed against George's hip.

'It not just that, man.' Lara pointed again. 'The blimp change the view, man. It stick up in de eye and it stick up in de stomach. Chilren growin' up with this kinda nonsense hangin' over them? Like the crime problem is their fault? Their Daddy's fault? How it go help dem? How it go make them proud, break out?'

'Like you did?'

'Yeah, man.'

'What does a boy from a poor village do if he can't play cricket?'

'Go to Foreign, man. Take a trip.'

'Or shoot his way out.'

'Or shoot down the blimp.'

'Quite.'

'Hot air. That what keep it up.'

'Do you ever go back to the village where you were born?'

'Sometimes.'

'When you see a cricket match set up in the street, or on a vacant piece of land, all little boys, all that talent, what do you think?'

'I pray they all have a father like mine.'

'We know there's only one of you. But actually there could be many more. I hope you don't take this the wrong way, Mr Lara, but in my time, I've seen many as talented as you, little boys playing in the streets. This whole island is crawling with boys like you once were. Imagine what your life would have been if your father hadn't had the gumption to put you forward.'

'I would be vexed,' he nodded.

'Disappointed,' George added.

'The kinda man the blimp suppose to be watchin' all now.'

Lara made a gun with his finger and pointed it at the blimp, pressing the trigger. 'Pow.'

At home, Sabine was watering dog shit off the grass. Jennifer vacuumed up a live gecko from the wall. The dogs stared up at the coconut tree, waiting for the iguana to fall. Sebastian was at the computer, emailing a colleague in London. Lunch would soon be ready and after lunch George would write up the Lara interview. Forget the cricket World Cup, the future goals of the West Indian team. The blimp – Brian Lara and his strange ideas. Spot on. Bravo. George had his sources, too; he'd check the facts. But if Lara was right . . . Wow.

Brian Lara: the truth about the blimp.

Mossad agents in the jungle.

A spy ship for the Americans.

*

Sabine thought George was acting odd. He'd grown thinner; his shorts were hanging around his arse a little. He was more secretive than usual about his work. But then he'd left the Sparrow interview spread open at the right pages on the kitchen table, as if to show it off. Something was going on. And she felt bad about the dog. Beating it like that – for what? Her arm still ached. She went out to the garage and stared at her newly polished green Raleigh bicycle; it had started to gather rubbish again, newspapers piled on the basket, laundry folded and left on the saddle. George had loved her on that bike, riding down to the dock to greet him after work, weaving through the hot dusty streets of Port of Spain. Charlotte Street, the great open air market, buzzing with life, mountains of fruit. No market now. They couldn't afford to buy fish these days. She'd been brave and free on that bike. But something was up with George. George had always been so confident; he'd never suffered the classic male crisis mid-life. He'd never had any self-doubt. Maybe he doubted something now? Had the letters given him a jolt? She vowed to be nice. To *try*. To find more common ground. A great commotion broke out on the other side of the house: the dogs barking and gnashing, great stems falling from the coconut tree.

'Oh gorsh, dat damn lizard,' shouted Jennifer.

*

George stripped off his clothes and struggled into his trunks. He went out onto the balcony, and surveyed his oasis. The sight of the pool water brought a need for the peace it promised and he went quickly down the stairs. He stood poised at the pool's edge, arms raised above his head in a V. Hovering for a moment, as was his custom, he took a huge breath before launching himself, with the grace of a hippopotamus, across the blue surface, hitting it with a mighty *crack*, slapping the water into shock, sending waves crashing to the side of the pool. Katinka flew out to attack the tsunami. The keskidees scrambled a party of fighter jets out to dive and swoop. George surfaced, strands of long wild hair plastered to his face.

There'll be water in heaven, he promised himself.

CHAPTER EIGHT

SOCA WARRIORS

Gabriel Chowdry was a good lawyer and an old friend. He listened carefully to the story of Talbot and the police thugs who beat him up, of Bobby Comacho and his garlicky breath, his threats. When George finished his story, Gabriel leant back in his wing-backed leather chair and clasped his hands together.

'You're pissing in the wind, George.'

'Why?'

'No witnesses.'

'What about the photos we took?'

'No witnesses to the injuries. No witnesses, no case.'

'Bastards. They knew what they were doing.'

'I'm afraid so.'

'I still want to go ahead. It's important to at least *try* to make a case against them.'

'George, I advise against it. You're not alone in this. A few others have tried. Not many, but one or two. And you know what – sometimes the police don't even answer letters sent to them by lawyers. Letters get lost, go missing. It's like cat and mouse. No one can touch the police. These police assault cases get *nowhere*. You're asking me to take on a closed case. And – it will cost you a lot of money. Hundreds of thousands of dollars, even. They will find ways to stall the case. Then you'll lose. Talbot has no case. No proof. Now – if you had witnesses, photographs – then – I could help. Even then . . .'

'But I could make sure it would be all over the press.'

'So what? Think they care? George, even so – it could take years.'

'I still want to do it. It could encourage debate. Embarrass those fuckers.'

'George Harwood versus the Chief of Police. Harwood versus the present reigning PNM government elected by the people? Why?'

George coughed. He knew why. Maybe it was the wrong reason or maybe it wasn't, or maybe he just wanted to do one thing right. One final thing. 'To impress my wife.'

Gabriel laughed. 'What?'

'Something like that.'

'George. Go home and drink a rum.'

George stared at his friend; his neighbour when they first arrived in Trinidad. Gabriel's wife Helena had been an educated woman, also East Indian, a lawyer, too, serene and aloof; she hadn't lasted long in Trinidad, no place for women like her. She had left him, disappeared without even a note.

'I'm lucky Sabine never . . . left me.'

Gabriel nodded.

'Have you had any news?'

'No.'

'Sabine was right about it all. I wanted to stay, I'm selfish. Now she barely speaks to me. And Talbot's face. He was almost killed up there on that hill. Left to die. This sort of thing is common now.'

Gabriel pursed his lips. 'So you think you're a white man with money, contacts, that you could help him?'

'Yes.'

'George, impressing your wife is the wrong reason to pursue this.'

'Sabine or no Sabine, I want to do this. Someone should. I have money in the bank. What else am I going to spend it on?'

'I want you to know that as your friend I strongly advise against it.'

'I want you to know that I still want you to go ahead. Please.'

Gabriel managed to look confused and disapproving and amused and happy all in one face. He shook his head. 'OK,' he said, slowly. 'OK.'

On the hill, Talbot was up and about, bandages still wrapped around his ribs. His eyes were brighter, the bruises were fading. Jennifer was in the kitchen, making callaloo. Conscious music boomed from across the road. George hovered in the doorway behind her. Talbot sat down at the kitchen table.

'I saw a lawyer this morning, Talbot. We can proceed with your case. I just wanted to come up and let you know. You can relax, though. It's going to take some time.'

'Mummy say she see a police car cruise past de house two night past. She say de car stop an' park up just dong de road, dat dey watchin' us.'

'Is that so?' He turned to Jennifer.

Jennifer shrugged. 'Police car park up fer an hour or more, not far from here. Dey never come up here fer no reason. What dey doin'? Makin' joke?'

'Tell me, Talbot, are you *sure* no one saw what happened to you? It would make all the difference if there was a witness.'

'No one, Mr Harwood. Just de hills up der.'

'The hills,' George mused. Sabine had said that, too. Shacks in those hills. Squatters, Rastamen, simple folk, dotted all over those hills. Some of the shacks were very far away, across the valley, but the sound would have carried.

'Talbot, there are shacks, people living in those hills.'

Talbot nodded.

'Is it possible? You know, that someone at least *heard*?'

Talbot shook his head. 'Even if dey hear somptin, no one go speak out.'

Jennifer came forward. 'Dey mus have already tink of dat and go rong to dese people to treaten dem.'

'Do you know any of these people?'

Talbot shook his head.

'Dey is bush people,' Jennifer said. 'Simple bush people. Dey ent sayin' nuttin.'

'Potential witnesses,' George pressed.

Jennifer looked at him with large calm eyes. 'Mr Harwood. Dis a small place, eh; you watch out who you go and visit. Everyone know everytin goin' on up here. You tink people ent talk about you comin' all de time to see Talbot?'

'I'll stay away from now on, then.'

'Das de best ting fer now.'

'Or maybe we should move Talbot?'

'No,' Jennifer insisted. 'He staying right *here* in de house where he born.'

'OK, OK.'

'Mr Harwood, wait till people find out about de lawyer and ting. De court case. Den . . .'

'Then what?'

Jennifer steupsed. 'Den dey go find out. Nuttin scarin' me away . . . and dem across so . . .' She nodded at her nephews out the window. 'Dey go be our family bodyguards. We had our own police force.'

Sabine lay horizontal on the sofa, chain-smoking, staring into space. Sebastian had flown back to London the day before. She smoked and stared, voluminous in her mourning, in her sack-dress. His son was right: Sabine was dripping, melting.

George still never knew what to say. He took himself out into the garden, where her sighs hadn't spread, picking a hibiscus from one of the beds. Under the soil lay the bones of two dead dogs, the pets which had been poisoned by neighbours of that old slave woman. Sabine was right; they'd never been safe here. Now it was worse. He placed the flower in the crook of the mango tree above, just as Pascale had as a little girl.

I'm sorry about what happened with the ship, he said to the tree.

It's not your fault.

Pascale's fault. We missed it.

It's not your fault.

She could have left. On the next boat.

She loved you.

I love her.

She still loves you.

Does she?

She is sick from loving you. Go to her.

She refuses me.

Take her in your arms.

Impossible. He re-envisioned the liner slipping through the First Boca, past all the green and rock.

She won't have me.

Go to her.

George returned. Sabine lay in state, grieving. Her eyes were pooled. He hovered over her. Something small, he could say something small: dramatic and to the point.

'Shall I warm up some leftovers?' he asked.

'I'm not hungry.'

'You should eat something.'

'Just leave me.' Her voice was leaden.

In the kitchen he opened the fridge, took out a Pyrex dish of leftover curry and stuck it in the microwave. The dogs came wagging their tails to the kitchen door to see what he was doing.

'Hello, boys,' he whispered.

Their whole bodies wagged and they pressed their muzzles close to his legs. But they didn't cheer him up. He left the kitchen with the bubbling curry on a tray and turned on the CNC news, watching Carla Foderingham present the latest about the Soca Warriors. The big match was the next day. Trinidad and Tobago versus Peru, the friendly game. He had tickets but he hadn't mentioned this to Sabine. He looked over at his wife laid out full-length on the sofa. Maybe he should tell her about the lawyer. His articles, polishing up her green bicycle, nothing seemed to please her. The familiar reverberating sound started up, a gentle puffing sound, as Sabine began to snore.

Clock and George wore red T-shirts to the match. They arrived early, parking in the Movie Town car park opposite the stadium. George helped the little boy across the busy main road, a steady flow of football supporters straggling across it.

Everyone wore red. Flags hung from shoulders, faces were painted with the Trinidad and Tobago colours. Conch horns bellowed. Vendors greeted ticket holders well in advance of the entrance, hawking wristbands, T-shirts, whistles, car stickers. George and Clock dodged them, drifting up the main corridor towards the stadium entrance, stopping to buy cherry-flavoured snow cones. Four in the afternoon and the sun poured down. They climbed the stairs to the balconies, arriving at the top, gazing out onto the scratchy yellow-grass pitch.

The stadium looped around the pitch in a lazy oval of turquoise seats.

'Wow. It like a big snake,' the little boy gasped.

'Let's get a place to sit,' George suggested.

The stands were filling. Supporters who had already gathered were buoyant, batting Carib, Stag. Picong flew, nerves and laughter in the air as the fans discussed the match: Trinidad's possibility of success that day, let alone in Germany. Umbrellas opened everywhere to ward off the sun. The stands crawled with salesmen. Rastamen were pelting small brown bags of peanuts up the rows and red dollar bills were passing down in return on a chain of arms. Men roamed with plastic buckets of beer on ice. The air was a cacophony of calls.

George and Clock made their way down an aisle and across a row of seats. George opened his giant golf umbrella and they sat under it eating their melting snow cones and warm peanuts, watching a fat man dressed in a red satin suit and red cowboy hat goose-stepping around the pitch.

Clock didn't know much about football, so George explained the rules. Then he explained the business with the Dutch coach, how he'd got the team this far. He described each of the players and their backgrounds: Shaka Hislop in goal; the wondrous Russell Latapy; how the white boy, Chris Burchill, often tried to score from the mid-field. How Latapy and Dwight Yorke cried on this very field when they lost to the Americans in a World Cup qualifying match sixteen years ago; how Trinidad was the smallest country to qualify for the World Cup.

'Can we win?' Clock asked.

'No, we can't.'

'Why not?'

'Because many teams out there are giants.'

'David felled Goliath.'

'But we aren't David.'

'Who are we?'

'The Soca Warriors.'

'They go fight and fête?'

'Yes. That's our basic strategy.'

The sun began to sink and the sky mellowed, blossoming to ibis pink, the clouds scalloped with heavenly gold. More spectators arrived in crowds of red. Calypsonians sang and pranced on a makeshift stage. Indian dancers shimmied, children in carnival costumes paraded around the pitch. A man in a chicken costume skipped around. The Carib Girls ran a chaotic circuit, waving their pom-poms, abandoning their routine. The Trinidad Cadet Force marched and farted out a tune on their trumpets and tubas. The Peru team trotted on in their white strip. Each player was announced by name and position. Then the Trinidad team appeared.

The crowd roared, rising to its feet. The Prime Minister, Patrick Manning, led a small band of dignitaries onto the pitch to shake hands with each player.

'Asshole.'

'*Booo.*'

Manning's presence provoked jeers from those sitting around them. Then, a gigantic shadow fell across the pitch, across the whole stadium.

'Jesus Christ,' George muttered.

Above them, not so high up, was the dragon-like underbelly of the blimp.

'How the fuck did it manage to sneak up on the entire stadium like that?'

'It lookin' like a space ship,' Clock gasped, peering up.

The blimp was vast, sailing across the sky with stealth, with grace, not the plump comic bump in the sky seen from far off. Huge, hovering, it brooded in the air; it caused a feeling of guilt to spread through his veins.

'Fuck off, you bastard,' George shouted upwards.

Appreciative laughter came from all around.

Then the whole stadium rose to its feet to sing the national anthem. '"Side by side we stand, islands of the blue Caribbean sea . . ."'

The stadium lights banged on. The starting whistle shrilled. The spectators sat down.

Picong started up.

'Dong de road. Dong de *roaaad*,' men yelled.

'Pressure. Pressure.'

'Nah, man, look, dese Peru players cyan kick. Dat de *Macarena*.'

'*Kill* de hafling!'

A very drunk Indian man in front of them with a Latapy T-shirt shouted, '*Olé, olé, olé*, barbeque. *Olé, olé, olé*, powder puff.'

The Powder Posse scattered white talc in the air. A Mexican wave started up, a red bulge moving across the stands. George and Clock stood up, raising their hands as it passed.

'Again, again!' Clock shouted. Skinny black girls in tiny red vest-tops shook their chac-chacs.

The Soca Warriors were awful.

'We're going to get our arses whipped in Germany,' George cringed.

It was a friendly match, but the Soca Warriors played like saps, pissing about. They weren't even showing off. They ran about the pitch like harassed bachac ants while the Peru players were professional, disciplined. When the Peru team scored the stadium went silent.

Half-time was called.

George took out a strip of aspirin from his top pocket.

'You have a headache, Mr Harwood?'

'A stinker.' He knocked back two pills with the dregs of his snow cone. The hills behind Diego Martin twinkled.

'It pretty over der,' Clock marvelled. 'Like a galaxy.'

The players came back onto the pitch.

'Dong de *rooooaaad*,' shouted the fans.

'*Olé, olé*, cheese sticks,' shouted the drunken Indian man.

Talc puffed and floated in the air. The whole stadium was on its feet. The Soca Warriors kicked the ball around like a bunch of fuckwits.

'*Do* something, nuh, man!'

'Dey dancin' over you.'

George gazed across at the covered stand opposite, at the VIP section. Patrick Manning was watching, too. Same place, same time. Manning, son of Williams, son of the PNM. No one knew much about Patrick Manning. He had studied geology at university, become a career politician. He joined the PNM at the lowest rank, climbing his way up. He was unimpressive when he spoke, something foolish in his eyes, in his lopsided grin. Ears like the handles on a Toby jug. Like Williams, Manning had surrounded himself with cronies.

A hush fell. George's vision blurred. He missed the scuffle on the pitch. His head thudded. He rubbed the back of his neck. *Dear Dr Williams* was tapping on the walls of his skull. The Peru players lined up in front of the Trinidad goal. A penalty shot. Who was taking the kick? He couldn't tell. The line of players reeled.

The stand erupted.

A goal for Trinidad and Tobago.

People leaped up and down, hugging each other, whistling, shouting, the stands shaking with joy. Horns blew. Men were crying. Talc filled the air. The drunk Indian man waved an open bottle of water over his head and water looped above the crowd.

Clock danced up and down on his seat. George hugged him; the noise of it all sang in his head. Whistles screamed. His vision blurred.

When the crowd contained itself, he sat down.

'You OK, Mr Harwood?'

'Yes. I'm fine. Too much waiting in the sun.'

He didn't see the end of the match.

Everyone around was standing up, blocking the view. *Dear Mr Williams* knocking at the walls of his skull. *Dear Mr Williams*, the words an incessant thrum. George held his head. A swell of nausea surged up from his gut. He battled to keep it down.

The end-of-match whistle blew shrill. One all. Instantly, the stands began to drain. Clock sat down next to George.

'I'll be fine in a minute,' George reassured him.

Clock fanned him with a styrofoam tray he found on the floor.

'Come on, then.' George pushed himself up. He stood and wobbled, looking around. His vision had sharpened. Slowly, they climbed the stairs back up to the balcony. Then down more stairs. George clung to the railings, his palms damp. He staggered over to a vendor, asked for a bottle of water and drank greedily from it, pouring water over his face.

'Don't you worry about me,' George smiled.

The boy's face was serious.

'I'm fine. Let's get out of here.'

They proceeded down the second flight and out through the open turnstiles. The red river moved slowly, flowing towards the road.

George jumped at a loud explosion in the sky. He looked up. The sky was alight with flowers of green and yellow and pink, sparks cascading. A war of fireworks in the air, bangs and flashes like machine-gun fire. The air cartwheeled, spilling smoke and sulphur. George clasped his hands to his ears and shut his eyes. Clock's small hand was on his back, steadying him. The little boy clutched at him, stretching the material of his T-shirt, struggling to hold him up. George knew he was going. His legs buckled.

'Mr Harwood, Mr Harwood!'

He heard the little boy's shouts for help, the fizzing bombs erupting in the sky. The boy grappled and grasped at his T-shirt. George fell slowly and heavily to the ground, landing with a cushioned *thud*.

'Mr Hardwood, Mr Harwood, wake up. Wake up!' The little boy's voice was pleading, desperate. George wanted to take hold of his hand.

'Mr Harwood. Mr Harwood.' Another voice, a woman's, closer to his ear. Her face was blurred. Two men in uniforms hovered near by.

'We need to get him out de way,' the female voice directed.

'Easy now. One, two, three.' Hands lifted him to his feet.

George moaned. 'Eric Williams. I'm going to talk to that . . .'

'Mr Harwood, you fainted.'

'Did I?' He squinted, woozy. He recognised the woman, a friend of Pascale's. Pretty thing. Maureen Boos.

Carefully, he smoothed the back of his head. 'Did someone clobber me?'

'You fell over,' Clock explained.

They sat him down on a kerb, put his head between his legs.

'Mr Harwood, you know me. I'm a friend of your daughter's. Can I call Pascale?'

'Oh no, please.'

'She can come and pick you up.'

'I'll be fine. Just had too much sun. Drank on an empty stomach.'

'Where's your truck?'

'Very close. Please don't worry.'

George struggled to his feet. 'I'm fine now. Please. Don't look so worried,' he said to Clock. 'Maureen, this is my friend.'

Maureen stared with suspicion at the little black boy.

'We'll be fine.'

Clock put an arm under his and together they staggered off into the moving flow of red.

George parked the truck in its usual covered spot beside the kitchen. He didn't get out straight away. He rested his head in his hands, elbows on the steering wheel. *Thud, thud, thud* inside his head. He couldn't remember the drive home, only that it was slow and that the boy said nothing. The tiny Virgin Mary gazed expectantly at him, palms outstretched.

'George?'

Sabine stood at the door of the truck. 'I've been watching you from the kitchen window.'

'Oh. I was just thinking about you.'

'What happened? Pascale rang. A friend of hers said you fainted at the football match. You didn't even tell me you'd gone.'

'I'm fine.'

'She said you collapsed on the ground.'

'I slipped.'

'You were with that little boy from the church choir. George.

150

You go to a football match and don't tell me. You collapse. What am I to think?'

'Think what you like.' He was tired. He wanted to go to bed.

'Pascale's coming over.'

'Well, I'm going to bed.'

He opened the door of the truck and tried to move his legs.

'George!'

'I'm fine.'

'You're white as a sheet.'

'I just need to get some rest.'

Sabine put her head under his arm, helping him out. 'Oh darling, you can't walk.'

'I can.'

His legs were weak. Sabine staggered with him to the kitchen steps and together they zigzagged through the living room and up the stairs to the bedroom, where they fell heavily on the bed.

'George, I don't like this at all. I'm calling Dr Baker.'

George closed his eyes. The headache sizzled. He wanted to say something, but the words wouldn't come. He lay on the bed, managing to wriggle around so that he lay on his side with his head on the pillow. He wanted to curl up, to sleep for a long time.

Sabine came from the bathroom with a cold flannel, pressing it to his forehead.

'Oooh,' he gasped. It felt good. But the flannel warmed in moments, absorbing the heat.

He heard Sabine go downstairs and return, this time with a bowl of ice cubes.

George closed his eyes. His wife's hands on his head, his wife tutting and fussing over him. He wanted to tell her he loved her, but his tongue was thick. She pressed the cold damp flannel to his forehead and it stuck. She sat next to him on the bed and he could feel the warmth and weight of her, wanting to touch her. After a minute or two she peeled the flannel off, dipping it into the icy water, wringing it and pressing the compress back onto his forehead. He mumbled, half-conscious.

'What is it, dear?'

'I *do* care, you know . . . about people.'

'Yes.'

'I'm not a heartless beast.'

'Don't worry about this now.'

'I do care . . . I didn't know . . . you were quite so unhappy.'

'I wasn't.'

'We missed the ship.'

'Yes.'

'I never wanted to get on it.'

'No.'

'I'm someone here.'

'Yes.'

'In England I'd have been as unhappy as you are here.' He moaned. 'I'm selfish.'

'Yes.'

'I'm sorry.'

Sabine took the flannel from his forehead, resoaked it and placed it back. George reached for his wife's hand and clenched it tight.

The next day George sulked out on the porch. He'd refused to see the doctor. That Dr Baker was a quack. Giving Sabine those pills for all those years. He'd punch Sebastian Baker down. He wasn't going to see him. Lousy charlatan. Ladies' man. Did Sabine love *him*, too? Who were her other fantasy men? Did she love Dr Baker, want to fuck him, too? No, George Harwood was fine, thank you very much. They could all fuck off. He felt a lot better in himself. The big dogs were stationed near him: his dogs.

'Good dogs.' He fondled their ears.

When Pascale arrived she kissed her father on the forehead, sitting down on one of the rattan chairs next to him.

'So. Mummy tell mih you won't go to see Dr Baker.'

'I'm not ill.'

'If you don't, I'll bring him here to see *you*.'

'You women are making a lot of fuss over nothing.'

'You chupid old man. You collapsed! Maureen said you were out for several minutes, dead as a Fred. It damn well lucky you ent hit your head. Lucky she was there. You stubborn, yes, an' if you don't go and have a check-up, I'll make you have one. It can be done.'

George looked away.

Pascale lit a cigarette, inhaling a smoky blue plume. 'You look like shit.'

'Thanks.'

'I don't want you to die.'

'Don't be ridiculous.'

'I need you for ever.'

'You're being dramatic. Like your mother.'

'I need you to tell me the secret of how to stay married for a long time.'

George sighed heavily.

'Why did you marry Mum?'

George was taken aback. He stared at his feet. 'Because she was a dish,' he said finally.

'The world is full of beautiful women. Why her?'

'She was for me.'

'What do you mean?'

'Your mother filled up the frame. I couldn't see anyone else but her, no one around her or past her.'

'Did that ever wear off?'

'No, it got worse.'

'How?'

'Well, then love comes. You can fancy lots of other people. But the heart is small and fussy: it knows exactly who it wants. You only have room in it to love one or two people in a lifetime.'

'Love happens to you.' Pascale nodded.

'Yes.'

'It a tough bastard, isn't it, Dad?'

'Ha ha. Yes. And it lasts for years.'

'The other person's spirit climbs into you.' Pascale sighed. 'You feel so much for them. If they get hurt, you hurt. If you hurt them, you hurt yourself.'

'Is that how you felt about the man before Jacques?'

Pascale's eyes filmed. 'Yes, Daddy.'

May. George's favourite month. May, the time of trees. Pomme-arac trees in season. The branches dangled with bell-shaped, woman-shaped fruit, a lewd magenta in their colour, like a harlot's lipstick. Beneath the trees lay a fine carpet of magenta stamens, covering rooftops, wall-tops, pavements, lawns. The birds feasted on them and those stupid enough to park under a pomme-arac tree in May found their car splattered with magenta dye. The pink pouis were out, too, like glamour models, tall thin trees with strawberry afros exploding along the savannah, heralding the coming of the rains. The flamboyants were short and squat; black trunks and horizontal sprays of scarlet blossom. These trees were dancers, arms in the air, flashing their ruffed sleeves. In May, the mango trees were heavy with blushing fruit. Breadfruits bulged in an obscene manner. Bougainvillea brawled from balconies and walls. If a stick was thrust into the earth, it would surely flourish, such was the fertility of this humid heat. It shimmied in sheets up from the blistering road. Everywhere the grass was turning to an ashen dust-brown, the earth beneath became dry and crumbled.

In May, black people were sensible and took umbrellas when walking outside, holding them high. White people drove around in air-conditioned cars. They ran between their cars and shops. They feared what might come. Sometimes, at night, Sabine woke George up.

'Can you hear that?'

'No, what?'

'The green woman, she's restless. She's going to roll over.'

'Good. Maybe she'll squash those condominiums across the road.'

Hurricanes brewed far out. May, the month before the official storm warnings. May, the dry season finale, trumpets blowing, confetti showering from the trees. The air clapped and cheered. By the end of the month the murder toll had reached a hundred and sixty.

The next day, Jennifer was shifty. Sabine had gone out to play bridge. Jennifer avoided George, which was unusual. Was it the court case? Was she unhappy about keeping it from Sabine? Had more police cars appeared? Just as it was time for her to go, she appeared on the porch. Her face was pinched, her eyes bleak. She held a Hi-Lo brown-paper bag in her hand, crumpled up.

'Have you baked another cake? Hidden it from the dog?' he joked.

But Jennifer's face was grave. Very grave. He didn't like it.

'Jennifer, what's wrong? You look very awkward. What's wrong? What is it?'

Jennifer crossed the porch and came very close. She never stood so close. She stared at him in a sombre, caring way. He had the feeling she was going to say something unthinkable.

'Jennifer?'

She thrust the paper bag into his hands. It was heavy, something metal inside.

'What the . . .?'

Jennifer's eyes were huge. 'Talbot keep it under de bed, Mr Harwood. I doh know where he get it. But he have it long time. It when he get mix up. He keep it. He woh trow it away, he cyan get rid of it. I doh wan it in de house. It go make more trouble fer us. You keep it, Mr Harwood. Give it to de lawyer man. Keep it safe and away from us.'

Jennifer's eyes were wet and imploring.

'Yes, of course.'

He looked inside the paper bag. In it was a heavy bundle in waxed paper and he knew what it was before he began to unwrap it, shaking his head, knowing deep down that a gun was the last thing he wanted in his house, not now. This was bad. Where would he hide it? Where? And then it came to him.

'Of course, Jennifer. I'll keep it safe.'

CHAPTER NINE

MANNING

Ray rang later in the day. 'Eh, eh, ah have news for you, George.'
He sounded tense.

'Oh no, am I in trouble?'

'Not yet.'

'Manning's office ring us. He plannin' to delay local elections.
Dey offerin' us an interview. Furs time dey do dis, man. He rarely
give press interviews. Dis a big ting. He aks for you specifically.
He like de way you write. Tink yousa poet.'

George whistled. 'Has he *read* my last two interviews?'

'Ah assumin' so. De boys here vexed. Dey all want a pop at
him. He only want to talk to you.'

'He wants *me*? A white man?'

'Yeah, man. Will you do it?'

'How much will you pay me?'

'Name your price.'

'Don't be stupid. I'd do it for free. Of course I'll do it. When
does he want me?'

'Tomorrow afternoon.'

'Where?'

'At Whitehall.'

'Oh. House of Bobo.'

'What?'

'Nothing.'

Sabine was furious. 'You're not going anywhere to interview *anyone*.'

'Don't be ridiculous.'

'You mustn't exert yourself.'

'I'll be sitting in a chair, talking to the Prime Minister.'

'You're not well enough. What if you black out?'

'I won't.'

'What if you do?'

'I won't.'

'You can't drive there. I'll have to drop you.'

'Sabine, I'm fine.'

She shot him a look of reproach.

'I'm going to interview the Prime Minister of Trinidad. Now's your chance. What would you like to ask?'

'Ask him this: How much does he treasure his balls?'

'Mr Manning, do you treasure your balls?'

'Inform him your wife wants to cut them off.'

'I'll put it on my list.'

'Good.'

'How's your head?'

'Fine,' he lied.

*

Patrick Augustus Mervyn Manning wanted to use him, George knew that. Despite his last two interviews, in which he'd railed, asked tough questions about the blimp, Manning thought he was harmless. The Prime Minister wanted a PR job. Silly white fool in love with Trinidad. He'd never written an unkind word about anyone. But George already knew Patrick Manning, knew him intimately. Selfish bastard; not a political animal. Manning thought economics, he thought of money. He'd heard the talk. People said Manning had worshipped Eric Williams, was in awe of him. People said that whenever Manning was in a tight spot he asked himself: *What would Williams have done?*

George arrived early at Whitehall, a gaudy wedding cake of a mansion made of Bajan coral. It was one of the cocoa-baron homes around the savannah, once the family home of his gormless son-in-law, Jacques: Bobo the Clown.

The dead-eyed security guards at the mansion gate didn't like the look of George's rusted truck.

'Who are you?' They fingered their batons.

'Press.' George flashed his pass.

The guards were troll-like. They wore tiny woollen toques atop their bulbous heads, itchy woollen jumpers and commando-style boots. One wielded a machine gun. Grudgingly, they beckoned him through.

George parked in a space under the shade of an illustrious Samaan tree. From the glovebox he retrieved a flask of Vat 19 and a packet of Panadol Extra, knocking back two pills with two swigs of rum. He knocked back a third swig for good luck, a fourth for courage. Then a fifth, larger swig. Instantly, he felt much happier.

He wiped his lips, checking himself in the rear-view mirror: his hair was still stuck down with Grecian 2000. His eyes blazed, fire in them. Handsome fucker, still.

George walked back to the entrance, the trees on the savannah saluting him with puffs of smoke: violet, lemon, snowy white. A guard led him up the steps, into a vestibule of polished teak. He sat down, twiddling his thumbs.

'Mr Harwood?'

A young woman appeared in a suit and high clicking heels. 'Come this way, please.'

He followed her up a wooden staircase to a vast parlour room with a long balcony overlooking the city's great park. The floor was hard, polished wood, the antique furniture stood sparse and ill at ease against the walls. The windows were shut, the massive panes of glass magnifying the sun's heat. He recognised a silence of being watched: cameras, guards, servants padding about.

'Do sit down,' the young woman said. 'Can I bring you anything?'

'A glass of water, please.'

George began to perspire in his too-tight threadbare suit. His hair was unfurling from its sticky trap. He ran his hands roughly over his head several times, smoothing it back.

'Bugger,' he whispered, seeing he'd smeared grease on his trousers.

The woman returned with the glass of water. The minute she disappeared he glugged two long, greedy gulps. He took his flask from his pocket, wafting it under his nose; the rum's astringent vapours were like a slap in the face, sobering him up. He knocked back a hefty slug. This was how the fuckers did it, of course.

Leave 'em to sweat. This went on in every great house of power all over the world: the waiting. He loosened his tie. Damp had spread in patches under his arms and a ripe salt odour rose up around him, mingling with the scent of mothballs. He checked his briefcase for his tape recorders, setting them out on the table, unaware that Patrick Manning had entered the room behind him.

'Good afternoon, Mr Harwood.'

George jumped, shooting straight upright, causing one of the tape recorders to clatter to the floor. A ripping sound exploded somewhere in his suit and, as he leant over to shake the Prime Minister's hand, he knocked the glass of water over, water running off the table.

'Oh, God. I'm sorry.' He suppressed the urge to fart.

Manning stifled a grin. 'Maxine,' he called. A woman hurried in with a cloth and wiped the water up, taking the glass.

Manning extended his hand once more.

'Pleased to meet you.' George shook it, shuddering. Manning was tall and well-built with caramel-coloured skin. A footballer's physique. He grinned from ear to ear, which meant nothing; this was his habit. That lopsided grin. The Prime Minister sat down with his back to a pane of glass, the heat blazing in, onto his shoulders.

'I'm a big fan of your writing,' Manning breezed.

'Thank you,' George said stiffly, hatred blossoming in him. It was a surprise to him; he hadn't known his own feelings.

'I liked the interview with Brian Lara recently. Mossad agents in the jungle!' Manning laughed, genuinely tickled.

The twit was already getting the better of him. Manning was relaxed, at home and George was so hot he could hardly speak.

This was no Eric Williams. Williams was better dressed, for a start. George leaned forward and switched the tape recorders on.

'Yes – the blimp. What is it?'

'Eh, eh.' Manning looked taken aback. 'Howyuh mean?'

'Is it a US-backed spy ship?'

Manning laughed out loud.

'Well, *is* it?'

Manning suppressed a knowing smile and stared hard at him.

'Chávez,' George pushed. 'The new threat. The new Castro in the Caribbean. It's not so far-fetched. Trinidad's oil installations out at sea. It must make George Bush rather nervous, no?'

Manning looked away and kept smiling, as if the questions would just go away.

George studied him.

'You have a wild imagination,' Manning said, finally.

'I have my sources.'

Manning sighed. But he wouldn't be drawn. George knew the blimp was also used to show off, to prove a point, like at the match the other day.

'Did you enjoy the football match?' George tried.

'Oh yes, indeed. You were there?'

'I went with a friend. We were sitting right opposite you, in fact. We enjoyed the day. Pity about the football.'

'Well.' Manning steupsed. 'It was a friendly game, nuh.'

'Eric Williams was a keen footballer. What do you think he'd make of Trinidad and Tobago in the 2006 World Cup?'

'Ah . . . Eric? Pleased as punch.'

'Fifty years of the PNM. Quite a year, eh?'

'An exceptional year.' Manning grinned. This was more what he had come to talk about. The football in 2006, the cricket World Cup in 2007, the economy booming. Panday, the leader of the opposition, arrested on corruption charges. The Prime Minister beamed with all this good fortune.

'You must have been, what, about ten years old when the PNM came into power?'

'Yeah, man. Just a boy.'

'A son of the PNM, would you say?'

'Very much so.'

'Yet in the past, you've called yourself the *Father* of the Nation.'

Manning stared, grinning.

'Eric Williams' – George put steel into his voice – 'I would have thought, took that title, no?'

Manning's grin faded.

'The little boy I took to the football match needs a father.'

'I'm sorry to hear that.'

George read from his notes. '"Between 1991 and 1995 the PNM did not spend enough time looking after its own children."' George looked up. 'Do you know who said that?'

'I can't remember offhand, no.'

'You did.'

Manning shot him a fierce stare.

'"I assure you that shall not happen again,"' George read.

Manning's forehead glistened. The tape recorders whirred. He took on a careful, studious expression.

'Ten years have passed. That little boy. Born poor. He'll stay poor.'

Manning huffed. 'Trinidad's economy is booming,' he rehearsed.

'Trinidad is healthier, thanks to all the foreign investment. Plus we have a Social Vision for 2020. You must have heard of it.'

'I've read about this vision on the PNM's website. The 2020 Vision pages are empty.'

Manning checked his watch.

George removed his reading glasses. 'I haven't been such a great father myself. I've been selfish. I got rich here, you see. Easy to get rich in Trinidad, for some people.'

'Have your children forgiven you?'

'Oh, one hates me, one adores me. My wife despises me, though.'

Manning looked puzzled. The sun's gaze, through the glass, was beginning to get to him.

'She despises you, too, of course. And Williams. Eric Williams broke her heart.'

'Did she *know* Eric?'

'We *all* knew Eric. Tell me,' George pressed, 'don't you ever feel uncomfortable in this house?'

'Why?'

'A slave owner's house. My son-in-law's former family home, in fact. Yet you're using it as the seat of government.'

The Prime Minister steupsed, irritated.

'There was a moment, Mr Manning,' George continued, 'when everything could have been rethought, way back.'

'That's naive.'

'Or revolutionary.'

'Revolutions! Pah. Look at what happened to Haiti. Cuba. We didn't have to fight for power, anyway. We were handed it.'

'I don't need a history lesson.'

'What's your *point* then?' Manning snapped.

'Trinidad needs a good government. Not a bad *father*. Not a father at all. Leave that to the man in the street. Stop patronising the people of Trinidad.'

Manning's eyes shone. The interview would soon terminate, George could see that. He didn't care: now was the moment. *Win her*.

'I don't mean to speak out of turn,' George persisted. 'But if you'll forgive me, Prime Minister, things could be so different.'

'Then why don't you start up a political party of *your own*?'

'I asked my wife the same question once.'

'Sounds like she's been an influence.'

'Yours too, no?'

'Leave my wife out of this.' Manning stood up; he looked down at George. 'You stink of rum and yet you talk *down* to *me*?'

'I'd hardly talk *up* to you, would I?' George joked. 'In general.'

The Prime Minister's eyes were hard, treacherous, his lips pursed. The tape recorders grinned.

'Dictator,' George blurted.

'What?'

'Opportunist!'

'This interview has come to an end,' Manning spat.

'I know you,' George slurred. 'I know your type. You greedy, selfish . . . *colonial*!' The headache broke through the shield of rum and pills, arriving in hot waves, up the back of his skull.

'Takes one to *know one*,' he sneered. 'The police, beating people up every day. No one important ever complains. They're a squad of *thugs*.'

Manning bent down, level with his head: eye to eye. His teeth were bared.

'And you?' he rasped, gazing at the tape recorders. 'I know

MONIQUE ROFFEY

you, too. We've all seen your type. White man in the West Indies. Second-rate, eh? Never management material in the UK. Here, a big shot. A hot shot. Couldn't face going back. Stayed too long, eh? Too long in the sun. Drank too much rum. Came here years ago to build and take. Take, take, take. You're nothing special, Mr Harwood. You're common. You are the past and you can stick your critique of my government, elected by the people, for the people, up your pathetic old white ass.'

Outside, the sun was so intense George feared venturing past the steps. The light scalded his eyes and they bled tears. He hid in the shade of the long sweeping porch. The bored security guards eyed him with a sense of purpose. One walked towards him but he smudged. George wiped his eyes, blinking. He couldn't see anything, just smudges and light. He clung to the wall, a hammering in his head.

'Sir.'

George tried to speak. The headache scraped into the back of his skull. Tears of pain flowed, pain and fatigue. He wanted to sleep. His legs were melting, melting from his bones; a slow feeling poured over him, over his tired body. He felt himself falling, sliding down the wall, and was unable to stop himself as he fainted, down beside a large potted fern.

*

Sabine clasped her daughter's hand. The scanner room was quiet, the floor cool, a buffed puce hospital-pink. The room made her nervous; that aloof, sterile atmosphere of all medical institutions.

The MRI scanner loomed feet away, a hollow white tube. George lay on a trolley about to disappear inside it. White robe, a tag on his wrist. His face was pale, his forehead damp.

'There's nothing wrong with me,' he insisted. 'This is ridiculous.'

A whirring sound started up; the trolley moved forward, taking George into the tunnel of the machine.

'I don't see why I should be here,' George complained. His voice was muffled.

The scanner screen stood to one side of the tube. The technician switched it on. Snap, snap. Snap. It took grainy black and white images of George's skull. The front, the back. The side.

Sabine gasped.

The tumour was immediately apparent, even to the untrained eye.

'Mummy, *that's* what it is,' Pascale sobbed.

Clearly defined, snuggled neatly into the left side of his brain, a growth. Dense, meaty. How could it be there? Something so big, without forming a lump?

'My poor love,' Sabine wept.

Pascale wiped away tears.

The machine clicked, snapping shots; macabre smeary black images of a skull, of the matter it contained, of the presence of the parasite tumour. It was present from every angle.

'How can we take it away?' Sabine said, her voice officious.

'Come on, Mummy.' Pascale led her out of the room.

Sabine sat down. Her hands buzzed with nerves, her feet, too. Aches in her throat, her ribs, her wrists. What *was* that thing growing inside her husband's head? Had she seen right?

The surgeon came to speak to them while George got dressed.

'It's been there for years,' he said. 'You have to decide quickly what you want to do. If we don't operate soon, he won't survive.'

The iguana tumbled from the coconut tree. The dogs barked and crashed after it. Sabine went to put the kettle on.

Jennifer steupsed. 'Go sit outside,' she commanded. 'I go bring de tray.'

Sabine joined Pascale and George on the porch. Pascale's eyes were glassy, dreamy; she was only half-listening to what George was saying about the Prime Minister.

'Stupid arse. I read him a piece of one of his *own speeches*! Didn't recognise it at all. I was scared, though. Whitehall's a big place. Almost farted.'

Pascale laughed.

George fished out the two tape recorders, placing them on the table near by, patting them.

'Ray will be pleased.'

Sabine looked at her daughter, who looked just like George. She was bold like him, clever like him. A Trinidadian, like him.

Katinka waved her fluffy tail. Sabine bent down to scoop her up, sitting the animal on her lap. George rambled on about Manning. The sun sank, setting itself in crème tangerine. The keskidees chattered and swooped above the pool. Jennifer brought out a pot of tea and slices of ginger cake.

'W'appen?' she chided. 'Dis place like a funeral parlour. Eat, nuh. I don't want to see allyuh ent eatin' mih cake. Ah bake it *fresh*. I goin' home.'

'OK then, Jennifer.'

Jennifer disappeared, steupsing.

Sabine watched George talk, his eyes crinkly. Radioactive with life. The pleasure of knowing him, of being with him all this time. The knowledge of loving him; she could never speak about it. Why had she taken up with George? She didn't know. She was still deciding if she *liked* him, that was the truth. After all these years, George and her, a mystery; a love affair she had never fully got the measure of. What was he thinking? She understood: George didn't want to know what they'd seen in the scanner room. It didn't matter to him.

George said he was going for forty winks. He disappeared into the bedroom, slept soundly for hours. Sabine talked with Pascale. They decided the operation should be performed in Trinidad. That he shouldn't be flown to England; they'd never get him on a plane.

'Do you want me to stay here?' Pascale asked.

'No, I'm fine. I'll be OK. I'll speak to your father later.'

Sabine wandered the house, drifting across the back porch. The two tape recorders were still on the table. Should she press play? Listen in? Fifty years. She still wondered about him, about what George got up to when he wasn't with her. The little black boy: his friend. Their relationship had been full of secrets. Could the surgeons extract the lump? Could they remove the blame he'd harboured all these years?

The rains arrived that afternoon. The yellow pouis had been exploding in the hills for weeks and this meant certain rain. And yet, when it came, Sabine was surprised: she'd forgotten about rain. Rain in the late afternoon was rare. It brought on a mixed-up earthy smell. The garden sighed. The Robber Man came to her, from years ago. *Send yuh back in chains*. Just like a slave. And yet she'd remained. Jennifer's Aunt Venus had mocked her for the articles she'd snipped out. *He a good man*, she'd said about Williams, all those years ago. Now Venus lived in Peckham. Those days of her life, with Lucy and Venus, when the children were small and delicious. Pascale with her afro of bubble-curls, Sebastian all buck-toothed and freckled. When she couldn't wait to see George at the end of every afternoon, cycling out to greet him on her green bicycle. Riding to the dock. Eating snow cones smothered in condensed milk. Foraging for the long, hard seed pods fallen from the flamboyants: they played pretend fencing matches. The end of the dry season then, too. She'd forgotten everything between those days and the day she saw the malicious tumour in George's head.

And what if George disappeared? Her husband of half a century. Vanished. Dead. One minute there and then not. What would she do? The thought alone evoked the onset of nerves, a swell of crisis in her stomach. A dead-dull feeling inside her, as if parts of her, her core, her inner stuff, would also cease to generate. Her nails, her hair might dry out. The hum of life would fade inside her. She might cease walking; she could halt mid-sentence, mid-step, even. One day Jennifer would find her just stopped, like a watch, sitting on the floor, or maybe under a tree in the garden. If George died she might stop living, too. That happened to couples who'd lived together as long as they had. One dies and the other fails to continue. It was that simple. Would that happen? She felt sure it would. Weeks later, she would be found sat upright, eyes closed, under a mango tree.

Jennifer sat moping in the kitchen. The big dogs stood in the doorway, noses twitching, wanting attention.

'Jennifer, stop moping.'

'I ent mopin'.'

'The silver needs a polish.'

'I ent polishin' no silver.'

'Then go home. You said you would.'

'Eh, eh, what wrong wid you?'

Sabine huffed and sat down on one of the stools around the kitchen table. She rubbed her eyes. They were dry and red.

'How's Talbot?'

'He walkin' and feelin' better in himself.'

'And those thugs still wearing uniforms.'

'He keepin' to himself. He ent looking for trouble.'

'Don't have children.'

Jennifer laughed.

'I need a stiff Scotch.'

'When de last time you and Mr Harwood take a holiday?'

'I don't know.'

'Go, nuh.'

'Where? Up the islands? More beaches? Nah.'

'Go to England.'

'George would never come.'

'Take a tour. It good for you.'

'It's too late.'

'Howyuh mean?'

'I don't feel like it any more.'

'I ent ever take a holiday.'

Sabine looked at Jennifer; she was dreamy-eyed. 'Where would you go?'

'Germany.'

'Ugghh. I hate Germans.'

'To see de Soca Warriors. Take mih family. Chantal and Nathalie-Anne and Talbot. Everyone. Stay in a hotel. Watch all tree games.'

'Mr Harwood just saw them. He said we're going to get a beating.'

'I doh care. It would be great to see dem.'

'It's a big thing, I suppose.'

'It de biggest ting I ever know.'

'I wish I could afford to send you all. I fear it's too late for tickets.'

'Can I bring de kids dong here to watch de games on TV?'

'Of course.'

'We can pretend it's Germany.'

'Mr Harwood would like that.'

Sabine came awake in her dream. Germany: the Trinidad striker Stern John was steaming down the pitch, England players falling and tripping by the wayside as they tackled him. He thundered past, but couldn't get far enough down the pitch to score. The ground slipped beneath him, shaking, tipping him backwards. She woke with a start, eyes wide open. The bed trembled.

'Jesus Christ. George!'

She clasped his hand.

'George, an earthquake.'

The bed bucked. The earth hummed, building to a larger sound, a growl. Dimly, she was aware of groans outside, the trees, the walls of the house creaking, the grass flinching. Menacing sounds, like something was going to snap. The dogs whimpered and whined, clawing at the glass sliding doors, trying to get in. The ground heaved and swelled, a giant ocean wave.

'She's moving again!' Sabine shouted.

George was awake, holding her hand tight. They were pinned to the bed by a force pressing them down.

'She's rolling in her sleep.'

'Christ, it's a big one. Sabine, don't try to move.'

'I can't.'

A framed photograph crashed to the floor. Perfume bottles leapfrogged across Sabine's dressing table. The bed swayed, throwing them together so they clutched each other.

'Stop! Stop!' Sabine commanded. Every moment was a minute, each second she expected the green woman to stop thrashing her hips. But the shaking didn't stop. Outside, the rushing of palm fronds. *Wallop.* A tree smashing to the ground. The dogs clawed and barked. There was a sense that the ground would open up, that the house would fall into the jaws of the earth. *Marie, pleine de grâce*, Sabine prayed. *Protégez-nous, gardez-nous.*

Then, silence.

They remained clutching each other. Sabine was in tears. George held her in his arms whispering soothing words: how much he loved her, loved her from first sight, how much he'd loved their life together, how everything would be all right.

'You're not dying, are you?' Tears glistened on Sabine's cheeks.

'No.'

They lay for several moments on the bed which had lurched a foot from the wall. Perfume bottles lay smashed on the floor; scents of Chanel and Dior hung in a heady cloud. Sabine and George gazed at each other, like they had a thousand times before.

'I'm still yours,' Sabine whispered.

The dogs barked and clawed outside.

George kissed her on the cheek and rose. Sabine lay on the bed, closing her eyes, remembering Stern John. This time he belted the ball into the goal. Red everywhere, erupting. Jennifer jumping for joy. The green woman, her lush rounded curves bucking and jolting. She could never compete, never win her husband's heart back from this bewitching country, not now.

*

The dogs clambered over George and he couldn't do anything until he'd fed and reassured them. Inside the house, paintings and pictures had crashed to the floor. Glasses had jumped from shelves, plates had fallen and smashed. Outside, the damage was much worse. A coconut tree had fallen down; its head draped in the pool, the long fronds like hair. The dogs padded round to stare at it. Katinka sniffed and woofed, her fluffy tail up like a flag. The three dogs escorted him on his tour of the garden and its walls and yes, two of the walls had long rambling cracks. In one, the crack was so wide he could insert the tips of his fingers, tracing its length from ground to top. Another tree had fallen down in the front garden, an old lime tree; limes like yellow golf balls were scattered over the lawn. Out behind the walls, electricity cables were down. The heavy-legged vulgar condominiums across the road were still standing, though.

'Jesus God,' George uttered, staring at them.

Jennifer's home.

George ran to his truck, driving out the gate in moments,

speeding along the empty road. Everywhere trees were down and cracks had split the road. Tarmac pushed up in unstitched scars; telegraph poles were leaning, wires slack. He accelerated. Talbot, Chantal, the little baby girl, he hoped no one was hurt, that no one was asleep inside when the quake hit. Pelting down the road, he took the turn by the gas station, the tyres screeching. La Pompey stood in the forecourt, the only person about. He laughed as he saw George's truck burning rubber and waved a fistful of red dollar notes. George floored the accelerator, roaring up the steep sharp bends of Paramin. No cars coming down. No one around. People were still indoors, too frightened to venture out. Tremors often followed. Up and up and up and then right, then up again, until he was upon the bend where her house had stood for a hundred years or more, since slave days over. Up here the slaves came to recover from those times, grow yams and cassava, spend their days in blissful contemplation of the clouds, watch the grass flourish, their children grow fat.

The house laughed at him. Jennifer sat on the top step. She laughed, too, when she saw him appear, so worried. Baby Nathalie-Anne sucked her thumb, sitting on her grandmother's lap. Talbot appeared at the door and stared.

'What yuh doin' up here, Mr Harwood?' Jennifer's face lit up, triumphant. 'I tellyuh already. Nuttin go lick dong dis house. No hurricane. No earthquake. Nuttin. It steady as a *rock*.'

CHAPTER TEN

DEPARTURE

In the kitchen Sabine soaked raisins in rum. She'd sprinkle them over coconut ice cream for dessert, some fresh pineapple, too. Incredible that the quake hadn't tumbled the shack down Paramin Hill. Imagine that, forty or so shacks thrown into that great open valley; imagine the disaster if a really monstrous quake hit. One day, one day, it just might. Imagine the tenacity in those wooden limbs, those posts laid down as temporary. Slaves like chattel, like cows. Granny Seraphina. Bless her soul. What will she do with George? George never liked Granny much, afraid of those sour yellow eyes. Poor Granny. Poor George.

Kersplash. The sound came from outside, of George diving into the pool.

The dogs woofed, running round.

The doctors had told him to swim, but *not* to dive. Silly, silly fool. The operation was at the weekend. Eight hours it would take to remove the tumour. That morning George had talked of taking a holiday, after he recuperated, a trip to London or Paris.

The raisins kept for weeks. Irit had taught Sabine how to do them. Excellent sprinkled into fruit salads, cakes. Always a jar of rum and raisins in the fridge. Good with almost anything.

She stopped.

'George?'

A knowing, right there, between her shoulder blades. The garden was too quiet. None of the usual splashing.

'George?'

'George,' she said louder, wiping her hands on her dress. 'Are you there?'

She put down the jar of rum and raisins, striding from the kitchen, through the house, calling his name, seeing the dogs behaving oddly, their tails lowered, cowering, nervous round the pool. Then she was running and shouting, *'George!'* He wasn't in the pool. Where, where was he? Was he in the garden? Had he stepped out? Was he tinkering with his barbeque? Could he have gone round to the back door?

'George!'

The dogs whimpered and then she was struck, immobile, yards from the pool, feet nailed to the ground. The dogs could see, they knew. Sabine willed herself forward, walking towards the pool.

George was there, at the bottom. His hands were outstretched in a V, in the diving position, as if he'd died mid-air, as if he'd dived and died and fallen to the bottom of the pool. Sabine couldn't hear herself screaming. Then she was in the pool, trying to reach George at the bottom, holding her nose and diving and trying to reach him and coming up for air and screaming and then the big dogs, out of fear and excitement, jumped into the pool, paddling round in circles and barking. Katinka jumped in, too, snapping at the water. The keskidees flew out in a party, swooping and squawking and dive-bombing the dogs, who barked louder and struggled for the sides, unable to get out. Sabine managed to haul herself out, her dress sodden. She screamed and bellowed for help and jumped in again, holding her nose, this time reaching the bottom, enough to grasp a handful of George's hair and move him a little before she burst up for air. She hoisted herself out again, finding the pool scoop, trying to poke at him, dig up under him and raise him up, all the while screaming and the dogs barking and paddling round in circles and then at last the neighbours knew something terrible was happening. They came running.

Floris and Edmund Knags arrived first. They heard the commotion and saw Sabine in her dress, soaking, standing at the side of the pool with the scoop and the dogs barking, trying to get out.

Edmund jumped in, diving to the bottom. He brought George up.

'My love, my love,' Sabine sobbed, kneeling at the side of the pool, grabbing for her husband's body.

Edmund pushed and Sabine pulled and George's body heaved forward in one movement, falling onto Sabine's lap. She bent over him, kissing him. 'No, no, no. Get him a blanket!'

George's long hair lay like strands of seaweed down his face. His eyes were closed and he looked like he was only asleep. Peaceful. 'No, no, no,' Sabine wailed. A blanket arrived and they wrapped him up as best they could. More neighbours turned up in twos and threes and Sabine couldn't see them through her hurricane of tears. They gaped, appalled, saying, *Oh, Sabine, Sabine.*

No one knew quite what to say or do. Sabine wailed and rocked her husband's wet body.

Quickly, the house was full and the driveway chock-a-block, cars on the driveway, on the grass, on the verge outside the house. Passers-by would assume there was a party going on inside. Sabine sat by the side of the pool with George on her lap, wrapped in a blanket as if to warm him back to life, warm his bones. She wouldn't move or let anyone take him from her. She sobbed and rocked and choked and kissed his head. 'My love, my love, my love,' she cried, and rocked.

The house bustled. Phone calls were made to the district officer, the undertaker. Someone telephoned Pascale. Someone else telephoned Sebastian in London. Someone called Dr Sebastian Baker.

Dr Baker came immediately, hurrying up the drive and through the house. He gasped when he saw Sabine and George by the pool. He knelt down next to them and put his hand on Sabine's bowed head.

'I'm so sorry,' he said as he kissed Sabine on the forehead. Sabine let him examine George and pronounce him dead, saying his heart had gone, saying he'd do the paperwork, get the certificate ready. He'd have to go back to the office, he'd be back again soon.

Sabine couldn't see Dr Baker through her grief. She only remembered the dances at the Country Club, all those years ago, how he had held her close, how things were so different then, a different life for her and George. Dr Baker bent closer and held her tight for a few moments but had no words, nothing to say to her.

'I won't last long without him,' Sabine whispered thickly to his ear. 'I won't last too much longer here.'

Pascale flew through the house and saw her father lying there, wrapped up like a mummy. She ran to Sabine and only then could Sabine let her husband go and stagger to her feet.

'He's dead, he's gone,' she wailed and the women locked in an embrace, clutching each other tightly. Pascale sobbed and Sabine groaned like an animal. No one knew what to say and so they left the two women by the pool with the large dead man wrapped in a blanket, his long wet hair flowing over his peaceful face. They held each other and talked to him and waited for the undertakers to arrive. The dogs were wet and exhausted, whimpering and lying flat on the grass, not too far from George. They whined, a nervous desperate sound, wanting to know what had happened. Someone went over to comfort them and lead them away to the front garden.

Sabine stood on the steps of the red and vanilla church in the pounding sun, sunglasses clamped to her face. Her beautiful son Sebastian had flown back from London the next day. The house was still full of people when he arrived: neighbours, friends, friends of Pascale's. People had brought food, soups and hops and ham and pelau. Jennifer was shocked; she kept uttering *Oh gorsh* and dropping things. The dogs were quiet. They kept looking into the pool. Sabine hadn't slept for days. She kept repeating the story of finding George dead in the pool again and again, to anyone who'd listen, as if convincing herself that it had happened. Pascale had gone mute and was staring all the time, staring into her future. How could George be dead? He was much too young; he had more time, surely? She still had so much more to say to him. It wasn't right. How could George die? That lump in his head – they hadn't finished arguing.

The hearse appeared. The sombre-faced pall-bearers hovered round the back doors, Sabine's son amongst them. Sebastian wanted to do it, wanted to carry his father's body inside the church. The same church where he was baptised, where he wanted to have his own funeral. Sabine and Pascale moved towards the entrance, where they stood waiting for the other mourners; they resembled soft statues, statues of themselves in the process of falling. They tried to hold each other up but their shoulders and knees sagged. They held hands and didn't speak. Those who came to pay their respects kissed them softly on the cheek, whispering their regrets.

The coffin slid out on a trolley. Everyone waited inside the church. Sabine and Pascale and Jennifer sat in the front pew. Six men carried the coffin. Frank Farfan was one of them. George's younger brother had flown in, too, three of George's regular bridge buddies and Sebastian. Sabine fought waves of nausea and remembered the *Cavina* and the day they arrived on the island, those big black birds circling overhead. They could take her now. Pick her bones clean; strip her of her sins, of her bitterness. Eric Williams, on the bandstand that day in Woodford Square so long ago. Tears fell.

The men linked elbows under the coffin for support and carried it slowly up the church steps, stopping where the pews began. The organist began to play and the congregation rose. The singing in the church chilled Sabine's bones. It was somehow too intimate, too damn intimate. One voice seemed to be leading the choir, clearer and higher than the rest, a crystal voice. This one voice penetrated Sabine, slowed her breath and made her body soften. She dared not look towards the choir stalls; she kept her head bowed, eyes lowered. The coffin was laid on a stand waiting next to their pew. Sabine didn't look up or around. The singing was getting to her, gnawing at the very edges of her. Sebastian slipped into the pew with them. They all stared upwards, towards Father Andrew who was conducting the service with great reverence. The priest had come to their home every Wednesday night to play bridge with George, too, every Wednesday night for decades.

The boy's voice entered her. Only then did she let herself gaze across to the choir. Clock stood with one hand over his breast, peering down at George's coffin. He sang like a bird, pure and high and lucid, like a nightingale alone in a tree. He was singing his heart out. His eyes were big and black and baleful, as if he knew of things others didn't. Did he know her secrets? Yes, probably. He was George's friend, after all. The boy sang and her heart rose and fluttered and the boy sang for her, for her only, so that she could remain upright.

The next morning, Jennifer was late in. Sebastian was asleep. Katinka had been digging a tunnel into the neighbour's garden and was covered in dirt. Sabine picked her up, dumping her into the deep scullery sink out the back, dousing her down with water and squirting her with shampoo. Stupid little dog. She scrubbed and lathered the dog up so she looked like a poodle, all white balls of froth. She rinsed and then dried her with an old towel, scattering flea powder on her, watching the fleas jump off. Katinka was a present from George, years ago; George had always been good with presents. Sabine hadn't slept. It wasn't possible to sleep, or think clearly. Adrenalin still coursed through her, she could feel it like a river. Adrenalin and caffeine and the hundreds of cigarettes she had smoked in the last few days. Her head pounded and yet somewhere, inside her, she knew she wanted to close her eyes.

A creak sounded at the gates. The dog yapped.

'Thank God, Jennifer's here,' Sabine told her.

Jennifer appeared but didn't say hello at first. Her face was puffy, eyes red with tears. She assumed Jennifer was still crying over George. Then she realised something else was wrong. Jennifer looked frightened.

'Jennifer, what's happened?'

'Nuttin.'

'Jennifer. Don't say that. What's wrong?'

'Oh gorsh, nuttin.'

'Don't nothing me; I'm not in the mood.'

Jennifer's eyes were filmed over.

'Come on, out with it.'

'Dey treaten Talbot.'

Sabine stared. 'Who . . . what, who's threatened Talbot?'

'One o' dem police fellas. He see Talbot las night up on de hill. Talbot say dis police fella was lookin' fer him. Talbot doin' nuttin. He just walkin' dong de road, mindin' himself. De police man stop his jeep and he tell Talbot he go dead him de next time he see him. Next time four eyes meet.'

'Four eyes meet?'

'Next time dey meet alone. Eye to eye.'

'Jennifer, this is serious. One of those police thugs threatened to *kill* your son.'

Jennifer nodded. 'Talbot 'fraid to go out. He hidin' all now in de house. He 'fraid, madam. I 'fraid for mih son.'

'Quite. A policeman has threatened to kill him.'

'De policeman say an ol' white man come to de station two weeks ago and vex de Superintendent. Bobby Comacho, dis Superintendent, he know de white man. Mr Comacho give dem hell.'

'Oh God. Oh no. George. What did he do?'

'Madam, who else would it be?'

Sabine exhaled loudly. 'Oh my dear George. Oh Jennifer, I'm so sorry.'

'Mr Harwood tell mih he go pay for a lawyer to help Talbot.'

'What?'

'Yes. He tell mih not to say anytin to you. Keep it secret.'

'George said that?'

'He was goin' to pay for a lawyer, to defend Talbot.'

'How? In court?'

'Das what he say . . . he want to help.'

'Oh dear Lord. He never told me half of the things he did . . . Mr Harwood had a separate life . . . oh God . . . that stupid man. I mean, oh God, what was he thinking?'

'I tink he doin' it for you, madam . . . in a funny way.'

'What do you mean?'

'I ent know exactly, it jus my feelin' . . . he want to make good.'

'Oh George!'

'Talbot 'fraid dese fellas bad, 'fraid dey come back, but Mr

Harwood say he go protek him. Now he die and news mus get out. Dese fellas come back fer him, treaten him. How Talbot goin' to get by now Mr Harwood dead?'

'Jesus Lord.'

'Mr Harwood dead. Now Talbot, mih son go dead too.'

'No!' Sabine shrieked. 'I give you my word. No one is going to touch your son. No one.'

Jennifer had tears in her eyes. She steupsed and went towards the kitchen. 'I goin' to mek tea.'

Sabine gazed across at the garage wall. The newly polished green bicycle stood against it like a child waiting to be noticed. She had ignored it, purposely, to hurt George, to make a point. It had collected even more carrier bags full of junk since she last inspected it. Stacks of newspapers had been placed over the wicker basket in front. Strange. Like someone had tried to cover the bike again, cover it up. She went over and began to relieve the bike of its cargo, the bags of garage tools which hung from the handlebars, wiping the dust that had gathered. She lifted the newspapers out of the wicker basket and peered inside. In the basket she saw a crumpled brown Hi-Lo bag. She reached down and pulled it out, feeling it was heavy in her hands. She looked inside and saw the smaller parcel, wrapped in waxed paper and instantly knew what it was, what George had been hiding in the basket of her green bicycle.

'Mrs Harwood, you *crazy*. You go make tings *woss*.' Jennifer followed Sabine to the gate as she wheeled the bike out.

'Please, please doh go.'

Katinka followed them, smiling, tail up.

'Jennifer. Yes. I'm going to make things very bad indeed for those bastards down there.'

Sabine opened the gate, swinging one leg as if to mount the bike, hearing a loud crack in her knee. Her leg didn't reach. It was too short all of a sudden. She'd shrunk over fifty years.

'Jennifer, come and help me.'

'No.'

'Jennifer, come on. Do what you're told.'

'Oh gorsh, you go kill yuhself on dat ting.'

'Come on, help me on.'

'No.'

'Please.'

'Oh gorsh, man.'

Jennifer came forward reluctantly, heaving and pushing, and in a moment Sabine was upright on the bike, her toes barely touching the ground. She glanced at Jennifer as if to say, *How do I look?* and then she was out, on Saddle Road, the main road into town, into Winderflet, cycling full pelt. The wind was in her hair and all the workmen on the vulgar condominiums opposite were looking down and heckling her and laughing and people in cars passing were watching her like she was mad. An old white woman on a green bicycle riding down the road, like she was in France or Italy or somewhere. A seventy-five-year-old white woman, mad as hell and riding down to the police station in Winderflet. Four herons perched on the bridge railings stared at her. The man at the fruit store on the bend in the river stared. The woman selling Caterpillar boots on the oil drums on the verge of the road stared. At the People's Place parlour a whole block-lime of men with their feet cocked up against the wall stared and smirked. She knew they recognised her. Mr Harwood's wife, *as crazy as de mad-assed white man himself.*

Sabine cycled past them all, head up, turning right into the police station in a wide fast arc, knowing it would be hit-and-miss when it came to stopping, and she crashed straight into the station's front steps. The bike clattered to the ground, Sabine leaping from it like a cowgirl from a horse. She walked into the station carrying the brown-paper bag.

Bobby Comacho loitered at the front desk, liming with the officer on duty. His back was to Sabine: a tall solid black man, obviously the man in charge from his uniform, the peaked cap.

'You!' Sabine bellowed.

Superintendent Bobby Comacho wheeled round.

'I take it from that stupid hat you're the *oaf* in charge.'

Bobby's face fell, his eyes went dark, murderous.

'Don't you look at me like that, you evil pig,' she spat. She held up four fingers. '*Four*, do you hear? Four of your disgusting thugs beat up my maid's son! Put him in hospital. Did you know about that?'

'Lady, you watch yerself. Yuh foolish husband already come here. I ent know what you talkin' about,' Bobby warned.

'Oh no? You know all right and you don't care because you've done it *yourself.* Haven't you? Isn't that how you got your captain's hat? Bullied your way up the force, you fat bastard.'

Bobby glared.

The officer in charge gasped.

Sabine frothed, her small white teeth flashing.

'Lady, get de *hell* outta here,' Bobby growled.

'I will not.'

'I'll have you trone in a cell.'

'One of your stupid illiterate policemen has now threatened Talbot with *his life*. One of your men, a man on your force. What's his name? Tell me. I want to speak to him. Last night he threatened to *kill* Talbot and now, guess what?' Sabine broke. She was relaxed. It was like singing or swimming or crying, a relief to be there. From the brown-paper bag she brought out the gun and held it high, level to Bobby's enormous chest. She smiled and tightened her grip on the gun.

Bobby stared.

The officer in charge quivered.

'Nobody move,' Sabine ordered.

She held the gun firm, her arm straight. Her frame heaved gently, like an ocean swell, as her breath slowed. Bobby shook his head slightly. Sabine smiled and nodded ever so slightly. She squeezed and the trigger gave and she heard a sharp deafening sound as she fired not one, but two, and then three bullets. The three bullets sank without a sound into the body of Superintendent Bobby Comacho, responsible for the safety of the citizens of Winderflet. His body sank lifeless to the floor. The officer in charge gawped. Sabine turned and walked away, out into the station forecourt, into the blazing sun, the light dazzling her for a few moments so she wasn't sure exactly where she was. She raised her hand and shaded her face and looked upwards to see that, up above the church, above it all, in the blue serene sky, the blimp was gazing down at her, gazing precisely down.

TRINIDAD, 1956

CHAPTER ELEVEN

ARRIVAL

The sky that day was unusual. A vast expanse of white puckered cloud which had spread low, very low, over the Gulf of Paria. Here and there, a vein of greyish-blue cracked through, but that was all. This white blanket reflected the sea's brutal glare back down onto itself so that you felt trapped under it. But then, further off, to the east, the cloud formation had changed, whipping itself into towering sculptures.

'Like huge galleons,' someone said, pointing.

'An armada in the sky, moored from the sea,' said another passenger.

'Cloud galleons.'

'Sailing ships.'

That day a curious fleet welcomed us, a spectral armada hovering over the mouth of Port of Spain's harbour. It was mid-morning when the banana boat, the *Cavina*, slipped through the First Boca, the narrow strait between the north-west tip of Trinidad and Monus Island. Trinidad surrounded us, hilly and bushy, boisterously green. This greenery marched straight down the steep hills to the sea. No beach or strip of land in between, just this wild green and then the black sea. When the ship passed closer to the land, I noticed hundreds and hundreds of tall pale trees flourishing up from the rocks. Liana vines dangled from their skinny branches. Some, I know now, were the poisonous sea-salt-loving manchineel; their acid fruit is lethal, corrodes the gullet if eaten. Don't stand under a manchineel tree in a rain shower – the fruit fumes mix with water and can melt the skin. I noticed sea-almond trees, too; also tall and rather ragged cacti, hog-plum trees, naked-Indian, all manner of deciduous trees, some with spiked trunks, others with thick, tongue-like leaves; a miracle jungle sprouted up from those dark arid rocks.

Black scavenger birds floated high overhead. Corbeaux. Fifty or sixty spiralled and swung against the thick white cloud. We sailed past a single blasted tree, one limb left on it, bent in a curve and withered. Some of those big black birds sat hunched along it, watchful. Their red-rimmed eyes were speculative, watching me.

'That must be Gaspar Grande,' George said, peering forward. George had done his homework, all right. Before our voyage, he'd purchased maps and shipping charts from Stanford's in Covent Garden. His suitcase bulged. Books on birds and butterflies, mammals, reptiles and insects of the Antilles, marine life, geology. Architecture, cricket. Rum distilling, cocoa planting. George knew what he was arriving to, oh yes. *La belle*. Beauteous Trinidad, a country already encrusted with charms. Bejewelled Trinidad – oh, George's lust fantasies had commenced long before he even met the island.

'Savannah grassland,' he had murmured in his sleep.

'What, my love?'

'Rainforest and mangrove . . .'

'George . . . what are you talking about?'

'Four hundred and fifty-three birds. One hundred and eight mammals.'

'Yes, my love.' I stifled my amusement.

'Manatee. Golden tegu lizards. Purple honeycreepers.'

My husband was already lovesick, already caught up with the idea of what lay awaiting him. George knew what he'd chosen, what he was coming to.

We passed Carrera next, once a prison island just like Alcatraz, a lonely rock harbouring a few dilapidated barracks, a long narrow chute down one side to the sea. Then a flotilla of tiny islands appeared port side, five in all; this was Five Islands, also covered in the same bushy greenery. Above these tiny rocks, more cor-beaux tumbled out of the white sky.

'They've been staring at me,' I said to George. 'I swear they have. Wanting to peck at me. I must look plump and juicy.'

'You're very juicy indeed.' George laughed, putting his arms around me. 'Don't you worry, my love, I'll take care of you, you'll see. You'll have servants and a big house and you'll eat ripe pawpaw and guava for breakfast, dropped from the trees in our garden. Here, you'll be a queen.'

George had brought me to Trinidad, all the way across the Atlantic Sea. He'd talked me into it, into him accepting a nonde-script clerk job in a faraway country I'd thought was India, at first. The shipping company, Forbes-Mason, had offered George a job he felt he was unable to refuse. One evening he brought home a map of the world and unfurled it on the kitchen table, pointing. 'See?'

I stared at the continent named *INDIA* on the map.

'No, not there, silly. Here.' He pointed to a speck, miles away and to the west.

'There?' Trinidad turned out to be part of a chain of islands, the Antilles, a long and curved archipelago, set into the Caribbean Sea.

'Yes. There.'

'You're kidding me.'

A long brown shed with a rust-red galvanized roof squatted on one of the Five Islands. Indentured labour arriving from Calcutta had once been quarantined here: thousands of souls had sweltered in the heat for days with little water and food, awaiting entry to work the cane fields, for the ex-slaves had said, *Enough is enough*. Thousands had huddled in those sheds in the hostile heat but George didn't mention this to me. The boat slipped along. By then, all the passengers had congregated out on deck, only about a hundred and twenty people: teachers and bankers and businessmen and others, like us, with three-year contracts newly signed. Even Miss Jamaica was on board, a frizzy-haired white girl newly wed to a Trinidadian French Creole. The *Cavina* bore the last boatload. That's who we were: the last colonials ever to arrive in Trinidad, before things changed for good. It was 3 January 1956. We didn't know about the young Eric Williams, that he was about to launch a new political party to thousands in Woodford Square. We arrived just as this small country had found a charismatic new leader, as it was gathering its collective will, just as Trinidad was bellowing, *Go back, get out, colonial massa*. We arrived in the same month Eric Williams launched his campaign. But not even George knew that yet.

The *Cavina* shifted out into a long channel marked with buoys. George became excited, his eyes glittering, his nose twitching with the sea smells. Port of Spain harbour glimmered into view. The hills of the northern range encircled the harbour, immense, draped in cloud-shadow and what looked like blue-green velvet – these mountains once part of the mighty Andes chain. George gasped in open admiration. *Bitch, muse, hypocrite, friend* – I knew not what to call Trinidad.

To the right, I noticed a long bank of low-lying darker green vegetation which ran right up to the wharf.

'Caroni Swamp,' George said.

A swamp? I was taken aback. Caroni Swamp lay along the entire port side of the entrance to the harbour, trailing off into the distance. But how wide was it, I wanted to know. And did it spread across the island's interior? Was Trinidad mostly a deep muddy bog? And what lived inside such an unwelcoming environment? Anacondas, alligators?

Of the hills surrounding Port of Spain, one stood out. Only one hill appeared to be inhabited, busy with red roofs and glinting flashes of silver. Laventille Hill. The community looked intriguing from the ship, the only sign of civilisation because the city itself lay flat behind the harbour, invisible from the ship's deck. I imagined this was where we might settle. Imagine! *Quelle idée*. Laventille: the city's slum, where the slaves congregated after emancipation. It was windy up there, and indeed it was named accordingly: La Ventilla. The ground there was spongy, the air infused with the foul scents of the swamp.

A lighthouse stood on the wharf – at last something familiar. Small, toy-like, more a decoration than anything else. Broad daylight. Yet the lighthouse was like a magnet to the boat and we sailed straight towards it. By then everyone was enthralled and we clung to the starboard rails of the ship. Some pointed.

'How big is the city?'

'How many people live in it?'

'A few thousand, a few hundred?'

'I hear it's very poor.'

'No, it's rich.'

'It's dirty.'

'I hear you have to watch your step.'

'You can't walk around at night.'

'Rubbish, it's ruled and built by the British. It's well-ordered.'

'It's like Bombay.'

'It's like Jamaica.'

Laughter.

I crossed myself. *Protégez-nous*, I whispered. My stomach was twisted up into knots. I imagined this was the case for all of us. Nothing spoke to us. Only George seemed unperturbed. The sea fell more silent and a blanket of white cloud pinned us down. A brown dried-up coconut floated past. Grizzled pelicans perched on the marker buoys, regarding our entrance with indifference. The stink of the swamp reached us, a strong salt odour mingled with the scents of dead fish, dead dogs, decaying mangrove. Its own smell. We put our hands to our noses and laughed off our unease. George's eyes gleamed. But I stared uncertainly at the small famous port, those encroaching hills; the hairs on the back of my neck stood erect. Sixteen days at sea. We'd arrived to this: Port of Spain. So quiet and self-contained and green.

Eventually, the white cloud-blanket evaporated. A second, even more hazardous sky revealed itself, overearnest, a blazing staring blue. The sun hurled lancing rays at us and I felt I had to get out of the way. The *Cavina* manoeuvred closer to the dock. I crept downstairs to our cabin, getting down on my knees. I prayed to the Virgin:

Je vous salue, Marie, pleine de grâce,
Protégez-nous,
Nous sommes seuls ici,
Nous avons besoin de votre aide.
Gardez-nous.

I was frightened, all of a sudden unsure of myself. What if I refused to get off the boat, refused outright to descend to the dock? What if I changed my mind? I could, couldn't I? Explain to George I'd had a change of heart. The ship would fill with its outbound cargo of bananas and head back to Southampton. We could stay on board. What if I failed the test of Trinidad? The heat had chased me down into the cabin, invading the small space. My skin was slippery-damp. Water in my hairline, a rivulet of water trickling down the nape of my neck. Lightly, I pressed my fingers to my forehead, then my cheeks, inspecting my glistening fingertips. I pressed the palm of one hand to my chest and wiped away more perspiration. I practised breathing: in, out, in, out. I peered into the dresser mirror and saw another woman, her face steamed and plump.

I sat still on the small bunk bed, eyes closed. Italy, France: already this was very different. Hot countries I knew, European countries. But this heat was indecent, like breath or fingers. Hands on me, touching me.

'Get away from me,' I rasped.

I returned to the deck to find our ship pulling alongside the Queen's Wharf. I could see black people milling around and custom houses and cranes and other ships docked. A halo of pale yellow dust hovered in the air. Voices shouting. The sky shouted. Butterflies swarmed in my stomach. I clutched George's hand tightly. George's face was smooth and pale and calm. He showed no outward signs of distress from the heat or anything else.

We had arrived. Travelled all the way from Harrow on the Hill, from our new home, a wedding present from George's parents, from mid-winter, frost still on the ground, from family and friends. I couldn't believe it. We brought very little with us. Two suitcases with some summer clothes, a crate of favourite bits and pieces, which we had labelled *FRAGILE*, and, of course, my green Raleigh bicycle.

On land, the heat was stupendous. Show-offy, acrobatic; the air was somehow mobile, writhing from all the sun's stunts. My lacquered hair, I feared, was turning to kindling, the skin on my shoulders sizzled. I thought I might actually be cooking, just like a pork chop. The pavement smouldered up through the thin soles of my sandals. I wanted to return immediately to the ship.

'Are you all right, my love?' George asked.

'Mmmm . . .'

'Darling, you've lost the ability to speak.'

He was right: I couldn't find the breath to form words. A stout red-faced Englishman came forward from the crowd to greet us, sweat trickling in straight lines down his temples. He dabbed at his forehead with a handkerchief.

'George and Sabine Harwood.' George grinned, stepping towards him, ushering me in the man's direction. We all shook hands briefly. A car was waiting near by, a Chevrolet. Perspiration had collected in my eyelashes and my sight was blurred. I was close to fainting. And the smells! Heat and fruit and the strong ripe musk of Negroes. Black people everywhere. I tried not to stare. I'd never seen so many of them before. They were strangely quiet and distanced, as if they only existed in the background.

A commotion started up near the hold. Directions were shouted, people beckoned others loudly, calling those on the dock to come forward to retrieve their crates. My green bicycle appeared. Two men wheeled it down the ramp, laughing and making a fuss over it, as if it were some novelty toy. A steward pointed in my direction.

'Lady, lady,' they called. 'Bring it fuh she. White English lady.'

I blushed, thanking them profusely.

'I'm *French*, not English, you know,' I said to one, but he only laughed.

We recognised our crate emerging, too. A young stevedore

tossed it from the ship's belly to the wharf. The crate landed with a thud in the dust. George ran to rescue it. But I was shocked, checking myself: maybe these people couldn't read English?

The Chevrolet swept us along the foreshore, along Wrightson Road, to a hotel opposite open parkland called the Queen's Park Savannah. This was the Queen's Park Hotel: the grandest in Port of Spain. My spirits lifted. A curious building; the main part resembled a Victorian country house, though one adapted for the Caribbean, constructed from rainforest hardwood, with wide verandas and jalousie shutters. One wing was art deco in style, tall, with scalloped windows. We were shown to the older rooms. Inside, slow-moving ceiling fans stirred the thick air. In the corners there were nests of softly faded white wicker furniture, feather-stuffed chintz cushions. Persian rugs thrown down onto wide polished wooden floors. An atmosphere I immediately recognised. Two macaws clambered along the veranda rails, one turquoise, one scarlet.

Qui est là? Qui est là? One spoke in French. I was delighted.

George squeezed my arm. Here I could collect myself. We went upstairs to our room and collapsed on the four-poster bed. The ceiling was high and our balcony overlooked the huge savannah opposite; a light breeze fluttered in. I loosened the mosquito net hanging above the bed.

'Other wives,' I said.

'Who?'

'I'm *not* like those other expat wives, am I?'

'No, my petal. You're not.'

'I won't want to leave, I promise.'

George was already drifting into sleep. 'That's right,' he muttered. 'That's right, my darling.'

I watched George sleep, pressed my lips to his warm belly. Of course, there had been an interview in London. George's bosses at Forbes-Mason had wanted to meet me. Other wives hadn't liked it. The firm had found it impossible to keep its employees long in Trinidad. Three couples had quit before us, all lasting months, not years. Men loved the West Indies. They had something to do. Usually they enjoyed higher positions than they did in England. They loved the climate and the people. The wives hated it, though. I knew this. But I wasn't put off. George wanted to show me off, to show them that I was different. And I was. I knew that, too. I was bilingual. I was comfortable with a mixture of tongues and races, different cuisines and cultures. I had lived in a hot place before. I was gay, vivacious. It wasn't hard to reassure his bosses. They only had to take one look at me, my olive skin, my Mediterranean nature, to see that I was different. I impressed those grey men. Three years: we had nothing to lose. A house was thrown in. We signed the contract. I thought: *I'll show them.*

I drifted off, too, dreaming, of all things, that I was riding my green bicycle along the road to my new home in Harrow on the Hill. The road was frosted; it was January. I was wrapped up in a tweed coat and gloves and shivering with the cold, riding home to meet George. Happy, newly wed. Eager to see him. As I rode, white flecks tumbled from the sky, graceful and mesmerising, reminding me of something: black flecks I'd seen somewhere else, against a blanket of white. The white flecks became black flecks. Black birds spiralled and wheeled ahead of me, littering the sky.

*

We stayed exactly one week at the Queen's Park Hotel. The company wined and dined us dutifully and we received an invitation to tea with George's new bosses and their wives. Bonny and Miriam amazed me: they wore hats and gloves and stockings.

'Where are you from, *originally*?' Bonny probed. Her creamy oval face was rather stern; a shadow of dark hair crept along her jaw.

'Antibes.'

Tight, forced smiles.

'And did you have a good trip out?'

'No,' I laughed. 'I was seasick all the way.'

'Did you bring much with you?'

'Just my bicycle.'

Their eyes shot wide open. Miriam smirked. 'I suppose you'll buy a *vehicle*,' she said.

'I don't drive.'

Looks of horror.

'Do you play bridge?'

'No.'

Froideur.

I grinned and puffed my cigarette smoke into their eyes. I had so many questions but it was clear they weren't the right women to ask for advice. They thought I wouldn't last. This only concentrated my resolve. We would not only stay but do well.

That first honeymoon week ended. Only then did we find out that the home we'd been promised hadn't even been built! We were expecting the key. But when we arrived, the entire subject was tacitly avoided. I pushed, gently. We were taken to view a tiny apartment on Bergerac Road in a district called Winderflet. Near Chen's Pick and Pay, a supermarket, and the Country Club.

'Handy for six months or so.' The company didn't even apologise.

When we opened the door I yelped. Black shiny cockroaches, fat as mice, scuttled up ceilings and across the floor.

'*Qu'est-ce que c'est?*' I shrieked.

'Just beetles.' George tried to placate me.

'Beetles? They're not *beetles*. They're demons!'

George stormed in yelling and stamping on as many as possible. The flat was in a shocking state. The mattresses hopped with nits, the refrigerator was mottled with mould. The walls flaked grey paint.

Tears welled and ran down my cheeks. 'Take me straight back to the hotel,' I commanded.

George nodded, his cheeks flushed. 'Sabine, I can't understand this . . . Really. There must be a mix-up.'

The company weren't even ashamed. At my insistence, the flat was quickly scrubbed and repainted, new furniture was delivered. A bed, a table and four armchairs. A new fridge. Those tight forced smiles: my first taste of what those dour English women didn't speak of. Chin up, don't mention it. A large glass of rum. In the afternoons, a little Valium.

I was determined not to be bored in Trinidad. When George was at the office I tidied and cleaned our minute flat till it was spick and span. I decorated it with the few precious knick-knacks we brought out with us. I went shopping every day at Chen's, the dark and ramshackle supermarket near by. My first shopping trip was difficult. My simple shopping list read:

bread, one baguette
milk, one pint
cheese, cheddar, half a pound
butter
apples
tomatoes
biscuits
sugar
tea

Chen's appeared deserted at first. Outside, a row of rusty shopping trolleys burnt molten hot in the sun. I managed to disentangle one, pushing it ahead of me like a shield. At the entrance, I stopped. The shop bore a tangible air of melancholy. A dank earthen odour hung in the aisles and the two bare light bulbs leaked a wispy light.

Immediately, I came across the fruit-and-vegetable section. I saw a large heap of root-like bulbs, dirty and hairy, like potatoes or coconuts. I looked for a label but found none. Next to them, a pile of bananas and hills of green beans, forlorn and shrivelled. I found tomatoes, too, grown locally, small and yellow, a little rotten; also some cauliflowers, heat-tired and turning brown. Oranges, I recognised oranges, except they were green. I picked one up and squeezed it. It was solid. I pushed my trolley past this section several times. Overripe mangoes exploded like hand grenades, fizzing with their own juice. Flies buzzed over them, over everything. Nothing even resembled an apple.

The wooden shelves were dusty, their contents sparse. Boxes of flour and tins of Carnation condensed milk. Tins of corned beef. Other brands I recognised: Heinz, Bachelors soup. Tins of orange juice and garden peas. Fray Bentos pies. Bags of rice and pulses. Split peas. Black-eyed peas. Gungo peas. Tubs of ghee, bottles of cooking oil. Bottles and boxes of local products: Matouk's, Bermudez. Towers of wooden crates of Coca-Cola bottles; bottles of rum. Cockroaches flitted along the shelves. I turned a corner.

A fridge! Thank God. In it, four pats of butter. Six packets of Birds Eye fish fingers. No milk.

I decided to ask for help, steering my trolley to one of the checkout tills. A young black woman with stencilled-on eyebrows and a hairnet sat there, half asleep.

'Excuse me.' I smiled as charmingly as I could. 'I'm looking for milk and some cheese.'

Her huge black eyes blinked. She looked at me with a profound blankness, somewhere between depression and contempt.

'I'm new here,' I explained.

She looked away, muttering inaudible words.

'Sorry?'

Again, she muttered.

'I'm afraid I can't hear you.'

'We ha' no *cheese*.'

'Oh.' I perspired profusely.

'Milk?'

She stared through me.

I waited.

Finally. 'Ovuh der.'

I didn't understand. I cringed.

She pointed to the aisle where I'd seen the tins of condensed milk.

'I want *real* milk,' I explained.

She looked mystified and then sullen, as if offended.

I returned to the aisle and found the condensed milk. I threw a tin into my trolley. After that, I hurried. Too ashamed to return to the till empty-handed, I bought anything to fill the trolley, pulling boxes and tins off the shelves without looking at prices, wanting to escape quickly. On the way out, I passed through a different checkout. I didn't even glance into my basket until I returned safely to our flat. When I emptied it, the contents were very different to my shopping list.

One tin of Carnation condensed milk

One box of Crix crackers

One tin of peas

One bottle of rum

One packet of Birds Eye fish fingers

One jar of Matouk's marmalade

One bottle of Limacol

One bunch of bananas

One big brown hairy bulb

That evening, George laughed at my haul and reluctantly I did, too. We sat on our balcony and drank rum and ate fish fingers and peas. We devoured the bananas.

'They're a little tart, don't you think?' George commented.

We discussed the bulb; George found one of his botany books and we decided it was either a yam or cassava. I wanted to talk about the young black checkout girl's attitude but didn't know how to bring up the subject. George would only say he didn't know what I meant. But I wasn't imagining it. She wasn't exactly rude or unhelpful; it was her complete refusal to engage, as if I were an irritant. I pushed the subject to the back of my head as best I could.

We played Scrabble and I won.

'Damn!' George leapt from his seat in feigned anger at his loss, burying his head in my lap, taking the material of my skirt in his mouth and tugging at it like a lion might tear at a kill. I shrieked as he plunged his head deep between my thighs and somehow, between my protests and then moans, he managed to tear the skirt from my hips with his teeth. We made love on the floor. George whispered thickly into my ear, *I love you, love you, love you, Sabine*. I never quite managed to mouth the same words back. Most times, I went near to unconscious in his hands.

In the morning our stomachs were bad. The bananas, we discovered, were unripe plantain.

CHAPTER TWELVE

THE HIDING CLUB

Every morning I waited on the balcony for the postman. The Bergerac Flats, a neat row, six on top of six, ours on the top floor, number twelve. One morning my neighbour was waiting, too. I liked the look of her. Intelligent green eyes, a still and candid regret in them that she couldn't hide. She had dusk-brown skin, a mixture, of Indian and something else, and a poised demeanour; a subtle and aloof manner which made me want to win her favour. She smoked, too, like me. Even in the morning, in her silky blue kimono, she appeared fashionable. I'd noticed her husband, a sprightly, always-smiling, dark-skinned Indian man, bounding up and down the staircase, taking the stairs in twos. We'd exchanged brief hellos.

'Anything for us?' I called down to the postman.

'No, ma'am.'

I sulked. No post for her either.

Until then, George had been my only companion.

'We've just arrived,' I ventured.

A wan smile. 'Me too.'

Her accent was American!

'We're from England. Well, I'm French, but we came from the UK. My husband has a contract to work for a shipping agent, Forbes-Mason. They service the cruise boats.'

'I'm from Philadelphia.'

Her face was fully made-up even though it was so early in the morning. Painted-on eyebrows, rouged lips. Her hair was reddish from henna, combed back in a chic Hollywood style.

'My husband is Trinidadian.'

'I see. What does he do?'

'We're both lawyers.'

I was stunned. She saw this. A resigned expression came into her eyes.

'I'm Sabine.'

'Helena Chowdry.'

'We've signed up for three years.'

She nodded.

'I am finding it all very interesting.'

Helena looked at me carefully with those discreet green eyes. I didn't mind. I was starved of company. 'I've lost ten pounds. The heat! I am melting.'

She smiled, but only the corners of her mouth turned upwards.

'How do you keep looking so glamorous?' I gushed. 'I've given up.' I wiped the perspiration from my face.

But Helena, like George, was cool-skinned. 'Oh, I know, it's *terrible*,' she drawled.

I babbled on and gradually Helena thawed. Even so, I extracted little from her: they were newly married, too, her husband's name was Gabriel. He'd studied law in England. They were settling in Trinidad: no contract, no end date. Helena was proud, guarded in her manner. I didn't understand why, not then.

In one of the flats below lived Irit, a Hungarian Jewess. Her thick Hungarian accent was luxurious. Irit *oohed* and *ahed* and *dahhh-linged* and rolled her 'r's. She even spoke a little French.

'Sabine dahhhling,' she purred. '*Viens ici*, come for a *petit* cocktail, *oui*? *Où est* that husband of yours? Out on his *petit vélo*? What does he expect you to do? Ride on the back? Like some English beatnik? Eh? *Viens*. I am making some rum punch.'

Irit's flat was chaotic, full of paintings and books and headless dressmaker's mannequins pinned up with satin or chiffon. It reeked of garlic and heady Guerlain perfume. Pets were forbidden, but Irit had smuggled in Mao, a violet Persian cat with a rude plume of a tail. She was married to John, a much older Englishman, who'd helped her escape Hungary during the war. John was besotted with her and she was devoted to him. Irit was ravishing with her rich-chocolate hair, cut short; her angular cheekbones. Her eyes were only ever half open and peered up through long inky lashes.

My green Raleigh bicycle saved me. Without it I was stuck. I rode it everywhere in my shorts and halter-neck top. It gave me freedom. I rode it through Boissiere village and then round the savannah. I loved to ride past the big mansions there, the former estate houses of the cocoa barons. Most stood empty, one was a school, Queen's Royal College. The house on the corner looked like a Rhineland castle, another like an eccentric gunboat, all spires and cupolas and oval windows. One was like a wedding cake made of coral. Another looked like a French chateau. All mimicked bygone European architecture; all seemed ludicrous rather than stately. A castle on the savannah? A chateau surrounded by coconut trees? The owners had arrived, grown rich and then constructed eternal landmarks in an effort to reassure themselves that they were still European. These houses gave me a sense of comfort; like me, they were hopelessly at odds with their environment. I often rode to the savannah just to gaze through their high gates, to conjure up the families who once sat at their dining tables. Little did I know that my daughter would one day marry the descendant of one of these families.

One friend led to two, three, four. All in the same boat, all women, all from other countries, mostly Europe. All stranded. We swapped our histories and tips on how to get by. Oona was Irish, Myra was Scottish, Leila was Russian. Jews, Catholics, Protestants, a mixed community; all young, all marooned, our husbands there for the opportunity. The last exploiters? Yes. I can admit this now. I measured myself against these women, determined not to complain too much. They seemed to complain an awful lot. Even so, I welcomed their camaraderie.

We met at the Country Club, which was a short walk from the flat. A Samaan tree spread itself like a cloud outside the front door, its shaggy beard caught up with orchids, dangling to the manicured lawn. The Club spoke of British colonial order, of former French flamboyance and grandeur. Marble sweeping stairs and wide teak verandas. Fountains and a pool and an enormous dance floor. We went every afternoon, when the sun sank, to sip Bentley cocktails. Or we lunched on flying fish and breadfruit chips under cover of the bar area. We used the pool. Every Saturday, the Club hosted a dance and we wore full evening wear, dancing all night.

Uniformed black staff glided about behind us, again in the background of these adventures. Their wordlessness made me feel self-conscious. The staff never spoke unless asked a question; silence, of course, an ingenious form of resistance.

Once, when a waiter brought over a cocktail, I decided to try my luck at conversation: 'Thank you so much. I'm Sabine,' I smiled.

'Yes, Miss.'

'Do you live far from here?'

'No, Miss.'

'I understand it will be carnival soon.'

'Yes, Miss.'

'Carnival here is famous, I'm told.'

'Yes, Miss.'

'Do you like carnival?'

'Yes, Miss.'

There was no possibility of a real conversation. But these people weren't wordless, quite the opposite. I often saw them chattering to each other. Like the girl at the checkout at Chen's, they just didn't like to speak to *us*. Besides, I often couldn't understand their language. *Eh, eh, oho. Mash it up. Watch meh, nuh. Oh Gooood, Oh Gyaaad*. They sucked their teeth when cross. This even had a word: *steupse*. There were many new words to learn, some African, some Africanised French: *Bobbol*, meaning scandal. *Mamaguy*, to make fun of. A *langniappe* was a child born after a long gap. *Tantie* this and *Tantie* that. Every older woman was a *Tantie* someone; the word was a form of the French for aunt. French was my first language and I spoke English fluently; I was a good mimic and had a keen ear for an accent. But the black people I had come across spoke their mixture-language so quickly and so quietly it was almost a whispering.

At the Country Club whites played, blacks worked. No one asked questions. Neither knew nor cared about each other. Unnatural, but accepted; the rules had been written somewhere long ago, in blood, in sweat. An aloofness existed in the Club's atmosphere, a *Keep your eyes averted* code of conduct prevailed. The large Indian community were absent; they neither worked nor played at the Club. An official colour bar existed: no black human was allowed membership. But the black staff, in their own silent way, made us pay for this.

At the poolside, we European women chatted.

'Where can you buy sausages?'

'Ha ha. Are you mad? You can't.'

'What about bacon?'

'Try United Grocers, in Frederick Street.'

'Lettuce? The ones I've seen are like weeds.'

'That's all there is.'

'And clothes?'

'Johnson's, in town. But you'll only find two rails.'

'Shoes?'

'Bata.'

'Bata?' Laughter. 'Just for sandals and what the locals call *washicongs*. Plimsolls.'

'Shirts for my husband?'

'Aboud's.'

'Pots and pans?'

'Kirpilani's.'

Over by the other side of the pool the local white French Creoles were as distant as the black staff. Haughty, even. One, in particular, was the queen bee: a tall, dark-haired woman with cactus eyes and aquiline features. She refused to acknowledge me when I smiled in her direction. In Europe she would never be considered white. She was yellow-brown.

'Who's *she*?' I asked Oona, who'd lived in Trinidad the longest.

'Dr Baker's wife. Christobel.'

I was intrigued. 'I'd like to meet her.'

'Oh, they're not friendly.'

'Why?'

'Because we're not staying. We're birds of passage. There's an age-old resentment, too.'

'Why?'

'Well, *they* ran things for a short time until the British took over. They can be very snobby, too, worse than the Brits. Some claim they are descended from the French gentry.'

'Don't tell me they *like* it here.'

'Of course they do. They're Trinidadian. Been here for donkey's years.'

'But they must have been like us at one point.'

'A hundred odd years ago. Yes. But the French Creole planters set Trinidad up. They're the native aristocracy. What do you think the Country Club is?'

'What?'

'Home of Poleska de Boissière, the snobbiest of the lot. This place was once the hub of French Creole society. Blacks have *never* been allowed here.'

'But Christobel isn't exactly white.'

'Of course not. But mostly.'

'Don't they yearn to go back to Europe?'

'They're no longer European. Not even the ones with pure European blood. Besides, they don't fit, socially, in Europe.'

'Why not?'

'Here, they're high society. They once owned all the estates, those big houses in town. When Christobel opens her mouth in England people stare.'

'You mean she speaks just like *them*?' I pointed to one of the waiters.

'Yes. More or less.'

George bought a scooter. Every day he rode it to his office down near the docks. He was very dashing in his American Ray-Ban sunglasses and penny loafers. In those days his hair was a mop of russet and his skin was very pale, though he became much more freckled. Even so, he never needed to acclimatise. George found nothing strange about Trinidad, he saw no reason for complaint. He was at ease with his fellow white expatriates as well as the man in the street. He spoke to both with equal courtesy. He often brought home titbits of office gossip, or sometimes local vegetables for me to cook: okra, christophine. I stared at them, not knowing what to do with them, not caring. They shrivelled. I threw them away.

'Here, darling.' Once he brought home a present; the present was wrapped, a book. I snatched at the paper while George looked on, blushing.

'Oh darling.' But my voice was thin, betraying my displeasure at the sight of the gift. It was a cookbook of local cuisine.

Most of my new friends employed a maid. Even Irit, living in all her chaos. Our flat was so small I thought it unnecessary.

'Oh, *mais oui*, you *must*, dahling,' Irit advised. 'Do you think I lift a finger? No, I have enough to do with myself, never mind wash and cook and clean. And besides, a maid is so cheap. You want to be sexy when George comes home, no? You want to be happy, have dinner ready, wear a nice dress?'

'I'm a lousy cook.'

'Exactly. These women can cook.'

'But only local dishes.'

'Oof! What do you mean "only"? My maid Glory is an artist.'

She disappeared into the kitchen, returning with a pot of a creamy mixture.

'Try this.'

'What is it?'

'Breadfruit, dahling. It's called oildown. No fat whatsoever in it. Breadfruit and pig's tail. Fresh.'

I tasted it.

'*Délicieux*, no?'

'*Oui.*'

George and I had been surviving on toast and fish fingers. I hated to iron his shirts.

'How do I find a maid?'

'Easy. I will ask Glory and she will send you her friend. Leave it to me.'

I was pleased.

Two days later, there was a knock at the door.

I opened it.

'Hello, madam, I am Venus.'

The woman in the doorway stood six feet tall at least. Buck teeth. Her hair a riot of pigtails fastened with blue bobbles. Black as the cosmos, the whites of her eyes shining like lamps.

Venus giggled. 'Venus Gardener. Miss Irit tell meh you need a maid.'

I nodded.

'I does cook good and clean good, too, Miss. I can mind chilren. Glory mih sista.'

Glory and Venus.

'What's your mother's name?'

'Maria. Like de Virgin. She live in St Lucia long time.'

'Oh. Well – my name is Mrs Harwood. Do come in.'

Venus stooped to enter. In our small flat she was a giantess. I didn't know what to do or say, if I should offer her a Coke. I had never employed a servant before. Venus wore an A-line skirt and flip-flops, a thin cream shirt, all as a kind of ready-established uniform. It was clear that she had never done this before either. Her face strained to contain a well of natural mirth; her facial muscles twitched, wanting to grin from ear to ear. She was struggling hard to control this inclination.

'I need a cook and someone to iron my husband's shirts. Maybe do a little cleaning, too. But, as you can see, this flat is minuscule.'

'Yes, Miss.'

'What can you cook?'

'Callaloo, macaroni pie, curry crab. Plantain. Anytin. I learn from mih granny.'

'What's her name?'

'Seraphina.'

'Good heavens.'

She giggled. 'Yes, Miss. Granny a heavenly woman. I de younges. Only gyals in de family. No bruddah.'

'How old are you, Venus?'

'Twenteh.'

Five years younger than me. But she could have been any age. Eighteen, thirty-five.

'Do you live far?'

'Just up so, in Paramin. I walk here. I does like to tek a walk. It good fuh de blood system. Good to keep slim.'

'I ride my bicycle.'

'I see you, Miss. Everybody know you already.'

'Who?'

'Everybody. I tell dem I go fine a job with de white lady on de green bicycle. Nobody believe meh. But is true. I see you ride pas' every day. With de basket in front.'

I blushed.

'You is famus, Miss.'

An impish expression crossed Venus's face. At any moment she'd giggle again and this was infectious. I didn't know what to think of this information: that I was being watched. So, these people *did* look up. On the sly. I'd never noticed anyone looking at me on my bicycle. I hadn't felt uncomfortable, yet. Within minutes I liked Venus: positively *liked* her. She was the first black person to speak more than two words to me, the first black person to make me feel welcome. Perhaps she would make me understand things better.

'Can you come three mornings a week?'

'Yes, madam.'

'Then come tomorrow, at eight o'clock. Dress as you are. I pay what Miss Irit pays. I will give you lunch, too.'

'Thank you, Miss.'

One afternoon, I cycled round the savannah, marvelling at the trees. The yellow pouis were just coming into bloom, the dry season arriving. On my bike in shorts and plimsolls, with the sun beating down, I soon found myself down in Frederick Street and then weaving into Charlotte Street, before cycling abreast of an open-air market.

There were people everywhere, hawking their wares on the streets: sugar cane and green bananas, fish and mountains of yams and sweet potatoes. The market resembled a mass of bees swarming, the air thick with the smell of forest honey and coconut oil and human sweat. The sun shone and polished the black bodies. At last, life – I had been so cut off in that tiny flat. I knew I was missing out, missing this: the thrum of the population, out here, in the street. I sailed by, a white ghost in their midst. My heart beat hard in my chest; many of the traders looked up and stared, silent and curious. Instinctively, I knew it would be wrong to stop, let alone roam in the market without a guide. My face flushed with the embarrassment of not knowing the rules. I smiled and broke into perspiration.

Then, something caught my attention: a white man standing on a street corner. A white man holding a shopping basket in one hand; in the other, he held the hand of a black woman. She was smartly dressed, not one of the market women. A white man with a black woman, walking down the road, clearly together, buying vegetables. I stared. Another white person amidst all the black people. What seemed impossible, was then, fleetingly, possible. The sight disturbed me, stirred my imagination. I almost rode straight into a lamp post. I cycled on, past the market, dizzy, dizzy with the idea that these two people could be together, might even be in love with each other.

Very quickly, Venus became my closest companion, my educator. I had so much to learn from her, and yet so much went unspoken between us. Venus was a secret. She gave easily and concealed everything. But often I felt I asked the wrong questions. I had no idea of Venus, of who she was or where she lived, of her ambitions. She talked to me and didn't; it was a given that we spoke only on one level: of the shopping, the cooking, the house, the life of women. Her silence, when she chose to be silent, was impregnable. I left her to her silences. She divulged what she wanted, taught me what she thought I ought to know.

It was Venus who got me cooking. She introduced George and me to creole cuisine, which she called *blue* food: sweet potato, eddoes, cassava, yams.

'Good old-fashioned stodge,' George called it.

Venus brewed up drinks, too – a red cordial a bit like cranberry juice: sorrel. Another, from the bark of a tree: mauby, a green liquorice-type medicine we choked back. In months, our diets had changed for ever. Venus devised our menus. Instead of reading the cookbook, I hung around the kitchen.

'What are you doing?' I asked, peering over her shoulder. She was stripping down the stalks of some large leaves.

'It dasheen bush.'

'What's that?'

'For callaloo.'

'Can't you just chop them up and put them in the soup?'

'No.'

'Why not?'

'You hadda take out dis vein furs.'

'Why?'

'It trouble de throat. Make it itch.' Her eyes shone.

I stared. Venus nodded and smiled, suppressing her amusement.

'And what's *that*?' I asked. At the end of the callaloo-making process she took a tiny crinkled-up red pepper and popped it into the mix.

'Doh ever let dat buss,' she advised.

'Why not?'

'Den de whole ting spoil. You cyan eat nuttin at all if de pepper buss.'

'Really?'

She steupsed, as if it was such common knowledge it was hardly worth mentioning.

'No man can eat dat pepper when it buss, boy.'

From Venus I learnt the necessity of seasoning: how to spice the poor cuts of meat, often the only cuts available. Venus taught me what to do with dried salt fish, how to souse pig's trotters, how to make root vegetable fritters.

We gossiped, too, tentative with each other at first. We had a mutual curiosity. Even though I knew she carefully selected and edited what she said, I was grateful for what she allowed. I looked forward to her stories of Granny Seraphina and Glory and was shocked to learn she lived without running water or electricity. I couldn't imagine her home up in the hills of Paramin. It could be cold up there at night, Venus told me. Cold?

'So how do you bathe, if there's no water?' I asked.

'From de stanpipe by de road. I does pour a bucket ovuh mih head. Tek a showa every mornin.'

'But you're so tall!'

'Ah does use many buckets, madam.'

'And Granny Seraphina?'

'She a natural lady, she tek only rain bath or sea bath. Or she bade in de river.'

'Where?'

'When we does tek she to see she friend in sout.'

'But what about every day?'

'Granny proud. She doh like to bade in de road.'

'I don't blame her. I wouldn't like to either.'

Venus nodded. 'Granny a big women, she have big brain, yes.'

'Like Mr Harwood?'

Venus snorted.

'Like who then?'

'Like Eric Williams.'

'Who's *he*?'

'Granny's boyfriend.' She laughed.

'Granny has a boyfriend?'

'Yeah, man. She love de Doc.'

'What does this Dr Williams do?'

'He already a famus man, Miss. Granny love him. He have a big brain, too. He go save de contry.'

'Then maybe Granny would like Mr Harwood, no? He has a big brain.'

Venus erupted into laughter at the idea. But I didn't mind; watching Venus laugh brought me pleasure and made me laugh, too, even though sometimes I wasn't sure why. When Venus laughed her eyes lit up, her black skin glowed phosphorescent. Why didn't she hate me as the others did? What made her happy to be my friend? Because we were of similar age? Because we were girlish, foolish, secretive together, compulsively talkative – maybe. Venus and I were not long past our teens, women in the making.

George joined a cricket team. The team was mostly light-skinned men, many fellow expats. They played for hours on the savannah on a Sunday or travelled south to play in San Fernando. He adored playing against the local island teams because, of course, they played much better than those who'd taught them. One afternoon I went to watch him play on the savannah in Port of Spain.

Those green sloping hills were all around, the sky blazing a Holy Virgin's blue. Far off, above the eastern slums, corbeaux spiralled. The grass was pale and crisp. Men dressed in white, men both dark-skinned and light. My husband amongst them, his skin sizzling, his too-long auburn hair hanging like a flag. Most wore hats to ward off the sun. The air was heavy with itself, so full of moisture it caused a slowdown of movement, of the senses. I sat with the other wives under the pouis trees. I watched George as he walked out to bat.

The bowler was tall, straight-backed and coal-skinned. He and George nodded, only just perceptibly, at each other. They took their places at either end of the pitch. For a moment they almost bowed. Then the bowler turned his back and walked slowly in the opposite direction: ten, maybe twenty paces further away from the designated spot. *A fast bowler*, someone muttered. My stomach trembled. A murmur went up amongst the spectators. But George stood eager and braced.

'Poor man,' said one wife.

'Dear God,' said another.

The bowler began his run, slow and loping at first, his steps somehow halting in the air, his feet light when they touched the ground. They went invisible as he quickened his pace. His arm flew back and his whole body arced with the curl of his right arm. The ball was released while the bowler was still airborne. The throw was like a javelin hurled, like an act of war being committed.

'Oooooh,' came the gasp from those watching. People stood up from their chairs.

George turned the right side of his body to meet the ball and smashed with all his might, sending it far into the centre of the park. *Smack*.

'Yesss!' came a roar of relief from the onlookers.

A fielder tore after it. Two others followed. Mayhem erupted on the pitch.

Blind in the heat-haze, I clapped as George made four, five, six, seven runs. Moisture ran down my face, trickled between my breasts. The men in white blurred before my eyes.

'Well *played*,' said a wife.

I sat down in my chair and fanned my face. 'Well played,' I whispered, breathless. I knew nothing of cricket, hadn't even known George was so interested before we arrived. But I saw his reason for loving the game that day, playing it there, of all places on earth, on the savannah in Trinidad.

Trinidad had its own rules. I spent those first months learning them fast. One afternoon, I spotted Helena on her balcony. We'd developed a strange balcony-only friendship, chatting most days while we waited for the postman. Now that George and I employed Venus I felt more confident as a hostess. I wanted George to meet Helena and her husband, was sure that they'd get on.

'Will you and Gabriel come over for dinner?' I asked one morning.

'We'd love to.' This broke her from her reverie. She smoked on her balcony a lot. Distracted, glacial.

'I've employed a maid. She's teaching me so much. Her name is Venus. I'm no longer losing weight – we're eating like horses. I'll ask her to make something nice.'

Helena looked troubled.

'How is Gabriel enjoying his job?' I hedged.

'Well enough.'

'George loves what he does. England was so dreary for him. He's settled right in. The men have something to do.' This was it, I'd guessed. 'You must miss working.'

She nodded.

'What kind of legal work did you do?'

'I worked for a small private firm. We worked on social welfare, housing, domestic issues for women.'

'I see. Will you work here?'

'There's no such work here.'

'Couldn't you work with Gabriel? Or start your own practice?'

Already I was asking too many questions. In trying to make conversation I'd glided, in moments, onto thin ice.

'I could never work with my husband and we don't have the capital for me to set up on my own.'

I could tell she was bored and needed cheering up. A refreshing Bentley cocktail would do the trick.

'I'm going to the Club. Will you come?'

Her eyes blazed and her body stiffened. 'Which club?'

'The Country Club. It's very nice. There's a pool, a bar. We could walk.'

'Sabine, I can't go there.'

'Why not?'

'I'm not the right colour.'

'What do you *mean*?' I exploded, laughing. Then, in a moment, realisation came.

'They don't allow coloured people in,' Helena said, stonily.

'They mean *black* people.'

'I'm of colour. Gabriel is a dark-skinned Indian.'

'But they don't mean *you*.'

Helena looked incredulous.

'Don't be silly. Come with me, I'll get you membership. Half the local French Creoles who go there aren't exactly *white*. It's very flexible.'

'Even if they did let me join, Sabine, I couldn't go.'

'Why not?'

'Its membership policy is derogatory. Racist.'

I'd never heard the word before. I was shocked.

'Trust me, they wouldn't let us join.'

My cheeks flushed. 'I don't understand.'

'Sabine, it's no different to anywhere else in the world. The US was just as bad. Haven't you noticed?'

Helena shot me an impatient half-smile.

'But n-not everywhere has a colour bar,' I stuttered.

'Sabine, *everywhere* has a colour bar. There are places for you and places for everyone else.'

'That's demeaning.'

'Precisely.'

'No one can stop us from being friends. I won't go to the Country Club again.'

'Or anywhere else?'

'No.'

'Sabine, this is my problem, not yours.'

'I'm *hated* here.' I blurted out what I'd been thinking all along. 'The blacks won't even look at us. And when they do, it's with faked feeling, politeness they're paid for. Except for Venus.'

'But you pay Venus, too.'

I had somehow overlooked that. But Helena was right. Maybe even Venus didn't care that much.

'You know what?'

'What?'

'I go to the Country Club to feel *safe*. It's a hiding place. It's the Hiding Club.'

'Well, I hide here. On the balcony.'

'Who are we hiding from? Each other?'

'Yes.'

'I'm sorry. I'm ignorant. Will you still come for dinner?'

'Yes, of course,' Helena smiled. 'We'd love to.'

But even so, I still went to the Hiding Club. I hid there, like the rest of those women. I wasn't proud of myself.

CHAPTER THIRTEEN

THE UNIVERSITY OF WOODFORD SQUARE

I never attended university. I escaped school at eighteen, after completing the baccalauréat. In those days I learned by rote, copying everything down to be regurgitated – that was the way we learnt. I then worked as a secretary with an English accounting firm and picked up the language as well as touch-typing, shorthand, that kind of thing. Education was over.

I met George in Antibes, at a party on the seafront. George was a flashy dancer, dipping and twirling all the other women around the dance floor. I'd spotted him earlier – well, you couldn't miss George with his fierce cobalt eyes and his mop of red hair, which was much too long, almost like a hippie, even though that wasn't the fashion then. His face was captivating, all angles, his nose long and arched, hawk-like. His jaw was strong and he had a wry smile on his lips, as if in a state of permanent appreciation of all around him. His skin was lightly freckled, just like a boy's. George was a handsome man back then; an extrovert, a bookish English eccentric. Our eyes met across a bowl of champagne punch and George brought over a glass.

'I've been trying to make you jealous all evening,' he confessed.

I tried to swallow it – smiling placidly. 'I'm not the jealous type,' I said but the words fell flat. I tried to walk away, but George grabbed my elbow and pulled me towards him.

'Would you like to dance?'

'No.'

'Please?'

We danced. Out of sheer impishness, I bit George hard, on the shoulder.

'Ouch!' he exclaimed.

'Oh, have I hurt you?'

'Yes.'

'Good.'

He looked at me, as if I'd thrown down a challenge: who could say the boldest thing, the most direct.

'Will you have babies with me, then?'

I stared.

He winked.

'Yes,' I replied and meant it.

He laughed and we danced for the rest of the night.

Our courtship was very swift. We won each other, you could say. We were each other's prize. People liked us, we were one of those couples; other people enjoyed having us around. Parties were gayer when we were there. Others basked in our happiness, envied our devotion. We brought out the potential in each other. George, in those days, gave me the experience of being at my best; moments, hours, days, a long period of complete happiness.

I'd loved a man before George. I'd lived through the Second World War as a young girl and I'd seen a thing or two. I was confident in myself. But never, oh never, had I been stopped in my tracks.

One day, soon after we arrived, I rode my green bicycle down into Port of Spain. It was late afternoon, so the sun's smile had faded from the sky. George's office stood near the wharf and I'd wanted to surprise him; maybe we could go for a walk along the dock.

I flew round the savannah that day, the breeze catching my hair, and noticed that Venus was right about the looks. Glances. Smirks from people in the street. As if I was an oddity, or a crazy person. *You is famus, Miss*. I rode down into Frederick Street. The tarmac was still hot, the road dusty and almost deserted. Usually the streets of downtown Port of Spain were raucous, a cacophony of street vendors hawking cotton candy, snow-cone vendors weaving through the streets, ringing their hand bells, cars honking them out the way. Madmen in rags often directed traffic. Taxi drivers stopped to chit-chat.

That afternoon, Frederick Street was silent. Momentarily, I was unsure. Had I come down the right street? I wobbled, looking for landmarks, a shop I knew, and then the jail loomed up on the right. Yes. This *was* the right street.

I saw crowds up ahead. Lots of black people milling about. Something was going on. But this wasn't market day or the market street. I didn't think to turn back. Curiosity pushed me onwards.

Then, I was afraid. There were throngs. Thousands? Thousands of people up ahead.

In moments, I had wheeled into the thick of a mammoth crowd. All black people, all gazing into Woodford Square, the big green park in the middle of town, off Frederick Street. The park was usually a genteel setting, benches and a bandstand and a fountain, neat and well ordered, just like the kind you might see in parts of London. That afternoon it was jam-packed. People perched in trees, clung to the spiked railings, others dangled from street lamps, from rooftops. Some of the onlookers waved bal-isiers, heliconia. Big brash crab-claw-like flowers, monsters in the already monstrous gardens of Trinidad. These plants collected water. Snakes hid in them. A strong odour of musk, of bodies steaming. The crowd spilled onto the road and I couldn't get through, round or past. I trailed my toes on the ground, so I could walk the bike.

'Father, father,' a woman shouted.

Others looked towards the bandstand. There was an atmos-phere of rapture.

I was suddenly afraid to catch an eye, to look directly into any one face. I didn't want to draw attention to myself. Was this a military operation? Some general speaking, maybe a British dignitary?

The crowd erupted, clapping, answering a voice amplified through a microphone.

I was stuck, conscious of my shorts and T-shirt, my blonde hair, my white skin. Faces in the crowd glistened in the heat. Everyone was turned towards the square, like during Sunday mass when the priest is blessing the host.

'What's going *on*?' I dared to ask an old woman.

'Dr Williams is speaking.'

'Dr Williams?'

I'd forgotten what Venus had said about him. I'd forgotten everything in the heat.

'Who's *he*?'

'Our leader. Eric Williams.'

I stared. Every person in the square was magnetised, all ears pricked, listening. I was heat-dizzy. I wanted to sit down, go home. But there were too many people. I spotted some railings which weren't clogged, wheeling my bicycle towards the gap. I peeped through.

Hundreds of people, the town's people, were crushed around the elevated bandstand in the centre of the park. The bandstand doubled as a hustings, decorated with those menacing balisiers. A row of people sat on it, behind a table; they were also listening to the person speaking, hands folded on their laps.

Then, I saw him: a small besuited black man with thick spectacles. He was standing on the bandstand, in the middle, fronting the group. Surely, *he* wasn't the man they were listening to? His hands were thrust deep into his pockets, ever so casual. Two microphones stood in front of him, pointing downwards to his mouth. Yes, this *was* the man they were all listening to. This was Eric Williams.

'We have the honour,' Eric Williams proclaimed and my shoulders shivered, 'to put such a party at your service. We stand or fall by our programme, a comprehensive social security programme for the general welfare of the people of Trinidad and Tobago.'

A roar from the crowd. Hands reached up to him.

'Father, father,' they chanted. Some people held up balisiers like crosses, waving them. Eric Williams gazed out onto the crowd, nodding, a discerning smile spread across his face.

'Nor are we an *ordinary* party in the accepted narrow sense of the word,' he continued. 'We are, rather, a rally, a convention – of all and for all!'

'Yessss,' murmured the crowd.

'A mobilisation,' Eric Williams proclaimed, 'of all the forces in the community, cutting across race and religion, class and colour. Hence our name, the People's National Movement!'

Clapping burst out like thunder. The ground shook. Others were stunned, as I was, staring. Nothing like this had ever happened in downtown Port of Spain.

'Hence our programme, the People's Charter!'

'Yessss!' The crowd gasped.

'We repudiate imperialism, colonialism and racialism in every shape or form. We want self-government NOW for Trinidad and Tobago, in internal affairs, through a reform-based constitution.'

Another roar from the crowd. My skin was electric. I was nervous and sick to the stomach; it was like the nervousness of being aroused, of that kind of love. Charisma, oh, the trick of it. The lure of it. Somehow, also, I was miserable, scared and miserable and elated all at once. This man spoke words like poetry, tender and precise; the crowd was moved by the force of his conviction. Was he a doctor? Some kind of businessman? A lawyer? He appeared smart: white shirt, red tie, a black suit. Forty or so. He stood with one foot heel to toe with the next. He looked relaxed. *Relaxed.* Eric Williams was a political animal in his natural habitat, up there in front of thousands. Explaining his vision for the future. This Eric Williams beamed down at his people, speaking slowly and deliberately, all the time in the world on his side.

'People, we are here together. Let us unite, let us take our time, take back the future . . . shall we?'

His voice was jovial, rich, educated. He made jokes here and there at the expense of his opposition and of the colonial government. The crowd laughed, moving minutely together. Williams gossiped, too, as if letting the crowd into secrets high up in the order of things, as if sharing classified information.

I couldn't leave, couldn't tear my eyes from him. I was stuck, immobile. Wanting more, just like the crowd.

'Father, father,' people wailed.

The air was charged. Here he was, the man come down from the university, sharing his wisdom.

Eric Williams laid out his plans: a British Caribbean Federation, eradication of colonial political corruption, elimination of racial discrimination, promotion of education.

The crowd nodded, awestruck. They had never been given a man like this, not just for them; never heard these kind of words spoken, not for them.

Eric Williams spoke with clarity and confidence. His party, sitting behind him, were mixed in race. One was even a woman, bookish-looking in her horn-rimmed spectacles, her skin light brown. What was going on in Trinidad? George, my friends at the Country Club, had never mentioned this Dr Williams.

People around me started to notice my presence.

'Go away, white girl,' a man rasped.

'Massa here,' another shouted.

I edged the bike through a thinner part of the crowd, towards the next street, mounting quickly.

I pedalled fast, down to the dock. Everywhere the streets were deserted. The whole of town was in Woodford Square, listening to this messiah, his ideas for the future of Trinidad. Eric Williams' words rang in my ears. *Repudiate imperialism, colonialism.* I felt like I was new, like I had been shaken.

Forbes-Mason was three blocks away. As I arrived George was leaving. He was surprised to see me; then he noticed my reddened eyes. He tried to hug me but I didn't want to be hugged.

'Darling, what *on earth* have you been doing?'

'Did you know about this man?'

'Who?'

'Dr Williams.'

George's face dropped. 'Of course. You can't miss him. Haven't you been reading the newspaper?'

'No. I haven't. There's a mass of people in town, a huge gathering. In Woodford Square. All listening to him.'

'Yes, I know. There've been rallies. He was there last week, too. He's there quite often. Causes quite a stir.'

'And you never told me about him?'

'I didn't want to worry you.'

'I'm not a *child*. I'm not stupid! They want to *get rid of us*. We're not wanted here any more. They hate us. We came too late, George. Three years. We won't last that long. This is the end of things.'

'Don't be silly. It's OK,' he soothed. 'The British *want* to leave. They've been planning self-government for years. Their plans for a federation will go ahead. It's all been discussed. We *will* go. This man, Eric Williams, he'll be their first leader.'

'The British *want* to leave?'

'Yes.'

'But you said the British were going to stay for at least three years.'

'They will; this isn't all going to happen quickly.'

'The British no longer care?'

'The war left them in debt. These islands are like rocks around their neck.'

'What will happen?'

'Nothing. The people will inherit what we leave them. They can do what they like with it. It'll be peaceful here.'

'They won't kill us?'

George laughed.

'George, I want to leave.'

'We will.'

'I mean *now*.'

'Look, we're quite safe. We've only just got here.'

'Then why am I shaking?'

'You've had a shock.'

'That man was quite something. They all loved him. Was he a slave?'

'Of course not! There's no slavery any more.'

'They killed all the whites in Haiti. I know that.'

'Two hundred years ago.'

'They stuck white babies on spikes. Raped the women.'

'Dear God! You're mad. This isn't Haiti. You're talking rubbish.'

'But we're just as hated.'

'You could see it another way.'

'How?'

'This was bound to happen. You should be *pleased*.'

'Pleased?'

'This is exciting. Eric Williams is quite an orator – exceptional, in fact. We should be glad they have him and not some half-educated hooligan. Or a man who's decided to call himself a prophet, with a light in his eyes. He's not some crazy. He's using democracy, calling for a new order. We should be thankful it isn't worse.'

I was exhausted, my face caked with dust.

'I hate this place,' I rasped.

But George wasn't thrown. 'Come on, let's go home,' he said, caressing my hair.

I was twitchy until Venus arrived the next morning. I pounced before she had a chance to put on her apron.

'Were you there yesterday?'

'Where?'

'In Woodford Square.'

'Oho, de University.'

'What?'

'Dey call it de University of Woodford Square.'

'Why?'

'Dat is where Doc Williams go to speak to us. He speak about political tings. He like to educate de people. He der long time, man. Many times he speak. Granny Seraphina, she go to hear him.'

'I went there, too – yesterday.'

Venus's eyes bulged.

'I was on my bicycle. I rode into the crowd by mistake.'

'Madam, you crazy, in trute. Dat no place for you to be.'

'Never mind that. Have you been?'

'Once or twice. With Granny.'

'What does Granny think of him?'

'She tink he a great man. He been to Oxford University in England. He does write books and ting. Granny, everybody tank de Lord for Eric Williams. De contry will be safe wid him.'

De contry.

Dr Williams spoke in the same preposterous dialect even though he wore a suit and tie. The local English was spoken in an infectious sing-song. It wasn't just the way they spoke, that mad fusion of Europe and Africa, but how.

I was determined to be serious and speak the Queen's English. I didn't need education from Eric Williams, a man who couldn't speak properly.

'The country,' I tried to correct Venus, but she was inspecting the fridge.

'It empty, Miss. How ah suppose to mek food?'

I blushed.

'Let's go to the market then.'

'In Charlotte Street?' Venus stifled a grin.

'Yes, why not?'

'You wanna go der, Miss?'

'Yes, of course, I was there the other day. On my bicycle.'

Venus laughed out loud and slapped her thighs.

'What's so funny about me riding that goddamn bike?'

'Nuttin, Miss. You tink I sit behind you on dat green cycle. Nah!'

'Of course not. Don't be silly. Let's call a taxi.'

*

Charlotte Street was more hectic than the last time I'd ridden past. The market was even bigger than I'd guessed, sprawling across a whole block. I followed Venus into the midst of it, where vendors displayed their produce in a maze of long wooden trays used as tables. Weighing scales stood on each tray, blocks of rusted weights. Baskets the size of bass drums were all over the ground. Jars and jars of spices: nutmeg, mace, powdered ginger, star anise. Vermilion salted prunes, magenta dried mango. Castles of brown-sugared coconut candy behind glass cabinets. Bundles of blue crabs trussed up in string. Kingfish and snapper and careet. And fruit! Oh, once you could buy fruit in Trinidad, not like now. Trinidad was a garden once. Fruit was piled up like towers of jewels. I marvelled, wanting to pick up mangoes the size and smoothness of babies. I wanted to pinch them, squeeze them.

'Madam, you feel all right?'

'Yes. I feel fine.'

I stared, bewitched. Breadfruit and jack fruit and sapodilla plums. Guavas and jars of dark unguent which was guava jam. Custard apples. Pawpaws, which were rude and pendulous, somehow still growing. Tamarinds in their rough-smooth suit-cases. Choko and okra and bodi and pumpkins. Limes like grapefruit and grapefruit like cannonballs. Bananas still on their stalks, great emerald hands.

I followed Venus as she picked her way through the stalls. She knew exactly who to buy from and what was what. I tried to look natural.

I spotted another white woman, someone I recognised from the *Cavina*. Only weeks had passed, but it felt like an era.

'Gladys!'

'Sabine, hello, what a surprise.'

I almost jumped into her arms. 'How are you coping?' I asked.

Gladys was a thin, delicate-looking woman, her skin the colour of paper. Her shoulders were burnt, peeling, her hairline was damp with perspiration, her arms blotched with mosquito bites.

'I'm OK.'

I wanted to tell her about Eric Williams. 'Can you understand the people here?' I laughed.

'No!'

'I've already employed a maid. She makes me feel better.'

Gladys raised her eyebrows.

'She cooks. We were starving. She brought me here. Do you know what anything is?'

'No.'

I hugged her.

'Where are you living?' I asked.

'Winderflet.'

'Me, too.'

'This is Venus.'

Venus came forward.

'Venus, do these people here go to the University?'

'Yes, madam.'

I suddenly felt ashamed, on edge.

'What university?' said Gladys.

'In Woodford Square.'

'Oh, *him*. Yes.' An astute expression crossed her face.

'You're a teacher. What do you think of him?'

'He's doing a good job. No one can touch him. The *Trinidad Guardian*, as far as I can see, backs Gomes, his opponent. But Eric

Williams is an original. An ex-pupil of QRC, where we teach. He's revered there.'

'I saw him speak,' I blurted out.

'Gosh, that was brave.' I could see she was impressed.

'It was an accident. It's made me feel very different. Are you going to stay?'

'Yes. For now.' Gladys looked sad, though, her eyes a little wet.

'I want to go,' I said.

'But you've just arrived.'

'I can't stand the heat. And I don't feel . . . right, either.'

'Why?'

'We're not wanted.'

Gladys nodded. 'I know.'

'I'll stick it out, I guess. Three years.'

But Gladys wasn't listening.

I began to read the *Trinidad Guardian* avidly, a broadsheet not unlike the *Daily Telegraph* in layout, allied, of course, to the colonial government. Even so, it followed Eric Williams' campaign. I wanted to know what he was saying. And who was Gomes?

'Darling, you've taken a sudden interest in Eric Williams,' George commented one day, when he returned from the office.

The *Guardian* was spread out on the table. I was reading an article about Williams: *PNM and Women*.

I blushed. 'I'm just keeping an eye on him.'

'Yes. You and Sir Edward Beetham, eh? The Roman Catholic Church and the CIA.'

'What do you mean?'

'Everyone's keeping an eye on Eric Williams. Everyone is hurling abuse.'

'Why?'

George snorted with faint impatience. 'They're afraid he's a Communist, a nationalist, a Marxist, you name it. He's *uncommon*, that's all. In fact, I hear Sir Edward Beetham regards him with some esteem.'

'The Governor? Really?'

'Yes, dear.'

'Don't "yes, dear" me.'

'Sorry, dear. I mean, it's quite possible the British think highly of him. He's an Oxford man. But Williams doesn't like the Governor, or white people in general, even though he has a drop of white blood.'

'No! Really?'

'Yes, of course. It's common knowledge. His mother is a Boissière.'

I was shocked. 'You mean . . . like the woman who owned the Country Club?'

'Exactly the same. The illegitimate children lost the noble "de". Williams' mother was Eliza Boissière. A relative of no repute. An unwanted connection.'

'So he's part ex-slave, part aristocrat?'

'You could say that. Probably a prevalent mixture on this island.'

Later, when George was out of sight, I cut the article out and put it in a shoebox. And so that day I started my first shoebox file on Eric Williams. I was very careful to conceal my spy work from George. He'd think it very odd – he seemed to understand everything implicitly. Who was this black-white-slave-noble-man? I read everything I could about Williams. It made me less anxious. The more I knew, the less I feared him. The more I knew, the more I came to be intrigued by him. Eric Williams hated the likes of me, but I found I couldn't hate him back.

I quizzed Venus extensively about Williams. I wanted to talk to Granny Seraphina, too, know what she thought. But Venus was evasive; she often went quiet on me when I asked her about Granny.

'Can I meet Granny soon?' I pushed.

'Granny doh like visitors.'

'Oh, I see. I don't want to be a nuisance. But I'd love to meet her.'

'She fonny so, fonny about dese tings.'

'About what things?'

'Political tings.'

'Why?'

'She waitin', das what she always say. She doh like to talk much. But she waitin'.'

For some reason, I knew what this was like. But I didn't know what I'd been waiting for all my life. Images of Williams plagued me constantly: up there, on the bandstand, the crowd around him. Balisiers waved. My breath slowed just recalling that day. What he had to say, all those people listening to him. *Father, father.* And Williams so casual and self-contained. I was distracted by it all. I wanted to make love to George more. He was delighted with my new fervour.

One night, after a particularly vigorous session in bed, both of us spent and covered in sweat, I looked down at my husband.

'No one can touch him,' I whispered.

'What?'

'That's what Gladys said.'

'Touch who, darling?'

'What . . . what did I say?'

'You said, "No one can touch him."'

I stared.

George looked puzzled.

'Who, my darling?'

'Oh, nothing.'

I bent to kiss his mouth, covering my mistake, writhing and working George slowly back into a state of passion and all the time shutting my eyes tight, blocking Eric Williams from our bed.

CHAPTER FOURTEEN

THE ROBBER MAN

A month later we were invited to a garden party at the Governor's residence, one of the estate mansions on the savannah, next door to the Botanical Gardens. John and Irit were invited, too. Stockings and hats and gloves were in order, suits and ties for the men. We went together in John's Hillman, all a little nervous, the men in the front, women in the back, Irit clutching her hat on her lap.

'These stockings encase my legs just like sausages,' Irit complained. 'Why do the English insist on keeping up these bloody stupid formalities even in this heat? They are mad. I bought the biggest hat and most horrible loud dress just to annoy them. What do you think? It will be like an umbrella on my head, no?'

The brim of Irit's hat was almost a foot wide. Her dress was fussy and gay, made of fuchsia silk. 'I made it special,' she winked.

John indulged her every whim. 'You could wear a bag of coconuts on your head, my pigeon, and still look stunning.'

I wore a lace dress, gloves and a cloche of black feathers. George said I looked as if a dead corbeau had fallen from the sky and landed on my head.

The party was a grand but staid British affair. We made an entrance, Irit in her hat and inappropriate pink dress, me like a high-class call girl. Pale English women stood around in shapeless flowery tea dresses, hats and white gloves. Most looked about to faint.

'They look sick,' Irit whispered. 'Look at them. Half of them are ill. No colour. They look like they are dead.'

Mute black waiters glided about, trays of champagne flutes in their hands. Their silence was like the aftermath of an argument: righteous, powerful. Irit stopped a waiter. 'Ugh,' she choked, tasting the champagne. 'It's warm. Like cider. May I please have some coconut water instead?'

The waiter nodded and disappeared, returning with a glass of opaque liquid. 'This is better. Thank you so much.'

People stared.

Irit was indignant. 'Half these people are low class. They come from nothing back in England. They are no one. They come out here and are big fish. But just look at them. Half have no breeding, you can see it in their faces. They are peasants. And they think they are higher than the blacks. They treat them terribly. Give us all a bad name.'

A tray of canapés appeared. It was hard to pick anything up in gloves. Irit took hers off, swiping a vol-au-vent.

'Open wide.' She popped one in my mouth.

The men had wandered off. The invitation came through their bosses and they were obligated to circulate; this was our formal welcome to Trinidad. I didn't recognise anybody. Here was the colonial old guard: bureaucrats, civil servants, the Police Commissioner, his cronies. Hummingbirds hovered near the vases of Bermuda lilies, blurs of iridescent green, their wing-beats like a hurricane's fury. The cucumber sandwiches had curled, the stuffed eggs perspired and glistened like fat men, the salmon mousse had collapsed into itself, making a revolting pink mess. Ice in glasses vanished in minutes. Everything disappeared as we avoided the subject of the heat.

'I must try to behave myself, for John,' Irit smiled.

I recognised Bonny, one of the manager's wives from my first week. She blossomed from the crowd of pastel dresses, a flute of warm champagne clasped to her breast. Her eyes sharpened when she saw me.

'So.' She looked me up and down. 'How are you coping?'

'Well,' I pretended.

She forced a smile.

'This is my friend, Irit.' I gestured, turning to include her.

Bonny nodded stiffly, barely glancing at her. 'You've been to the Country Club?'

'Oh, yes. It's very nice.'

'And where else?'

'The beach, Maracas. It's beautiful.'

'Oh, my *dear*. You can't swim there. The currents will drown you.'

'I've swum there quite happily.'

Bonny grimaced.

'And I've been to the market in Charlotte Street.'

'Ugh, that dreadful place. I send my maid.'

'And to the University of Woodford Square.'

Her eyes widened. 'You can't be *serious*.'

'Yes. Eric Williams is a very interesting figure. Don't you think?'

'I can't stand him.'

I grinned. 'I think he's quite original. Inspiring, in fact.'

'Ugh, that awful man.'

'Why do you say that?' Irit stepped in.

'He has a chip on his shoulder. He's a racist. He only appeals to the masses. He'll do nothing for the whites here, the business class, those who've built and run Trinidad. He'll destroy what they've done. We will be forced to leave.'

'And go *where*?' Irit said, suddenly terse. 'Back to your mansion in England? To your big house in the country?'

Bonny stared.

'Back to your English servants there? Your butlers and chauffeurs? Your gardeners, eh, your serfs?'

'Eric Williams will destroy this country.' Bonny's eyes hardened.

'Oh really? He's a well-educated man. He's been to Oxford. He's an historian. How many people here can claim that? Do you think there's one person in this garden with a university degree?'

Bonny quivered, a snarl on her lips. 'Williams is *obsessed* with slavery. It's all about the past. He can't let it drop. He should forget about it. It's *so* boring.'

'What? Forget about the past, just like that? No one would *dare* say that to a Jew!' Irit growled.

Bonny was thrown.

Irit became ice-cold. 'Forget the Holocaust? Six million gassed. Oh, just forget about it. Get on with it?'

'That's different.'

Irit laughed. 'Yes, it is. At least they killed us lousy filthy Jews *quicker*. Six million in only five years. *Poof!* All in the oven. Slavery went on for hundreds of years. *Huuunndreds,*' Irit purred.

Bonny paled. 'Slavery and the Holocaust are two different things,' she stuttered.

'Yes,' Irit spat. 'But both barbaric genocide.'

Irit's fists were clenched. I was proud of her then. Bonny backed away from us, blending quickly into the crowd of tea dresses.

John lent us their car and we drove to Maracas Bay, a remote beach tucked into a curve along Trinidad's rugged north coast. This beach was famous for its strong currents and rough waters, just as Bonny had said. It was late afternoon and the waves were rolling onto the shore in measured swells. I chose a spot where the waves looked calmer and swam out far and dived deep and cried into the sea.

I hated Trinidad. I felt constantly misled, constantly in a state resembling grief. I didn't understand anything. And just when I thought I did, it was snatched out from under me. *Three years. George loves it. I'll do it for him.* The sea absorbed my tears. The water buoyed me up, made me light. It communed with the water in me. In the sea I became peaceful. I was a sea-creature. I sprouted fins on my ankles. A tail to swish. I swam somersaults and backflips.

George came out to me, paddling like a dog. 'I never knew you were such a good swimmer.'

'I've always loved the sea and the beach. We spent summers at the seaside, always.'

'The Med is flat, though.'

'Yes.'

'You're not scared of these waves?'

'It's the currents you need to be wary of. But you can see them.'

'I'm proud of you.'

'Good.'

'Are you OK?'

'I'm not sure. What kind of place have you brought me to?'

'Another world, a world we Europeans made.'

'It doesn't feel like Europe at all. Nothing makes sense.'

'But isn't that interesting?'

'No.'

'What don't you understand?'

'Everything.'

'Really?'

'I feel as if I have to learn everything again, what to say to who, who is who and why. Why I'm so funny on my bicycle? I wish you'd told me it would be so . . .'

'So what?'

'Restrictive.'

George looked sad. 'Just enjoy it, my love, while we're here. This island is rich and very, very beautiful. I'll show you round; you might change your opinion.'

'Just bring me here, to the sea, from time to time.'

'I will, my darling.'

We kissed and frolicked for an hour or so, till the sun began to set. We sat on the dry, warm sand wrapped in towels, watching the display – shades of mango, paw-paw and hibiscus swam in the sky. We drank a rum-cocktail mixture from a flask and I felt a little better. I loved my husband. Maybe he was right: don't ask questions. I squeezed his hand and he kissed my fingers.

'Paradise,' George said, hugging me.

That first year we wanted to watch the carnival bands. This meant a whole day in the sun. I decided on my favourite Chinese coolie hat with cherries on one side, a gift from George purchased on a trip to Paris. I wanted to dress up.

'I shall take Grand-mère's fan,' I decided. 'It'll be so hot.'

Grand-mère's fan, a prized possession, a hundred years old at least. Whalebone and lace, it resembled the wing of a decayed red admiral butterfly. Grand-mère used it in the high summer months, batting it against her chest. As a child, she let me snap it in and out, play coquette, stamp around her flat shouting 'Olé!', hiding my eyes dramatically behind it. Grand-mère's Chanel No. 5 still lingered in the fabric.

We parked at the nearest corner of the savannah and walked towards town. It was mid-morning and we joined the gathering throng; everywhere groups of people drifted in the same direction, towards Fredrick Street, some in costume, others like us. Open-top cars, full of white people, toured the savannah beeping their horns. They looked gay and happy and festive and black people stared at them as if they were the outsiders, a little odd and foolish.

In those days the carnival masquerade bands were small and fairly segregated. Whites and other light-skinned people stuck together. They played pretty mas by day and their bands were well ordered, parading in lines down the centre of the street or across the stage in the savannah. Some had brass instruments,

trombones, trumpets. Their costumes were fairly innocent: farm-
ers, cowgirls, sailors. The whites behaved in an orderly fashion, as
though attending an English country fair.

The black bands were more alive and seemed to be more spontaneous in their revelry. This was carnival born from the barrack
yards, the jamette class, a spontaneous festival of foolery and
trickery devised, years back, to ridicule the rich whites with
transvestism and piss-stained sheets. Carnival wasn't just dressing up, oh no, nothing so simple. It was first fuelled by ill-feeling,
by the loathing of the black man for the white master. As I
approached the top end of town it was with a sense of thrill mixed
with threat, a spectator and yet also an object, the spectacle itself.

The black masqueraders jumped in the streets, their bands accom-
panied by kings and queens, huge papier-mâché statues on
wheels pulled along by a cavorting man or woman. Enormous
butterfly creatures, fantasy insects, grasshoppers, begemmed
praying mantis. Contraptions of netting and sequins. In Frederick
Street we stopped, standing on the pavement outside Sa Gomes,
watching the bands parade past. I was grateful for my fan, hiding
behind it to watch. Men and women danced in a lewd manner,
rotating their hips in full circles, thrusting their backsides rhyth-
mically in and out, often inches apart. *Wining*, they called it.

A Spanish Armada floated past, papier-mâché galleon-head-
dresses bobbing on the sea of afro heads. Classical costumes, too:
the planter and the planter's wife, Dame Lorraine, a stock character still much lampooned. Statues of Donald Duck and Mickey
Mouse bobbed past. The American marines based at
Chaguaramas were unpopular. Little boys, painted blue or red,

tiny horns stuck on their heads and with pointy wire tails, ran around causing havoc. Devils. Jab Jabs.

I forgot to hide behind my fan. I wanted to join in, but didn't dare. I turned round to dance with George but he'd wandered across the hot road to take photographs. I waved at him and he waved back. I moved to the music, enjoying myself, closing my eyes, letting the rhythm take effect, climbing up through my soles, grasping my calves.

So I didn't see the ol' mas band arrive with its donkey carts and the men's faces blackened with coal; didn't see the Robber Man on his way through the streets, the carnival band in the street scattering. I heard his whistle, though, an ear-splitting screech.

My eyes shot open.

A tall black man stood in front of me. My heart faltered. He wore a wide-brimmed Cavalier's hat, a black ostrich plume curling from it. His silk cape was voluminous, covering his shoulders and torso. He carried a small box the shape of a coffin.

'Eh, eh! Look wa' we have here! A real life Dame Lorraine,' he said, looking at me. 'My God. Ting self, man! Look she fan and she hat. She dan dan.' He pranced around me, showing me off.

His entourage laughed. Children gathered round him, half frozen with fear, half awestruck. I was quickly encircled. At first, I wasn't too scared.

'Let me introduce myself,' he proclaimed, taking my hand as if to kiss it. 'I am the Night Invader, the Unthwarted Bandit of Paramin, the King of the Verdant Hills, Conjurer of the Clouds, Highwayman, *Body Snatcher!*' The children squealed. He bent to kiss my wrist formally, but snarled and slobbered instead.

I tried to snatch it back.

'Oho. She try to wriggle free.' He clasped my hand in a steel grip. 'Madame Lorraine doesn't like to look at me. Why so? She 'fraid? She does not know who I am? Why, Madame, wid dis whistle, I can call hurricane from de sout. I can break up de lan' wid earthquake. I does mash up de sea wid big waves, calling dem ovuh de norden range, over de hills of Paramin. I does wake up de dead!'

His henchmen crowed. The children darted about in circles. One poked at my shoes. The Robber Man clutched my hand.

'Eh, whitey. You here by yourself? Eh, eh, *she pretty like pretty self*. Doux doux. Sweetheart. Look how she blush and fan she face. You like it here in Trinidad? Have you sampled any of de local *delicacies*?' He rolled his hips, leering. By then a crowd had gathered, others joining his band, whistling, egging him on.

He stood up straight, about to make a speech.

'Eh, you like it here in Trinidad? Well, Miss, lemme tell yuh somptin: yuh days *numbered*. Go back to where you came from. De Doc go put allyuh on a boat. Send you home pack up head to foot, pack you tight, *in chains*. And if you doh like it he go pitch you overboard. You tink I make joke? Go back, white girl. Take my advice. It time for de people to have der day. We go run dis place, den you go see how yuh like it, eh? Maybe you get taste of your own *treat-ment*. Maybe we go bury you up to your neck near a red-ant nest! Paste your pretty mout wid *honey*.'

The crowd erupted, jeering.

The Robber Man lowered his head; we were eye to eye. 'Or *wossssss*. Fill dat lovely ass of yours wid *gunpowder*.'

The children shrieked.

'Blow you up like a cannon!'

He thrust his face close to mine and smiled sweetly. 'Eh, doux, doux?'

I trembled.

'De Doc, he does read books. He know a ting or two. Nature speaks in louder tones dan philosophy. Lightning announce thunder.' The Robber Man threw his cape back.

'I tell you dis. Plenty lightning now. He has appeared. Come to save his vexed and oppress children. He has come forward, cast down he bucket. Everywhere people will bless de name of de hero. *Eric Williams.* Trophies will be raised in his honour.'

I backed up against the shop front in a cold terror.

'Time to pay up, my plump white chicken!' The Robber Man opened his coffin. Inside, rolled-up banknotes and coins, a packet of cigarettes, bracelets.

Intentionally, I had left my handbag at home. George kept our money; he was nowhere to be seen.

'I h-have nothing to give.'

'Oh no?'

I shook my head.

The Robber Man stared lasciviously at Grand-mère's fan.

'No! You can't have this.'

'Oh, no?'

One of the children jumped up. Quick as a flash, the child snatched it and threw it in the coffin.

Wap. The Robber Man snapped the coffin shut. He smiled and bowed and doffed his fine hat.

'Good day to you, Madame Lorraine.'

He blew his whistle again. The band moved on and the Robber Man vanished.

When George reappeared with his camera, smiling, he found me dazed and limp, and then furious for no reason as I'd been happy on my own.

'What happened, darling?' he quizzed me.

'Nothing,' I spluttered. 'Nothing I want to talk about.'

Eric Williams: that year carnival was Eric Williams. I couldn't avoid him. A young calypsonian called Sparrow erupted into the public consciousness. Lean and hungry, Sparrow was a mesmerising showman, possessing a powerful baritone. When he laughed, a canyon laughed, deep and echoing, and it was hard not to laugh with him. Sparrow pranced and wined on stage in tight suits, his arse as rotund and muscular as a stallion's. Gold medallions nestled in his chest hair. In the papers I read that he had won both the Road March and Calypso Monarch competition that year. 'Jean and Dinah' blared at every public fête, pulsated from every corner parlour, every rum shop in the villages across Trinidad. He was the people's *other* hero, photographed everywhere with Eric Williams.

Eric Williams starred in my dreams. Sitting on the veranda at the Country Club, dressed in tweeds, silk tie, polished leather brogues, white waiters attending his every need. Bonny, the bitch, serving him tea and digestive biscuits on her hands and knees. Eric Williams was perusing the grounds of his ancestor, Poleska de Boissière, a white attendant taking notes as he spoke. Eric Williams preparing a speech. *I am going to let down my bucket where I am right here with you in the British West Indies.*

My shoebox file grew bigger. Cutting round the articles in the *Trinidad Guardian* that contained him. If I pressed and filed Eric

Williams he'd go away, he would stop pestering my thoughts and daydreams. Knowledge was power and with power I could conquer my preoccupation with him.

'Madam, you *crazy*. Why you put Dr Williams in a box?'

'That's where he's safe.'

'Why you 'fraid him so? He a good man.'

'I'm not *afraid* of him. I agree with you. He'll make a big difference.'

'Of course. Granny love him.'

'Will he give Granny what she's been waiting for? Running water, electricity?'

'Yes, madam. Everyting go change. I will have bath and light bulb and we go buy a stove. Granny Seraphina been saving for it all now. She keep her money safe under she mattress.'

'I'm sure she's right.'

'Yes, madam.'

'You think you can trust him?'

'Madam, if we cyan trust him, den who?'

I wanted things to change for Venus. I couldn't imagine her home. A shack? A shanty, up that cold hill in Paramin? I couldn't bear to ask. How many shared it? Two or ten? If she bathed in the street what did she use for her ablutions, her time of the month? The whole subject was her secret life, which we never discussed. Besides, we were only visitors. Who was I to distrust or, for that matter, give a damn about Eric Williams? Even so, I kept my cuttings. *Snip snip snip* round that homely scholarly face, the thick-rimmed spectacles. *Snip, snip snip* round his speeches, his meetings.

Once, George almost caught me. A shoebox was on the table,

stuffed with clippings. The words *ERIC WILLIAMS* and the year were written on the side of the box facing me.

'New shoes, my kitten?' he asked.

I quickly put my newspaper down, covering the box.

'Yes.'

'Can I see?'

I blushed. 'No. I was hoping to surprise you.'

His eyes filled with tenderness.

The box of notes on Eric Williams lay on the table between us. I almost told him then. Almost opened the lid and said, *See? I'm going mad here. I want to leave. I've lost my senses.*

George came forward and I stood. He put his arms around me and kissed my face, my neck, my mouth. I felt a swoon of love for him, the same swoon as on the first night we met.

And George *did* try to show me the sights. Friends from his office invited us to Toco, the very north-eastern tip of the island. A rough and ragged coastline. Choppy waves. The air fresh with the tang of salt and sea-grapes. But when we reached the beach house the tiny cove was secluded and the sea a lazy lace froth. Some of the froth looked irregular from afar, some of the bubbles bigger than the others. We didn't go into the sea at first. We dined at the house on the cliff-top, drank rum and ate buljol with Crix. We gossiped.

Later, I wandered down to the cove alone. The surf lapped the shore. On the sand, left behind in the wake of the waves, was something very strange: huge glutinous sacks dotted here and there along the shoreline. Bags of fluid, a frilled ridge along the top. The bags had long tentacles trailing back to the sea. These tentacles were black-blue and several feet long. Not one or two of these jellyfish, but many; I walked along the small beach counting as many as twenty. I looked out to sea and saw that the bubbles in the sea were in fact these jellyfish. Hundreds? Hundreds, like a fleet about to land. Was it the season? I turned and hurried back to warn the others and on the way I came across a gang of skinny children in the narrow lane leading to the house. One was a little Indian girl with long black hair, hanging to her waist. She was elfin, her eyes were black pools. She wore a pink dress and she was gesturing to me while holding out her other arm at a right angle to her body.

'Come an' see,' she said.

I froze.

'Get that *thing* off you!' I shrieked.

The little girl didn't have long hair at all. Along her outstretched arm she had arranged one of these lethal sea-creatures. The milky bag lolloped dangerously on her puny bicep. The tentacles were spread along her arm and dangled from it, like long black hair. The girl smiled, as if pleased with her magic, her ability not to be stung. She came towards me, as if to let me touch it.

'Keep away!' I gasped. But the little girl ran away with the huge jellyfish on her arm. Off to scare another. The other children shouted and laughed and chased after her, up the lane.

When I returned, I told the others what I'd seen.

'Portuguese man-o'-war,' said one of the locals in our party.

'Really?'

'Yes, it's the season.'

'So many?'

'Sometimes.'

No one believed me about the little girl, not even George.

'You're imaging things, darling.'

I wanted to throw my glass of rum in his face. He was always right about things. He had the facts. I didn't. He understood Trinidad. And I was always seeing what he didn't see.

We moved house. Forbes-Mason were still building a place for us and when I kicked up a fuss we were allowed to find another. Our new home was twice the size of the flat, tucked down a narrow street right opposite the Country Club. I danced around its empty shell. Three bedrooms, a dining and living room, a patio, a small garden. Furniture, too: new beds, tables, chairs, a proper fridge, a stove. A back yard. High walls and a driveway and suddenly there was space to breathe and be alone. Venus came with us and I could hop and skip to the Country Club.

The rains arrived. Not a drizzling affair. Not a piddling, piffling, pitter-pattering. Not a drip, drip, drip. Not the extended misery of an English winter, where the skies are always shrouded and sullen.

The rain came in a moment. From nowhere. A roar. The hair on the back of my neck stood on end, like needles. Goosebumps rashed my arms. It was a flood hurled from the sky. I shivered and felt guilty about something I'd done, searching my conscience. I sat in the living room and reached for a cigarette, puffing anxiously as I stared through the louvres at the sheets of belting water. What had I done wrong? What? Pools collected on our new lawn. I watched the green mountains all around. Voluptuous, the undulating hills of a woman. I saw her everywhere, this green woman. Her hips, her breasts, her enticing curves. Shoulders, belly. She encircled us. She laughed at us when it rained, shaking her hair. Birds stopped their chatter. The roar was deafening. The rain, when it came like this, was a lashing, a bombing.

Afterwards, the deep drains behind the house bubbled with brown water. Winderflet River flooded; it became bruised and swollen, the roadside gutters ran riot, engorged, bobbing with stolen goods: shoes, dead snakes, broken-up furniture. Potholes like tiny lakes appeared in the road. Crapauds lumbered out from under stones, burping, licking up the insects hurled from the trees. Mosquitoes, newly hatched, marauded in gangs, clouds of them. It was then I had my first conversation with the hills.

Feel better now, I spoke in a whisper.

Yes.

Feel relaxed?

Yes.

Well, I don't. I'm on edge.

Relax, she soothed.

You're beautiful, you know that.

So are you.

I hate you. My husband loves you.

They all love me.

How long will this rain last?

As long as it lasts.

Will there be a hurricane?

No, not this far south.

CHAPTER FIFTEEN

HE WANTS TO BE ONE OF US

April: a time of leatherback turtles. We were staying in an apartment on the north coast. I'd persuaded George to come for a swim with me not long after daybreak. The sky was still pale and the surf was tea-green. We sat under a coconut tree to dry off. I huddled in a towel in George's arms. He stroked my hair as we contemplated the surf. My skin was salt-tight. The swells were hypnotic, bulging. Then, near the shore, a dark shape broke the waves.

'Look,' I exclaimed.

The shape surfaced again, something like a small submarine. And then, in a moment, the animal appeared whole-bodied, its shell sleek, its limbs ancient and elephantine. A head like a boulder, a flash of razor gums. The creature heaved itself from the surf, its fins scraping at the sand, oddly mechanical in its gait. She didn't notice us, or, if she did, she was too exhausted to care about our presence. She shambled past us and began digging not fifteen feet away, her fins tossing up clumps of sand into the air.

George pressed his lips to my bare shoulder and I felt a thrill spread through my spine. He moved nearer. In minutes the creature had dug a deep well. She manoeuvred herself so that her tail hovered over the pit. I drew closer, too, following George. Then I understood why she didn't see us. Slowly, George waved his hand in front of her face. No response. She was in an altered state, a birth-trance. The creamy eggs cascaded from her womb. Eyeless, perfect, benign. The sight of them brought on a tender feeling. George reached forward and stroked her blind head. 'Good girl,' he whispered. His eyes were also glazed, his face placid: the monster between us was mute, almost desultory, a monument raised from unknowable silt depths. I wanted to put my hand out and catch one of her eggs, steal some of her mystery for myself.

When she was done, she sealed up the hole. We watched from a distance. When she disappeared back into the waves she left a distinctive pattern on the sand, which George carefully swept with branches from a nearby palm. We watched the ocean again and this time I felt an inexplicable emptiness. I felt separate from George, not closer for the experience. George stood at the shoreline and gazed after her for a long time.

George changed. Gradually, over the weeks and months after arriving in Trinidad, I noticed a difference. He stared up at the hills more and more. He would drive up there, up into the spine of Trinidad, past Arima, up to where waterfalls trembled from the green hills. He returned with stories of enclaves of Caribs still living in those hills, of shamans, of ordered mile-long lines of bachac ants, of butterflies the size of birds, blue morpho, of scarlet mountain roses.

George pored over maps, plotted days out, to central Trinidad, the east coast, Manzanilla, Mayaro, once a cocoa estate, where miles of coconut trees arced gracefully towards the sea like crowds of slender girls. Or to the famous Pitch Lake in the south, where thick black tar welled and oozed from the land. He wanted to see the golden tegu lizards at Asa Wright, the agouti, the honeycreepers, the plantations of christophine which covered the hills. Often I went along on these trips. I observed Trinidad as he did, this landscape parading its fertility, a banquet of eccentric delicacies. I had never seen a tiny tree spouting from the parched dried husk of a beached coconut; never seen fireflies, like fairy lights, like minute oil lamps, etching out the garden trees at night. I saw what George saw and knew, finally, that I had competition.

In June, when the rainy season arrived in earnest, the skies swelled and remained dark for most of the day. I didn't ride my bicycle. George bought a small Ford saloon and I took driving lessons. We found a new club. St Andrew's Golf Club was higher up in Winderflet. George played mostly in the early mornings in the rainy season. We socialised there on Saturday evenings, especially if there was a tournament. A barbeque, rum punches round the bar. Once, I came up to the bar to meet George and found him standing with a man I didn't know; his dark hair was slicked back with brilliantine. He was light-skinned, his eyes alert, teasing.

'Darling!' George broke off. 'Come and meet Sebastian.'

We shook hands and, either because he held a cold drink, or because my hand was damp, a crackle shot between us. Momentarily, it was embarrassing.

'This is my wife, Sabine.'

'You!' Sebastian dashed his electrified hand to his forehead. 'The white woman on the green bicycle! This is *your wife*?'

'Yes.'

Sebastian shook his head. 'Jesus Christ. Well . . . What a surprise. I'm very pleased to meet you.'

He smiled at me, a mixture of wonder and regret. '*Everybody* wants to know who you are. You've been causing a commotion. We've all been dying to know your identity. You cycle past my surgery. You stop traffic. Cars crash behind you. Haven't you noticed?'

'No.' I was too busy watching out for Eric Williams.

'You must be the only white woman *ever* to ride a bicycle through the streets of Port of Spain.'

'I come in to shop or meet George.'

'How long have you been here?'

'Six months.'

'Sebastian is a doctor, Dr Sebastian Baker, the best in town, I hear,' George explained. 'A good golfer, too.'

'Oh, I think I've seen your wife. At the Country Club,' I said.

'Christobel? Oh, good. She's on her way.'

My stomach tightened. I'd been intrigued by her, but also put off. Christobel hadn't changed her attitude over the months. A wordless communiqué between us: *Keep your distance*.

When Christobel appeared I stood my ground.

'Christobel, I believe you know Sabine.'

Christobel Baker towered several inches taller than me. Up close she looked even more regal, her skin honey-brown and buffed, a décolletage so voluptuous it was hard not to stare. Her dark bobbed hair was pushed back in a bandeau, revealing a high smooth forehead. Her eyebrows were arched and fine, eyes outlined in kohl. She peered down her long nose.

'Pleased to meet you, at last.' Her accent was local, sing-song, but nothing like Venus's broad dialect. Her voice was languorous, like her manner.

'This is the woman who's been cycling all over Port of Spain,' Sebastian chuckled. 'This is *her*.'

'You?' Christobel's eyes creased with mirth. 'Yes. I've seen you at the Club. We've never been introduced. But you're *famous*.' Her face cracked into a smile crossing the width of her face, dissolving my reserve, bewitching us all.

George, the fool, was completely smitten.

'Is there something wrong with cycling?' I asked.

'Well, no.' Sebastian was politic. 'But no one else would do it here, no white *local* woman.'

Christobel examined me. I felt the heat of her gaze, wished I'd made up my face, worn a more stylish dress, higher heels. My hair was wet after a shower, plastered to my scalp. I couldn't meet her eyes. I sensed she was wondering if I was attractive enough to steal her husband.

'How long are you here for?' she probed.

'Another two years.'

'Minimum,' George chipped in.

'Maximum,' I snapped.

'You're *already* counting the days?'

'I didn't mean that. It's just everything is so different here. Like my bicycle. I keep getting things wrong.'

'Where are you from?'

'I'm French.'

'Ah, my family were French, too. From Martinique.'

'Parlez-vous français?'

She shook her head.

I was disappointed.

'Christobel is fourth generation,' Sebastian boasted.

A fine specimen, too, I thought. The perfect hybrid to withstand
the West Indies. Her blended skin, her Afro-European features,
her demeanour. Proud of all this.

'What makes someone a Creole?' I asked.

'It's a birthright,' Christobel explained. 'Everyone *born* here is a
Creole of some sort, except the East Indians. They arrived with
their own culture intact. The rest of us have all been seasoned.
We've lost our native language. No one here speaks Spanish or
French or African any more. A little of French patois exists here
and there, in remote places. We're transformed from what we
were.'

'How?'

'The landscape, the sun. The temperature. The heat gets to us
all in the end, especially the Europeans. We've seen so many come
and go. Mosquitoes like white skin. George, you like it here?'

'Yes. This country is *ravishing.*'

I almost hit him.

'I love the sun, the temperature. I don't seem to notice the mosquitoes,' George smiled easily.

'You like the rum, too, eh?'

'Of course.'

'What about society?' Christobel said this with her nose in the
air, her chin set square.

'I'm bedazzled. In love with every creature made in Trinidad.'

'Really?' She batted her lashes.

'Trinidad is a place where God came to design the planet earth.'

'You are romantic, no?'

'This is where I want to live. Maybe even die.'

They were getting on my nerves.

'What do you think of Eric Williams?' I intervened. I studied Christobel, wanting her to answer this question, for it was a new question. I wanted answers.

'Oh *him*. Ha,' Christobel snorted.

'I've seen him speak, in Woodford Square.'

'That little *runt*? You couldn't pay me to go der.'

I was almost personally insulted. George looked awkward, but Christobel kept her cool.

'He's not a runt at all,' I retorted. 'He's been to Oxford.'

'That man, that bush nigger in a suit?'

I stared, incredulous. Her face was marked with bitter contempt. I had never seen such a look of superiority.

'Why do you hate him?'

'Hate him? He hates us – he wants to *be* one of us.'

'Well.' I looked her up and down. 'Isn't he?'

Christobel barely concealed a snarl. I flashed my eyes and smiled and quit the subject, not daring to ask what I thought: *Are you and Eric Williams related?*

When we got home I hurled a banana at George's head. It was in protest at his fawning.

'*Ravishing*. Oh God! Your eyes were on stalks!'

'So what? I can look, can't I?'

'She'd eat you for her dragon's breakfast.'

George was thrilled at my jealousy. 'Now, now, there's no need for that.'

'She was breathing fire all over you, you stupid man.'

'What about *him*?'

'Who?'

'Sebastian. He couldn't keep his eyes off you. He practically jumped out of his skin when you appeared. I bet he's got a pair of binoculars in his desk drawer. I bet it makes his day when you cycle past.'

'Oh, be quiet. She's such a snob. *She's* the jumped-up bush nigger. What makes her white and Eric Williams black? They're both a mixture. What gives her the right to look down on him?'

'It's a class thing, mostly, not colour,' George explained. 'Christobel is from the class of the master. Williams is from the class of the slave. She is a queen and he is a servant, that's the unspoken class structure between them. She doesn't like the roles reversed.'

'Well, *someone* in her family slept with the servants, that's for sure. Maybe that's what she doesn't like. That Great-Grandpapa was a common philanderer.'

'Very likely.'

'This place. French Creole, British, master, slave. A tiny fickle inward world, more snobby than England. Did you hear what she said about Williams? Do you think *she's* got much of an education? And I'm now supposed to stop riding my bicycle.'

'I love you on your bicycle. Please don't stop riding it.'

'Oh George! I *hate* Trinidad.'

'I love you.'

'I'll ride my bike for you, then.'

'It will make my day, puddle duck.'

'Oh, get lost.'

'Come here, duckling.'

Once, Venus was silent for a whole day. I couldn't penetrate her mood, no matter what I tried or said. I left her alone, which was always the best thing to do. She chopped vegetables loudly, and sighed heavily. We had become close, but I had still never met Granny, or visited her home up in Paramin. I had grown increasingly curious, but never dared invite myself or offer Venus a lift home. She lived in my house and knew my world, but her home and her world were none of my business.

'Oh God, Venus, what's wrong?' I blurted.

'It Granny.'

'What about her?'

'She join de PNM.'

'What?'

'She gone political, she say she done done. She sign up wid de political fellas.'

'That's a good thing, no?'

'She go see Mr Williams speak all over de country. She sleep out on de street. She gone for days, down sout, over in Arima. She gone mad.'

'You should be proud of her. Eric Williams will lead Trinidad. Maybe he'll employ Granny. That would keep her out of trouble.'

Venus giggled.

'I mean it. I hear he is very pro-women. He has very progressive ideas. How old is Granny, anyway?'

Venus went quiet and shook her head. 'Nobody know. She ent even know. Granny old.'

I smiled just at the thought of such a formidable pair of colleagues. Eric Williams as Prime Minister and Granny Seraphina as his deputy. Granny was still a mystery.

'I'd love to meet Granny.'

'Granny woh come here.'

'Then invite me round for tea.'

Venus rolled her eyes.

'Trust me.'

But Venus went silent again. No deal.

Late one Friday afternoon, I was cycling past the big church in Abercrombie Street when I spotted a commotion up ahead. I sailed right into the knot of cars, without a thought, finding myself behind a large flashy American car, a Buick. The car had stopped at the lights or maybe the lights had broken down or maybe there had been an accident, I'm not sure. I pulled up much too close to the left-hand side of the car and noticed a chauffeur in the driver's seat. I was wearing shorts and a halter-neck top, as usual. Up ahead I saw the cause of the hold-up: crates of oranges had fallen from the back of a truck.

'Eh, eh,' the chauffeur steupsed and beeped his horn. I peered surreptitiously into the back seat. In an instant, I recognised him. Eric Williams. The suit, the thick black glasses. He was sitting against the cream leatherette, composed – and looking straight at me! He was sizing up my backside. I turned quickly, head facing front, trying to think of a way past. My shoulders, my back, my legs blazed with fury. And yet, with the same sense of intrigue, the words he'd uttered that day, up there on the bandstand, came to me. *Repudiate colonialism.* I felt his gaze on me.

'Hurry up!' I shouted at the people ahead. Eric Williams was appraising me, his eyes shooting hot lines up and down my back. Another truck had driven across the road, blocking us.

The chauffeur beeped his horn. The second truck reversed back enough for me to slip past and I pedalled frantically, only to find the American car trailing me, beeping, trying to beep me out of the way.

Others began to notice who was in the car and a path cleared. I pedalled harder, refusing to get out of his way. His huge car caught up with me and then, for a moment, or maybe two, the car tracked my course, along the hot narrow street towards the dock, towards the Red House. That's where he was going, I presumed, for a meeting with those he was to replace.

I glanced across.

Eric Williams nodded. I wobbled and looked ahead. I glanced again. This time, he was abreast of me. His face had a studious expression, his head was tilted, as though wanting to ask a question. I had so many questions for *him*. I wanted to shout them across through the window. But our wheels moved forwards, both of us gliding as if on magic carpets, up Abercrombie Street. I wanted to scream but the words were caught up in me. *We're not wanted here. They hate us. We came too late, George. That little runt, that bush nigger, he wants to be one of us.* Panic rose in me, for no reason. And I was enjoying his eyes on me, squirming with the pleasure of his curiosity. I wanted him to look, yes; I wanted his eyes on me.

*

Riding home, I looked up into the hills of the green woman of Trinidad. She surrounded our home. Venus and Granny lived somewhere up there, hidden in the discreet folds of her thighs.

I understand nothing of you, I whispered to her.

One day you will.

I'm not planning on staying that long.

Go away, then.

Before I go, I'll venture up.

Like your husband does.

What?

He comes to look at me, all the time.

Really?

Of course.

I knew. I knew.

That night, George and I drank rum cocktails and dined on crab-backs and curried kingfish. Pepper and rum stung my lips. George lounged on the sofa with a novel and I stood by the open door, restless, looking out onto the porch. The night sky was alive, ablaze with fiery stars, with a ripening moon; the air was very humid. I turned to face my husband.

'George?'

'Yes, my love?' Casually, he looked up.

Slowly, I began to unfasten my blouse from the bottom upwards, pulling it open delicately, as though the fabric were opera curtains.

'Look at me.' I revealed the stage.

George's eyes lit up.

I pulled the blouse wider, exposing my flat belly, my breasts, which were firm and snug in a fine black-lace bra.

George gazed at me.

I shrugged my blouse to the floor and unhooked my bra, the cups relaxing. I held the bra to my breasts, gazing down at myself, the feast of me, and then flicked my eyes back to George, raising my eyebrows to make sure he understood that I was a gift, that he must never take me for granted. I smiled, dropping the bra. Moonlight fell on my shoulders. I caressed myself under the moon-curves of my breasts, running my palms over my nipples until they stiffened to points. I loved my young body. I turned slowly, so George could look at the shapes of me, the swells and swoops, my slim waist, the S of my back. My breasts, like fruit, like pears, soft and swollen in that first skin of youth. I lifted up my arms and arched my back so they moved like naked dancers.

George stopped reading his novel, oh yes. He came towards me on his knees.

CHAPTER SIXTEEN

THE HOUSE IN PARAMIN

Irit had opened a boutique at the top of Frederick Street, Zandolie, and it was a great success locally. It reeked of heady scents, the musky incense sticks she bought from Rastafarian vendors on the pavement: orangewood, frankincense.

'Like a holy place, no?' Irit laughed.

She served strong cardamom-scented coffee to regulars and had arranged a peacock-backed wicker throne in one corner which encouraged customers to sit and chat. We often gossiped while she sewed behind her tiny desk. Most of the dresses were her original design. She sold locally-made accessories as well as expensive smuggled-in watches and jewellery and crystal perfume bottles and handbags. The boutique was half cave, half Burlington Arcade. You could buy Cartier and Rolex watches and brooches carved from a coconut husk.

'Guess who came yesterday?' Irit gushed one day.

'Who?'

'Eric Williams.'

'No!'

'*Oui.*'

'On his own?'

'Yes, of course. Late, after I'd closed. Earlier I'd received a telephone call from his secretary. She asked me if he could come then. He likes to be private.'

'And he came?'

'Of course. He has very good taste. He likes to give presents.'

I couldn't hide my amazement.

'He bought several things, all the most expensive. He knew exactly what was what, has a very good eye for what a woman might want. He even asked me to order something, too, something from New York. He chose all the finest quality.'

'What was he like?'

'Charming, natural. I liked him. We talked. He sat down and drank my coffee.'

'I don't believe it.'

'Yes. I am a Trinidadian citizen now. I will vote for him in September and I told him so.'

I felt heat blossom in my face, heat in my chest. 'I bet that shocked him.'

'No. He has whites in his party, some influential French Creoles. He's not stupid; he wants his party to appeal broadly. And he's a man, he likes women. I fluttered my eyelashes at him.'

'He's married, no?'

'Yes.'

'He bought gifts for her?'

'I didn't ask! He has many friends, I expect.'

'Where did he sit?'

'Where you are. Right there.'

'Williams sat *here*?' I almost shot straight out of that great peacock-backed chair.

'My dear. You're blushing like a child.'

'Don't be ridiculous.'

'Well, nothing wrong with that. I blushed, too. He will be in charge. Run things. Power, *ma soeur*. I had to go home and have a cold shower afterwards.'

'I saw him speak a few weeks ago, down in Woodford Square.'

'Yes – I know.' Irit's eyebrows rose. 'Good for you.'

I wanted to tell her about my boxes of clippings, how I'd been following Eric Williams' career. I wanted to confess, as though it were a sin.

'The PNM will win this election in September and then all the British will leave soon afterwards. Give them a few years. Then the PNM will run things, formally. The Queen will come and shake hands and say bye-bye. Williams will be Prime Minister.'

'We will leave, too.'

'Oh yes?'

'Yes. Our contract will be up by then.'

'And you think George will leave his new job and all that is happening here? Go back to that dreary weather and all those grey, sick-looking people in England? Live in the suburbs? Why should he go back?' Irit levelled her long lashes at me. 'What's there for him? Why don't you like it *here*?' Irit spoke like a villain, like she was in cahoots with the PNM, part of their secret force. And for a moment I didn't doubt that she had charmed Eric

Williams. I could see them conferring, thick as thieves, both cool and glamorous and serious in their intentions.

In September 1956, Election Day was fraught: a British warship was anchored in the Gulf of Paria, another off San Fernando in the south. Eighty per cent of the population turned out to vote with long winding queues all over Trinidad. Schools and community centres were packed. That evening the masses rallied in Woodford Square, baying for Eric Williams to be with them, beckoning him from a cool shower, his hot dinner. Euphoric, he went to speak to them again, taking the bandstand. His public speeches had already made him an iconic figure: in a year, he'd caused a revolution without spilling a drop of blood. Eric Williams' PNM won thirteen of twenty-four seats; it was all announced on television.

Irit was exuberant. 'I'm glad for them,' she toasted the PNM. 'I'm glad they will kick those fat horses out. Hooray for Trinidad and for Eric Williams. I gave Glory the week off. It's like carnival again this year, eh? Mas in Port of Spain, everybody drunk. I think the people are shocked. This is historic, no? *Viens*, come over for some rum punch.'

Helena was cautious. 'So now maybe the Country Club will accept me as a member.' She smiled her serene, distanced smile. 'I'll be the first to put my name down. Or maybe I won't. I'll see. Maybe now I'll have the choice.'

Venus was overcome. 'We goin' to de Red House to celebrate, madam. Granny gone already. Ah meeting her der. She cryin' all day, she overcome. She dancin'. De house decorated wid PNM flags, wid balisiers. Oh gorsh. Dis a good ting, madam. Carnival in tong in trute.'

Carnival, the Robber Man, bloody Eric Williams and his big flashy car, his robber talk, the people of Trinidad absorbing his every word up there on the bandstand. I thought of that hot day in Woodford Square, of his queer stare through the window of the car, his eyes on me. Something wasn't right and I couldn't put my finger on it. Eric Williams now had the chance to deliver what he promised. Love? Oh God. The people of Trinidad were in love with him, all right. Somehow, we all were – such was the need for him then and there, at that particular hour in Trinidad.

I was happy for Venus. This was her victory. Even so, we stuck to our own kind. We entertained a lot at home, socialised with our own type or Trinidadians of our own class, those with light skins who went to the clubs, others from George's working world. We refrained from talking politics.

We drank more rum.

I brooded. When we'd left Southampton eight months earlier, I hadn't bargained for this. I thought we were coming to a friendly charming island. Palm trees. Beaches. I hadn't bargained on sullen black women in the supermarket, on being laughed at on my bicycle, on 'racism', on snooty French Creoles, on seas infested with man-o'-war, or this Eric Williams and all that came with him. I wanted to make sure George was on board, that he too would be looking forward to getting back to a life in a temperate country.

'I want to have a baby,' I informed George one morning.

'All of a sudden?'

'No. I've been thinking about it.' My thoughts were that once children came along, George would see sense, pack up and go back to England at the end of our contract. 'I want *your* babies, remember?'

'Of course.'

'And I want to leave in two years, before we're sent back all tied up in chains.'

'What do you mean?'

'Like the Robber Man threatened. I want to come and go in peace.'

'We will.'

'You'll be sad, won't you?'

'Yes. I'm not afraid of the Robber Man.'

I inspected my brown skin. It was impossible to stay indoors all day. I was changing, too, in some indistinct way. The heat made me weary, less me.

'I don't want our children to be Creole,' I told George. 'It's far too complicated. I want them to be English, European. I don't want my children to be part of this.'

'But "this" is exciting.'

'I want to leave.'

'But we've just got here. Remember, a few months ago. I'm doing well in the job. The boss is already talking promotion.'

'Really?'

'Yes.'

'But you said three years.'

'And you said you were flexible.'

'I was. Before I got here.'

Two months later, I was pregnant. With my son in my belly, I rode past the same spot where our crate marked *FRAGILE* was tossed onto the dock, where the old Chevrolet waited for us. I gazed out at the Gulf of Paria, wanting to jump in; I could have happily swum back to England. My head was full of ideas and possibilities, and of what lay ahead, of what I would do when we got back to England. Two years away. I thought of the new woollen clothes I'd need in England, new shops I'd visit. Shops! And theatres and cafés and everything would be familiar and I could say I'd once lived in Trinidad, but it was a strange place. That the people there were waiting; that they were somehow *en train d'attendre*. And that I'd never felt at ease there. We had arrived at the wrong moment. Eventually, I'd acclimatise, get used to England again. Eventually, I'd forget Trinidad completely.

My son was born in the month of August. *The Mountain*, a Spencer Tracy film, was showing at the Starlight Drive-In at the shopping plaza in Diego Martin; we didn't see it all. My waters broke halfway through, flooding the car seat. George sped me to the Park Nursing Home opposite the cricket oval in St Clair. Dr Sebastian Baker met us there.

'Here we go, Sabine,' he smiled, all scrubbed and gowned. Sebastian Baker had a talent for doctoring, especially this kind of hands-on work. In his green theatre gown, he was no longer the ladies' man, the limer, drinker, raconteur. He was tense as a scholar in his approach, gracious in his bedside manner. His eyes glinted and he smelled of antiseptic soap.

'No wriggling,' Dr Baker joked softly, placing my legs in the stirrups. My son had curled up inside me, his backside pointing downwards as if he were already suckling my breast. The midwife remained mostly silent yet I understood her every instruction: breathe, push, pant, strain, push again. George had brought me in at half past ten and by two in the morning there was still no progress.

The baby was stuck, unable to turn around. Dr Baker grew calm, and calmer still as the evening wore on, as I panicked more.

'This may have to go Caesarean,' Dr Baker muttered.

'No!' I cried, more frightened of the knife than anything. 'I don't want a big scar. I want to wear a bikini!'

Dr Baker raised his eyebrows.

'I'm serious!' I shrieked. I *was* serious. I'd seen other woman with Caesarean scars, a great mess on their stomachs, as if clamped back together with coat hangers.

Dr Baker fell quiet. Sweat beads popped on his forehead and the air was a fog despite the jalousie shutters. The delivery-room lights dazzled like radiant sunshine even though the clock showed the dead of night. But I'd more strength left in me.

'Please, no knife, no cutting,' I begged.

The midwife steupsed and turned her back, busying herself in the corner.

'Please,' I whispered.

Dr Baker nodded.

I lay back on the hospital bed and prayed, opening myself up wide. His hand slipped inside me, enough to get a gentle grip, enough to turn my son round. Oh, he was quick as a fish. In and out and then he caught my son as he slipped from me in his coils and fluid.

It rained. It rained my son. When the storm broke, relief surged through me, racking my body in aftershock. I bucked out the rest of what was inside me, the swell sending me into a stupor, a grand and intoxicating relief, the relief of all births, of all deliverances. I wanted to sleep heavily and immediately but George ran in from the waiting room, speechless.

'A boy!' he cried. George kissed me, weeping, his warm tears falling onto my damp face. Dr Baker and the midwife attended our new baby.

Venus was delighted with our firstborn.

'Watcha go call him?'

I had already suggested the name to George, on the way home. He'd agreed. It was a fine name.

'Sebastian. Sebastian Wilfred Harwood.'

'Madam, he so handsome already. How he get so handsome?'

Two years later, again at Park Nursing Home, I gave birth to Pascale. She was bonny and bright-eyed from the day of her birth. We took her home and she fitted right into things. George had persuaded me to stay *one more* year. I agreed.

Now we were four. A family. This was a new time for us. My children were both born on the island. They were Creole. I was only dimly conscious of this, at first. Venus mothered them almost as much as I did, hugging them to her black breast, singing them her African lullabies, loving them as her own. They wore her smell as much as mine, they knew her voice, obeyed her wishes. They kept her in their eye, tracked her movements. She could hush them when they cried. So my children knew two mothers: one black, one white. They extracted love from us equally, needed us equally. I wasn't troubled by all this, not at first. I was glad of Venus's help. In her large extended family an infant was always being nursed. Venus owned a natural passed-down wisdom when it came to mothering and I observed her. I came to care for her sons, too. Granny Seraphina looked after them mostly. Granny Seraphina: by then she had become a fabled luminary, such was the reverence with which Venus spoke of her. I saw Bernard and Clive now and then, Venus's children, when Venus brought them over. Even so, my relationship with Venus's children was different. They didn't wear my smell on their skin.

George and I made love often, sometimes twice a day. Once, George returned home from work early, full of passion. The children were asleep, Venus was preparing dinner.

'I've been thinking of you,' he whispered into my neck, as he pulled me into his arms.

In the bedroom he peeled off my clothes, gasping at my still-swollen belly, my milk-laden breasts. I was overripe, vulnerable, fruit exploded and fallen from the branches of my former life. George fed on me, just like an infant, even more love-struck with the mother-wife I'd become than the girl he'd met on the beach-front. He delighted in my body's changes; he was intoxicated with my new shape and smells. Our lovemaking was full of hope for the future.

In the early hours of the next morning, the room was still dark and the day still unbroken when George moved over me.

'I know you're all relying on me,' he whispered. 'I know only too well. And you can trust me. I'll be there for you, all three of you.' But he sounded lost or somehow sorry for himself.

The children learnt to swim before they could walk. We tied a foam bubble around their honey-brown bellies and tossed them in the sea. Both swam like dolphins. The four of us often went to Tobago to swim in the flat transparent waters at Pigeon Point.

'They'll be so different from the other children when they return,' I commented. 'Like little urchins.'

'Sea urchins,' George laughed.

'We can send Sebastian to your old school.'

'Indeed,' he agreed.

I was happy then. I saw us moving back to our house, a wedding present, in Harrow on the Hill. I saw the children living at home with us. They would have dual nationality – born in the Caribbean, but able to get British passports because of George. I saw them integrated and settled back into a more civilised lifestyle. Little did I know that George's old school took boarders.

But we stayed on – signed another contract. Forbes-Mason promoted George to managerial status. George persuaded me: he was so eager about the new position in the company.

'And our children are so perfect, like you,' he whispered. 'You have made me rich. Let me repay you. Let me make something of myself here.' We fell into a swoon of success: George's new position, a bigger salary, our beautiful children. I was almost happy in that small house opposite the Country Club. The babies distracted me.

'I want to show you something,' George announced one day.

'Now?'

'Yes.'

'What is it?'

'I'll take you there.'

'But the children . . .'

'Venus is here.'

I went to get my handbag and sunglasses, rather excited, hoping George had bought me a present.

He drove me down Saddle Road, way down, past St Andrew's Golf Club and then past Andalusia Estate, where the road became very broken and full of potholes; then even further down into lower Winderflet, following the river, driving towards the turning for Maracas.

'Are we going to the beach?'

'No.'

We turned a corner. Ahead of us lay a stretch of badly surfaced road, a wall of mountains to the right, to the left what had once been a cocoa estate, Perseverance Estate, now fallen into ruin. George drove a little further and stopped the car.

'Why have we stopped?'

'To look at the view.'

'What view?'

'Of our land.'

'*What*?'

George got out and walked over to my side, spreading his arms out, gesturing across a wide expanse of bush. 'What do you think?'

I stared.

'George, what do you mean?'

'All this is ours.'

'You're joking.'

'No. I paid one dollar per square foot. I've bought three plots, all this right along the road.'

I didn't get out of the car. George got back in and started the engine, driving slowly past his purchase, examining it with pride. I was silent, trying to understand. We'd passed this stretch of bush many times on the way to the beach. I had ignored it; it was meaningless.

'Don't you like it?'

I laughed.

'It's prime property.'

I glared at the land. Impenetrable scrub; the grasses were neck high. It wouldn't have been possible to walk on it.

'What do you think you're going to do with it?'

'Build a house.'

'*What*? You're *crazy*. Oh no, no, no. Here?'

'Yes. Why not?'

'I'm not living here! In this jungle.'

'We'll raze it all, clear it off. You'll see.'

'Nobody lives out here, George. I'm not living out here on my own, with you at work all day. Are you mad?'

'Others will buy. We're the first.'

'We already have a home. In England, remember?'

His eyes glazed over.

I understood it then: now that I had babies George thought I was content *for ever* in Trinidad.

'Stop the car,' I commanded. George stopped. I got out and slammed the door, stalking back the way we came, down the broken tarmac.

George ran after me. 'Sabine, Sabine, I'm sorry, darling . . . please . . . I thought you'd be excited. Try to see, try to think ahead. It'll be beautiful here one day.'

I turned and bashed his chest with my handbag, hitting him again and again. Then I slapped him hard across the face.

'You fool,' I shouted. 'I won't live out here. What do you think I am? You think you can bring me out here on a *safari*? You think I'm made for this, all *this*,' I screamed, pointing up at the dense glowering hills which surrounded the land he had bought. 'You think I've gone native, too, like you. Creole? Eh? You think I like this island as much as you do? No. I'm not living here, *ever*. Do you understand? You're a fool, a stupid English fool. It's time to go anyway, George. Can't you see that? It's time for us all to go.'

Later that day, after Venus had left, I drove into Port of Spain to shop. On the way back, I spotted her carrying a heavy bag on her head. She'd been into town, too, and was on her way home. It didn't occur to me to drive on, that she didn't want a lift from me, that this was how we had arranged things over the years, every-thing separate after working hours. I slowed down.

'Venus,' I called across. 'Want a lift?'

She looked askance at first.

'Come on. Hop in,' I urged. 'I'll take you to the bottom of the hill, if you like.'

Venus gave in, smiling. I could tell the bag was heavy.

'Tanks, madam.'

And then she was in the passenger seat, me driving her, the two of us outside my home for the first time since we'd met five years before. We drove along in silence. Quickly we came upon the spot where I had agreed to drop her off, but I turned left rather than stopped. When she didn't complain I accelerated, up Morne Cocoa Road, which once connected the plantations in one valley with other plantations; the road wound and rose steeply.

'I shall take you home,' I said, decidedly.

Venus made a wry smile. I took this to mean I could come up. It wasn't exactly an invitation. I was delighted. Even though I wasn't a confident driver, I managed those hairpin curves.

'Stop,' Venus said suddenly, as I approached a particularly steep bend.

'Here?'

'Yes.'

I looked across.

Back from the road, surrounded by bush, was a house. Or, more accurately, what was left of a house, an old chattel house, its exterior so ancient it seemed somehow silken, as if settled on by thousands of moths. The roof was made of sun-bleached planks nailed haphazardly. Remnants of heat-soiled fretwork clung to the eaves. Once, there had been sturdy posts for legs. But now the house balanced. On rubble, on broomsticks and bedheads and planks of wood jooked up into its under-work. Beneath the house rose piles of flat river-stones which had been carefully laid on top of each other to make columns. One corner of the house jutted into thin air. A flight of skinny concrete stairs ran from the ground up to the front door. But there was no front door. Instead, a grey and ragged sheet, knotted in the middle, hung as the door. Despite its utter disrepair, its bone-bare exterior, the house had a faint air of contempt. The house gazed down at me.

Venus saw the concern on my face.

'Madam, six generations borned in dat house,' she said. 'Dat house steady as a *rock*.'

'I'm sure it is.'

'Yeah, man.'

I laughed. It was late afternoon, still light.

'Granny,' Venus shouted upwards.

I was nervous at the prospect of finally meeting Granny Seraphina. I looked around. Outside the house, on the well-swept dirt floor, a living area had been set up, four battered plastic garden chairs in a circle, a blackened coal-pot near the concrete steps. A cockerel and some chickens pecked about. Other homes crouched in the long grasses near by some were wooden and decrepit, just like Venus's house, designed to be movable once, years ago. They had become grindingly permanent, part of the hill itself. The neighbourhood was silent and the immense and hovering Paramin mountainside seemed to cause this silence.

The sheet curtain at the door quivered. A thin dark figure appeared on the top step, a toddler clamped to one bony hip. She wore a plain shift dress and her white-wool hair was covered by a red headscarf.

'Granny,' Venus called up. 'Come down and meet Mrs Harwood.'

Granny stiffened, perceptibly, at the sound of my name.

Venus smiled at me. 'Doh mine Granny.'

I nodded.

Granny began a stiff-legged climb down the concrete stairs; it looked somehow theatrical. Her legs were so spindled that she took each step slowly and emphatically, one by one, making us wait, as though she were a dignitary.

'Sit down,' Venus offered, and gestured to one of the plastic chairs by way of hospitality.

'We have Cannings sweet drinks in de cooler. Big Red, Mango Solo. Cokes.'

'A Coke would be wonderful,' I said, sitting down.

Venus disappeared round the side of the house.

I sat with my back facing Granny. Sweat sprang in my palms. When she appeared all at once, in front of me, clasping the toddler, I rose to my feet.

'Hello, Granny, I've heard so much about you.' I fought the urge to curtsy. Granny didn't put out her hand to shake mine, didn't even say hello. She simply nodded, presenting herself, as if no further introduction was necessary.

So, this was Granny Seraphina. Her face was small and rounded, a concoction of mahogany curves. Her eyes were hideous, a crystalline yellow-gold, the eyes of a wary jungle cat. The expression in them was stern, derisory. It was impossible to tell her age. Ninety? A hundred and fifty? Granny was no slave – but her parents, yes, certainly. Clive, Venus's oldest child, a two-year-old, clung to her hip and stared at me with a look akin to Granny's.

'Sit down,' Granny ordered.

I sat again and she sat too, heavily, with the child. I smiled and sweated and tried to meet her gaze. We sat for what seemed like minutes.

'Venus tell meh you been to de University,' Granny said, abruptly.

I was amazed that Venus had mentioned this.

'Yes.'

'Hmmmmm.' She nodded, clicking her throat.

'He's quite a speaker, isn't he?'

Granny nodded slowly, as if at something else, as if she wasn't quite with me.

I was determined to keep up a conversation. 'Venus tells me you're now a member of the People's National Movement.'

Granny smiled, full-toothed. 'Tink you might join, too?' Her face broke and she grinned: a trick question.

'Would the PNM have me?'

Granny's eyes glowed; they searched my face. 'Join, nuh, see what happen.'

'I'm afraid I'm not as devoted as you to their ideas. I'm only a visitor here. Eric Williams will be Prime Minister and we'll be gone by then, with many others, I imagine.'

Granny cocked her head. Her mouth set into a glum determined grimace. 'You like it here, in Trinidad? You enjoy your stay?'

I looked around. The shack seemed as if it might tumble down the hill any moment. I felt alone and humbled and wanted to tell the truth.

'No. I don't like it here.'

Granny nodded.

'Trinidad doesn't like me.'

She seemed pleased with this.

'Eric Williams doesn't like me.'

'No, man. Time fer change.'

'Yes, Granny. I can see that.'

'De Doc a smart man. De smartest man in Trinidad.'

'Are you sure about that?'

'Yes.'

'Have you met him?'

Granny clicked her throat. She shook her head.

'I think he's unique. So does Mr Harwood. A man like him comes along once a century.'

'Most white people doh tink so. Dey 'fraid he.'

'I know.'

'Jealousy.'

'Yes. Or nervous.'

'Dey is nervous, man.'

'Granny, I'm the same. Make no mistake.'

'You 'fraid de Doc?'

I nodded.

'Praise de Lord. Don't be afraid. Doc Williams de fadder o' alluh us. Bless Dr Williams.' Her face lit with reverence. Her yellow eyes rested on me, righteous and placid, as superior as Christobel had been. 'Eric Williams arrive too late in my life. But he' – she jiggled the toddler on her knee – 'he will grow up into a different society. Tings will be different for he. My grandson. Maybe even Clive will be Prime Minister one day.'

I looked at her carefully. 'Well, he has a good role model.'

But Granny's face fell as she gazed at the ground, at her feet, at a future full of promise. She was ready for it. And there was something in the way the child Clive regarded me, something so blank and evidently indifferent, which made me feel uneasy.

CHAPTER SEVENTEEN

MASSA DAY DONE

Eric Williams was bombastic as Premier Minister. Occasionally, he still delivered lectures in Woodford Square.

'He has a chip on his goddamn shoulder,' asserted Christobel Baker, just as Bonny had. All the local whites thought this. Granny was right, they were scared of him. They all despised him. 'It's all so personal for him,' Christobel sneered.

'He's got small-man's syndrome,' said another.

'He's out of his depth.'

'The son of a postman.'

Mostly, I made my cuttings late at night. In the kitchen. When Venus was asleep. George, too. I retrieved the out-of-date newspapers from the stack in the garage and cut around the stories of the day: Williams and the PNM; Williams and his plans for Federation. His private life, too: Williams and his daughter Erica. He was everywhere, the man-of the-moment. My shoebox files grew to six boxes. I knew it was strange, after all this time, still to be cutting him out. But I found I couldn't stop.

When Venus mentioned Williams was giving one of his lectures in Woodford Square and that Granny was attending, I decided to go along.

I left the children in Venus's care, quietly slipping out with the excuse of a shopping trip. I parked near by and walked into town, skirting Woodford Square, slipping in at the back of the gathered throng, peering through the railings.

The square was packed and Eric Williams was up there on the bandstand. My stomach churned. He had that effect. My heart thudded in my chest. Yet I was eager to hear what he had to say. It was March, 1961. The sun lashed down on us in that square. I'd brought a large straw hat and kept my head lowered under it. Long sleeves hid my white arms. Whites still didn't attend these lectures; George, my friends, would have thought me mad, irresponsible to be there. Maybe I was. That day, he was alone at the hustings, no party behind him. And I noticed he'd gained props: heavy dark glasses, a hearing aid.

I clasped the bars of the railings, peering through. Williams was in full flow, a preacher, a man of words addressing his people. There was a relationship between him and the crowd, a form of mass intimacy. I scanned the crowd for Granny and yes, spotted her there, amongst the sea of heads, halfway between where I stood and the bandstand, her white hair covered by the same red headscarf. She gazed upwards, a look of serenity on her face. The whole gathering was in a state of earnest admiration, gazing as one. Thousands? Yes, thousands gazed towards the bandstand; thousands were hanging on Eric Williams' every word.

'Massa,' he was explaining, 'was a symbol of a bygone era.

Massa was usually an absentee European planter who exploited West Indian resources, both human and economic. Massa came for the short-term. Massa pulled out when things got bad and sugar ceased. Massa often left the small islands as undeveloped as he found them. Wealth that should have been ploughed back into the island went everywhere else. All that Massa left behind was his name on the land or sometimes on a beach.'

I squirmed with the shame these words inspired. George and his piece of land. Harwood's this, Harwood's that. Would George also want to name pieces of Trinidad? My fingers gripped the railings of the park. Ahead of me, Granny raised her fist and shouted above the others. 'Yes, man. Down wid de damn blasted colonial Massa!'

'Massa,' Williams continued, 'used the whip liberally to control his workers. Two hundred lashes was *common*. Massa's economic policy was to grow one crop only: sugar. All else was imported for his table. The African slave kept alive the tradition of agriculture in the West Indies, growing food for his own subsistence. The one-crop policy stunted West Indian society. A Royal Commission in 1897 attacked Massa for making it difficult for the peasant to attain land. Massa ignored the Royal Commission, continued with his one-crop policy until 1930. Massa's economic domination of the region reduced the population to drudgery, giving them a profound distaste for agricultural endeavours.'

Cheers of recognition. I began to feel distinctly uncomfortable. Yet I couldn't leave the square. Where would I run to? The sun beat down on me, punishing me. Why should I run? I didn't even care to. Let them tear me apart if they wanted. Williams mesmerised me. He was animated, enjoying himself. Williams spoke with words which sang and lifted hearts. He lacerated and lampooned the old way of things, the old ideas. He moved all those around me. Granny's fist was raised in the air, a salute to him. Around me, faces gleamed.

But Eric Williams was cool in his suit and tie. He dressed just like my husband. His tone of voice was dry and sarcastic, as clipped as any Englishman's. Eric Williams lectured on and on and the sun beat down. The crowd swayed as if they might all faint as one.

'Massa,' Williams continued, 'had the monopoly of political power – this was why he could do all these things. He used his power shamelessly for his own private needs. Massa's economy was distinguished by a scandalous waste of labour: forty house slaves was common in Jamaican planter homes. Demeaning work, total contempt for the human personality. Massa developed a philosophy, a rationale for this barbarous system. He thought that the workers, both African and Indian, were inferior beings.'

Murmurs, nods of agreement. I dared not raise my head.

'Unfit for self-government, unequal to their superior master, permanently destined to a status of perpetual subordination, unable to ever achieve equality with Massa.'

Eric Williams was calm, self-assured. Desire stirred in me, fantasy. Everything would be different in Trinidad when he was made Prime Minister. He waved his clenched fists, breathing fire. Fire in his belly. Fire was what they all wanted. Fire gave fire.

'It was there in all the laws which governed the West Indies for generations. Those laws denied equality on grounds of colour. Those laws forbade non-Europeans to enter certain occupations and professions, whether it was the occupation of jeweller or the profession of lawyer. Those laws forbade intermarriage. They equated political power and the vote with ownership of land. Consciously or unconsciously, directly or indirectly, those laws attempted to ensure that the non-European would never be anything but a worker in the social scale . . .'

I couldn't believe my ears. Heat had been breathed into my entire being. He had that ability. Heat from his words, from his very body, spread into others. The crowd was inflamed. Williams said things George never even mentioned. Williams was right and George was wrong. George was selective in his intelligence. Williams lectured on and on in the hot sun. History. Revolution. The revision of history. He preached freedom of the mind, breathed hope, a new sense of opportunity into the souls of those listening.

'Massa day *done*!' Eric Williams declared, pounding the lectern. 'Sahib day done! Yes, suh, Boss day done!'

Wild applause.

Granny cheered and waved her fists.

'Massa stood for degradation of West Indian labour.' Williams was unstoppable.

'Massa stood for colonialism.' The crowd waved balisiers, hands reached out; some were on the verge of falling unconscious.

'Massa believed in the inequality of races.'

'Yes,' the crowd chanted.

'Massa was determined not to educate his society. Massa was quite right. To educate is to emancipate.'

I left quietly, hands clutched to my chest. I didn't want Granny to see me there; I wanted to go away, far away from the likes of Granny, from the mass of people gathered in the square. I sweated profusely, from the heat of the sun, from the heat of Williams' words. His words lit me, as they had lit the whole crowd. I floated on unsteady legs. Bombs had detonated in my head. I shook. I fanned myself. I was sad and sorry for myself all at once. Williams' words tolled heavily in me. *Massa day done*. It was all over. Trinidad had found its Saviour. I was happy, relieved. We would go. I would speak to George.

I don't know how I managed to find my car again in that white heat, how I found my way home.

Williams clarified my instincts and explained my inclinations. I vowed to be a better friend to Venus, I vowed to be better educated. Massa's time was over. George was Massa. So was I. That evening I told George I had sneaked into Woodford Square. I repeated to George what Williams had said.

'George, it's time,' I pleaded. 'We really have to disappear.' But George was glass-eyed and distant.

'Yes, dear, we will go. Soon. I promise.'

My green bicycle was no longer my only mode of transport. Mostly it leant against the wall in the garage, growing specks of rust. One day I wheeled it out into the sun to scour it with a wire brush.

'Madam, long time you ride dat ting,' Venus commented.

'I don't need it so much any more.'

'You 'fraid.'

I blushed. 'Don't be silly.'

'You used to ride it jus for relaxation.'

'I was younger then.'

'You young still.'

'I've had children.'

'It would tek off de extra baby weight.'

She was right. But the bike made me feel awkward. I couldn't even imagine riding it down into town any more.

'You were fonny on dat bike.'

'How so?'

'A white girl dress so casual, who ent care who look at she. Many wouldn't do dat.'

'Why?'

'White women 'fraid black men look at dem.'

'People *stare* now. They never used to.'

'Madam, tings different.' There was a look of caution in her eyes.

'I thought I was imagining it.'

'No, madam, maybe bes you don't ride down tong dese days. Maybe it bes you ride it rong close by us.'

I scrubbed and scrubbed until the bike shone. Venus's words nagged at me. What did she mean? What would happen if I rode my bike into town? Before I knew what I was doing, I had opened the front gate, mounted the bike and cycled out into the road.

'Bye-bye, Venus! I won't be long,' I shouted over the hibiscus hedge. 'Look after the children.'

Venus came to the kitchen window, mouth open, shaking her head. 'Madam, you mad! You watch yuhself.'

I tinkled the bell on the handlebars, pedalling slowly down the road, past the Country Club and down into Boissiere village, alert, watching out for those who might be watching me. Years had passed since I'd ridden my green bicycle into town. Years since I'd cycled to meet George at the docks, since my arrival. I was a different woman now, a mother, less innocent.

I rode down into Frederick Street in the midday sun. The streets were bustling, everybody on their lunch hour. Pigtailed brown-skinned schoolchildren in white knee socks and uniforms strolled along in groups. An old man, dreadlocks in his beard, leant on his cane as he promenaded down the hot pavement. I weaved in and out of traffic, down to Marine Square, to the cathedral there, right down to the dock, where I dismounted. I bought a snow cone from a vendor, wheeling the bike towards the lighthouse, all the while adjusting to the stark assessing gaze of those around me. It bored holes through my back. Worse, far worse than the sun. I kept moving, nervous, eating the sweet red cherry ice. People stared but I couldn't stare back. It wasn't dangerous or menacing; somehow it was worse, an ancient consideration. Or had they all been listening to Eric Williams in Woodford Square? Were they his students? Had his message settled in their hearts? Yes. I imagined them all waving balisiers. No one would physically harm me, no, nothing like that. This was covert, a group operating as one.

'Ayyy,' a man called from across the road. 'Come here, white meat. Lemme taste a piece, see if white taste different. Come here, nuh, lousy white pig.'

We mixed with the Bakers on and off at cocktail parties and dances. Christobel dwarfed me physically. Socially, too; her status was as good as aristocracy. Sebastian Baker's eyes fired up whenever he saw me and I played up to it. He'd delivered both my babies and I was comfortable around him, had an unspoken and natural intimacy with him.

'Come and dance with me, Sabine,' he said one night at a Country Club fête. He pulled me onto the tightly-packed dance floor. I wore a low-cut dress, a well-boned bra. I flattened myself against him and he groaned with pleasure. I laughed and let him enjoy the feeling of my young body pressed to his. He was light on his feet, an excellent dancer. We salsaed into the centre of the crowd.

'How are your children, Sabine?'

'Happy.'

'And beautiful?'

'Very.'

'Like their mother, then.'

One hand was cupped to my buttocks as he gazed into my face and ample cleavage. Our thighs were locked. A little tipsier and God knows I'd have reached up and kissed him in full view of George and Christobel. He smiled, guessing my desire. I let him pull me closer and could feel he was aroused. We danced well together, slowly, moving as one. I was happy to enjoy another woman's husband, who, up close, smelled of limes and whisky and brilliantine and the heat of the evening.

'You look ravishing this evening,' he whispered into my ear.

I pressed myself closer.

When we left the dance floor we were drenched in sweat, mostly other people's. Christobel had watched us and her face, as we approached, was bleak. She shot Sebastian a look of pure hatred.

'You minx,' George chided, dancing me back into the crowd, where I fell into his body, fell into step with him, in love with him again. I loved everything about George. His long slim hands, his boyish face, his eyes, so full of casual mirth. I loved his freckles, the strange rust shadow of stubble which appeared when he hadn't shaved for a few days. George's face glowed. It was that of an innocent, yet George was far too clever to be innocent. He gazed down at me with love-swollen eyes and this melted me. I loved George and no one else.

George spun me around, pulling me close. 'I'm your slave,' he whispered.

'Then take me away from here.'

He pulled me tighter, pressing his lips to my neck. 'Yes, my love. Yes.'

My skin had turned milk-coffee brown. I was shades darker. There was no escaping it. The Trinidad sun was mighty, omnipotent. And I perspired constantly. Whenever I showered and towelled myself dry, I was damp again within minutes. I sweated from doing nothing, just sitting. There were two seasons: the dry season and the rainy season. But it was *always* humid. I was always limp, half-hearted. I often walked around dazed, forgetful. The heat punished me, treated me with contempt. It leached away my strength. Venus, I noticed, hardly perspired, never complained. Mosquitoes never troubled her either. I itched all the time as they devoured me. TCP was my *eau de parfum*, Limacol was my *eau de cologne*.

We endured a plague of scorpions, tiny brown shrimp-like creatures with barbs held high above their heads. George trod on one and was off work for days. We found the nest under an old bench out in the tool shed. Bachacs were another pest, red ants which marched in unwavering columns; their razor-sharp jaws vibrated like an electric knife. They stripped one of our mango trees in a day, denuded shrubs in hours. They even made off with other, larger insects: cockroaches, spiders, often wriggling, legs in the air, like damsels in distress, carried up above the ants' heads. If you tried to block their path, they tramped around your trap like robots. The only way to stop them was to pour a lethal blue poison into their nest, but finding this was near impossible. Bachacs lived in colonies dug deep into the ground. They marched for days to hunt. Scorpions and bachacs and army ants and tack tacks, big black ants the Amerindians used as surgical stitches. Then there were Jack Spaniards, wasps with bums hanging at right angles to their torsos. Trinidad teemed with ferocious insects.

Nothing upset me more than the bats. At night, tiny pipistrelles swooped at great speed through the house. Leathery velvet rockets which hit the ceiling-fan propellers, splattering guts across the walls. The first time this happened, I cried. *Mon Dieu, mon Dieu.*

I became a murderess. I went mad with murdering these beasts. I whacked and bashed and sprayed Flit onto anything and everything which crept or wriggled. I nail-varnished caterpillars, hair-sprayed beetles. I stamped and kicked away all manner of scuttling black demons: wood lice, earwigs, centipedes. I mashed and mangled them to death.

Venus arrived one morning looking miserable. Her face was drawn, her expression preoccupied.

'Venus, what's the matter?'

She steupsed.

I didn't want to push.

'Are Bernard and Clive all right?'

She moped, nodding.

'Please tell me. I can't bear it if you don't.'

The whites of her eyes were huge, veined with red. Clearly she hadn't slept.

'What is it?'

'Water, madam.'

'What?'

'We ha no water for six days.'

'*What*? Why didn't you tell us?'

'De stanpipe in de road dry up. I OK. Ah does bathe here. But de chilren dirty. Granny cyan bathe. We cyan cook.'

'What happened?'

She shrugged. 'Me ent know. Dey tun off de supply for buildin' somptin.'

'And they've forgotten to turn it back on?'

'It seem so.'

'Why didn't you *tell* me? Why don't you ring the water authorities?'

'We ha no phone. Nor de neighbours.'

I blushed with shame.

'Oh Venus. Go and use the shower. When you're finished we'll go and get the children and Granny. They can all come here to bath. We'll get some plastic drums, fill them for you.'

Venus's eyes were full. I sent her off and found the phone book, searching for the number for the water services. I rang it but no answer; rang again and the same thing. I rang and rang until the phone went dead. I rang George.

'Hello, darling.'

'Why hasn't he done the most *basic things*?' I bellowed.

'What are you talking about?'

'Five years! It's been five years. What's he doing? What are *they* doing?'

'Who, darling?'

'The PNM.'

'Darling, you've gone mad. What's the problem, what are you talking about?'

'Venus has had no water for six days.'

'Well, ring the water authorities.'

'The cretins *aren't in.*'

'Well, I'm sure there's some good reason.'

'I'm sure there's *no* good reason. *For God's sake*: can't you see it? Nothing works. No one cares. Not even *they* care about Venus. They say they do. But they don't care. She's invisible. Eric Williams? That stupid hearing aid he wears. He's gone deaf in five years. He goes shopping at Zandolie, flirts with women. Granny Seraphina is saving for a *stove*. Do you think that she'll get current in her lifetime?'

'Darling, I'll be home soon. Simmer down.'

This put me into a wilder state. 'You stupid man,' I shouted and slammed the phone down.

Venus came up behind me, smelling of coal-tar soap. She smiled carefully, having overheard.

Fuming, I drove with Venus up Morne Cocoa Road to Paramin. When we arrived at the corner where the old house stood I sensed a stiffness come over Venus; I guessed she didn't want me to come in.

'Stay here a moment,' she muttered.

I parked and waited in the car.

Venus hopped up the steps, peering into the dark interior of the house. 'Granny?' she called.

No reply.

'Wait a while,' Venus called down to me.

I nodded.

She disappeared inside.

I sat for a moment contemplating the mountainside. *He used his power shamelessly for his own private needs.* The mountain was silent. Anger rolled around inside me. I wanted to kick the mountain, strangle Eric Williams. Bellow for order, for a hurricane to blow that old house down the hill. I got out of the car and waited down in the yard. I could hear a commotion in the little house, Venus talking in lowered tones. A toddler crying.

A skinny dog prowled near by. It didn't look fed.

'Venus?' I shouted, mounting the steps. 'Venus? Can I help?'

Venus's face appeared from behind the sheet-curtain, worried.

'Please, let me help.' I was halfway up the steps.

'It Granny . . . she cyan get up. Ah try to raise her up, but she too heavy.' Still Venus was reluctant to open the door.

'I'll come in then,' I offered.

It was gloomy in the old house, quiet and gloomy, everything cast in soupy shadows, shades of brown, ochre. A table in the makeshift kitchen. Pantry cupboards. Sheets draped as curtains. Plastic roses in a vase. A huge cross high up on the wall, pictures of the Lord and the Virgin in thick gilt frames. Everything so tidy, bare. Bernard, the baby, was asleep in a straw basket on the floor. Clive sat on the sofa, sucking his thumb.

Venus led me to the back of the house. A figure lay on a mattress on a metal-framed bed, very brown and small. Granny Seraphina. A sheet was pulled firmly up to her chin. Her lips were sucked into her mouth. She seemed to have been praying hard. Her white hair was covered in the same red scarf.

'Granny, Mrs Harwood here. She come to take you fer a bath.'

The old woman nodded minutely. Her brilliant yellow eyes were enormous, stripping me down.

Together we tried to help Granny to her feet. I saw what Venus meant: the old woman was heavy. Tiny, emaciated, but heavy. A bag of metal bones. With great effort we managed to raise her. No word of thanks; in fact, I got the impression she'd rather I hadn't come.

We struggled down the skinny stone steps to the car, propping Granny up. We helped her into the back seat, forcing her rough body to sit down.

'I ent goin' nowhere.' She tried to get out but we calmly forced her to sit. We went back up the stairs and picked up the boys and settled them in the car next to Granny. Venus sat in front with me, clutching a bag of spare clothes for everyone. My stomach swam; I thought of the Robber Man. *He has appeared. Come to save his vexed and oppress children.* Eric Williams: five years. What was he doing?

I peered into the rear-view mirror at Granny Seraphina, who stared out the window: waiting. She didn't want to look at me; she didn't like the look of me.

Venus took her sons to the shower adjoining the room in which she slept in our house. There was much squealing and squawking with delight under the warm jets of water. I collected their dirty clothes and put them in the washing machine. Granny sat at the kitchen table, resolutely silent. Her back was hunched and she stared into her lap, fingers laced together, a different person to the firebrand at the rally, to the woman I had met weeks before. This woman had come undone, temporarily. I began to prepare sandwiches, busying myself buttering sides of bread, deciding it best not to make small talk. Granny Seraphina. Made from what? Oil? From tallow wax? From old rope? What did we have to talk about? I matched her silence. Buttering bread, slicing ham, tomatoes. Cutting off crusts. Then I noticed she was looking past me, inspecting the four-ringed electric stove behind me.

'Venus tells me you're saving for a stove,' I dared, heat in my cheeks.

She nodded slowly.

'You must be thirsty. Would you like a cup of tea?'

She stared. A stupid question.

'I'm going to have one.' I turned the knob. The kettle always sat on a ring.

Granny studied my movements.

'Come and see,' I said.

She resembled a skittish horse, head held high, poised, eyeing me.

'Come and feel,' I encouraged, holding my hand above the reddening ring.

This invitation got the better of her: she rose slowly, mouth set. I lifted the kettle up.

Granny approached, hand out, palm down. The ring pulsed candy red.

She held her hand out above it, nodding, as if she knew.

'It goes hot quite quickly,' I said.

Cold yellow eyes, deadly with intent. 'Yes. We gettin' one a bit smaller.'

In the end the Queen didn't attend the ceremony. I was piqued. Instead, she sent her sister, Princess Margaret, who read out a message from the Queen, the usual starchy stuff. Even so, thousands flocked to Woodford Square to watch the ceremony one steamy overcast afternoon in August. It was 1962. Marches and parades in every village in Trinidad, euphoria in the streets. Eric Williams, Trinidad's new leader, read out his solemn pledge to the people. The Union Jack was lowered. The newly designed red flag of Trinidad and Tobago was hoisted onto a white pole in the Red House forecourt. A lump rose in my throat as I watched all this on television. Eric Williams became Trinidad's first Prime Minister. No longer a try out, a by-proxy affair. He and his party, the PNM, would rule undisturbed by the Crown.

I was moody all day. I clubbed cockroaches. I played with the children. I took a shower and sat down afterwards, plucking my eyebrows too thin. We'd been invited to a party to celebrate but I didn't feel celebratory.

'You're as jumpy as a cat,' George noticed.

I had an idea.

I'd write to him! My very own ritual to commemorate his arrival.

I found some writing paper and ink. I filled a fountain pen. In my cocktail dress, at my dressing table, I sat down to write. I stared at the pages but the words didn't come. I saw him on the bandstand. Standing heel to toe. Casual and sure of himself. The man who watched me through the windows of his flashy car. No words between us then. Something was wrong. So much placed on his shoulders. I thought of my young son, Sebastian. I would never want him to grow up to rule a world; would never wish this for any one man. I began to scribble down my thoughts and hopes and well wishes for the new government, giving them my blessings. My heart was full of trepidation.

Remember me? The white woman on the green bicycle. I know you saw me. I know you. Talk, talk, talk. Today, all that pomp and ceremony. Good luck. Kiss the hand that kept you down. You should tell them all to get stuffed, including that twit of a princess. Already you are adapting your words. You are letting them dictate the very way they allow you to take over. Is this the right way to get started? You don't know them like I do. My husband George, he's one of them. Quite mad. They're indestructible. Massa day done? Well, tell that to Granny Seraphina. Tell that to the old slave woman. She's the one you need to worry about. No water for six days. No current. When will it come? When will you remember her? Oh Father of the Nation. Granny can't write to you. She can't read and write. Why do I feel unhappy? Why am I full of mistrust? You're a child again, Trinidad. Not an adult. A child. Don't run, don't run away with yourself. Learn to walk again, walk away from them. Crawl and walk in the opposite direction.

TRINIDAD, 1963

CHAPTER EIGHTEEN

THE CASTLE

George built his hacienda out in the bush. His great-aunt died suddenly, and it was just the windfall he needed. A local architect helped him realise his dream. When he razed the land on that old ruined cocoa estate, he found he wasn't the first to build in that lonely godforsaken valley at the foot of that voluptuous hill. Miraculously, the roof of another house peeked from behind the tall grasses, right behind our plot. A mad French Creole had beaten George to it.

'I'm not going to live there!' I gasped, even when the land was cleared.

But George was silent. He nodded, unhearing, staring at the open space.

'I mean, George, I'll be *alone*, with the children. It isn't safe. This is bush! Bush all around. And me and just one other house?'

But George wasn't to be swayed, not at this point. Later, he unrolled the blue sketches of the architect's designs on the kitchen table. The house he wanted to build was impressive, with arches and courtyards and wide porches all around.

'It'll be a family home.' George's eyes glistened.

'We already have one – in England.'

'We can have two.'

'Oh God – you just want to make your *mark*.'

'What do you mean?'

'For ever. *Comme la Tour Eiffel*. A monument.'

George ignored this comment. I don't think he understood what I meant. And at that moment I didn't understand what was happening, how much my fate was bound to his ideas. My husband was in the act of staying. My dreams of leaving, of returning to Europe, were being reconfigured entirely. A team of builders was employed. George visited the site every morning, before work. Every evening he arrived home with news of the foundations being dug, the floors going down. But I remained resolutely indifferent to the building project: it happened without me, without my consent. I never even acknowledged its existence until the day it was finished and, even then, when George announced it was ready, I replied, 'What is?'

That green woman lying on her side, right in front of our new home, baring her hips invitingly; that broken-up road running past. I cried into my pillows at night, not wanting to leave our tiny home in which, despite it all, I'd grown to find comfort. That little house was a stone's throw from the Country Club, where I took the children every day to play; it was near all our friends, near town, near the savannah, near everything. I'd been happy there – in the short-term.

The exodus had begun. First, all the bigwigs left, the Governor and his household and political staff, his retainers and civil servants.

Then a wider circle removed themselves, those who'd worked in the public services, the police force, the hospitals. By then, George had been promoted to Deputy Director at Forbes-Mason. Most of his staff had packed up and joined the queues on the wharf. But the big bosses in London didn't want to close down the company and withdraw completely, not yet. We attended leaving party after leaving party.

'You're staying? Good luck.' This from so many of those leaving us behind, compassion and relief in their eyes. So many British couples who had become our friends boarded the liners.

'I'm not leaving.' Irit was adamant.

Helena was worse off than me. Over the last seven years I'd watched her dwindle, growing thinner, more fragile. A blank expression had crept into her eyes and she clung to her cigarettes. As a professional woman of East-Indian origin, she hadn't found a place for herself in Trinidad society, not amongst the wider European or Indian communities. Education was her own particular social stigma.

As the walls of our new home rose, brick by brick, my fantasies of leaving intensified. I dreamt of escaping Trinidad every night; I had visions of gangplanks. I saw myself walking out along one at knifepoint, goaded by pirates. I laughed and ran, jumping into the sea, plunging like a cannonball into the deep. I cried in my sleep. I was magnetised by the wharf. I became obsessed with news of the latest boatload, scouring the *Guardian* for faces I recognised. Corbeaux infested my dreams, hovering high up in the blue, waiting to pick at my flesh. I lay dead and silvery on the beach; the black birds descended in their dozens, squabbling.

Trinidad was becoming a new country. It was happening before my eyes; this virgin nation was developing a sense of self-awareness, of being part of the world on its own terms. A national anthem was composed. Trinidad and Tobago acquired a coat of arms! A small army was founded. A coastguard. And a national airline. Eric Williams flew around the globe on a tour of diplomacy, letting various nations know that Trinidad and Tobago had joined the world stage. Trinidad was small but rich, beautiful. This was now official. The PNM even had matching ties.

George became more ardent, wanting to please me. He could always be sure of the calming effect of his touch, his hands on me. He spoke words of love into my neck, into my hair. At night he clambered over me, parting my knees. His lips and hands caressed the tender skin along each thigh; he could spend an hour, easily, lost and whispering his love to me. Once, I sat up on my elbows, watching him. He looked up. We gazed long into each other's eyes. I always saw somewhere, in his face, an image of every man on earth, a virile and benevolent god. A smirk on his lips, like he knew things from another side of life; a smile of self-knowledge. I blinked hard.

He frowned. 'What are you looking at?'

But I never told.

George sighed. He buried his head between my thighs. He made up for things with his hands and mouth. He often wanted nothing in return for the sexual pleasures he lavished.

'You are my home,' he whispered. 'You are where I reside.'

And yet, my fears nagged. I wrote more letters to Eric Williams; letters I never sent. I wrote in the middle of the night, sweat dripping from my nose, tears in my lashes. I wrote to him about my childhood, asking about his childhood, wondering if we'd had any similar experiences. Anxiety churned my gut. I mumbled as I wrote.

Who do you love? Your little girl? Your dead wife, the second one, not the ones alive? That half-Chinese woman who died so suddenly, so young? She coughed up blood and was gone in days. Who do you think of at night, last thing before you sleep? Who do you care about? Who is your guide? Who consoles you, Mr Williams? I'm anxious to understand my fate. I'm anxious because something is happening to my family. My husband has changed, and you know what? I'm changing, too, leaving myself behind. It's a strange and uncanny metamorphosis. I cannot fathom what manner of moth or butterfly I'll become. A beauty or a horror? How much longer will I survive?

Like George, my children loved the island. Both were boisterous and sociable, both spoke with a song in their voice. Pascale's hair was an afro of matted curls, Sebastian refused to wear shoes.

'But your feet will grow wide,' I complained. 'And then you won't be able to wear shoes at all.'

I grabbed him and pinned him down, inspecting his toes, his heels which had grown rough. His soles were already calloused.

'You'll turn into a *goat*,' I warned.

'Or an agouti!' he laughed. He liked the idea that he was half boy, half wild animal from up in the hills.

Pascale never let me comb her hair. At the nape of her neck it became clumped, just like a Rastaman's. Every week, Venus and I would have to catch her to groom her. Once, she saw us coming and ran from us, screaming. Venus tore after her, through the house, shouting, 'Oh gorsh, Miss Pascale! Shit, man, dis chile *crayzee*, madam, w'appen to dis chile?'

Pascale had disappeared. We searched high and low calling her name, trying not to sound threatening. Then, we had the same idea.

We entered her bedroom on tiptoe. Venus put her finger to her lips. I nodded. We both knelt down and slowly lifted the bed's counterpane. Pascale was sitting underneath, her back to the wall, her eyes wide and defiant.

'Pascale, come out,' I said as calmly as possible.

She shook her head.

'Pascale, we won't hurt you.'

She glared and sulked. 'No.'

Venus steupsed. 'Pascale, get yuh *ass* outside de damned bed right NOW!'

'Noooo!' Pascale wailed.

We reached under the bed, each clasped one skinny leg and yanked, dragging her out kicking and screaming. Venus paddled her backside and then we carried her out to the porch. Venus sat on her while she continued to wail, laughing at her protests. 'Ah go squash yer flat as a pancake, Miss Pascale. Yer want a squash?'

'Noooo.' Pascale continued to thrash.

I went to fetch a bowl of water and the shampoo and a thick afro comb.

Eventually, Pascale squealed herself hoarse and was quiet. Exhausted and hot with tears, she sat as we snipped and untangled the clumps. Venus ran coconut pomade through her hair and cane-rowed it back. Eventually, Pascale was happy with this new hairstyle.

Seven years. I'd smudged. Incrementally, against my will, I was becoming part of things, part of the island. I could no longer take a clear look at Trinidad. I was hemmed in. It was an uneasy relationship, the kind of love which made me on edge all the time. Like an infection, a festering, niggling, burning sensation: an insect bite. I fought more with George. Our lovemaking became fierce.

'Kill me off,' I once taunted.

He found this exciting. When he came towards me I slapped him hard across the face.

'Owww. Why did you do that?'

'To wake you up.'

'But I'm not asleep.'

'You *sleep*walk through the day. You don't care to see what's going on, all you care about is that damn house in the bush.'

'I love you, Sabine.'

I slapped him again. It felt good.

'Please don't do that.' His eyes were sorrowful and innocent. He didn't know how to please me outside the bedroom.

Eric Williams wrote and published a book, *The History of the People of Trinidad and Tobago*. It was available in all the bookshops in Port of Spain. George brought home a copy and sniffed at it. Famously, Williams wrote it in a month, wanting it to be used by common citizens, by students. He bequeathed it to Trinidad as a kind of first book of information. But Granny Seraphina couldn't read.

I hadn't seen Granny since the time of the water shortage. I thought about her often, though. I understood she didn't want a close connection, not like I had with Venus. One day, I made an excuse to visit Venus in the hope of speaking to Granny. I was in luck. Granny was sweeping the yard, a studious expression on her face. She was bent over, sweeping, sweeping the already bald dirt ground outside the shack with a palm broom cocoyea. I'd parked further down the hill and appeared on foot. But she was so deep in thought I had to cough loudly to announce myself. She looked up from her broom and froze, as though she'd clapped eyes on a ghost.

'Hello, Granny,' I said politely. 'Venus forgot Clive's sandals. I thought I'd drop them by.'

Granny looked vexed. Whatever she'd been thinking about was still dwelling.

I wanted to say something, to get to the point of my visit. I wanted to ask her most recent opinion about Eric Williams, about all this nation-building, the new jets, the Party tie. But there seemed to be no way of making small talk with Granny.

She glared. Maybe she already knew why I'd come.

'"I will let down my bucket here with you in the British West Indies,"' she said in a calm voice, enunciating each word precisely.

A chill ran through me. I knew those words and who had said them.

'I der when he say dat. I der, man.' She steupsed, looking down at her bare feet.

'I know, Granny, I know. Granny, things *will* change. Soon. I know they will.'

Granny nodded with her mouth pulled down, as if she knew that, too.

'Ah already wait a long time.'

'I know.'

'Seven years pass.' She steupsed.

'Yes. I think . . . We need a hurricane.'

She stared me down.

'To blow everything away. You know. Demolish all that has passed.'

Granny clicked her throat and contemplated the idea. 'Yeah, man.' She nodded slowly. 'A hurricane in trute.'

'But we don't get them in Trinidad, do we?'

Granny shook her head. 'No, man, wind pass furder up.'

Trinidad gained independence – and slowly, steadily, red rust encased my green bicycle. It stood propped against the wall in the garage. I didn't have the heart to give it away. Every day I saw it and ignored it. The basket filled with old magazines, plastic bags full of old tools hung from the handlebars. I piled worn-out sheets on top of it, bags of outgrown children's clothes. It came to look like a Chinese junk, as if it had just arrived from long and lengthy travels across seas, continents.

We moved in June 1963. Two lorries parked up outside the smaller house. Four removal men packed up our life and moved us out to the bush, to live next to that mad French Creole out on the beach road.

Venus came with us, leaving Granny Seraphina to look after her sons during the week. George had included servant's quarters into his grand design, a spacious, well-ventilated room next to the kitchen. Venus had her own door and key so she could come and go as she pleased, an ensuite bathroom. She was delighted. Venus lived with us, slept near us behind those high walls. George bought two Great Dane puppies as guard dogs and overnight we were an outpost there in the bush: a store-room, a pantry, and water tanks on the roof. The children ran about whooping like Red Indians. Our new home had wrought iron bars on the windows for security. I stood and peered through them, restless as a panther in a cage at a zoo. I often counted them: one, two, three. But then they would merge into many bars. I began to see thousands of them. Everyone could see our new home on the way to the beach; everyone mentioned it, discussing it at parties.

'Who's built out there?'

'George and Sabine.'

'Good grief. Poor woman.'

'He's mad.'

'The land was almost free.'

'On her *own* out there. She'll go mad.'

George loved his castle. He even baptised it Casa Familia. He commissioned a wrought-iron insignia, securing it out front, next to the postbox. He saw us as pioneers. He thought we'd grow to live in and love the hacienda in the bush. But I couldn't love it. I stared up at those massive hills, counting the trees in them just like I'd counted those trees from the deck of the *Cavina*. Millions, millions of trees in the hills above the house, countless varieties. In them, her hefty green shoulders, her giant head, cocked to one side, the holes of her eyes, her wild and bushy hair. By day she watched us and at night she came alive; all that lived up there in the green woman fed and mated and cried. Frogs croaked a call and response, crickets trumpeted.

George loved his swimming pool most of all. He swam in it every day, cleaned it with loving care, scooping the vermilion immortelle blossoms from its surface in the dry season, scattering all the right chemicals into it. He tested the water, vacuumed the pool's floor. He sat beside the pool for hours, on a sun lounger, reading, his white skin grilling like sirloin steak, drinking rum after rum. Jules, our neighbour, came over to welcome us but mainly to see if our home was any fancier than his, if we'd be any disturbance. Jules, dear Jules. He was fifty or so, kind-faced, grey wiry hair, wiry moustache. His skin, like so many of the local whites', looked diseased, had become a mosaic of brown flecks of melanin. He survived mostly off a small family inheritance. He was researching a family biography, he explained. His French family had fled from Haiti; they were once *ancien régime*, very grand, very much a part of things in the West Indies. Jules spoke a little French and I took to him immediately; he became my companion and ally out there in the bush.

George still went out to work every day on his scooter. George, so likeable and alert. When the big cruise ships came in, amongst other duties as Deputy Director he had the job of entertaining the more prominent passengers, those the company wanted to impress. Sometimes these were businessmen, once even a famous movie star.

'Darling, can you meet me at the Country Club?' he said on the phone, quite breathless, one day.

'When?'

'In an hour.'

'I'm not sure if I can.'

'It's important. We have an actor on the boat. Here with his wife.'

'Oh *God*. Do I have to?'

'Please.'

'OK. OK.'

'Wear a nice dress.'

I struggled into a green low-cut cocktail dress and powdered my face, half resentful. I drove to the Club to find some commotion outside, the car park jam-packed. The valet took the car and I was ushered in through the throng. I found George sitting at the bar. His face visibly shone when he caught sight of me. He rose and I kissed him on the cheek.

'This is my wife,' he said proudly to the man sitting beside him, who I recognised instantly. It was Cary Grant.

George's job took up more of his time, became more exciting. Meanwhile, I rattled about in that house. We didn't have enough furniture to fill such a large space. It was three times larger than the one we'd left behind, with smooth terrazzo porches all around. A huge parquet living-room floor George had intended for all the great fêtes we would host. Our four armchairs were scrawny in the living room. Our tiny television set, our one coffee table, our sideboard, all like doll's furniture in a museum.

'Go out and spend.' George waved his chequebook at me. 'Go and spend my money, woman.'

And so I hunted around for all we needed for our new existence. Irit helped me. Rugs and lamps and paintings and sofas and patio furniture and two of those peacock-backed chairs Irit had in her boutique. Even a big fish tank on a stand, full of coral and angel fish. Irit wasn't the least bit envious of our new home. She and John still lived at the tiny Bergerac Flats with their chaos and their violet Persian cat. She grew richer by the day, but her lifestyle never changed.

'Who go clean all dem frou-frou tings you have now, madam,' Venus pointed out one day. 'Not me,' she asserted. 'I ent polishin' no fish!'

Until then Venus had managed to hold herself in. But she was right; I was filling our home with mad things. Crystal, vases, all manner of cooking equipment for the kitchen, a soup tureen, a parsley grinder, a fish kettle. And all the while I stared through those bars, hundreds of them.

One afternoon, the front doorbell buzzed. The puppies barked and dashed out to the gate. I was alone with Venus, frightened at first. I made her gather the children before peeping out from behind one of the pillars in the courtyard. The bell rang again; I advanced cautiously down the drive.

'Who's there?'

'Hello,' I heard a woman's voice call through the wrought-iron bars.

The puppies danced and jumped up at the gate, woofing and wagging their stubby tails.

Behind it stood a woman dressed in a brown, much worn, maid's uniform.

I drew closer. 'What do you want?'

'I'm looking for work, madam.'

She was a big red-skinned Negro woman with frizzy grey hair. One eye was still, unmoving. Between us, the thick iron bars of the gate. Where'd she come from?

'What kind of work?'

'Cooking, housekeeping. I've work for many years as house-keeper. I have a reference.'

'Well . . .' Her face was open, placid. I could see she wasn't going to beg: she hadn't used the word *maid* and she spoke differently, a soft song in her voice, a version of the dialect which was milder than the way Venus spoke. Venus had come to me as lively as the puppies at my feet. This woman was at the other end of living, she'd slowed. Her girth was wide and her eyes were melancholy.

'I could use some extra help. We've just moved here . . .'

She nodded.

'Where do your live?'

'Just down so, in Santa Cruz.'

A rural area, full of grapefruit and orange orchards. You drove through the saddle cut into the mountainside to get there.

'What's your name?'

'Lucy, madam. Mrs Lucinda Bartholomew.' She thrust an enve-lope through the bars.

I took it from her and pulled out a letter, reading it; it was from an English employer just gone. I didn't know them. Lucy had lost her job when they departed.

'Come in, Lucy.'

That day, Lucy joined the fort. Venus was pleased. It meant she no longer cooked or cleaned, just looked after the children. Sebastian was six and Pascale four; they were a handful. Lucy stepped into the role of cook and housekeeper, walking in every day from the valley beyond the saddle. Venus and Lucy were as different as could be in age, appearance and demeanour, Venus considering herself above Lucy, even though, clearly, Lucy had accrued more gravitas. Venus had been with us seven years, the main difference; she was the Second Lady of the house and Lucy was content to let her see it this way at first.

Quickly, we got to know of Lucy's countrywoman genius.

A wart appeared on Sebastian's finger. I ignored it at first but it grew bigger and quite hard, bulbous. He picked at it all the time.

'Horrible thing,' I said to Lucy. 'So hard to get rid of. I'll get some acid from the chemist.'

But the next day Lucy arrived with some sprigs of a shrub she began to clean and split, the milky sap oozing.

'What's that?' I enquired.

'Cactus hedge, madam.'

I watched as Lucy made a splint from two milky stems and bound them to Sebastian's warty finger.

Three days later the wart had disappeared. Sebastian was amazed, assuming she'd performed a magic trick.

George chuckled. 'Our very own bush doctor.'

Venus changed her attitude to Lucy considerably. 'Granny Seraphina know dese tings, too,' she mused. 'It old time ting, dis bush medcin. It black people ting. Come from Africa.'

Like a Paris chef, Lucy was open and yet mysterious about her tonics, never revealing the entire recipe. When Pascale cut open her knee, Lucy boiled up pomegranate flowers into a tea for her to sip and the cut healed quickly. When the children had diarrhoea, she gave them pomegranate bark to chew. Colds and coughs Lucy cured with a cool beverage of hibiscus petals. Jackfruit, if they were constipated. Spinach leaves for poultices on boils. Ginger for gas, slices of aubergine, melongene, for minor sprains. All Lucy's cures worked. I wrote many of the ingredients down. She often explained what was what but, when I tried to boil up my own potions, they failed. I began to examine every leaf and blossom in my garden, trying to detect what was alkaline and what was acid.

'Half is an inherited knowledge, the other half is a gift,' Jules explained to me one afternoon. 'Not *all* of them use it or can use it. Venus would probably make a botch of things just like you.'

'Lucy is a very gentle soul,' I mused.

'You're lucky then.'

'Why?'

'I expect she knows poisons, too.'

'No!'

'Of *course*,' he laughed. Jules had a vivacious way of speaking, a sing-song accent like Christobel's, except more expressive, emphasising his words with great knowing. This was common amongst Trinidadians of every persuasion, this emphatic nature. No maybes.

'She wouldn't harm us, surely.'

Jules rolled his eyes.

'She doesn't seem the type. I sense she's had a hard life. She sings a lot and sometimes tears fall as she sings.'

'Listen to me. You have an ol' Shango woman in your home. You keep your eyes open.'

But Jules was wrong. I knew whatever wickedness Lucy could conjure with her herbs and plant tonics, she wasn't going to harm us. Something was amiss with Mrs Lucy Bartholomew, but she was past revenge.

Lucy, Venus, the children and the puppies, too. We were a household. Having Jules a tramp away, through the bush, made me feel safer. Occasionally, a car rumbled past, or a donkey cart pulled up at the gate selling milk from a large tin vat. The hill woman watched us, lying on her side, half earth, the other half mountains. Yellow pouis trees exploded like fireworks in her hair. Herons floated out of the canopy of her shoulders. Once, a wild duck arrived from the hill; it landed in the swimming pool. The children fed it chunks of bread and it became quite tame. Another time, two huge porcupines wandered in from the foot of the hill, across the porch, shooting their quills at the puppies who pranced and barked around them. We plucked quills from their muzzles for days afterwards. One hot sunny afternoon I spotted a long black shadow moving out near the front gate. When I got closer I shrieked and fled.

'A macajuel,' Venus identified it as it slithered away, the local name for a boa constrictor.

Birds flocked from that hill to the house. Red-bellied macaws chattered up in the palms and hummingbirds, colibri, hummed through the house, piercing the hibiscus I'd arranged in vases. The mountain above our home was not static or still. It provided cover and harbour to communities which were invisible from where I stood out on the porch. Communities of human squatters, of beasts and birds and reptiles. The mountain woman looked placid, but in fact the opposite was true. The mountain woman teemed with life.

Slowly, not overnight, conversation died between George and me. Our heads were filled with very different ideas.

'How was work, dear?'

Silence. George's head was deep in a book.

'How was work . . . darling?'

Silence.

I stood directly in front of him, miming his reply.

'What?' He looked up and smiled to be polite.

'Any new ships in?'

'No, dear.'

'What would you like for dinner?'

'Anything.'

I stared. 'Boiled cabbage? Jam sandwiches?'

He snapped his book shut. 'What's got into you?'

I want to leave, my heart whispered. These words in my throat, swirling in my mouth.

'Eric Williams has disappeared.'

'What?'

'Don't you agree? He's hardly ever in the country. Meanwhile . . .'

'Meanwhile, *what* . . . what are your theories? Eh? Please, enlighten me.'

I glared, standing above him, gazing down with contempt. *Pour l'amour du ciel*, I whispered. I turned on my heel and stalked away and then deliberately burnt his stupid English mashed potatoes. I thought about George less and less. I no longer looked to him for guidance. He had his cricket team, his books, his rum and his pool. I had Lucy and Venus. I thought about those hills more and more. About Granny Seraphina and Eric Williams. I often wrote to him:

This is a small place. You have made yourself accessible. Granny and I know you, have encountered you at the University. You went there to meet your people, heir apparent. Prince in waiting. You have encouraged a sense of familiarity. But now you have disappeared. Where are you? And what are you doing? I am interested, we all are.

*

My son Sebastian said *mash up* and *bol' face* and steupsed when he was agitated. Pascale was going the same way. I couldn't stop it.

'Watch at me!' Sebastian once called to his sister.

That was the limit. '*Look!*' I bellowed. 'Look at me!'

The maids did it. My children took on their mannerisms and repeated their jokes, believed their fairy stories. The maids spoke of jumbies and soucouyants, unearthly creatures, part firefly, part vampire. My children knew about dwens, children who lived in the forest, children whose feet had turned backwards. They ran around barefoot, the soles of their feet black and greasy. They sucked on pig's trotters; gulped down callaloo. They devoured pawpaws, guavas, mangoes and soursop ice cream. They were nothing like the children I'd dreamed of. They were white in skin but black in culture. Venus was their black mother. Lucy their black grandmother. When Venus's sons came to stay I was outnumbered.

'Here, drink this.' Lucy handed me a chilled red tonic one day.

'What is it?'

'It will help you, madam.'

I was suspicious.

'It make you strong. You will feel better.'

I took the tonic, sniffing it. It was sweet, syrupy. 'Thank you, Lucy.'

I slept soundly that night, hardly moving a limb, waking with the dawn. George snored lightly next to me and when I tried to get out of bed he hugged me to him, mumbling, wanting to keep me there. Instinctively, I pulled his hand up under my ribs, kissing it. I loved him still: or did I love him *again* after not loving him for a time? Either way, I loved George and my love for him felt like a memory flooding back, overwhelming me. Tears pricked in my eyes. Images came. George, when we met, dancing over to me with a glass of champagne. George, in tears, at the births of our children. George on the cricket pitch, smashing the ball and tearing across the pitch. His terrible dog-paddle swimming. His booming laugh. The time he stroked the sea turtle's head so lovingly. The first night we made love, so hot and urgent I was frozen, hands and limbs clumsy, grasping. We fell over onto the bed and then off it, to the floor. We knocked over potted plants, a small brass table, its collection of shells scattering all over the carpet.

George moved closer, curling round me, our curves fitting together like a puzzle. How had I come to reside in Trinidad? The *Cavina?* That day was hazy. I had been smuggled into the island, just like one of those great Samaan trees. A seedling on arrival, a sprig. I had taken root, grown into the earth of the island. George sighed in his sleep, and I sighed, in love with George again, filled with hope again. I lived in Trinidad now. I whispered these words to myself. I was different. And I still loved my husband. That old Shango woman had given me a love potion.

CHAPTER NINETEEN

VALIUM

George wanted to throw a house-warming party on New Year's Eve, 1964: a Spanish night for a Spanish house. The children were excited. Irit promised to sew us costumes, George and I would be Zorro and his wife.

'I will make you look gorgeous, dahling, in your little suits.'

Jules and George walked into the bush, cutting down some young coconut trees, dragging them into the house; they stood as pillars on the dance floor. George ordered a suckling pig for the spit. The maids received a Spanish cookbook with recipes for tortillas, paella and sangria; both were bemused. Lucy rose to the challenge but Venus thought we were mad, especially with the coconut trees. 'Allyuh white people tek too much sun, allyuh *crayzee*.'

A party. A fête. George had designed his castle for parties; they were what he loved best. Parties are all about people. You can serve spaghetti Bolognaise and cheap *vin de table* if the mix of guests is right. No one will notice. I made a list of all the best people we knew, those still left, amazed to see how many *hadn't* departed for civilisation, and not all were white. Our friends, by then, were a mix: remaining expats and a varied local creole society.

Everyone entered into the spirit. For a night, women were señoritas, hair piled high, tresses snagged in mother-of-pearl combs or draped with lacy mantillas, eyes kohled, drawn to look like a bird's. Lips were rouged, bosoms buffed and bulging from tight bodices. Cinched waists, long flouncy skirts. They snapped and batted their fans. Men dressed up as bandits in sombreros and ponchos and gun belts and moustaches were dabbed on with a burnt cork. George drew a straight line with black eyeliner across his top lip. He danced with every woman apart from me, and, to hide my annoyance, I danced with every man.

At midnight, we drank toast after toast to the New Year. There, in the bush, at the foot of those magnificent hills, fairy lights and champagne and dancing and Jules jumping into the swimming pool. His moustache melted down his face and his sombrero hung from his neck. He held up a glass of rum in his hand and sang, 'Sabine, oh beautiful neighbour, come to me.'

'You stupid French Creole.' I laughed and jumped in, too, and together, both quite drunk, we slow-danced in the shallow end of the pool, fully clothed, a bandit and his señorita, Jules proclaiming his love to me and serenading the stars. My mascara ran and my wet blouse clung to my breasts and I pressed my cheek against Jules' chest. Jules, a big man, was lovely to dance with. From the pool I watched my husband on the dance floor, dancing groin to groin with Vera de Lima, a half-Carib, half-white woman, her black hair piled high, her hips luscious, the hips of the green woman.

How could George resist? I watched my husband dance with another captivating woman, like all the women there at the party, like all the women in Trinidad. All the women on the island were made to be looked at.

I reached up to kiss Jules full on the lips and he kissed me back, tender and knowing and loving but not lascivious, not like the way George danced with Vera de Lima.

'You are my good friend, Sabine,' he murmured.

Oh, good and lovely Jules. He didn't want to take part in any-thing between his neighbours. We danced in the pool and sang French songs till we were shrivelled with water.

Our New Year's Eve parties became infamous and we threw many more. The 1960s beckoned a new era and, even in Trinidad, this meant a more sexually liberated time. Marriage wasn't what it had been. For those who were unhappy, marriage was no longer a life sentence. For those who were happy, the sixties allowed opportunity to experiment. Words like *wife swapping* buzzed at cocktail parties. We met couples who were *not* married, incredibly. White women and black men together – this was more and more common. Previously this was unimaginable, just like the couple I had seen at the market from my green bicycle. A love that was still taboo in Europe was unavoidable in Trinidad. I loved George but our marriage was always under threat. Other men wanted me and other women wanted George. This was both thrilling and worrying.

At a crowded party, once, I noticed a young Spanish-looking woman standing near to George on the opposite side of the room. Too near? Her skin was reddish-brown and polished, her black hair hung to her waist. Her face was small and intelligent. Her breasts were pert and bare under her gauzy dress. She stood next to George in a manner that could have been perfectly innocent and yet there was something in her manner, in George's manner, that spoke of an intimacy between them. Yes, they were *too* close, their bodies angled towards each other. I was just about to dismiss these thoughts when her manner changed. Quickly, nervous as a bird, she scanned the room. I moved to one side and partially hid behind another guest. Satisfied, she laughed and glanced up at George. From her Martini glass she fished out the olive, popping it into his open mouth. George blushed. He closed his eyes and relished the salt of the fruit. When he opened his eyes he smiled and stroked her face with the back of his hand. He didn't seem to mind her public act of daring. It happened in a moment and no one saw it happen but me.

I came to understand that George slept with other women. He did so in the name of modernity, of this new age's allowances and celebration of promiscuity, but most of all because of the feast that was on offer to him.

Black men frightened me. I feared them for reasons I couldn't articulate. I didn't realise it at first, but I also felt threatened by black women: this was jealousy. A sex-love existed between white men and black women. This was an old love, as old as the hills around me. For centuries, white men had spread their seed as they pleased, had taken as many of their slave concubines to their beds as they could: blacks, mulattos, women with skin the colour of coffee, cinnamon, muscovado sugar; women the colour of mahogany, so black they were purple. This habit hadn't ceased.

The white man *still* strutted, still behaved as father, overseer: the white man, I suspected, carried a deep carnal longing for the black woman. I saw it, smelled it, felt it, even understood it. But I couldn't compete. And what, just what did black women think of the white man's attentions? What did they say behind his back? I dreaded to think.

I wrote to Eric Williams. It was becoming a compulsion.

> *I think you've been right about a number of things. The white man should leave, should stop interfering with the course of things here in the West Indies. My husband acts like a horse put out to stud. He fucks whoever he wants. He behaves in a manner he wouldn't back in London, where he grew up. The women in England, those of his class, behave quite differently. He must know this. Here, he's in a pleasure garden. He knows he'll never leave. The plants, birds, animals, especially those on two legs, these are what he came for. He doesn't care for politics. He came to enjoy the sights and smells. He turns a blind eye. He doesn't really care about you – why should he?*

I folded the letters up. Sometimes secured them with ribbon or string. I kept the letters in a box hidden in the back of a cupboard in the office, camouflaged by stacks of papers. Once, George appeared in the office just as I was closing the cupboard door, arranging the stacks to hide the box.

'Hiding something, dear?'

I turned and scowled. 'Yes.'

'Oh, really? What?'

'Letter to my *love*r.' I let the last word drop. He stared. I felt a flush of pure hatred rise through me. On the desk in front of me was a heavy paperweight.

George was clearly taken aback. 'And what lover is this?' he replied, half jesting.

'He's young. Spanish. Black hair. He likes to tease. You know. At a party, maybe, he will put an olive in my mouth.'

George reddened.

I picked up the paperweight. 'You little *shit*,' I whispered as I took aim. I hurled the object as hard as I could at George's head.

George ducked.

The paperweight smashed on the wall behind.

Irit became a personality in artistic circles. She exhibited local art in her boutique; it was a liming spot in arty circles. She rang us one evening.

'Come to the Hilton, dahhlings, tomorrow night, by the pool. For a little drink. I'm organising a gathering for a friend to try and sell some of his paintings. Wear a nice dress.'

The Trinidad Hilton was famously built upside down: the reception at the top, the rooms underneath. We arrived around 6 p.m. as the sun was setting into a vast rose sky. The pool was floodlit, shimmering; the Samaan tree above it was an immense chandelier of fairy lights. Under it was a gazebo bar. Black barmen dressed in Hawaiian shirts mixed cocktails with the discretion of spies.

'Darlings.' Irit greeted us in a lilac kaftan. Her face was caramel brown, her eyes shaded with peacock blues.

'Look, look, look, at this view, look at Port of Spain. Come and see.' Behind the bar a narrow path led out to a glass-walled patio. We followed Irit along to a wide balcony. Port of Spain lay demure and diffident below us, acres of savannah grassland, the mauve city skyline further off. Beyond it the busy wharf, the Gulf of Paria. A cool breeze fell on us.

'What a marvellous country, eh?' Irit purred.

My eyes prickled.

'I am so *proud* to be living here,' she grinned. 'No wonder they called it the Paradise Estate originally. Imagine what this must have looked like when the Spanish first arrived, eh? And then the British. Imagine how they rubbed their hands. Now it belongs to the people.'

'White men are still buying up this island,' I snapped. 'Some now even belongs to George.'

'But George is *staying*,' Irit corrected me, winking with approval at my husband.

George nodded broodily.

I was in a foul mood, wanting no more of Trinidad; I wanted to jump from that wretched balcony.

When we returned to the bar area more guests had arrived, a mixed and fashionable crowd, black and white, young and old.

Then, a commotion behind me, a thrum of movement, voices raised, an Arrival of some sort. Standing not too far from me, under an umbrella, was a knot of besuited black men, drinking rum, laughing loudly. They were glamorous somehow, like a Trinidadian Rat Pack. Several moments passed before I recognised the figure in their midst. The thick-rimmed spectacles, the hearing aid. A small man, joking, the centre of things, enveloped in blue furls of smoke. My eyes photographed him. Eric Williams. Feet away. Relaxed and enjoying himself. Everyone, not just me, acutely conscious of his presence, as though he pulled invisible strings on the heads and shoulders of those gathered. Everyone peeped, they couldn't help it. Eric Williams gleamed with the success of himself. He was polished, scrubbed. Off duty.

A hot and miserable shame flooded up in me. Almost a decade of snipping and cutting him out. Writing him letters! Letters – as though he were God. *Papa.* Father of the Nation. Smoking and drinking rum and ol' talking and lapping up the adulation of his gang of cronies, some of whom I began to recognise.

'Darling, look who it is,' George said, thrusting a rum punch into my hand.

I wanted to leave immediately.

'Now's your chance. To go over and speak your mind.'

Eric Williams glanced in our direction. I quailed. Our eyes met briefly but he didn't recognise me at first, not from that day on the bike down in Abercrombie Street. I was all made-up, wearing a cocktail dress.

'George.' Irit appeared. 'Come, come with me. Come, Sabine, you too.'

George followed and pulled me along with him, stumbling, trying to resist. I watched as in a dream as dear Irit, with the grace of a giant butterfly, alighted on the group, parting it, introducing George to Eric Williams. Williams shook George's hand.

'And this' – Irit turned to me, her eyes twinkling with mischief – 'this is his lovely wife, Sabine Harwood. A French woman. Eric, Sabine is very interested in the PNM, aren't you, Sabine?'

Williams inspected me.

George inspected me, too.

The whole group, including Irit, inspected me, waiting for what I might say, what I could possibly say.

'So.' Williams addressed me in a patient, jovial tone. 'You're staying in Trinidad?'

The group waited. George looked bemused and delighted and a bit drunk.

'No,' I replied, stonily. 'We're not staying in Trinidad *too* much longer. I *don't* particularly like it here. I no longer ride my bicycle. And that's a pity.'

Williams stared. Only then, I could see, he remembered me and, oh, then did he remember me. His mouth fell open and he almost said it out loud: *So, you're . . .* He checked himself and digested the information silently, even flushed a little. I raised my eyebrows in recognition of his recognition of me. George noticed something had shifted between me and the Prime Minister. The group melted into the background.

Williams coughed.

'I'm interested in the PNM.' I found my voice again. 'But I confess I wouldn't have voted for you, Mr Williams, even if I had been able. Not like my good friend over there.' Irit had moved away and was ensconced in another conversation.

'That's a shame.'

My dress was low-cut, pinched at the waist, revealing the swells of my breasts and the curves of my waist and hips. My skin was damp, plump with the humidity. He gazed at me and his gaze brought on a swell in me. My breath slowed and I shifted, uneasily.

From somewhere I found the bravery to speak my thoughts. 'Why is there no water yet up in Paramin?'

Williams baulked, half smiling. I was delighted. I followed his gaze to my breast and let it rest there. I shot him a cool open stare.

'My maid, her grandmother, is a member of the PNM. They

piss in a bucket out in the bush behind their house. They live in a chattel house. You know the kind. No water, no current. Why?'

'Darling!' George interrupted. He glared at me as if I was mad. 'Leave the poor man alone.'

'No, please.' Williams waved him off. He cleared his throat but I could see he was a little embarrassed.

'It's not public knowledge yet, but I've recently commissioned a full report into the entire lower and upper Winderflet area including Morne Cocoa and Paramin. We are aware of the lack of commodities in certain parts.' His voice was suddenly Oxford, clipped and precise, overriding the situation. 'A major regeneration project will be drawn up. For most of the poorer areas like those you speak of, these issues will be addressed. Basic sanitation, etcetera. Rest assured, Mrs Harwood. We have the problem in hand.' This last word was said with a curt dismissal.

Heat rose in my cheeks. He was a professional politician. He sneered, letting me know this, and I felt vague and foolish.

'I'm glad to hear that, Mr Williams. I shall pass this on to my friends on the hill. They'll be glad of the news.'

'Please do.'

'I shall. Goodnight, Mr Williams. Darling . . .' I raised my eyebrows tartly at George, turned and left.

I overheard George say something to Williams. Williams laughed loudly, appreciatively. Immediately, the men were absorbed in conversation.

I left them to it, heading to imaginary friends on the other side of the pool terrace. Once there, I gathered myself and took another rum punch from a waiter floating past. I watched them both: my husband and Eric Williams, the Prime Minister of Trinidad.

Standing comfortably, side by side, talking comfortably, too, not about politics, of course, avidly avoiding the almighty subject. George, electric with his shock of burnished hair, his cobalt eyes, his skin the colour of red rum, his booming laugh. A bona fide card-carrying colonial Englishman. Eric Williams, silent, like a Mafia don, bold in a quieter way. God, I hated them both.

George was elated when we got home. I didn't want to hear about their conversation but he told me anyway. Cricket. They talked about *cricket*. I clamped my hands over my ears. 'I don't want to know what you talked about to that bloody man,' I shouted.

'Why not? He was very interesting.'

'Cricket! I can't believe it.'

'What else was I going to say, eh? Have a pop at him like you did?'

'Yes.'

'Come on, Sabine. Do you think politicians aren't corrupt in England or in Europe?'

'That's where Williams *caught* it from,' I spat.

'What would *you* do, then, eh? Miss Morally Superior. How would you sort the mess out, how would you have conquered the monsters left behind?'

'If I was Williams?'

'Yes.'

'The descendant of a slave?'

'Yes.'

'I would keep the sugar plantations going.'

'Oh, brilliant!'

'Redistribute the land. Turn them into collectives. Have the

Africans run them, work them, own them. Equally. Invest the profits.'

'Just like they did in Haiti?'

'Ugh. You arrogant pig.'

'Well, why don't you *write* to Williams. Tell him your ideas. Suck his cock, why don't you. He obviously fancied you.'

'Maybe I will suck his cock – in front of you.'

'Good. Suck the cock of the Prime Minister of Trinidad. Lucky man. More than I ever get.'

I slapped George hard.

'Owwww.' He was only half hurt. He was still drunk.

'You're *all* prick these days, George. That's why I don't suck your cock. Can't get my mouth round something that large.'

'Very funny, Sabine. You've changed, too. You used to be much more fun. Now it's all politics and bollocks to that.'

'God, you're boring.'

That stung him.

I smiled. I was pleased to hurt him, piss him off. He was so dead to things. Dead and drunk and stupid.

'Well, if you're so interesting and so interested in politics, why don't *you* form a political party?'

'Because I don't *want* to be in this tinpot country, with its tinpot politics. Eric Williams can be King of this country. He can fuck himself.'

I wrote again to Eric Williams that night:

Have I fallen in love with you? Or am I falling into a hatred of you? I can't tell. I am confused, always. One minute gone, the next, like the

*mountains, you're everywhere, even at the Hilton. You're in the papers
every day, on the radio, on the television. Everyone talks about you.
And what are you doing? Commissioning reports? I shall tell Granny.
She'll be interested to know that. My husband won't leave Trinidad. He
has built a house, a big house with a swimming pool. Ducks come to
swim in it. He is turning black, just like you – we both are. Everyone
is leaving. And we are staying behind. Are you like George? Have you
forgotten yourself? Massa day done. Big Brain, they call you. Well, let's
see. I'm watching you. I'm not afraid of you.*

I went to see Dr Baker. I called him one morning and he agreed to
squeeze me in as his last appointment.

'I'm having difficulty. Sleeping.' I couldn't meet his eyes. I
twisted my wedding ring. Was he faithful to his wife? I imagined
Christobel had him on a tight leash.

'Sabine, how's life?' he asked carefully.

I looked down, unable to reply. Tears fell onto my skirt. I wiped
them with my fingers.

He handed me a box of Kleenex.

I took one, blowing my nose. 'I'm . . . *stuck* here,' I stumbled. 'I
never wanted to stay this long. Now we have this big house and
the children. George is the Deputy Director now. We know people
and it's all more than I'd planned on . . . so many others have left
or are leaving. I can't get back.' Tears fell heavily, racking me.

'My dear girl.' He spoke softly. He didn't touch or comfort me,
just waited until I collected myself.

'I hate this place. I always have.'

'Come now.'

'I don't *belong* and I don't want to belong either. I don't mean any disrespect. I'm always too hot. I can't stand the heat. I can't stand it any more. My children speak like . . .'

'Does George know how you feel?'

'He *loves* Trinidad! He wants to die and be buried here, in his bloody house, in the garden.'

Sebastian looked at me, concerned, wanting to say more. He exhaled heavily, reaching for his pad, writing me out a prescription. 'Take this as you need it,' he advised. 'It'll make things a little easier.'

I looked at the prescription and read the word *VALIUM* on it, relieved. It was what I'd come for.

Valium pills, rum, my conversations with the mountain woman. This became my other, private life. I scribbled a letter to Williams every day.

Something's not right here. Something about this island. Those who came before, those who've left, slinking off. Something can't be fixed. Am I right? Are you coming to the same conclusion? Hard to put right the many wrongs of the past. Granny Seraphina, the green woman who watches me. They know. They're patient. Don't mess with them. Hard to put it all right again. Hard to paint it all out. George doesn't care, not any more. I can't remember the day I arrived. That day has vanished from memory. I dream of departure every day. Sailing back. Something isn't right here. You know what I mean, don't you?

It was the first week of the summer holidays when Sebastian disappeared. We only noticed at lunchtime, I hate to admit. I thought he was playing with Pascale in the front garden; Venus thought he was out at the back. It was Lucy's day off. No one noticed the gate was ajar, not even when we called him in for lunch.

'Pascale, where's your brother?' Pascale shook her head, not the least bit interested. She'd been in her bedroom all morning, playing with her Barbie doll. At five, she already liked dressing up, dragging around her tiny handbags, bangles up her arms. She'd developed a bad habit of drawing on the walls and furniture with her pink felt-tip pens. We confiscated the felt-tips, so she drew with biros and crayons instead, even my old Rimmel eyeliners.

'He wasn't playing with his GI Joe?'

'Nah.'

'No, Mummy,' I repeated.

I wasn't worried. The garden was big enough. I wandered out the front and saw Venus out by the gate.

'Madam, de gate open.'

'What do you mean?'

'De dogs out on de road. I had to call dem in.' Both were sheepishly following Venus up the drive.

Venus was trying not to look anxious.

'Do you think he's gone out?'

'I don't know, madam. Maybe he see de schoolchildren walkin' past, on der way to de village dong so. Dey pass every day.'

'But he wouldn't *go* anywhere with them.'

'I see him talking to dem one time, tru de gate.'

'To those children?'

'Madam, he lonely for friends his age. Who he go play wid here when mih sons not visitin'? I feel he go out wid dose chilren.'

'What?'

Winderflet village was up the road and round the corner, quite a walk for a seven-year-old.

'Venus, you stay here, call Mr Harwood, tell him to come home immediately.'

'Where you goin'?'

'To find him!'

I ran to the garage and threw the newspapers and old clothes off the bicycle.

'Madam, on dat ting?'

'What choice have I got? He could be anywhere. Call Mr Harwood.'

I cycled hard down the hot tarmac and round the corner, calling out his name. Winderflet village was more ramshackle then. A collection of squatters' shacks and half-built concrete homes clustered to the winding river. Emaciated stray dogs lay about in the dust. A caged rooster balanced on an old oil drum, crowing in indignation. I rode along the pavement, shouting for my son, tears welling up, sweat dripping from my hairline.

'My son is lost!' I shouted. 'Has anybody seen a small blond boy?' A woman sitting in her window, watching the world pass, stared at me. I stopped, angry. 'Have you seen my son?'

She shook her head, nonplussed.

'A little blond boy. He came through with some schoolchildren.'

She was sucking a salt prune and spat out the orange stone into a crumpled tissue. She lifted her finger. 'Try up so.'

She pointed behind her, into the thicket of shacks, where back yards met each other, where there was no pavement, just a labyrinth of shanties made of galvanized tin and salvaged wood.

'Thank you.'

I hopped off and wheeled the bike through the narrow paths and passages, under washing lines and past an outdoor hair salon, a woman in curlers shaving a man's afro. I blushed, calling out, '*Sebastian.*' Someone was cooking: cumin exploding, tumeric, green peppers sizzling. Somewhere, a radio on, Lord Kitchener singing 'Tick, Tick,Tick', an old calypso. A dog barked at me. A woman smoking on her porch steps smiled at me and clicked her throat: everywhere this attitude. As if I was funny, or crazy. Everybody stared at the bicycle. No one spoke to me or came forward to help. I wanted to throw down the bike and scream, *Why, why won't anybody help?*

Then: a yard clearing. Four shacks backing onto a small square. Three skinny black boys shooting marbles in a ring drawn in the dirt. A blond boy was with them, eyes squinting in concentration, ready to shoot.

'Sebastian!' Rage choked in my throat.

His marble shot across the circle, knocking others out. The boys whooped. Sebastian looked up. His face paled. He turned and scarpered, vanishing through the maze. I dropped the bike and ran after him, yelling, threatening to kill him. He darted like an antelope through the narrow lanes.

When I caught up with him it was by the scruff of the neck. He fought viciously and bit my hand. I slapped him hard.

'You are coming home *right now*, young man,' I hissed, marching him back to where he'd been playing marbles. The other boys had cleared off, too, though I noticed one staring at us from a nearby open window.

'Don't you come for him again!' I threatened. Swearing and cursing and shaking with anger, I walked Sebastian home, all the while wheeling the bicycle. 'Just wait till your father hears about this.' He was sullen and hot-faced and not the least bit penitent.

George greeted us anxiously. He'd sped from the office. When I told him the story he thrashed Sebastian soundly and sent him to his room. 'That'll teach him.' George was sure. But I was miserable. My bitten hand throbbed.

Out of guilt, I took the children to Maracas the next day. Sebastian was still sulking. Pascale was oblivious. The sea was how I liked it best: heavy rollers crashing in all over the place. I'd have plunged straight in under them, if it wasn't for the children. Instead, we spread out towels under a cluster of coconut trees next to the river at the western end, near the fishing village. I coaxed Pascale into the calm shallow river water, tiny fish flitting around in it. I left Sebastian moping on the sand, keeping an eye on him. Pascale was already something of an individual. It wasn't just the graffiti on the walls. She was scared of the full moon, howling if she saw it. She often slept with her bum in the air, as though worshipping Allah; most nights we'd have to turn her over. She was a fussy eater, hating milk and loathing eggs, especially boiled eggs. She was afraid of eggs. She already wanted to be a ballerina and all her swimsuits had tutu-like skirts of some persuasion, pleats, frills. She had one lazy eye which wandered when she was tired. She was precocious and clever, just like her father. She was all George except for her blonde halo. And her Trini sing-song.

With Pascale clinging to my back, I swam deeper to do our favourite submarine act. I dived down slowly, like a manatee, a cub on my back. I could swim quite some way with her hanging on to me, her little legs kicking.

'One, two, three,' I counted and we both gulped for air and plunged under the water, our hair silky and waving like seaweed. It was silent and green under there. Immediately I was relieved. The sea water had a dissolving effect. We dipped down and came up for air and dived again, paddling up the narrow river, our skin as slippery as a dolphin's.

'Again, again!' Pascale squealed.

We dipped and dived and swam and surfaced and dipped again. The river was peaceful, the scent of sea-grapes in the air, a heaviness like a narcotic. A rustling in the coconut trees as the breeze raked their dry brown branches.

We clambered laughing up the bank to find Sebastian no longer sitting in our camp.

'*Sebastian*!' I shouted, peering down the beach.

'Dear God, dear God, dear, God,' I shouted to myself. The same old anxiety flooded back. I turned and covered my eyes with my hands, searching up the beach towards the fishing village. And there, in the distance, out on a flat football pitch of sand, between two pirogues dragged up and chained to their moorings, lying on their sides, a group of small boys were kicking a football. One of them was blond and white.

Even the children were falling in love with Trinidad. I could fight George, but not them. A week later, I woke one morning unable to lift my head from the pillow. I couldn't move my limbs. My body was leaden and aching. It was as though I'd been attacked with a hammer; every bone in me felt broken.

'Dengue,' Venus muttered. 'It dengue fever, madam. Der been an outbreak in de village. Mosquitoes bad jus now. Der ent nuttin you can do, jus sweat de fever and in five days it pass.'

'Break bone disease,' Lucy called it, its other name. Exactly right.

By day, while George was at work, Venus and Lucy nursed me, bringing jugs of chilled lime juice, mopping my brow with damp compresses which burnt through quickly. I was delirious for days, writhing and sweating through the sheets. Their faces appeared distorted, as though I saw them through water; sometimes their voices grew distant. I fell into a stupor. Hundreds of faces swarmed around me, looming, glowering, Amerindians, Aruacs, Africans, all filing in to pick me over.

She sick.

Dey all sick.

Dem white people all sick, man. Dey sick in de head. In de blood. Dey sick like sick self and dey cyan shake what wrong wid dem. Not ever.

Dey sick, man. Look, she rollin' she eyes and mumblin', what she sayin'? Sorry? Eh? She a sick white woman.

Was this Venus or Lucy? Was this what *they* were saying?

Who was saying this?

The words fell from the air.

I wept and sweated.

Dey sick, dey bring sickness wid dem. Sweat, nuh. Sweat. Pray for your sins, for allyuh slaves, for all you have murdered.

'Lucy! Lucy!' I cried.

But Lucy was at home, asleep. Venus came to me. I couldn't hear her.

'Shh, shhh,' I heard, I think.

I trembled, afraid of Venus, what she might do, what she was thinking. George had left me alone with them. They could kill me, kill me in my sleep, in my fevered state. I tossed and sweated, aware of their hands on me. I shivered with terror. I knew they hated me. I sensed it. I heard them discussing plans to stake me out over an ants' nest, paste my mouth with honey. The Robber Man laughed at me. I saw his coffin box. *Wap!* Eric Williams in Woodford Square, on the bandstand. *Repudiate colonialism.* I wanted him to save me, save me from Lucy and Venus. Poleska de Boissière sitting in an old carriage with a parasol, making the rounds of her estate; she was ninety, or was she fifty? Eric Williams sitting next to her. The carriage, a huge baby's pram, just like royalty use in England. They were royalty, riding around together, waving like the Queen.

Venus was right. Five days later I lifted my head. I was thinner and weaker when I stood.

'Look at this!' I was suddenly scared. 'What have you *done*, what have you done to me?' I shrieked. All along my arms and legs, my stomach, an outbreak, a rash like measles.

'That a good sign, madam,' Lucy assured me. 'The fever leaving you.'

No way to atone for the sins of those who came before me, or even for my own sins, for George's sins: stupid foolish white man spreading his seed. The hills nodded down at me. Those great shoulders shook and heaved, laughing.

I was white. White in a country where this was to be implicated, complicated, and, whatever way I tried to square it, guilty. Genocide. Slavery. Indenture. Colonialism – big words which were linked to crimes so hideous no manner of punishment was adequate.

Or perhaps this eternal guilt *was* the only fitting retribution; a curse, yes, an agony. Daily, I held myself together in the face of this appalling history. I just wanted to get on with things, ignore it all, live as if all these crimes were a dream, long ago happenings. No white person I came across *ever* mentioned them: no expat, no ex-colonial, no French Creole, those flinty-eyed beauties like Christobel who arrived from Martinique, who once ran the estates. No white person spoke of these things.

I was naive. I dared not bring up the subject of slavery. The whites just wanted the blacks to learn from them, run things as the colonials had. They still wanted Europe in the West Indies.

'Get on with it, man. Stop being *the victim*. Slavery was appalling, but you can't blame it for everything. Get on with it now.'

'Slavery was *mild* in Trinidad. We were good masters, we treated them well. We looked after our people, looked on them as family.'

'Whites don't owe you a living.'

'The black man is lazy.'

'He can't govern himself.'

'Massa day done, eh? Now none of them want to work. What they going to do now?'

'They're getting rid of us, but they can't take over.'

Comments made by friends around the dinner table. Trinidad's whites felt no guilt at all. They'd done nothing wrong.

Eric Williams was the only person I knew who spoke of slavery. And so I wrote to him:

Papa, I hear they call you Papa, both in your cabinet and on the street. Papa. Father. Just like the white man. They were fathers, too, treated their slaves as children. You are the father now, a black man. You and

George: how different are you? Granny Seraphina is still waiting for electricity. Venus lives with us now and so she has running water. But there's no water in her village and their village school needs a roof and the villagers have tried to fix it and were told not to, that an entire new school would be built by the government. And guess what: that was two years ago. Still no school. It's been forgotten, hasn't it? How can you sleep at night? No one by your side, no one to oppose you in private. You make me nervous, Mr Williams.

George didn't like the new me. I was quieter, secretive. Resentful of his affairs. He knew nothing of my private world, the letters and the pills.

'What's got into you?' he quizzed me one day.

'I've told you many times.'

'You want to leave all this behind.'

'Yes.'

'Any more theories about Eric Williams?'

'Yes. Convenient how he's grown deaf.'

'Why do you care?'

'Maybe I don't.'

'Maybe you should stop being so juvenile.'

'Juvenile?'

'It's juvenile to have ideals. Man is an imperfect beast. Williams is a man.'

'I think about him a lot.' I said this without a thought. It was the truth. I thought about Eric Williams more than George.

CHAPTER TWENTY

QU'EST-CE QU'IL DIT?

Granny Seraphina. One day I spotted her waiting for a route taxi on the hot pavement near Boissiere village, umbrella held aloft. Eyes like yellow headlights on full, flagging me down. I stopped the car.

'Would you like a lift?' I called across to her.

The old woman nodded, as if she'd been expecting me. Granny closed her umbrella, folding her bony legs and arms into the front seat.

'I'm on my way into town,' I explained. 'Where can I drop you?'

'De Red House,' she replied, her chin set.

'Oh, you have an appointment?' I smiled, teasing her.

She clung to her handbag, staring out the windscreen.

I pushed. 'Do you go to the Red House often?'

She looked at me as if I were stupid. 'Yes,' she nodded. 'Friday las' of every month.'

I was shocked. 'Why?'

'Ah does go to give in mih letter.'

'What letter?' My stomach churned.

'De one Clive write fuh meh.'

'Clive writes letters for you?'

She nodded.

'Who are you writing to?'

'Dr Williams.'

'The Prime Minster?'

The old woman nodded, glancing shiftily at me.

I almost stopped the car but managed to drive on. 'And you . . . take your letter in by hand?'

She nodded.

'Do you ever get a reply?'

She made a small dismissive gesture: again, a stupid question.

'What do you write about?'

'Ah aksin' for somptin.' Her voice was curt, anger smouldering in it. She was tired of waiting.

'Granny, you will get what you want. I know you will.'

But Granny's eyes were distant and she kept her mouth clamped shut. I was afraid of her then. I drove on, changing my course so I could take the old woman right to the steps of the house of power. Big stone hall, painted blood red, burnt to the ground at least once and rebuilt exactly the same. Granny climbed out, clutching her brolly and handbag. She didn't say thank you or goodbye or anything like that. I noticed she was more gaunt and bent than the last time we met, as though she could only look downwards.

I sent my son away at the age of eight. I posted him off to England. I wasn't the only mother to do it either; we all sent them off, those who stayed on. Little blond creole boy; I sent him to get an education. To prepare him for when we'd join him in England – right then I *still* held hope that one day we would leave. Maybe I sent him to get a taste of what I wanted, bring it home with him? We chose a small preparatory school in Kent. Blazers and boaters and short trousers and ties and knee socks and a games kit and plimsolls and new underpants and vests and *shoes*. Shoes with laces, two pairs; one for best. I spent hours sewing name tags into every single garment and towel, every sheet and blanket. *Sebastian Harwood. Made in Trinidad*.

After Sebastian's first term we went to Piarco Airport to meet him off the BOAC jet. I wore large sunglasses to hide my wet eyes.

'That's him, that's him!' I cried, seeing a blond boy emerge at the top of the flimsy BOAC staircase. He appeared unsure of himself, climbing down each step with purpose, as if just woken from sleep. He frowned as he descended, something on his mind.

'Darling, it's *him*. Thank God!'

George was immersed in a magazine. My heart thudded, eager to have my little boy in my arms again. Several mothers stood there, waiting anxiously. The BOAC aunties guided our children back and forth. I ran to greet Sebastian, bombing him with kisses, squeezing him so hard he yelped. Poor little boy: wordless, dazed, unable to answer the hundreds of questions I fired at him.

'How was the flight?'

'The food on the flight?'

'The other children on board, did you know anyone?'

'Are you tired, my love?'

'Hungry?

He nodded, sleepy-eyed, in reply to all my questions. Lucy

had made his favourite dinner: callaloo and fried plantain. 'Just wait till we get you home.' I hugged him tight.

Venus was in the kitchen when we returned.

'Eh, eh, Look who *back*! A big young man. Look how tin he get and how white. Eh, Mr Skinny Pokey?'

She laughed, hugging Sebastian even though he didn't want to be hugged, holding himself back. Quickly, though, he was full of tears.

Venus bent down to his eye-level, wrapping her arms around him. He clung to her, sobbing hot florid tears. Tears in Venus's eyes, too, as she knelt in the kitchen, holding my son's grief and homesickness.

'Oh gorsh, nuh. Oh gorsh, w'appen to you, yousa big man.' But she hugged him tight, holding on to him in a way which comforted herself. His little frame shook.

I turned away, leaving them.

George stood at the bar, mixing himself a rum and soda. He didn't like all the fuss, he hadn't missed our son. He held a frosted clinking glass up towards me. I shook my head, passing him.

In our bedroom I switched on the air conditioning and lay down on our bed. I turned on my side, water spilling from my eyes onto the pillow. I should have escaped then, in those early days, I should have packed up, said goodbye to George and to Trinidad, taken our children back to civilisation.

Sebastian never needed me again, not really. He arrived and departed for boarding school three times a year for the next eleven years, but he was never the same again. I'd abandoned him. And he'd abandoned his need for me.

He was bilingual for many years. He learnt to speak impeccable Standard English from his schoolmasters and friends, in self-defence. The boarders were allowed pets and his pet crapaud was replaced by a black bunny called Bouncer that he kept in a hutch. But every time he stepped off that BOAC jet onto the tarmac at Piarco, his first language rushed up his throat. The sing-song came alive, that demented vocabulary. He *eh*, *ehed* and *ohoed* and steupsed and said *mash up* and *bol' face*, ran about barefoot and never mentioned a word of his school term, as if it hadn't happened. In his adult speech, no trace of this island language remained; he spoke the Queen's English. All this broke my heart so much we never sent Pascale away.

George purchased another piece of Trinidad. This time it was a strip of land with some beachfront and a sand-spit and its own little island, a rather ragged-looking rock, I saw from the photographs, off the Blanchisseuse coast. I didn't want to go to the beach any more, what with my skin the colour of teak. Most afternoons I slept heavily, after two Valium. George would disappear, returning home smelling of grass and spices. That scent, I came to know it well; he came home often wearing it like a cologne, like the scent of another woman. Sometimes he wanted to make love to me, even when I was drugged.

'How *could* you?'

'How could I what?'

'You know! Get off me.'

'Darling. What's the matter? You know you like this. You like me.'

'I'm not in the mood . . .'

'Really? Are you sure?' He ran his hands up my legs, up into my skirt. 'You're always in the mood.'

I twisted away. 'Not after you've been with *her*.'

'I've been to the beach.'

'You've been with that *bitch*.'

'You're imaging things.'

'And you have no imagination at all. You're *boring*. You see nothing. Blinkers! Nothing. You're a boring man. Boring!' I screamed at him through my haze.

'Darling.'

'Get off me!'

He stood and stared, shaking his head.

Later, in the garden, I smoked. The green mountain woman peered down at me from her immensity. I knew.

He's been rolling in *you*.

Maybe so.

He's yours. Have him.

I don't want him.

Take him off my hands.

I don't want him.

He's in love with you and I don't blame him.

I'm very beautiful. Didn't you know?

Not till I came.

Your husband knew what he was coming to.

Yes. He's ruined now. Ruined.

I heard a soft laugh, laughter of wry recognition and exaltation.

I took more pills. Slept for days at a time.

Then, one day, George came home excited.

'Look at this.' He tossed a small booklet onto a patio table. A downpour had just stopped. Everything dripped and glistened and the keskidees were roused, making a fuss, asking their eternal question: *Qu'est-ce qu'il dit?*

I picked up the booklet, realising that it was a passport. Trinidadian. I opened it, reading George's name, his details. I flipped the blank crisp pages to a recent photo at the back. George's face had changed. His skin had crinkled around the eyes, his cheeks were more filled out and, yes, he was darker. Still a dashing man, though, his eyes azure against his new skin tone. At thirty-seven, George was in his prime. The passport was brand new.

'I picked it up this morning,' he explained.

'How did you get it, you're not *born* here?'

'I have to have it.'

'Why?'

'Europeans can't own land any more. Only Trinidadians can.'

'So?'

'So I've become a Trinidadian.'

'*What!*'

'I'm a Trinidadian.'

I looked at him, shocked. 'That's not possible.'

'Yes, it is.'

'How?'

'I've traded my old British passport in. They're allowing this.'

'You haven't.'

'I had to. It was that or sell up and get out.'

'But that's what they *want*. They're controlling who gets what, so that we don't get it all any more.'

'Well, tough, I own parts of Trinidad.'

'But you're English! How will you ever be able to get back into *England*?'

'Don't worry about that. I'm a born Englishman. By birth and blood. The British Embassy assured me. I *had* to do it.'

'And you didn't discuss it with me?'

'No.'

'Jesus, George. When are you ever going to see we're not *wanted*? You're hanging on to your job as it is.'

'I'm Trinidadian now, so are our children. We've lived here *ten years*. Our home is here. Others are building near by. Soon it'll be a neighbourhood you'll *like*. I'll buy more land. It's cheap as dirt. If I lose my job I can develop it. When are *you* going to see it all, the bigger picture? What do you want me to do? Go back to a desk job in the City? Commute with my briefcase, going to work in the dark, coming home in the dark, on the train and the tube like so many of those poor fucks. I can't do that. Here I'm *someone*. We know everyone. What do you want from me? To go back to Harrow on the fucking Hill?'

'I hate it here!' I screamed. 'I want to go back.'

'Well, *go*.' His eyes blazed.

I sobbed, facing him. George faced me back. An awkward fear churned in my gut.

I slapped him. He flinched and put his hand to his face. His eyes became calm and serious and at that moment he matched my heat with grace. I don't know where he summoned this grace from. A resolve that was his, that was a question of his self-worth, the high price he put on his own head. George valued himself in some way which was delicate, unshowy, tenacious. He knew himself. It was the cause of his magnetism. He nodded, careful and slow.

'If I push this, I'll lose you,' I said quietly.

He said nothing.

But I understood. He'd called my bluff.

Qu'est-ce qu'il dit, the birds outside squawked.

'Shut up!' I shouted at them. 'Shut up, shut up.'

Qu'est-ce qu'il dit?

'He said go, go. And maybe I *should*.'

Later, Lucy gave me one of her potions. I knocked it back with more Valium. I slept it off. George went out and got drunk. I wrote to Williams.

Corruption now is obvious! Everybody talks about it. Ten years you've had. Like me. Ten years. I'm still waiting for that report. Is that hearing aid even switched on? We all know about the deal with the foreign sewage company, how your ministers asked for more money for the boys, your closest advisers. They say you were shocked at first, to hear about this racket, but they talked you round. The beginning of the end. Now you take this extra cash just like they do.

Beware of Granny. She still shits outside. She's coming to your door, now. Beware her wrath. Even your old friend Sparrow has turned against you. His latest calypso says it all: 'Get de hell outta here'. I hear it all the time on the radio. My boxes have grown. Ten boxes now. I hide them in the attic of our office. George doesn't know. George can go to hell, like you. You were brilliant, excellent, once. Educated friends, C.L.R. James, George Padmore, Aimé Césaire. You knew them all. No wonder they fired you from the Caribbean Commission. No wonder. You were dynamite. Exactly what they didn't want, a firebrand, a demagogue they couldn't control. And

then you arrest C.L.R. James for fear of his subversive influence.
Arrest him! Your teacher, your friend.

I took more pills. That report into basic sanitation in Paramin was never written, maybe not even commissioned. I didn't care. To hell with it all. I was a fool. And I was married to a man who had carefully thought things through. I couldn't remember our home in Harrow on the Hill, couldn't picture it. Then one day I found out, quite by chance, that George had sold it – without telling me.

'Why?' I shouted.

'Because I needed the money.'

'Again, you never asked. Never consulted me.'

'Why should I? The house was mine, not yours.'

'It was a gift to *us*.'

'Bought with my parents' money. My name on all the paperwork.'

I'd never considered the implications of this. I owned nothing. My husband owned me, though. I was chattel, human chattel. I was stuck, truly stuck in Trinidad. The green woman gazed down at me, mute, but never sympathetic.

Still, we threw parties. Parties cured us. Pool parties, dinner parties, cocktail parties. Always Jules, always Irit and Helena and Gabriel, the Bakers. We were proud of ourselves and our home and our children and everything looked as though we were blessed: money, looks, rude health. Our life appeared charmed. And for those times, yes. Parties brought us back together. We flirted and showed off, alive to our desire for each other. Our physical appetite for each other never waned. Parties made us remember this and I forgave George his infidelities, which sometimes he even confessed.

'I'm so, so sorry,' George once wept, falling onto his knees. 'Forgive me. I'm so greedy. I don't love the others. I'm your slave, Sabine. You have me in chains. My heart is chained to you.'

George drank more and more. At weekends it was nothing to drain a rum and soda at 11 a.m., drinking throughout the day.

'The heat burns it off,' was his belief. He spent hours by the pool, reading, swilling the ice in his rum. He still cleaned the pool daily, lovingly, hoovering and scattering chlorine and squeezing blue drops into the water. He lived in shorts and cotton sports shirts, flip-flops. His transistor radio was always on, tuned into the local news or the cricket reports. He never lost his English accent, though. If anything, this part of him grew stronger. The whole island spoke in a mellifluous sing-song, in banter and picong, all playful and backward and uncompromising. But George boomed. His laugh was stupendous, a guffaw so loud people smirked at him, behind his back.

Still, I wrote to Williams, mostly at night, sneaking off to the study, when the house was dark.

Strikes everywhere, hundreds, one every day in the news, unrest in the oil fields, in the sugar factories. The PNM's response? To ban strikes! You are corrupt and so is George. Is this the island's curse? Did the Amerindians curse us all, condemn us to our follies, to what the island offers so freely? To lust and booze and failure to govern. A national inheritance? You've lost the plot. You are overwhelmed and overturned.

You are indentured. You are enslaved. You are colonial. You are stuck in the revolving door of all these past methods. All men are born equally stupid and greedy.

Granny Seraphina fell ill. Boils on her legs, open seeping wounds.

'She woh go to de hospital,' Venus said. 'She woh go to no doctor either.'

'Has this happened before?'

'From time to time.'

Their home on the hill was poorly ventilated. Now the boys were older, Granny slept on the floor. The boils appeared out of the pureness of poverty. We brought Granny home, her legs wrapped in bandages made from scraps of material. She slept in Venus's room, next to the kitchen. Lucy lanced and treated her boils, patching them with soothing herb poultices. Granny approved of Lucy's cures. The old woman lay silent in Venus's bed. Venus slept in Sebastian's room as he was away at school. Bernard and Clive came, too. For a week, we camped. The house was full. Pascale and Venus's sons whooped and ran wild. George made himself scarce. He didn't like Granny at all.

'That woman gives me the creeps.'

'I'm glad.'

'She's trouble.'

'Yes.'

'I don't want you encouraging her to stay.'

'She'll stay till she's better.'

'She looks like she's already dead.'

'Quite the opposite. Granny is very alive.'

One evening I peered in to see how she was and found her bed was empty. The bedside light bathed the room in tobacco-coloured light. Singing. I could hear singing, though. Granny? Singing, in high lucid tones. I crept into the room. The door to the small bathroom ensuite was open. The shower was on. Water fell like continual rain; the sound brought on a raw and guilty feeling. My shoulders crawled. The sound of singing and rain.

The shower curtain was pulled only half across. Granny's old dress lay crumpled on the floor. I dared to look, quickly, surreptitiously – and there she was. A black human cross. Granny Seraphina, arms outstretched, head back, the water bathing her eyes, falling into her nostrils, her open mouth. Singing all the while, her black body lathered with creamy soap. Granny, soaped and lathered and singing like an angel in my house.

Later that evening, Lucy came to me, finding me in bed.

'Madam, drink this.'

I drank her cooling tonics frequently. Most were innocent enough, no more than soluble aspirins. They tasted quite pleasant, too, and brought relief. This tonic looked different, darker, shreds of bark spiralling in it.

'What's this?'

'Drink it. It good for you.'

I sniffed and tasted it. 'Oooh.' I grimaced. 'That's *gosh*.' I sipped again, then looked at her squarely, balancing the glass on my knee.

Lucy always looked sad. Her sadness was like mine and this made me feel comforted.

'Lucy, what happened?'

Lucy's brown eyes were molten soft. She wasn't sure what she should say to me. The slope of her shoulders, the sag of her breasts, even her face was lopsided with grief. Her still eye bored through me. 'My daughter die, madam.'

'Oh Lucy, I'm so sorry.'

She nodded, as if to confirm the fact to herself.

'What happened?'

'Nobody does know. De doctors don't even know. She get sick. Some kind of brain fever.'

'How awful.'

'Yes, madam. She died in the car, on the way to the hospital.'

'No!'

'Yes, madam.'

'Why?'

'It all very sudden.'

'When did this happen?'

'Years ago, madam. She was a woman, she was twenty-two years old.'

A tear spilled down one of Lucy's cheeks.

'You weren't able to help her with your medicine?'

'I try. But nothing help her. There was nothing I know of to save her.'

I gazed into the tonic Lucy had prepared for me. 'Can you save me?'

'No, madam.'

'Sometimes I feel like I'm dying, too.'

'I can see that.'

'I'm homesick, you see. Can you give me something for it?'

'Yes, madam. Drink what I give you.'

'The Africans who came to the Caribbean on the ships, they were homesick, too.'

'Yes.'

'They never got back either, did they?'

'Some go back in spirit.'

'How?'

'They drink a broth. A poison.'

I looked at her, hopeful. 'Could you mix me up such a broth?'

'No, madam.'

'I'm sorry, Lucy.' I hung my head.

She left. I sipped her tonic and was soon asleep, dreaming of Sebastian and Pascale. They were waving at me from a spit of sand. Sebastian held a small clay urn in his hands. He opened it and began to scatter something from it. Ashes. Ashes fluttered down like birds, caught on the wind. Some fell and floated on the sea. I stood across a bay from them, on another sand-spit, ankle-deep in water. Some of the ashes floated on the surface, towards me. They made a dappled pattern. Large black flakes: *who were they scattering*? I didn't know. The ashes floated towards me, in on a tide, slipping between my feet. I danced backwards to avoid them, knowing then. It was George. George's ashes, wet and sodden and clinging to my shins.

CHAPTER TWENTY-ONE

DE MAN WOH BITE

It became more and more common to see black- and brown-skinned members at the Country Club, including Eric Williams and various hangers-on. They liked to swan about, drinking cocktails and laughing loudly at the bar. Mostly I avoided them.

One lunchtime, I was there at the Club alone. Sebastian was away at school in England and Pascale was attending primary school near by. I had taken to spending lunches and early afternoons alone at the Club, sunbathing near the fountain. I read and smoked and watched the iguanas scuttle across the grass. Or I swam lengths in the Olympic-sized swimming pool, sometimes up to forty. I was known to the staff and so when a waiter came over with a tray, I was surprised. I hadn't yet ordered a drink.

'Hello, Martin,' I said to the handsome young black man in a pristine white shirt.

Martin seemed a little nervous as he approached and when he lowered the tray I saw a white envelope. Martin and I looked at each other with mute and mutual curiosity. I raised my eyebrows and he pulled his lips down, miming a serious face. I opened the envelope and read the short note.

'Where is he?' I whispered, shocked, peering behind Martin.

'At de bar, madam.'

'Jesus God.'

Martin smiled, delighted to be the messenger.

I read the note again, lips moving.

I looked up towards the covered bar area. Yes, I could just make out a familiar figure sitting there. Suit and tie, dark glasses, hearing aid. A teenage girl was with him. His daughter, Erica?

'He daughter here from school in England,' Martin explained. 'He bring her here sometime. He like to be with her.'

'Martin. Good God. He's invited me up for a drink.'

Martin's face creased into a toothy grin.

I laughed to cover my fear. 'Are you surprised?'

'Yes.'

'Shit. What shall I do?'

Martin looked up towards where Williams sat, head down in a newspaper.

'Go up, nuh. De man woh bite.'

'I can't. I'm too nervous and I hate him.'

'He not so bad, Miss. He come many times. He good to us.'

'You *still* trust him?'

Martin's face fell to a slack uncaring expression. He shrugged.

I was wearing a bikini and I was covered in suntan oil and still damp from a swim. I peered upwards at the besuited blind-deaf figure and a murderous hatred stirred through me. Did he remember me from the Hilton? Did he connect me with Irit, with my husband?

'How does he think he knows me?'

'He aks meh if you is Mrs Harwood, madam.'

'Did he, now?'

'Yeah, de lady who ride de green bicycle down Port of Spain.'

I stared at Martin, stunned.

Martin's eyes danced and he stifled a laugh. 'You does ride a bike one time, madam?'

'Yes.' I felt sad all of a sudden. 'Yes, years ago. When I first arrived.'

Martin looked impressed. He shook his head.

I noticed Williams' daughter had gone down to the pool and was standing at the edge, about to dive in. Williams had dropped his newspaper and was waiting to watch.

'He's here *alone*? No bodyguards, no entourage?'

'He alone, madam.'

His daughter was thin and leggy, pretty. She executed a neat precise dive into the pool.

I sighed. 'Tell the Prime Minister I'll be up in a moment. I'm just going to change into some clothes.'

'Your daughter is a strong swimmer,' I said to Eric Williams as I approached. As it turned out, I had only brought a flimsy polka-dotted wrap dress with me, so I wore that, purposely leaving some bosom exposed. My short blonde hair was still wet and combed back off my face. My skin was somehow nuder for the recent swim and the sun cream. I wore flip-flops and I was tanned a honey-brown. On behalf of Granny I didn't extend my hand or offer any form of deference to who he was. I sat down in the wicker armchair opposite him and made myself comfortable. Martin glided to our table.

'A Bentley, please.' I smiled and Martin nodded.

'Another rum and soda for me,' Williams said, modifying his accent towards the Trinidadian of the educated classes. Around us heads were turned away but I was aware of ears pricked, of people taking notice.

'Is she here on holiday?'

'Yes.'

'At school, in England?'

'Yes.'

'My eldest, my son, is in Kent. He went back a few days ago.'

I couldn't see Williams' eyes through his dark sunglasses. I was conscious that he was cool, though. He studied me as I talked. His manner was attentive, courteous, as though storing private ideas. He was much more composed than I was.

'Has she her father's brains, too?'

'Oh, yes.'

'And her mother's looks?'

He exhaled a violet plume of smoke and nodded thoughtfully.

Everyone knew of Williams' second marriage to Soy Moyou. Soy was the love of his life: young, glamorous, half Chinese. She died of tuberculosis two years after they were married. Erica was their only child.

'Her mother wasn't just lovely to look at – as you are. She was a very bright woman.'

I blushed, despite myself.

Eric Williams shot me a wry considered smile, catching me off-guard.

'I used to be . . . so self-contained before we met, you know?

Some people can have that effect on you. They can make you *need* more than just the self.'

I nodded, a little ashamed. I wanted to flirt, to be in control again, but my throat had dried up. I was struck dumb by his aura of power and by this candid approach. He was working me. *Power, ma soeur.* I remembered Irit's words. But he was still assessing me from behind those dark lenses, gauging my reactions.

'Yes.' I steadied my gaze. 'I've always felt like that, about my husband, George.'

'Then he's a lucky man.'

'How long has it been since your wife died?'

'Fourteen years. She died soon after our daughter was born.'

'I'm sorry.'

'Don't be. Erica is my joy. She keeps me alive, especially on bad days. To have more than just the same old job,' he joked, swirling his rum.

'Once, if you'll forgive me, you were passionate about the job.'

'Yes.'

'I saw you speak. Twice, in fact. In Woodford Square.'

He looked genuinely taken aback. 'What?'

'Massa day done. I heard you say that. Four years ago.'

Williams moved around in his chair. Touché. I was pleased with myself; now *he* was off guard. I smiled. 'Now we drink at lunchtime in Poleska de Boissière's old home. A relative of yours, maybe?'

I could tell he didn't want me to speak like this. Not yet. But what had he expected? To gaze at my shapely figure again, to amuse himself while he was alone at the bar? Had he just wanted a female companion for an hour?

Eric Williams lifted his dark glasses. He propped them on his head, staring at me. His eyes were a bold coloured-in brown; the whites were shiny, like polished ivory, like the eyes of a man half his age. Clear and wide and open.

'You telling me *I* Massa now?' His accent dropped, he spoke like the man from those university-of-the-street days.

'Your words. You just said that.'

'Everyone say dat.'

'Would your wife . . . would Soy have said that about you, too?'

Williams stared and half laughed at my impertinence.

'I beg your pardon,' I muttered.

'Soy wanted nothing of politics. She never wanted me to go into politics full-time at all, not like this. If she was still alive I would never have got so involved. She didn't want that. It would all be different.'

'Who else, then, if not you?'

Williams shrugged. 'There are other people. Robinson. Others.'

'I've been here ten years. We arrived the day you launched the PNM. I've found this country . . . tiring. It's got the better of me, too.'

'Too? You think it's got the better of *me*?'

'Yes.'

'No running water for your maid who lives up de hill?'

'Isn't that the least of it?'

'You come up here to take another potshot?'

'I was invited.'

He nodded.

'Who criticises you, Mr Williams?'

'Dey all like to criticise; gossip is rife.'

'And you kill them all off, your opponents. Isn't that right?'

Williams gazed at my breasts. I let him look. I could have opened my dress, let him feast his eyes. I was suddenly turned on, and furious.

'You give your husband this . . . criticism?'

'It's good for him.'

'Why don't you leave? Trinidad is none of your business. You and your type, you and your husband. Why are you still here?'

'My husband has become a Trinidadian. He owns land now, and you have let him buy it. He doesn't care what the politicians do. He loves Trinidad the way you do. He loves it here. He'll die here.'

Williams snorted. 'White men. White men like George Harwood. They all take, take, take. All the second-raters, those who aren't good enough to survive in England, they come out to the West Indies and swan about. Buy land, build. Set up shop. They come and stay, ruin their second-rate minds. Is that what you want? To be married to such a man? A man who'll ruin you, too?'

I glared.

'He wasn't such a man when he arrived. George has changed.'

'Is this all personal enough for you now?' Williams smiled.

I stood up, trembling.

'*Think*. The oldest of twelve, your father in the post office. Oxford, teaching at Howard in the States. All those books, all that time you've had to think, all the time in the world to think up new ideas for Trinidad, to make a difference. Kick those fat horses out. But now all you want is *this* – this life, the old way. You never really wanted to change things too much. You can't be bothered.

All too much hard work, even though it doesn't really work for the people of Trinidad. You keep things ticking along. The Catholic Church has fought you and won. Your cronies are a bunch of thugs. You listen to gossip and you haven't managed to change much. You were brilliant once, just like George. Now you sit and drink rum at the Country Club, a place which once barred black men like you from even setting through the door. The Country Club should be blown up. Those bastards, those second-raters you talk about – they *made you*.'

Williams' face was set in a look of half fury and half disbelief. I sensed a grim mood sweep over him, that I had overstepped the mark.

I looked at my watch.

'I must go,' I said. 'I have to pick my little girl up from school. Goodbye, Mr Williams. I hope you enjoy the rest of your daughter's visit.'

I looked around the bar and noticed it had gone quiet, people straining their ears, pretending they hadn't been listening. I hurried, almost running down that path and across those splendid wide hardwood floors towards the Saaman tree outside.

I was unhappy for days. I couldn't ban Williams from my dreams or my daydreams. *He has appeared. Come to save his vexed and oppress children. He has come forward, cast down he bucket. Everywhere people will bless de name of de hero. Eric Williams.* I tossed and turned. The Robber Man, the Mighty Sparrow. Eric Williams. They harassed me in my sleep. I had nowhere to go, no home to return to in England or France. I took pills and they sent me back to sleep and I dreamed even more about Eric Williams, saw him mocking me, sitting in the white wedding cake on the savannah. Eric Williams wore a white suit. He was reading his own *History of the People of Trinidad and Tobago* aloud to Granny Seraphina and she was nodding, sitting at his feet, her face aglow with reverence.

George and I argued.

'What's got into you *now*?'

'What's got *out* of *you*? You choose to be blind.'

'You're crazy. Politics again, Sabine?'

'Am I crazy? At least I'm *alive*. Thinking. At least I'm not second-*rate*.'

George stared.

'Isn't that why you came here, why you accepted that lowly office job out here, a dot on the map? Out here you can be someone. You can be a master, invent yourself, a little king.'

George stood very still and calm; rage choked in his throat.

'We invented this island. Wasn't that the whole point of the West Indies, eh? A get-rich-quick scheme for Europeans?'

'Is that what you think I'm doing here?' George said, his voice steely.

'Yes.'

'I see.'

'You had it planned all along, didn't you? You shrewd bastard. You never planned to leave. You'd done your homework. You *came* to buy, didn't you? Build, settle, be the king of your castle. Drink rum. Fuck the local women. Keep the wifey sweet, kid her along. *I love you, I love you, Sabine.* Tell her anything, drug her up.'

I thought of the *Cavina*, those great black corbeaux in the sky ready to pick me over. George knew *then*. Dreams and ambitions he never dared reveal, not in one go.

'Well, why not? Eh?' George retaliated. 'OK, why not? Rather a king here than a little clerk in a company in the suburbs of London. Who did you think you were marrying? What did you want from me? Why don't you save yourself? Leave. Women want men to make them, save them. They get disappointed if we fail, if we do the wrong thing. But what the fuck have you ever done apart from bitch and complain and point out men's errors?'

'I hate you,' I spat.

'You used to be lovely, sunny, fun. You used to love me. I could feel it.'

George's eyes pooled. I had never seen him like this.

He was right. At that moment I didn't like, let alone love him any more.

We made love. Hot and passionate and desperate to find each other again. Eric Williams joined us in our bed. I was making love to Williams, too, not just George. I was disgusted, writhing and unable to escape the clutches of either man. This country, this house under the hip of the green woman, this backwards language, this heat, this mad fucked-up legacy of corrupt ruling. This island was cursed. Nothing, nothing would ever wipe away what had gone before. Granny, Venus, my children who were creole. It was all more than I could stand. I hated my husband as I fucked him, as I let myself be fucked; hated Eric Williams; saw them as the same, the same man.

TRINIDAD, 1970

CHAPTER TWENTY-TWO

BLACK POWER

Trouble had been brewing. Like an approaching hurricane in late August, when the keskidees fall silent and the clouds flee from the sky to outrun the winds, there were signs. Strikes, strikes in the oil fields, strikes on the buses, strikes and more strikes. March 1970, the sun was ferocious, relentless. The country was still delinquent, newly pregnant after carnival. There were marches out on the streets; black people marching in the midday heat. Enough was enough. Rallies out at St Augustine, at the university. A new movement was formed: the National Joint Action Committee. A charismatic student leader, Geddes Granger, spoke up for black disappointment, wanting *a complete change of the system of our way of life*. Trinidadians had a black government but no black power.

Granger was educated, angry and articulate. Halle-bloody-lujah! I was sick, sick, sick of it. First Williams, then Granger. The same thing all over again, the same man. Except Granger was a much more glamorous figure than Eric Williams; younger. A handsome, bearded black man in jeans and an African shirt, his fist raised. *Power to the black man*, he shouted. And yet, just like Eric Williams, his eyes were shrouded behind dark glasses and there was something about this screened-off demeanour that was all too familiar. I wanted to knock their heads together.

Venus was unhappy.

'Granny listen to dese Black Power fellers in Woodford Square. She too old to stan up all day in de sun, man. But she stan up and she listen to dem. She gone de whole day and when she come back she does talk a lot, man. Talk more dan ever about change, about startin' over here in Trinidad, a new time . . .'

'Maybe you should go, too,' I said, testing her.

'Nah! I doh want no trouble. Granny a mad crazy woman. Nah, not me in de street. Granny Seraphina tell meh to march, too, you know, Miss. She tell meh to quit mih job here, grow afro and be proud and go out and pelt bricks at de Red House. She gone *mad*, Miss. I 'fraid she. Boy, she vexed wid de PNM. She gone back to Woodford Square, dis time wid broomstick and she listen to de new leaders, what dey sayin'. I tink she go lick dong de entire buncha dem government fellas. She dangerous, Miss!'

The PNM had reacted badly to all this Black Power business. Stokely Carmichael, the great Black Power leader himself, was barred from entering Trinidad. His books were banned. And Carmichael was a Trinidadian! A black man banned by the black government. The PNM loathed him and his type. Everywhere afros and hippie beads like in America, everywhere *Negritude* on the streets, anger expressing itself in protest, in barely contained malevolence. There was even a chapter of the Black Panthers in

Trinidad. Holy God on earth. And thousands gathering in Woodford Square, all over again, this time marching to Shanty Town, all led by Geddes Granger.

I drank lots of rum. I paced about the house. George didn't seem to care.

'It'll all blow over,' he predicted. 'We need to sit tight, wait it out.'

I threw a glass of rum in his face.

'Why did you do that?'

I glared at him. 'It's all beneath you, isn't it, all this shouting and marching? Emotion is vulgar to you, isn't it?'

'You're being vulgar now, yes.'

I stormed off, slamming doors. 'This country can go and rot. Let them kill themselves.'

Lucy was stoic, calm. She walked in to us every day from Santa Cruz, over the saddle cut into the mountain. Sometimes she took a route taxi. But her fellow travellers harassed her when she asked the taxi to pull up outside our gate. *Leave dem blasted white people. You still house slave? House nigger to white people?* She told us of their taunts.

'Lucy, don't come in then,' I begged.

She wasn't bothered by it all.

'Dey can't stop me comin' to work,' she complained. 'I not angry, not like dese fellas.'

I scribbled furiously to Eric Williams.

Granny pelting bricks, Granny there with her broom, outside the Red House. You forgot her, didn't you? She's out on the streets. I can't go

out there. I am trapped in the house. But I should go out, too; join the
protests, throw bricks at you. I'm that mad. I have a bad feeling about
all of this. God bless Granny, keep her safe. I wonder what you are
doing with yourself; what you are going to do about all this?

The phone rang late one morning. It was Mrs Roberts, Pascale's schoolteacher. 'I'm sorry, Mrs Harwood, but we're sending the children home. It's not safe. We're closing the school for the rest of the week. Please come and collect her.'

'What's happened?'

'Riots. Riots down in Port of Spain. A Molotov cocktail hurled into the home of the Minister for Education. Shops on fire.'

George came home right away.

'It's true,' he confirmed. He'd sped through town; his hands were shaking. We left the house immediately, driving with all doors locked, windows up, towards Pascale's school lower down in Winderflet. Everywhere, black faces were leering into the car. Small stones hit the windscreen, the back windows.

I clung to the edge of the car seat. 'Their own government did this,' I cried. 'They did this to *themselves*. The white man left, quit, years ago. Why are they blaming *us*? What have we done? What have we done to this place?'

George was like granite, his jaw twitching.

'Fools!' I cried. 'We're stupid fools.'

We turned into Valenton Avenue to find a traffic jam, a long queue of cars. Black people standing on the pavement, glaring. More of them than us. I began to pray in English and then in French: *Marie, pleine de grâce, protégez-nous, gardez-nous, nous sommes* – CRACK! A cobweb of glass appeared in the windscreen.

'George!'

George wound down the window, shouting obscenities at a group standing on the corner, threatening to take them on, man to man, hand to hand. The line of cars began to move. George accelerated.

'That wasn't very clever,' I gasped.

'The fuckers.' George shook and sweated.

We were halfway up the hill. A white March heat. Trees, cars outlined in silver. The hairs on my arms quivered. We inched our way up the steep road. White people in a line, windows up, cars turning into ovens. White people melting and their hearts thumping and women shouting at their husbands. Arguments raged in every car on that hill up to the school. Women hurled abuse, praying, crying. Marriages teetered on the brink of divorce, ultimatums were being delivered. Mine would wait, till we got home.

We turned the corner, driving along the side of the school. All the classrooms were empty, the playground deserted. The teachers stood outside the sheltered back entrance with the children lined up in their forms, clutching the smaller children by their hands. Small frightened faces in pink- and blue-checked dresses. Khaki short pants. Two security guards waited with the teachers, both black. They peered at us through the hole in our windscreen.

'That's Mrs Roberts.' I recognised Pascale's form teacher. She saw us, our windscreen, her face gaunt. She gripped Pascale's hand. In a moment I was outside the car, hugging my daughter. I hugged Mrs Roberts out of nerves.

'Thanks so much,' I gasped.

'We'll call you when things change,' she promised.

Everywhere, mothers were hugging their children, cars were

nudging and edging forwards, horns beeping, white faces strained and sweating.

'You're OK now, OK, my love.' I hugged my daughter to my chest. 'OK, my love.' But Pascale was inconsolable. She didn't know what was going on.

I glanced at George. His face was stern, concentrating on how to get us back safely. Stupid man. His castle built on sand drenched in the blood of thousands of dark-skinned souls, those brought to Trinidad whether they liked it or not, forced to toil unpaid, all those who lived here before them hounded into extinction. But he didn't care to add it all up. No white man on the island cared to see that what was happening was natural: cause and effect. The sins of the white man now passed on, mutated, repeated by the black man. Enough was enough for Granny, Geddes Granger. I'd had enough, too. It was then, with my daughter sobbing in my arms, that I made my decision: I was leaving.

When we returned, Lucy was standing in the kitchen, reading an article about Geddes Granger in the *Trinidad Guardian* aloud to Venus. Venus was in her mid-thirties, no longer gawky; she'd grown into a tall, straight-backed, blue-black woman with a huge-toothed smile. Venus had raised my children. She was my closest companion, my confidante in all matters of the house. Lucy had reached sixty and had come to smile a bit more, cry less. They were our family in Trinidad: Venus, our friend and critic; Lucy, our wise woman.

'They threw stones at us,' I blurted, wretched.

George went straight to the bar to mix two stiff rums. Pascale went straight to Venus. Venus pulled my daughter close and she buried her face in Venus's long black neck.

I burst into tears.

Lucy clicked her throat and looked ashamed. She hid the newspaper behind her back.

George returned with the drinks and the four of us stood in the kitchen.

'Madam, don't worry yourself with all this.' Lucy tried to console us. 'This is nuttin, just some young people carrying on. They don't talk for everyone.'

'Granny Seraphina is out there with them,' I snapped. 'Why aren't you both out there, too? I'd go if I were you. How much longer are you going to wait for basic sanitation, for electricity? You don't even care! You're so used to having nothing you don't even ask. Why is it the young are the only ones who get angry? Or the very old? Why do we fall asleep in middle age?'

George stared at me, shaking his head.

Venus and Lucy looked embarrassed.

'Go on, get off your *backsides*! Go out into the streets and protest. You have nothing and this is your chance to shout about it.'

I knocked back my rum. I was absolutely certain then. 'I'm leaving, George.'

Venus and Lucy glanced at each other.

George winced into his rum. 'Oh, really? Where will you go?'

'Back to England. I'll live in Kent. Near Sebastian's school. He can live with me, no longer board. Pascale will go to school near by, too.'

'And money?'

'I'll work.'

'You won't get far on one wage.'

'Education is free in England. If need be they'll go to a state school. It won't be the end of the world.'

'So. You have it all planned.'

'Come with me, George.'

He shut one eye and peered into his glass as though into a long tunnel.

'Now's the time,' I pleaded.

'We'll see.'

'I mean it, George. With or without you. I'm leaving Trinidad, as soon as possible.'

I began to pack. I pulled down old suitcases and trunks from the tops of cupboards. Dust flew up all over the house.

'Oh gorsh,' muttered Lucy in disbelief. She stood behind me, watchful, silent.

'Lucy, stop staring!' I shouted. But she didn't move from her spot behind me. Everywhere I went, she followed.

'I'm *leaving*, get used to it.' I choked back tears. But she only stayed closer to my side, sat on the bed and watched. I didn't want to look at her, couldn't look her in the eye. I sang and hummed loudly as I rummaged from room to room. She followed me. Then Pascale joined Lucy. Both followed me round the house.

'Mummyuh, watcha doin'?' Pascale asked.

'Packing.'

'You goin' on a trip?'

'*We* are.'

'Where?'

I stopped and bent so that we were face to face. 'You and I are going on a trip. We're going to see your brother. Wouldn't you like that?'

She nodded.

'Yes, I thought so. We'll meet all his schoolfriends. You'll eat strawberries and cream.'

'Yippeee!' She tore off round the house, dancing with glee.

Lucy clicked her throat. 'Don't look at me like that,' I warned her.

Venus went silent and avoided me.

I stamped around. I opened cupboards, pulled out old clothes. I tried to give Lucy and Venus bundles to take home. Both refused. George sat by the radio and drank lots of rum. The house buzzed with hourly reports. A protest in San Juan. Bombings over the weekend at the US Vice-consulate. A march from Laventille to town. Throngs in Woodford Square. The PNM's University had become the Black Power Movement's People's Parliament. Rallies were held there every day, a bulletin of events pinned up on the railings. Granger on the bandstand, the crowds in love with him, and no wonder: this well-educated young black man, this fire-brand with connections to other black leaders, Stokely Carmichael in particular. All too familiar. The same man, all over again. He was dangerous. Dangerous to Eric Williams.

I wrote to Williams.

What about all this, eh? When slavery was abolished some blacks were already free. They became the black middle class. The rest, well, they'd had enough, they built shacks, shanties, slunk off to live a quiet life, piss poor. Most of them never revived their spirits, regained their sense of self-worth. Their descendants have remained invisible, enslaved. But now what? A slave revolt? Like in the old plantation days? Africans like a good ruck, and now you've got one on your hands. Good luck. An Afro-Saxon, that's what they're calling you. This young man

Granger – remind you of anyone? He's from Laventille. He's quite something. He was a boy when you canvassed around there, when you spoke in Woodford Square. He remembers you, you lifted his heart, lifted him up. Lifted us all. You educated him and now he's taken over Woodford Square. One of your students has come back to take you on!

We no longer lived alone in the bush. A settlement had grown up around us, as George predicted. Others had built, mostly white or Syrian. All owned big dogs, had erected high gates. We phoned each other and kept in touch. No one dared go to work. We kept the front gate padlocked, the dogs loose. Children threw stones through the bars. Pascale wet her sheets one night and came in to us crying. We huddled on our bed as though it were a raft. George and I hadn't spoken all day. Pascale was asleep between us. The air-conditioner had broken down. Those iron bars on all the windows were finally needed. A wrought-iron gate stretched across our private balcony like the doors of a cage. George opened the sliding doors for air. The night sky glowed, alive with stars. Crapauds burped, cicadas rubbed their legs together. We were far away from town, nowhere near the riots, and yet the air was full of trouble.

'Don't you feel it *now*, George?'

'What?'

'Guilt.'

'No.'

'I feel guilty for my sins. Like this is all our fault.'

'Don't be ridiculous.'

'It won't go away, George.'

'What won't?'

'This anger and resentment. It'll come back, again and again. No compensation for what was done to them. It's all swept under the carpet. The British didn't care. The PNM became like them.'

'Oh Sabine, I'm tired of all this bullshit.'

'Our love has changed, George. This is all too much for us. For me. You love it all more than me.'

'No I *don't*.'

'I'm unhappy and you don't care.'

'I do.'

'You drink, you block it out. I'm not happy, George. Not like this.'

'I'm sorry . . .'

'I feel heartbroken. Over us. Over Trinidad.'

'Oh God, woman. You're always so dramatic.'

'You see? You no longer care for me. That's why I'm leaving.' I rolled over, my back to him. Pascale was fast asleep. How she looked like George, how strong and stubborn she was becoming. Her accent was bold and rhythmic. She was half George, half the island.

Then, a rustle.

Voices out on the road.

The dogs barking.

George pulled a baseball bat from under the bed.

'Stay here,' he whispered.

But I followed him out onto the front porch. George stood in the garden, in the centre of the grass, lit by the moon, his bat poised. The voices were out past the garden wall. How many of them there: three, four? Our dogs were massive beasts, pacing back and forth, growling like lions.

A hiss. The whiff of petrol. Over the wall, in a wide arc, against the petrol-blue sky, a bottle. Its neck stuffed with doused-up, ripped-up old T-shirt. Graceful as a shooting star.

It landed heavily on the grass, exploding into flames.

'Come here, you *bastards*,' George bellowed.

Another bottle flew over, this one on fire, exploding in mid-air, glass shattering and raining down on George. The dogs barked like thunder, tracking the voices along the wall. A patch of grass erupted into fire; George bashed at it. Then another Molotov cocktail revolved through the night, flames spinning from it. George swung, hitting the bottle, hurling it backwards so it exploded against the wall. The dogs went wild. The neighbour's Dobermanns barked. Lights flicked on next door.

Freddie, our Syrian neighbour, rushed out into his garden in his Y-fronts. 'What goin' on?' he shouted over the hedge.

'They're hurling bombs at us!' I shouted.

Then, an engine. A motorbike starting up behind the wall. The voices stopped and we heard the peeling of tyres, the engine trailing off up the road towards Winderflet. Towards town.

George stooped.

I rushed to him. 'My love, are you all right?'

We held each other tight.

'Yes, yes, I'm fine.'

We began to pick up shards of glass. I switched on all the outside lights. A patch of white stuccoed wall was scarred black. A patch of grass was blackened, too. Glass in the grass. The stink of kerosene in the air, remnants of grey-black gauze all over the lawn. I called the dogs away, locking them in the back garden. Freddie appeared at our gate with his cutlass. We let him in. I was too shaken to cry, too nervous for nerves. He hugged me. 'Dem arses. Dem foolish niggers.'

'Why, why?' I groaned.

Freddie's face was murderous.

We sat in our kitchen with a bottle of rum, all of us smoking. Our faces were damp, shining.

'We can hire armed guards,' Freddie suggested. 'I know some fellas.'

'Black people to guard us from other black people?' I snorted.

'Dese Black Power people don't have de support of de entire country. What we gonna do? Sit here like ducks, wait for more mischief? Nah! I gettin mih own personal guard. Nobody go help us. Not de police, no one.'

George's eyes were bloodshot. Stupid man, out there on the lawn, guarding his castle with a baseball bat. What did he really imagine he would do? Break a leg? Smash a skull?

Venus had woken up next door. She appeared in the kitchen in her nightdress and dressing gown. 'W'appen, madam?' She stared sleepily at us.

'Niggers, dat what happen.' Freddie was drunk.

'Shut up, Freddie,' I snapped. 'We had some trouble, Venus. Some men tried to frighten us.'

'They did a bloody good job.' George drained his rum.

'Dis contry goin' dong,' Freddie added, maudlin.

'They threw petrol bombs over the wall,' I explained.

Venus gasped. She began to cry and mumble to herself, visibly upset. 'Oh gorsh, oh gorsh.' Tears fell heavily, wetting her hands.

'Venus, what's wrong?' I asked quietly but she stood there trembling. For the first time in fifteen years I saw Venus, saw her for who she was. A poor black woman, a woman entirely dependent on us, but who, when the chips were down, bore no allegiance to us at all. Venus, wittingly or unwittingly, could harm us.

'Venus,' I whispered. 'Did you *know* these people?'

'I tink I know dem,' she wailed. 'Yes, madam.'

'Jesus Christ.'

We all stared at her.

'Yes, Madam. Mih neighbours. Dey know summa dem Black Power people. Dey want to know about white people, where dey live. I hear dem talkin' once, but doh know what dey say. Dey know Granny.'

I glanced at George. His face was blank. He looked old, tired.

Freddie's mouth had melted into a grimace, his eyes surrounded with dark circles. 'Niggers,' he said again. 'You see dat? Livin in your own blasted house. Dat is niggers for you. Dey run de damn place, and den when dey cyan organise, dey blame de white people. Let dose young boys come again, man. Let dem come. I'll be ready for dem.'

The next morning I flew up Morne Cocoa Road, right up to where the old shack stood with its superior air and lopsided grin. Granny was standing on the top step, waiting, as if she had been expecting me. I parked and stood at the gate. I sensed my own presence there on the hill, the whole neighbourhood watching me; a hard hostile stare, eyes scrutinising me from kitchens, from street corners. Granny standing up there.

'Can I come in?' I called up. I was miserable from the night before. I rattled the gate and a dog barked. Granny nodded, making her slow crotchety way down the stairs, one step at a time.

She arrived at the high thin gate and stared at me through the bars.

'Granny, did you hear about what happened at our home last night?'

Granny didn't move. She made no facial gestures, said nothing.

'Two men came by on motorbikes and threw petrol bombs over into our garden. They frightened us.'

She clicked her throat; her yellow eyes were bold and clear, searching me, then beyond me. Finally, Granny was having her moment.

'Venus told us you might know who came by.'

'Venus say dat?'

'Yes. She said you know some people round here, people – involved in the riots. They want to make trouble.'

Granny inhaled a deep breath, resolute in her silence.

'Did you know these people?' I pushed.

Granny's mouth pulled down into a grimace. She wouldn't talk. I looked up at the old house behind her. It was treacherously old, carbuncular, hunched over.

'Granny, why don't you let me and Mr Harwood help you? We can help fix the house. Get builders in, shore it up.'

The old woman glared.

'I know why you're angry. But meanwhile that old house is falling down the hill. It will collapse one day, maybe even with you all in it.'

'Dis house nuttin to do wid you. Mine yer own affairs.'

'It does have something to do with me. Isn't that why those men came last night?'

'Dem boys dong so, dey sufferin'. Dey sicka allyuh. Alluyuh go

399

home. Comin' here. Go home, nuh. What you doin' up here? You come to offer me money?' She steupsed. 'Take your blasted money. I doh need it. I live here all mih life, all mih goddamn life. Dis house ent go brek dong. Not like you. You frighten too quick, man. An' you ent see *nuttin*. Plenty hurricane comin' soon, comin' now. Alluh us plenty ready to mek change. To hell wid de PNM. To hell wid you. Keep away from us. I ent know nuttin about las' night. I here in mih bed, alone. Clive, Bernard here, too. My daughter, she asleep in *your* damn blasted house. She sleepin' in home wid water and stove and she cook and clean for you an' she sometime forget us, forget we livin' here. Now you come and tellin' me you wan give us money?'

She smiled as she stared me down, enjoying her bitterness.

'I'm sorry.' And I was. I felt eternally trapped.

Granny turned and limped back towards the house balancing on rocks from the river below. I walked towards the car just as two young men came out from a house further down the road. One stared at me and whispered something under his breath. The second man laughed and looked me up and down. Sweat sprang from my palms. I found my keys and started the car, driving up and up and then over the hill, over and away, anything rather than drive past those villains.

The following days were full of violence. My packing intensified. I took some silver from the shelves, two candlesticks, a punch bowl. I wanted to show I was serious. I removed framed photographs, took pictures down from the walls. The others stared at me, as if at an actor. They didn't believe me. I only just managed to believe it myself.

We were housebound, relying on the radio and television for the latest reports. Thousands gathered in Woodford Square. From there Granger led a march south to Caroni and then on to Couva. The Young Power Movement marched on Whitehall and Balisier House. Williams made a public address, his voice crackling over our tinny transistor radio, saying that while people had a right to march they had no right to trample on others' freedom. The riots, he said, were part of a global revolt against traditional institutions.

More violence. Worse violence. Riots in Charlotte Street, the police using tear gas to disperse the crowds. Black Power leaders chanting *Power to the people* and the crowds pelting the police with bottles and stones.

George slept outside on the porch with his baseball bat. Venus went home. Lucy stayed away. Freddie hired guards. The dogs barked at everything that moved beyond the gates. Pascale couldn't sleep. We were running out of food. The woman up in the hills peered down, silently victorious. Nature always wins in the end, will always overturn men's wars. The heat declared war on us. We sweated through sheets, through clothes; the worst dry season in years. No breeze, no mist from the mountain tops at night. An eruption of bachacs, lines teeming from a nest newly built God knows where. Agressive red ants marched through the house. George bashed them with his baseball bat.

I took down more suitcases, dusted them off. George and I rowed.

'I'm leaving, I'll be gone in ten days. BOAC will take everything in the hold. I've checked.'

'Fine.'

'Stay here, die here. I hope you do.'

'Go back to England, then, see how far you get.'

'I can't compete with this island.'

'Why do you hate it so?'

'You're a drunk.'

'And you've become *black*. Like one of those Black Power people.'

We fucked and fucked. It was obscene. We tried to fuck each other into submission, tried to fuck things right again between us. It was our first language and our last, the only conversation we had left, and it proved useless.

I wrote to Eric Williams.

This isn't about jobs, unemployment. These protests are morally moti-vated. Your response? Throw them crumbs from the rich man's table. Levy taxes for the rich, give the poor a little more. An insult. They are angry with you, Mr Williams. The whites have no loyalty to these people and they still more or less run things. You've let them. You let George buy his land; he will build on it, get rich. Buy more land. Meanwhile, our maids don't even own the plots they live on. They're squatters. I've had enough of this. I leave here miserable. I leave with my creole children and I leave my husband behind. He is part of this place now, part of the island.

The riots spread to Tobago. A rioter in Port of Spain, Basil Davis, was shot dead by a police officer. His funeral was immense; like that of a head of state, his body carried aloft through the streets of Port of Spain, the crowd twenty men wide, the streets crammed with black people, afro heads, fists raised. Thousands mourned him, banging drums, waving flags, singing hymns.

Granny Seraphina attended. She let her white hair flow wild. She raised her fist and chanted, *power to the black man, power to the people*.

I started to pack in our office. My Remington typewriter. I wanted to take that. Plus some books, some papers, photo albums. And, of course, there were the shoe-boxes of letters to Eric Williams. Fourteen in all. Did I take them, too? Or burn them, every one, out in the garden, when George was out? No one knew of them but me. I could destroy the evidence of my past folly. I'd written them for company. Notes to self. They'd been a record of my loneliness and despair and now they were irrelevant and embarrassing. I'd burn them the minute I could.

We stayed at home for days. We nipped to Chen's when it was quiet. Bought the newspaper, milk, rum, food. We swapped gossip and news reports with neighbours. It wasn't safe for George to go to his office.

I came into the kitchen one morning, unlocking the kitchen door. The dogs weren't there. Immediately, I was fearful. The dogs were *always* there when I opened the door, waiting to be fed, to greet whoever woke first with their wet noses and handsome heads. Both had grown waist-high, the colour of peanut butter, their muzzles musky black.

I called their names. Neither appeared. I whistled, walking out towards the driveway, calling them. I stopped: the dogs lay out there on the drive.

I called their names again, this time quietly, as though calling to a naughty child. Neither moved. I approached them, wiping tears from my eyes; then I was standing above them. Their tongues lolled blue, engorged, their eyes had rolled backwards. Flies buzzed around their muzzles. They were stiff with rigor mortis. Dead for hours, dead in the night. Nearby lay some of the raw meat thrown to them. I left the dogs there in the morning sun on the driveway. Two immense creatures, laid out like big game trophies, waiting to be stuffed or made into rugs.

I returned to the kitchen, putting the kettle on. I made a pot of tea and took the tea tray into George. He was sitting up in bed with the papers.

'The dogs are dead,' I said.

'*What*?'

'Poisoned, I think. Please don't go out, not now. I found them dead, on the drive.'

'No!'

'Yes, I'm afraid so.'

George's face was a little boy's, incredulous.

'*Both* of them?'

'Yes.'

'Dear God.' His face sagged, his eyes pooled.

'They threw meat for them, poisoned meat. In the night. They're quite dead now.'

'Oh, *no*.'

'I'm sorry, George.'

George's frown slid down his face, his lips slackened. Tears came and he wept like an infant. I sat down near to him on the bed and held him in my arms.

CHAPTER TWENTY-THREE

EMERGENCY

George and Freddie dug two deep graves in the earth out in the back yard, under a mango tree. The dogs were so stiff it was like burying two tables. The men dug for hours and sprinkled lime into the pits. Flies swarmed over the dogs' mouths and eyes and genitals. I didn't let Pascale see them; I told her they'd eaten something which had made them sick and that they'd gone to heaven. She bawled and flung herself on her bed, kicking and screaming, sobbing into her pillow, saying they were her best friends, her very best friends.

Pascale insisted on a funeral. When the men had shovelled all the earth back into the pits, when the dogs were completely hidden, we gathered around the graves. Pascale had decorated their collars with ginger lilies. She knelt near the freshly dug earth, reading out a poem she had written on a piece of paper in felt-tip pen. A poem for their souls in heaven. George, Freddie and I stood behind her.

Solemnly, Pascale placed the dogs' collars in the crook of the mango tree, then pinned the poem to the trunk. I sprinkled grass seed over the raw-earth plots. George smoothed the seed over with his spade. Freddie cussed under his breath. Pascale was brave; this was her first funeral, her first encounter with the dead. Later I promised her I would plant a pink hibiscus bush to mark their graves.

The house was much quieter without the dogs. George was wordless, struck dumb. Pascale was tearful for days. I continued packing in a trance-like state, trying to stay clear-headed, trying to decide what we'd leave, what we'd take, even packing a case for George, hoping he might come back with us.

Then, it all happened at once. Riots erupted in Port of Spain, the angriest yet. A flurry of phone calls from friends, all with businesses in town. A hundred businesses had been fire-bombed overnight; cars overturned and set on fire down in Independence Square. Many of the old French Creole enterprises were destroyed by the mob. Foreign companies were also targeted, whole office blocks smashed up, those run by the light-skinned middle classes, the bourgeoisie of Trinidad.

'Can't see why they'd attack Forbes-Mason, down by the dock. We've always treated staff well, always worked with the boatmen down there. They know us.'

But George received a telephone call from the Director of the company. 'Forbes-Mason has been hit. It's on fire.'

George phoned London immediately.

'The office won't be rebuilt,' they said. 'We're not going to open elsewhere, either. It's time to call it quits. Sorry, George. The *Southern Cross* is still in the harbour for the next day or two. We'll pay your passage. I'd get on the boat.'

'*What* boat?' I wanted to know. 'WHAT boat? George?' I stared, shaking, unable to think straight. Had he deceived me?

George sighed. He didn't look at all guilty.

'Please tell me.'

'There's a cruise ship in; it hasn't been able to get away because the captain went to stay with friends of his family for a few days. Now he can't get back. It'll be leaving as soon as he can.'

'There's a *ship* on the dock?'

'Yes.'

'And you didn't tell me?'

'No.'

'*Why* not?'

'Why do you think?'

I was sorry for him then, for the coward that he'd become. This was our last chance. 'Come *with me*, George. Please, I beg you. I haven't yet booked the flight. This will be quicker, easier. All of us together.'

George hung his head.

'Can't you see it's all over? This is the hurricane. It's come. The old ways will be swept away.'

I saw him struggle to stay in control of himself. He never planned to leave. The riots, the Molotov cocktails, the dogs rotting under the earth; now he'd no place of work. I could see it was all beyond his thinking. All these years he'd rejected my ideas, the things which were invisible, but there, always.

'Yes. I can finally see what you mean.'

'Then *come. Please.*'

'OK.'

'Oh thank God!' I hugged him.

'You've won, Sabine. I'm so sorry about all this. It's all gone wrong.' He sighed heavily; his sun-drenched, rum-drenched days were over. 'I'll go back with you, of course.'

'George, we'll start again, we'll be with Sebastian, we'll all live together. It won't be as bad as you imagine. When's the boat leaving?'

'In two days.'

'Oh *mon Dieu*, *merci*. Thank God.'

We packed till late into the night. I rang Irit to see if she and John might like to live in the house, rent-free, asking her to be its keeper until we were settled in England.

She was delighted. 'I will be Queen of your castle,' she purred.

'Irit, are you all right, over there?'

'Of course, dahling.'

'What about your shop?'

'It's higher up, the riots are further down, near the dock. So far so good.'

'You're staying?'

'Of course. This storm will pass. It is disgraceful what the PNM are doing. They are all at the Hilton, *hiding*. Williams is at home with his little gang of advisers. They are drinking rum and Port of Spain is burning. I like this Granger. Handsome, no? I hear there'll be trouble tomorrow; they're calling in warships from England and America.'

'No!'

'Oh yes. You wait. Tomorrow is a big day.'

'But our boat is leaving soon.'

'Ha ha, you may have to swim after it.'

We slept fitfully. Baseball bat by the bed. Sweating through the sheets. Mosquitoes buzzing, our legs blotched with red lumps. The

hills around us shifted, groaning with the hotness of the earth. I
went outside and stared up at the green woman.

So, we're leaving finally. I'm taking him back, I said to her.

Yes, it's time to go.

He'll miss you.

Don't worry about that. Look, you see, you won in the end.

I'll miss you, too, in a way.

You can always come back.

Never.

You never know.

Never.

Good luck.

Our suitcases stood in a line downstairs, bulging. Twelve of them
bound up with straps. Lucy had slept the night on the sofa.

At dawn, we switched on the radio. The Black Power leaders
had been arrested. All except Granger, who'd disappeared.

'Treachery,' I muttered. 'That fucking hypocrite. How could
Williams do this to his *own people*? His own students?'

Police occupied the Red House. Riot police had invaded
Woodford Square, cleared it with tear gas. Warships were on their
way. A curfew had been imposed from 6 p.m. in the evening till 6
a.m. the following day. A State of Emergency was declared.

Venus managed to get a message through to us from a payphone.

'Ah cyan come in. Granny tek Bernard and Clive into tong, she
take dem on de marches. Dey peltin' stones at de police. Ah cyan
come. All rong me upset. Everyone out. Dey burnin' down de
place. No taxis on de road. Granny gone mad.'

'Do you have water?'

'Yes, madam.'

'And food?'

'For now.'

'I'll come over when I can, in the next day or so. I'll bring you some ice for the cooler.'

'Don't come, madam.'

'Why not?'

'It not safe.'

Bernard was nine by then, Clive eleven. Good little boys. I imagined them marching down Frederick Street with Granny, their fists raised. I imagined she was filling their heads, lighting fire in their souls; that one day the boys would be just like Geddes Granger.

I wrote to Eric Williams:

So, Port of Spain is on fire. American and British warships on the way to help you out. You are at home, with your little gang. Granny taking her grandsons into town to be part of this. Granger, your alter-ego? Granny, your shadow? It all comes back to those ideas of yours, out there in those days. Woodford Square. You had ideas and they were good ones. They lit these protests, they lit Granny and Granger. They are seeking vengeance for their disappointment. I am escaping, finally. I am sorry for you, sorry for George. You don't get to have it all, not forever.

Stupidity is also an ingredient of revolution. Eric Williams, the most unpopular man on the island, expected the nation's troops, most from poor black families, to put down a popular uprising.

At the regiment base in Teteron Bay posters of Stokely

Carmichael and Malcolm X were pinned on the barracks' walls. The young officers saw the Black Power protesters as brothers and so they mutinied. They refused orders to clamp down. Instead, they arrested their commanding officer, locking him up with all other higher officers, those who didn't flee. They broke into their ammo bunker, rallying the six-hundred-strong regiment. Chaos broke out in Camp Ogden, too, the army base in Port of Spain. This news came over the radio.

'George, now I'm frightened.'

'Don't worry. We're going.'

We had nothing to eat. I piled what we had left on the kitchen table. Half a box of Cornflakes, two bananas, some stale Crix crackers, a jar of pickles.

'I'll go to Chen's,' George offered.

'I'm coming with you like it or not.'

We left Pascale with Lucy, promising to be quick.

Very few cars were on the road in Winderflet. The world looked the same, except noiseless, lifeless. The rum shops, the parlours were all closed, boarded-up. The school lay silent; the petrol station had been abandoned. The T-junction at the petrol station – usually so chaotic with people clogging up the kerb, hands out, route taxis stopping to pick them up or just have a conversation – was deserted. No vendors selling kingfish by the roadside, no fat women ambling down the pavement holding their umbrellas high. Our Lady of Lourdes peered down on an abducted parish.

'Something has died,' I muttered.

'Stop it, Sabine. It will all spring back to life.'

'I'm glad it happened, at last. The old way of things, all that will go.'

'We'll see.'

I looked at my husband thoughtfully. He knew Williams, too, knew the course of things in a man's world. They knew things I didn't.

We drove on past the reservoir, past Andalusia, towards Chen's, arriving to find metal gates drawn across the entrance, shopping trolleys overturned out front.

'Let's try Hi-Lo.' George accelerated.

Hi-Lo was also closed.

'I don't think we should go any further, George.'

'It's now or never,' he urged. 'We'll need food for the next couple of days. Let's push on.'

We passed Boissiere village, also silent, motionless. We drove round the savannah, past the entrance to Belmont, glancing down Jernington Avenue, the road leading in. The road was scarred black in places, debris scattered, broken glass, banners erected, graffiti sprayed on walls. On the savannah, pink and yellow pouis blossom like blood, strange carnival-coloured blood, all over the ground. The trees were magnificent, above it all. Flamboyants, immortelles, African tulips, yellow flames: out in force, cheering with the rioters. The air stank of chaos, of petrol and smouldering tyres.

'I know somewhere that might be open,' George muttered, turning towards the top end of Port of Spain. Both of us were in a stupor, drawn to the horror. I knew why George had ventured this close. I kept quiet, morbidly absorbed, wanting to see what it was like too, especially the Forbes-Mason offices.

We crawled down Edward Street, heading for the dock. A black pall of smoke hung over it, the shape of Trinidad. The air had turned acrid. I covered my nose and mouth. I wanted to push on as much as George. The Red House loomed, surrounded by riot police in tin hats like those the English air wardens wore in the Blitz, rifles cocked. They eyed us. Two came forward.

'George, look out. Turn left!' I commanded.

George turned quickly, avoiding the men, and in a minute we came upon Woodford Square. The square was eerily empty, heavily guarded. More men with those ludicrous tin hats stood around not knowing quite what had happened or what to do. There were heavy padlocked chains on the gates. The square was still cloudy with tear gas. The bandstand was empty, chairs overturned in the rush to escape.

'How could he?' I gasped.

My eyes smarted. Tears fell. Cycling into the crowd on my green bicycle. Hundreds gathered to listen to Eric Williams announce a new era, the crowd spellbound. Balisiers held up like crosses, hands stretched out towards him. Lifting me. Lifting the entire nation. Tears fell for those cleared off by Williams that very morning. The protesters who'd rallied there, fists raised. *Power to the people*. I whispered a prayer for Geddes Granger.

More inept riot police loomed – buffoons! More frightened of us than the other way round, aiming their rifles at us. We sailed past. More chains, Woodford Square was wrapped up in chains. Silent, ruined.

Still more police advanced, waving their rifles, instructing us to vacate the area. George complied, screeching away from the Red House, across two streets, cutting down towards the dock, towards Forbes-Mason.

'I just need to see it with my own eyes,' he said.

I nodded, *wanting* George to see the worst. We drove towards the black clouds. The streets were empty, shops with their guts smouldering, plate-glass fronting smashed everywhere, cars with windows beaten in. Menace hung in the air. Nerves fizzed in my gut. I clutched George's hand. We rounded the corner into Independence Square. Riot police stood everywhere, on edge. Police vehicles, the fire brigade. Smoke, a fire still burning in one shop.

Further up, on the left, Forbes-Mason, gutted and hacked.

'Dear God,' George murmured.

There was glass all over the pavement. We drove abreast of the block, peering in. The floor was black with soot and ashes. The chairs and desks were charred, overturned. In-trays and telephones and Rolodexes and ring binders blackened, broken, flung across the floor. Paper, reams of blackened paper. Magazines, Manila folders pulled from shelves, hurled across the room. Petrol fumes, like a bee swarm, hung over it all.

George stared across me, shaking his head.

Three armed policemen walked towards us.

'Come on, George, let's go.'

George was sombre, as though he had been personally attacked. We accelerated, turning straight across the square, down Chacon Street and then out, out of it all. And there, beside the Queen's Wharf, like a massive swan: the *Southern Cross*, milk white, spotless, glistening in the white heat. The cruise ship towered above the dock, its tiers of decks like folded wings, the glittering windows of the bridge a tiara nestling on its brow. A fantasy vessel banked alongside the smooth flat wharf. It was moored, the gangplank up. Even so, riot police were guarding it.

'George . . .'

'We'll be on it.'

'Thank God.'

'I'll arrange it when we get home.'

We sped past and away from Port of Spain. Out in the Gulf of Paria, way out, I spotted the smeary outlines of grey ships approaching, a small fleet. Pelicans sat regarding them, too, with the lack of interest they show everything. Eric Williams: surely this was the end of him. We drove up through Woodbrook and then past the cricket oval, missing Long Circular Road where Camp Ogden was ablaze, the firemen unable to put the fire out due to low water-pressure.

Trinidad. Even in revolution it was a farce. Mutiny. Antique tin hats for those who *would* defend the state. A trickle of water to douse the fires of discontent and half the government hiding at the Hilton.

We found a small supermarket open on the way back, its shelves mostly bare. We managed to buy bread and condensed milk, some cheese, a dozen eggs, four tins of baked beans. Plantain too, a bottle of rum, a bag of pomme-aracs. We arrived home to find Lucy making up a jug of freshly squeezed orange juice, sprinkling it with Angostura bitters. She'd carried in a bag of oranges on her head.

Lucy was silent, her eyes welling, glossy and black.

'Lucy, how are things in the valley?' I asked.

'Quiet, Miss. This stupidness only happenin' in town.'

'It's not stupidness, Lucy. They've burnt down Mr Harwood's office, burnt it to the ground. He can't go back there now. We're leaving the day after tomorrow. On a big ship. We're all packed. Miss Irit is coming to live here.'

Lucy stood like a statue over by the sink, motionless. Mountainous.

'Lucy, don't cry.'

She wiped tears from her eyes with her apron.

'I go lose mih job, Miss, lose Miss Pascale. I go lose you and Mr Harwood, and Venus. It not easy to fin' a work at my age, Miss.'

'Lucy!' I went over and hugged her. 'I'll pay your wages for the next six months. I'll tell Miss Irit you're here, too, to look after the house with her. You'll be a team. You'll like her.'

'OK, Miss.'

'I'll write and ring when we get to England. Pascale will write, too, and we'll send you photos and keep in touch with you and Venus. Have you heard from her?'

'No, Miss.'

Her good eye was roving, trying to keep up with events.

'Lucy, we have to go. People like us, we're not wanted here. We're part of the problem. Trinidad is changing. It must change.'

'Oh gorsh . . .' She sighed heavily.

'All those tonics you've given me, eh? I've been unhappy for a long time, always because of the way things are. You've helped me, but Trinidad's problems won't be fixed with one of your tonics.'

'No, Miss.'

'I'll miss you.'

'Yes, Miss.'

It was a day of goodbyes. The phone rang constantly. Jules came over at midday, already drunk. Freddie and his wife came over, too. Other neighbours heard we were leaving and rang the doorbell. They brought rum and Scotch, buljol and Crix. A fraught, chain-smoking lime started up round the bar. Trinidadians are impressive this way: they can lime under any conditions. Ol' talk, make jokes. Soon we'd migrated to the swimming pool, drunk on nerves as much as alcohol, recounting stories about Molotov cocktails and offices set on fire. Freddie's textile shop on Duke Street had been badly hit, too.

'Dey say Williams in a *state*. Dis hit him hard,' said Jules.

'But *of course*,' Freddie replied. 'He hated by everyone now. De poor blacks and de business community. Dis a disaster for de country. Set us back ten years. We back where we started. Damn, blasted Africans.'

George was bleary-eyed, utterly overcome. 'I met Williams once, you know, at the Hilton. I liked him. Very bright man. Sabine has always . . . found him interesting, haven't you, darling?'

Heat rose in my cheeks.

'She attended his lectures in Woodford Square, didn't you, darling?'

'Jesus Christ, you went der?' said Freddie. 'Yous one madwoman.'

'Woodford Square, man,' said Jules, sozzled. 'Alla dat lecture bullshit. Williams can kiss my ass.'

I went quiet. I didn't like that George had exposed my secret. That I had seen him talk. George didn't know, he hadn't witnessed the man in full flow. I was there. Granny too. Even though he didn't merit sympathy I couldn't help but feel sad. *Williams in a state*. I was disconcerted by this news. It's a woman's curse to love bad and foolish men, even when they fuck up so miserably.

CHAPTER TWENTY-FOUR

THE GREEN BICYCLE

I slept heavily that night. I dreamt of corbeaux, spiralling in the sky above our home. They picked at me, but no flesh came off my bones. One by one they flew away, leaving me whole. In the morning, more news came over the radio: Granger had been captured that morning, while eating black pudding and fried eggs in a snack bar in Couva. The coastguards were escorting him to Nelson's Island, another rock-like prison island in the Gulf of Paria; it would be hot there, the rock would be arid, barren of water. The government was locked in negotiations with the army. Port of Spain was still patrolled by riot police.

'The ship is still there, isn't it?' I asked, nervous.

'Yes, of course. It leaves tomorrow.'

I decided to take Venus some ice. I hadn't seen her for days but knew she had been hiding in her home up the hill. I was worried. I thought about Granny: up to no good. Bless Granny, bless her soul and let her get on with it, with the business of burning down town. She wanted me gone, dead and buried and gone. What had Granny been up to?

I didn't tell George. He'd never let me go up there alone, not then. But Venus was stuck, too, she might need provisions. I could give her a lift to Chen's when it opened, or bring her and the children home. I stopped and parked the car several yards from the old creole house.

'Venus,' I said aloud before realising she couldn't hear me from the road.

'Venus!' I called her name as I approached, my voice thin and somehow ludicrous, a false voice. 'Venus,' I called again, noticing a face at the window of a house near by, another face at an open door.

'Venus!' I called. Damn. I'd left the ice in the car, in a cooler.

'Venus.' I was closer to the house. The gate was closed. Granny Seraphina appeared on the top step. Her hair was unleashed, sprays of grey and white flames. She nodded minutely.

'Granny, I came to see Venus. Are you all OK?'

The old woman stared past me, down the road.

I turned slowly, trying to see what she could. Nothing at first. No sound and this struck fear into me; no sound. The afternoon was still, mute with heat. I turned back to look at Granny again but she continued to stare past me. Like a cat stares into the night, hearing sounds in the shadows, except she stared into the sheets of heat, down the empty road.

'Granny,' I whispered.

Then, the faint clatter of voices. Brown figures danced into view; a crowd of people, twenty or so, appeared at the bottom of the hill. They had come from the main road, from down by the petrol station; they were excited and talking loudly and fast, fists and voices raised, all returning from the savannah. Sticks held aloft. In the heat they were slow, far off. But my limbs were heavy and sluggish. I saw men and women and children advancing up the road, melting together. They were coming towards me and had sealed off the road behind them. I wanted to get on the other side of that tall flimsy gate into Granny's yard. I shot Granny a pleading look.

But Granny's face was vacant, glazed with concentration. My car blistered in the sun, halfway down the street, halfway between me and the crowd.

The voices grew louder as the throng approached.

Clive, I spotted Clive in amongst the crowd. Bernard, too. They were excited and shouting chants against the PNM. Venus's children, little boys I knew. I didn't see Venus. I shook, holding onto the bars of the gate.

'Please, Granny. Let me in!' But she was in some kind of trance, a fascination. I closed my eyes, wanting to sleep, wanting to end it all. They could have me, tear me limb from limb. I was sick of being scared.

'Eh, eh,' I heard.

The crowd had spotted me. Clive spotted me. A jeer went up and the throng surged forwards.

The first stone stung my leg through my dress. The second was bigger, falling harder, a sharp grazing blow on my stomach. I grasped the gate shouting God knows what but Granny didn't move. I was pinned there, flat to the gate of the old shack and there was no escape. More stones, people in the crowd bending to pick stones from the road, from the gutter and then more stones flew, hitting me, a hail of stones and I held my arm up to my face, clinging to the gate.

'Granny,' I shouted. 'For God's sake!'

I saw a child bending down to pick up a stone. Clive. I saw him bend and stare me down, a smirk on his face as he took aim and hurled it at me. Clive, an eleven-year-old boy, jumping for joy when his stone found its target. The crowd jeered.

I gasped and cried out, pleading. Clive's eyes met mine.

'Clive!' I shouted. 'Clive, stop that, it's me, it's me!' But he didn't care or even seem to hear. He picked up another stone, hurling it like he was shooing away a dog.

Clive was shouting and laughing and running to pick up another stone. I closed my eyes.

Those big black birds, those big black birds, finally descending to pick me over. The crowd squawking and fighting one another: who first, who first, which one to gouge out an eye. The carrion-crowd pecking at me, stones hitting me, those black birds closing in to scrape at me. I was the rotten waste, the dead meat of Trinidad. I was no longer scared, only relieved. Finally they were coming.

Granny Seraphina. I was aware of her at the gate, her hands on me.

'Clive, get inside.' Her sharp brittle voice. 'Allyuh move, leave she,' she said to the crowd. 'Allyuh get away. Move, nuh. Stop dis nonsense.'

Clive fled past me.

Then, no sound.

My flesh stung. Granny put her calloused hand to my forehead, briefly, as if to feel for fever.

'Wait a while,' she said. And I waited: moments, minutes? I don't remember, only that she helped me to the car.

Clive was just a boy. Excited, swept up in it all. I drove home, shaking. And took a shower straight away. I bathed my grazed skin with witch hazel. Nothing broken, just my pride. How stupid had I been to go up there? Break the curfew. I didn't tell George about what happened. I lay down on our bed and turned on the air-conditioning and prayed to the Virgin. *Marie, pleine de grâce, gardez-nous.* Nothing mattered any more. Nothing mattered. We were leaving Trinidad.

Later that day, I went out again. I decided to visit the home of Eric Williams. I knew where to find him; everyone did, at the official residence in St Ann's. The house would be heavily guarded, but I decided to go anyway. I'd no plan, not even a hope of a conversation. I went to pay my respects, or maybe to gawp, to make some kind of pilgrimage. I was tired and my skin still stung from the stones.

The famous street was cordoned off and so I parked some way away and advanced on foot. I spoke to one of the soldiers in a tin hat who was guarding the house, making a point of sounding officious yet urgent.

'Please tell the Prime Minister that Mrs Harwood is here to see him.' The guard looked a little shocked. I smiled prettily. He came back with a nod and I was swiftly taken into the spacious home of the Prime Minister. Three soldiers flanked me to the door.

A silent maid in uniform showed me to a cool dark room with few furnishings which looked out onto the patio and a garden. I went out onto the patio and sat on a white garden chair. The house had the feel of a place already deserted. None of the gang was there, none of his cronies puffing on Benson & Hedges cigarettes and drinking Black Label rum. I had expected a cell in disarray, the debris of men's talk, of the business of revolution and of the chaos out on the street. But the house was quiet. It had been cleared of such matter. There was no hostile atmosphere, but no tangible feeling of anything else, either.

Eric Williams appeared quietly, unannounced, through a glass sliding door. He came over and shook my hand, then sat down opposite me and put his glasses on his head. His eyes were red raw and his suit crumpled. It had clearly not been removed for days. He lit a cigarette and the maid arrived with coffee. I didn't say anything at first. When the maid left us, he rubbed his eyes and yawned, looking at me. He poured the coffee and I felt awful, truly awful watching him. Still we didn't speak. No ideas or reasons for my visit came to me. He knew nothing of my letters, of my thoughts and feelings, of my misery, my imminent departure. And yet he'd let me in to see him. He looked trampled upon, like he'd given in. I wondered about his dead wife Soy, about her not wanting him to go into politics. I still had a million things to say. A whole gamut of emotion; I wanted to pelt him with stones, wanted to kick him in the shins, speak to him with anger, talk to him calmly, too.

'Thank you for coming to see me,' he said.

'I don't know why I came, really. We're leaving. Tomorrow.'

'You must be pleased to go.'

'Yes. I am.'

'On that big cruise ship still in the harbour?'

'Yes.'

'You must feel vindicated.'

'Not really . . .'

'You must feel like I'm the fool, like you were right about me.'

'I don't seem to feel anything.'

'I've thought about what you said from time to time.'

'I'm no politician.'

'You saw me in Woodford Square.'

'Yes.'

'I can't remember those days any more.'

'I can't remember either.'

'You must be vexed.'

Tears came. 'I have been.'

'De whole of Trinidad vexed.'

'Yes.'

'Burn de place down. I ent know what to do right now.'

'It will blow over; my husband says so. You could start again.'

I looked at him, knowing that this wasn't possible. He had run onto the rocks, run aground on himself. He was a ruined man and intelligent enough to know it. He would not learn from this, or pull himself together, pull together another PNM. He had successfully silenced and locked up the opposition, his political son, Geddes Granger. It would be so easy to spit on him, spit in his face. George was right. I was naive. This was the way of things.

'I'll continue to think of you . . . from time to time. On that green bicycle.'

'You gave me quite a shock.' I smiled.

'Gave *me* a goddamn heart attack.'

'I'm sure I'll think of you, too. From time to time.'

'In Woodford Square.'

'Yes.'

He steupsed and took a slug of coffee.

'I was there, by chance, with my husband, yesterday.'

He hung his head. He looked like he might fall asleep right there, fall off the chair.

'I must go now,' I said, standing.

Williams stood to shake my hand. A small man, even smaller that day. I saw grief in his eyes. A man close to his own death.

I didn't let go of his hand. Instead, I pulled him towards me and he fell in close. I put my arms around him and held him tight, unhappy for him and for myself and for all that had happened and knowing no words to bridge the gap between us. Nothing as simple as a few well-chosen words of condolence; I had nothing to say to him. I held him close for moments which felt like minutes. I pressed my lips to his neck and felt him shake. When the maid came in we parted. I said goodbye to him and he sat down and I left as quietly as he had come.

The next day was to be our last in Trinidad. The garden bragged: whorish moussianda flirted their open-bloused petals to the earth. Chaconia flounced and waved their long scarlet candles. The tough savannah grass crawled across itself. The berries in the palms oozed, bringing birds squabbling onto them, spitting the stones onto the ground.

The dogs' graves had lost their freshness, leaves dropping onto them, the soil dry and crumbled. Their two collars, though, were still wedged into the mango tree; their plaits of ginger lilies turned crisp. Pascale visited the graves every day, reading out her poem.

There were a hundred phone calls still to make: banks, accountants, lawyers. Standing orders to cancel, bills to pay, names to be transferred on accounts. Phone calls to Sebastian's school, to George's family in London, to friends there, too. A nest of nerves in my stomach. George hadn't shaved in days. I drew him a bath, handing him a shaving stick, razor, comb, glass of rum. I couldn't eat. I smoked.

Then, a noise out by the gates, the sound of them dragging open. No dogs bounding out to investigate. I peered from behind one of the pillars in the courtyard. A black figure passed up the driveway; I caught a glimpse of black legs. My heart pounded: dear God. Then, a voice I recognised.

'Venus!' I ran towards her. 'Oh Venus.' I was hysterical, jumping up, not quite licking her.

Pascale flew out, too. 'Venus!' she squealed.

Venus's face was grave. 'Oh gorsh, Miss, oh gorsh, I hear what happened, I came straight away. Oh gorsh, ah sorry yes, ah sorry. Oh gorsh, my boy Clive. He doh know what he do. He a little boy. Oh gorsh,' she sobbed.

'Shhhh.' I didn't want to know. 'It's OK, Venus. Yes, he's a little boy. He got caught up. It's OK, it's OK.'

'Oh gorsh.' She blew her nose. 'He get licks, Miss, he get licks for what he did.'

'I'm OK, I'm fine,' I reassured her.

'No, Miss, it not OK. He by me, Miss, and when tings die down he go come to say sorry.'

'Venus, come inside.'

We sat her down at the kitchen table, gathering round. Venus had come undone. Her hair was unbraided and plucked up in frizzy clumps. Her beaming face was misted over. Her eyes were larger, the whites whiter and wet. Tears leaked from them, slipping like hot silver down her black cheeks.

'Why, Miss? Why all dis trouble? Why dem Black Power fellas go trouble up tings so. Oh gorsh, oh gorsh.' She held her head in her hands. 'Granny get de boys into all kinda mischief. She get dem into all kinda trouble. I sorry, yes.'

Pascale hugged her.

Lucy clicked her throat.

'The dogs died,' Pascale informed Venus, climbing onto her lap. 'They ate green bananas and got bellyaches.'

Venus looked at me, her mouth pulled down.

'Venus. We're leaving tomorrow. On a boat. Miss Irit is coming to live here. You can stay if you want. Lucy is staying.'

'You goin'?'

I nodded.

'When you comin' back?'

'We aren't coming back, Venus.'

Glass droplets bulged and broke, falling in lines down her face, down her wide snubby nose, dripping from her chin. 'You ent comin' back?'

'No.'

Pascale's face was pale and expressionless.

Lucy turned away.

I couldn't cry. I had no feelings.

Night fell. Venus had brought pigtail and dasheen bush and pumpkin. She made callaloo and we ate it with white rice and fried plantain. We sat in the kitchen. The radio buzzed. The government had given in to the army's demands, had reinstated Colonel Joffre Serrette as Commander in Chief. The hostages were released. A tight curfew was still in place.

Lucy and Venus didn't go home. Both insisted on staying with us.

Bats whistled through the house. I lay in bed next to George but all my nerves had fled upwards. I couldn't think. A flurry of voices competed, conversations taking place; banks, bills, getting up in time, leaving on time. George was awake, also unable to sleep. We hadn't spoken much all day. He was avoiding me. Things were blowing over, as he predicted. The hurricane had passed. The damage had yet to be assessed. I went to the study and took a pen and some paper, sitting down to write to Eric Williams for the last time.

I think about you a lot. I think of your drop of white aristocratic blood. I think about your aloof mother, Eliza Boissière, your enormous family, twelve children. So much placed on your shoulders. Your failure was preordained. You were set up. And your late wife was right: politics is no place for men of substance. Stay out of things. Look on and get on with important tasks elsewhere. I'm sure you will continue to run things here. I'm sure of that. I can't wait to get on that boat. I'll leave nothing here, not a piece of me. Goodbye. Keep safe.

I signed this letter with my name and put it in a stamped envelope knowing this would be the only letter I would ever send to him.

The keskidees woke us at dawn, squawking over the berries in the palms. We'd moved together in the night and lay for several moments, limbs entwined, holding hands. Pascale came in to us and joined our knot. On the bed we were dozy, dopey, not ready for the hours ahead. I fingered her afro of bubble curls, her cheek on my stomach, her lazy eye wandering. Pascale was honey-skinned, skinny as a crab. George looked at me, speculatively. I smiled. He kissed me on the shoulder.

'Time to get up,' he said.

Venus cooked us bacon and eggs, toast, brewed a pot of coffee. We sat at the round table out on the porch, eating in silence.

The taxi arrived at 7 a.m. Freddie insisted that his guards escorted us to the dock. They drew up in a beaten-up ex-police squad car. The men loaded the suitcases into the vehicles. Some bags were strapped to the roof.

Lucy and Venus watched, wordless. They'd agreed to stay at the house until Irit and John arrived. Freddie came over. Everything happened slowly, quietly. The sun blossomed, spilling warm liquid nectar onto us. I began to perspire, dabbing my face with a tissue. Pascale was in a daze. She hugged and kissed Venus and Lucy but didn't say much. George hugged them, too, unable to look either of them in the eye. He hugged Freddie briefly. I couldn't speak, couldn't even look at Venus and Lucy.

I returned to check the house for the last time, wandering through the rooms, ensuring we hadn't left anything behind. What wasn't in our suitcases was stuffed into high cupboards. We were in the act of vanishing, taking our lives away. All the wrong feelings marched forward. Guilt over Pascale and George. A sense of loss. Yes, loss. I'd never see that mother hill again; observe the swell of her fertile hips, her wild hair. I spoke to her.

Goodbye, my friend.

Goodbye.

I'll never see you again.

No.

Time for me to go. We should have departed long ago. Now it's time.

Keep well.

I'll think of you.

The keskidees squabbled. I was leaving them, too. George had built himself a dream out here, a false dream. The saplings he'd planted had grown luscious. Pink grapefruits so heavy they exploded on the branch, smashing heavily to the ground. Avocados had arrived in their hundreds, dark and bell-shaped, wanton and lascivious up there in the mottled boughs. They bombed the grass for weeks. We gave them away in bags, mashed them up and froze them. The lime trees spat yellow globes. The coconut palms were tall, lustrous, occasionally playing up, hurling a green nut at the dogs. The hibiscus hedge, a row of red trumpets heralding the sun. I wasn't leaving, I was retreating. Beaten by it all.

The others sat in the taxi, waiting for me. Lucy and Venus stood beside the cars. I came out with my sunglasses on, a knife twisting in my gut, twisting. Tears fell freely, blinding me behind the huge lenses.

'I'm so sorry . . .' I hugged Lucy. 'I'll write, I promise.' But my words were meaningless.

Lucy nodded, stepping away from me. She bowed, looking at the ground, holding herself in. Lucy, my saviour. I came forward again, wrapping my arms around her tightly. 'Thank you, Lucy. For all your help,' I whispered. I pressed my nose to her skin, inhaled her warm reassuring scent of coconut oil and Lux soap.

Venus stood straight and tall, quivering, dabbing her eyes with a hanky. I went to hug her but we dissolved, clasping each other. We held each other tight, shaking.

'Venus, Venus,' I choked.

'Madam, don't go.'

'Listen to me. Listen. I want you to have something of mine.'

'Yes, Miss.'

'I want you to have my bicycle.'

'Oh gorsh, Miss.'

'I know you've always liked it. I want you to have it.'

She nodded, shivering, shaking into her hanky. 'Yes, Miss.'

'Think of me when you ride it.'

'Yes.'

We separated, bleeding tears. I blew my nose. I kissed her cheek one last time – her skin was hot and wet against mine. Blind, I got into the car. Freddie opened the gate and waved. George squeezed my hand. We drove through the gate and Freddie waved us off. I didn't look back through the window.

We drove in convoy towards the dock, the guards trailing us. Pascale sat between us in the back seat. Trouble still festered. A few people had ventured out to look around. They stared at the ex-police car.

'I need the toilet,' Pascale announced.

'You'll have to hold on, it's not too far,' I told her.

'I need to go!'

I looked at George. He grimaced.

'Why didn't you tell me before, darling?'

Pascale began to cry with nerves.

'Oh God,' George groaned. 'Can't she hold on?'

'No!' Pascale wailed.

We were passing the Country Club.

'Can you turn into the Club for a moment?' I asked the driver. He turned and the guards followed. I leapt out of the car, pulling Pascale up the steps, racing across the wide polished floors to the veranda.

'Hello, hello,' I called. But the place was closed, no one there. We ran across the fountain courtyard, coming upon the bar area, where I had met with Williams, then down the steps to the changing rooms. Toilet cubicles there. Pascale went inside one. She peed for what felt like minutes.

'*Pascale, dépêches-toi,*' I urged.

When she'd finished I dragged her back up the stairs, hurrying her across the courtyard, back across those wide polished floors where we had danced on Saturday nights. The mute black waiters. Mute black slaves had never danced across this floor, never attended the grand fêtes held by Poleska. A shiver. I stopped to look behind me.

'Who's there?' I called out.

No one called back.

I ran, pulling Pascale along, Poleska de Boissière chasing me, one bony finger reaching out to poke me between the shoulders. *Get out, get out of my house*, she whispered. *You skinny white bitch, you traitor. Go, get on that boat, you weakling. Run away. Like the white cockroach that you are. Take your white Creole girl with you. Run away.*

I jumped into the car, heart thudding. Pascale was frightened, too.

'What took you so long?' George was sweating.

'I couldn't exactly make her pee faster, could I?'

The taxi driver stepped on the gas. We swung round the immense statue of the Samaan tree.

I peered backwards.

The figure of the dowager Poleska stood there, dressed in mourning black. Eliza Williams stood next to her, a younger, darker version, equally severe. They waved me off.

We drove on, past the half-burnt-down army barracks in St James, past lines of police. The sun blazed onto the car roof. I began to feel it at last, gentle waves of relief breaking over me. I was leaving Trinidad. I imagined scones stuffed with clotted cream and damson jam. Harvey Nicks. The coolness of an English spring, the chaste pastels and pinks of apple and cherry blossom on the trees. Red buses and red post-boxes. Bobbies on the beat. Everything around us glimmered silver in the heat. Everything blurred. Port of Spain had disintegrated in the sun's rays. I was in the very act of escape. We floated along Tragarete Road, then into Woodbrook, past bewildered black faces, past more police, then out, finally, onto Wrightson Road, the road which ran along the seafront.

'Shit,' said George.

A roadblock up ahead. Military vehicles across the road, barring our route.

'What on earth can they be doing?'

George scrambled for our passports and papers. 'They must want to know who's heading for the ship.'

'Oh God!'

'Or it could be anything. They might be looking for someone.'

'Oh Jesus, George. We'll miss it!'

'No, we won't.'

I began to sweat. Pascale curled up tight in a ball.

'We could take a short cut.'

George nodded. 'Go *left*,' he urged the driver.

The taxi swerved up, again, into Woodbrook, the squad car following. The driver tracked along parallel to Wrightson Road and then stopped dead. A traffic jam. George got out and ran up to see what had caused it. He came back panicked.

'A car's broken down, further up.'

The driver beeped his horn.

'Go right!' I shouted.

The taxi veered right and shot down the narrow street, joining the foreshore again.

'Thank God.'

George looked behind us. 'We've lost our guards.'

'And half our luggage,' I groaned.

'It doesn't matter. Not now.' George was just as nervous as me. I believed, then, I was minutes from freedom. I imagined separating him from the island. George on deck, with his arms around me, just like when we arrived. We were leaving those bushy rocks, those carrion birds on high.

The squad car appeared behind us.

We rattled along.

George looked at his watch and cursed.

I wasn't scared. A warm breeze fluttered off the salt sea, the sea heavy with thick scents of mudflats and swampland. River silt.

My breath tangled in my chest. The dock appeared, the cranes, the custom houses, the usual chaos somehow arrested in mid-flow. Police vehicles and dusty army vehicles were parked up on either side of the road. Armed police stood guard. I looked out, into the Gulf of Paria.

'The *ship*!' I screamed, but no sound emerged.

George gazed out to sea.

We craned our necks.

Out there, in the calm black sea, some way off, exiting via the First Boca, the *Southern Cross* was under sail.

'It's *gone*! It went, George! It left without us.'

The ship's decks glistened, its funnel trailed smoke. We watched as its beak disappeared, then its body, too, as the swan slipped past the green tree-crowded walls of Monus Island and the tip of Trinidad. The ship left behind a heaving wake which slapped itself and flattened out, rippling across the harbour, lapping to the dock, and then breaching the sea walls, lapping up as far as our car, wetting us, dousing us down.

Lucy drugged me up good. George hid my Valium. We missed the boat. It departed ten minutes before we arrived at the dock. I saw it slipping past those bushy rocks again and again. I saw myself on my green bicycle, riding after it. I fell into a profound sleep: unconscious for days. I didn't want to be awake. I refused to eat. In my dreams I smashed myself to pieces and threw the pieces into the waves. The sky went dark, dark with a million birds. Far out to sea, the winds picked up. Everything would be different. Everything in Trinidad would be different now; the winds would see to that. I saw a hurricane in the harbour. Boats thrown onto the dock. A pall of smoke, the shape of Trinidad. Men in tin hats. The government at the Hilton Hotel up on the hill above the slum; the government up on high, keeping watch. Eric Williams in his flashy American car, nodding at me, gliding past. Eric Williams collapsed and sitting on a white metal chair. *Repudiate colonialism*. I saw myself holding a gun, arm outstretched. I saw myself shooting a man dead. Holding a gun and shooting bullets into a man's chest. I saw another man being beaten half to death up in those mother-hills. A butterfly of bruises on his young face. My letters, my letters all burnt and floating, drifting on the sea. George dancing backwards, his shins covered in flakes of ash. George in a pot, a small urn. George and my letters, all turned to ash, floating away, across a sea as clear as gin.

One day, I decided to wake up. I took a pen and paper and began to write: *Dear Mr Williams*. I found I had so much to say. I wrote for an hour at least. I kept writing to Eric Williams until he died, eleven years later. Hundreds of thousand of citizens filed past his casket in the Red House to pay their respects. Granny Seraphina, long dead herself by then, couldn't be among them. The letters helped me to understand what was happening in Trinidad. George never found out about them. And he never went back to work. He developed the land that he had bought and that was occupation enough. Discreetly, he unpacked the bags. We bought new dogs. I was back in my old life and yet something had eternally shifted between me and George.

Not long after we missed the boat, Venus was in the kitchen making dumplings for corn soup. Pascale was helping her. Both chattered away. They looked up when I entered, their hands covered in flour.

'Mummyuh!' Pascale squealed.

Venus smiled.

'What day is it?' I asked and hugged my daughter.

'Tuesday. You been sleepin' for some time, a week or so,' Venus informed me.

I wandered into the garden with Pascale.

'We stayin' here, Mummy?' Pascale asked. 'We stayin' wid Venus?'

I nodded.

The shapely green hill looked down on me, silent. I scowled and felt sorry for my sins, whatever they were.

Hello again, she said.

Go away.

I'm glad you stayed.

You knew. You've got him back.

Is it so bad being here?

I'm not sure any more.

You're part of things now.

Maybe I am.

You might get used to the way things are in Trinidad.

I'll keep trying to understand.

You might even get used to the heat.

No. Not that. Never.

ACKNOWLEDGEMENTS

Many people helped to make this book. I'd like to thank Adrian Camps-Campins for unlimited access to his personal library and photographic archives; also Dr Hamid Ghany, for arranging access to the West Indiana Collection at University of the West Indies in St Augustine, Trinidad, and for his enlightening conversations about politics in Trinidad. Thanks also to Dr Selwyn Ryan for keeping our eleven o'clock appointment at UWI. I owe a debt of gratitude to Dr Jo Baker and Dr Lindsey Moore at Lancaster University for their meticulous guidance while writing this novel. I would like to thank my friend Katie Sampson and also Gilly Stern for their critical editorial feedback; also my editor, Francesca Main at Simon & Schuster UK, for her forensic editorial skills. Thanks to Steve Cook and the Royal Literary Fund for its generous financial support, likewise the Arts and Humanities Research Council. Linda Anderson, once again, provided instrumental support early on. The Black Sheep Housing Co-op, though now defunct, must be thanked for sheltering me, this time in the aftermath of a hurricane. I'd like to thank Sarah McCloughry for her advice and wise counsel at a most critical juncture; also Stephanie Anderson for cutting me free. Thanks also to my lovely agent Isobel Dixon at Blake Friedmann, always full of ideas and inspiration. Thank you, John and Antoinette Moat and the late John Fairfax, for giving me the Arvon Foundation, a place I have returned to again and again over the last ten years. Lastly, I would like to thank my mother and muse, Yvette Roffey, for a place to write and call home.